The
Malagasy
Tortoise

A Jim Morgan Adventure

by James Halon

IYHB

For inquiries or to order additional copies of this book, contact:

In-Your-Hand Books
P. O. Box 18614
Milwaukee, WI 53218-0614

Tel: 866-850-4000
Website: inyourhandbooks.com
email: sales@inyourhandbooks.com

With love to Margaret

Chapter One

My name is James P. Morgan. I'm over thirty and have an Engineering degree from Purdue. I cuss, drink J&B Scotch, smoke an occasional cigarette and cheat on my income taxes (just kidding). I also hold very dear the following reputation: "I'm the man who gets the job done." I slipped this candid observation into my last resume and – I got the job.

Physically, I'm a small person. I put on shoes before I weigh to reach 150. However, I tend to think of myself as a husky guy, the macho type, who walks into a bar and yells, "I can lick any man in the house." I actually did this – once.

This happened in Nome, Alaska at the Golden Nugget Saloon. That's where I got this scar, the one above my right eye. Ah, that magical land, Alaska. But I was much younger then, and yeah, the reddish scar remains today, a visual reminder of how easy it is to let one's mouth override one's ass. Yeah, I was young. But you know what? That youthful bit of brash stupidity has kept me from uttering such *like* nonsense to this very day. Like I was saying, I'm not a big person. At five-foot eleven and a hundred and fifty pounds I just don't *look* as rough and tough as I actually feel.

Intellectually, I hold my own with peers and almost every one of my Engineering cohorts. My GPA was high enough that I could have entered graduate school and began a doctoral chase, but I didn't. Some day? When my life slows down, I'll start the work to obtain my Master's Degree in Business Administration. However, for the time being, I'm content with who and what I am. Somehow… I'll contain my deeply seated desires to overindulge in the primrose world of scholastic gymnastics.

Morally, I think John Wayne, Lee Marvin and Charles Bronson make excellent role models for all aspiring Engineers. That ostentatious know-it-all mentality exhibited by those who hold their master's degree just don't hack it in the real world of getting things done. One must step on a few toes, kick some butt, cheat, lie and spit – when one must. These are the real moral values that one ought to follow. It's my hope to reflect much deeper upon these vagrant moral issues later – when I'm too old to kick ass and indeed get the job done.

Philosophically, I *am* the center of my universe. The real world revolves around me and me alone. I have pocketed enough money to allow myself this grand illusion. I have also learned to enjoy the little eccentricities that materialize when one holds such flagrant and powerful views of innate being. Aside from all this, I'm considered to be deeply pragmatic – yet laid back. – Especially by my significant others.

To be pragmatic and laid back is possible, I suppose. Hell, anything's possible when it's stated in philosophical terms. Isn't it? I still read Plato and that makes me appreciate much deeper those wonderful ideals proposed by that great entity, Aristotle. Hence, I see myself as a totally progressive thinker. But to what end? This I shall probably never ever know. Therefore, I am – James P. Morgan.

•   •   •

This adventure began several years ago with a scraggly written note attached to my bedroom door, "CALL EUNICE." I reached for the note with a fat mitten on my hand but was unable to grasp the tiny slip of paper. I had just entered the living quarters of Ice Hole Number Thirteen, an oil exploration site. I let the message hang and entered my eight-by-ten arctic bungalow and began the laborious task of removing my survival clothing: mittens, mukluks, parka, red scarf and three pair of woolen knee socks. I was nodding off as I undressed, a common occurrence when one finishes a twenty-four hour shift looking for oil under the vast and frozen tundra of the North Alaskan wastelands. With strewn gear and sweat-moist toes I buried myself deep in the old colloquial fart-sack, that soft fluffy haven where one feels like he's dog snuggled up against a big ol' heavyset cuddling woman. My last waking thought, "Call Eunice," was a simple and incoherent mumble that quickly turned to a snore.

And I dreamt – of tiny birds, little swallows winging in and out of adobe walls. White arches topped with red-orange tiles like those that adorn old Mexican missions – and they were. It was San Juan Capistrano back dropped below an azure blue sky, a sky of puffed laziness, of columned and tufted cumulus, of an ever relentless swooping, diving mass of frenzied swallows that chirped madly in their methodic annual celebration – their return home, their mass pilgrimage back to Capistrano, back to their avian Mecca.

And I moved, glided across State Highway 101. Ocean waves roared down on granulated sand beckoning me onward and onward, 'til a tern, a lone stationary foam-white sea gull floated genteel on an aerographic wind, sang, "Look, look 'round, look 'round and wait, wait 'round and you shall see." Then went away, in the way that terns do, with a graceful bank and one singular flap of its gray and white feathers was evermore departed.

An old convertible lumbered up from down on highway 101. It moved real slow – *tortoise* like – onward and onward. Its top was down to expose a heap of surfing paraphernalia and other odd beach junk. A green beach ball popped out of the back seat as the Chevy – I could now see that it was a Chevy – came to a bumper-jerking halt.

I watched as the ball began to spin, then stop, then soft bounce in a plop-dribble, dribble-flop. It then began a downward move zigzagging haphazardly toward the beach. It was a pogo-hop, a plop plopity dance that quickly turned into a deflated roll, a roll that ended at the feet of a most scantily clad sunbather, a woman, a good looking woman – *my* Eunice.

She grabbed up the ball, studied it, poked it, and then placed it on her nose where she snapped it into a rapid spin. The sight reminded me of a circus act, an act that I had seen once when I was a very young boy, and I felt amused, giggly. This was way, way out of character for *my* Eunice.

Hiding myself behind an orange tree, I watched her flip the plastic ball up into the air then catch it back on her nose while still in full spin. I screamed out, "Bravo," then slunk low into the tall coastal grasses in hope that she hadn't seen me. She began to clap her arms like a seal as the ball continued its spin. I was so enthralled I yelled out, "Clever Eunice, very clever." Then I sunk ever deeper into the lush grass in a controlled but contrite effort to further conceal my voyeuristic presence.

The ball slowed, then stopped. Everything became graphically still. I lifted my head to discern why, but couldn't. There wasn't any reason, at least that I could see. Then the ball fell with a flop smack onto Eunice's blanket. The ball appeared to be breathing. Yes, it was inhaling and exhaling, very deeply, as if it were an asthmatic on the verge of seizure. And then it changed color to a hot pink, a highlight pink, then it changed again, abruptly, into a bright reddish carrot-orange, and then – it began to grow.

Eunice jumped away, stood, startled, exposing fear, and much of her deeply tanned curves. She began to punch the growing, now turned scarlet, now monster, orb. Suddenly, in a fit of abject desperation, she threw herself physically on top the now fiery beach toy.

And the ball grew larger and ever larger. The polyurethane globe began to rise, carrying Eunice up and off the sand, ten, then twenty feet into the air where she called out, *screamed* out, an unrequited cry of abject desperation, "Help me, Jimbo. Help meeeeee."

I moved to help her but I couldn't. My feet were frozen, I couldn't move. I looked down to see that my feet were buried in an icy patch of tundra right up to my shins. I took hold of the blooming orange tree and began to hoist myself upward. It was no good. The only thing I accomplished was to shake down a ton of orange blossoms that rapidly transformed into snowflakes. I felt so doomed, so helpless, all I could do was watch.

I called out to her, "Hold on, Babe. I've got cold feet. See?" I pointed to my frozen feet. Surely she could see, right? The snow (orange blossoms) intensified. Huge oranges began to fall all around me. I picked one up and compared it to an apple. It was gigantic.

Eunice yelled out, "Quit comparing apples with oranges."

I challenged her, "Just what does that mean, Eunice?"

Her balance faltered, she dug her manicured fingernails deep into the fireball's magma, ripping and gouging in a violent, manic effort to deflate the yet expanding monster that she had precariously straddled. It worked. A horrendous psssss broke open the yet expanding plasmatic sack and sent her on a skyrocketing excursion of loops, dives and spins like no one person could ever, ever imagine.

She bumped a beachcomber stage left, then another sunbather stage right. It was madness. I heard her say, "Excuse me, sir." And then, calmly, "Pardon me, madam." And, to an old white bearded sage who attempted to grab her ass, "Watch it, Buster." Her face showed anger then, it was brief, pointed, and vehement; but, luckily, it didn't last for but a second, two at tops. Then it all ended. Eunice fell from the ball and flopped hard on the sand with her legs spread north and south. She began to whimper. Her auburn hair was a tangled mess. Yet, she looked beautiful – in a sick and demented way. She looked so helpless, abused – used up. She fell forward slamming her face full into the sand, and the earth began to shake echoing her inner sobs, sobs of fear and sobs of unspeakable helplessness.

And I woke, confused and disoriented, automatically groping around for a cigarette, that nasty little link to reality. Finding one, I lit it. Content to be back in the real world. I spent the next few minutes recollecting my dream and then, suddenly, recollected the tiny note, "CALL EUNICE."

Yeah, I still loved her. I could still hear her saying, "Go away, Jim Morgan. I don't want you." And I did go away. I went away because I did indeed love her, and now – I'm to call her? And out loud, I said, "Okay. I'll call you, Babe." I snubbed out my cigarette and closed my eyes on the artic darkness – a darkness that engulfed my entire being. And I slept, a much, much needed sleep.

Chapter Two

I woke that next day, the nineteenth of March, in a silent, groggy stupor. Immediately, my ears began to buzz from the deep quietness one finds on the frozen northlands. Snow had drifted up and over our sleeping quarters some seven months earlier and had brought with it a tomb-like, uncanny stillness. Ear ringing was a major malaise encountered by all of the twenty-two souls who chose to be invested there and I was no exception.

Switching on my defective lamp – some days it worked, some days it didn't – had forced me out of the bed and onto the cold tile flooring before my time. It was a bad lamp day and my only light would be that from a dim hallway bulb that was hung two doors away. The light was good enough to dress by and leave. It was ice hole routine – work, sleep, and then get back to work. My forty-dollar an hour salary made up for a lot of those remote Alaskan nuances, not to mention the doubling for overtime and the many frequent bonuses. Yeah, bathing in a bowl of melted snow and living with a defective lamp in a sunless, frigid land was quite enjoyable – especially when the Friday night eagle came bouncing in for its ritual, payday landing.

I put on my supervisor's hardhat and, although still numb-dumb, went off to find Sparks, our drunken ice hole radio operator. I soon found him, asleep, in the site's radio room. Drool was oozing out of his open mouth and had formed a small stream down his cheek, pooling on the fur of a parka that he had rolled up to act as pillow below his fermenting head. Sparks is an ugly person and is disliked by everyone. This cascade of slime was just one more of those little things that all add up to make him one repugnant personality. I had to look away from his opened mouth as the gurgling snore was turning my stomach. Yeah, Sparks is the site's biggest, most flagrant, alcoholic.

I backed out the door and began to pound on the red plywood wall, calling out, "Sparks! Sparks. Are you in there?"

His eyes opened slow, glazed from gin, or his favorite – Wild Turkey. Once, only a few days ago, I saw him chug-a-lug a whole fifth of Jack. He belched in a grotesque moist-lipped grin, and then fell dead on his face in a slow motion flop. Ten hours later, he was still lying where he fell. No one helped him. No one, not even me, cared whether he was hurt or dead. It was pathetic. No one acknowledged his sickness. His illness had simply progressed too far.

He began a cough, hacking himself into semi-consciousness, all the while pounding his fist on the metal desk. Then – reaching into an open desk drawer – he withdrew an open bottle of bourbon and took a deep bubbling draw. His movement was swift and continuous, all the time keeping his bloody eyes locked solidly onto mine. The bottle was then set deftly back into the drawer. In a deadpan grin he blurted out, "Hey Jim, what you need, ol' buddy?"

I could only stare at him in an appalled supervisory glare. He made a feeble attempt to stand but plopped back down, hard, onto the wheeled office chair. He slid backward several inches, fingers grouping for the desk edge – it was an all out effort for him to get balanced in a simple sitting position. I could only shake my head in a negative show of disapproval, of alcoholics in general, and of *him* in particular.

He continued, "Don't you know it's night, Jim? You should be sleeping, ol' buddy."

His words were drawled, slurred. The bad arctic joke ended with a muffled hiccup followed by a sharp burp, then a thin smile, a twisted smile, no doubt to show that, at least *he* enjoyed his own worn-out over-used bit of humor. He was hopelessly insane. He exhibited every sign of one, very, very sick individual.

Handing Sparks the note, CALL EUNICE, I asked, "Did she leave you a number where I could reach her?"

He took the slip of paper from my hand and studied it several seconds as if it were written in Greek, turned it one way, then another – squinting – then he says, "Yeah, she left a number, but I didn't write it down. I was *too busy*."

Sparks began laughing. He was in hysterics. His joke about being too busy was too much for his demented state and it was way, way too much for mine. I reached over the desk and grabbed up a fist full of plaid shirt, pulling him within inches of my own face.

He whimpered, "Don't," and his pink eyes began to moisten. He smelled of vomit and booze and there were black-headed zits all over his forehead and nose. I shoved him away. He hit his chair squarely and zoomed backward slamming into a filing cabinet. His head snapped back hitting gray metal, hard. He turned white from fear, then, clenching his teeth, said, "You're fucked now, Morgan. My dad's the VP of this operation – you're out of here, Dude."

Pointing my finger directly at his nose, I said, and meant it, "I'm going to knock out all your teeth, one by one, if you don't connect me with Washington, D.C. within thirty seconds flat, *Dude.*"

His face whitened again. I'm not sure that he believed I would, but I was fairly certain that he knew I could. In something similar to a whimper, he capitulated, "Give me two minutes, Jim. It takes that long to reach an operator. Okay?"

• • •

Eunice, nee Eunice May North, holds a Doctorate in Psychology from Stanford University. She is now considered "the" foremost authority in that little known and even less understood field of Intuitive Thought. She has written seven books on ESP, holds a co-authorship on Psychoanalysis and has penned another dozen or so works on the realities of intuitiveness. Recently she surrendered her full professorship at U.S.C. to become the Director in Residence of the recently founded Institute of Intuitive Thought, INTUIT U., located in Washington, D.C.

INTUIT U. specializes in parapsychology, ESP, intuitiveness, and most every other type of psychic phenomena. A major aspect of INTUIT U. is its collection of chemical compounds and herbal drugs that the institute has accumulated through anthropological field research. INTUIT U. is where ancient cures, potions, chants and even talismans – good or evil – go under the microscope for study and analysis and, ultimately, for sale to the general public.

Funding of INTUIT U. comes from the private sectors of industry where fully ninety percent of its capital stems from the bi-yearly compilation and sale of its world pharmacopeia. The huge pharmaceutical companies rely heavily upon the Institute's vast discoveries to support their own individual research programs and in-house developments.

Eunice also gets some covert funding from our CIA – I only know this because she wanted me to know, and this is *not* in the realm of public knowledge. In retribution for taking these covert funds, she personally keeps the CIA informed of the latest technology when discovered at, or around the Institute, which is quite considerable.

There are other sources of revenue but they are small in comparison to the monies generated by the pharmacopeia.

INTUIT U. employs some sixty full-time researchers and another sixty on an associate basis. With few exceptions, everyone holds a doctorate in this-or-that scientific field. The researchers live on campus in small groups of overly plush cottages. They are all considered to be volunteers but they are all taking home hefty paychecks. To be invited to volunteer one's service at the Institute is considered to be a great honor within the scientific community.

Eunice occupies a two story English Tudor that sits right on the Potomac River. The campus is maintained by outside contractors and is landscaped with such perfection that Eunice has considered opening the grounds to a private tour group in an effort to generate more funds.

Eunice has a full time, live in, domestic servant and cook whose name is Mureatha. Personally, maids make me uncomfortable. Furthermore, it amazes me to no end that people still hire themselves out for such mundane drudgery as cooking and cleaning. Didn't slavery and human bondage go out with Abraham Lincoln? Or was that LBJ?

●   ●   ●

Sparks passed me the radio's headset in under two minutes. He glared at me in a show of vehemence, then – with a wobbly arrogance – did a plodding strut out the door. No doubt to visit some other hidden watering hole.

A small metallic voice advised me to, "Please hold." And was instantly replaced with an equally "tinny" violin solo. I kept expecting my connection to be broken which is a ritual problem with arctic radio communications. It's common for some ham operator in Japan or Chile to come chiming in with, "Break, break, want to chat, Americans?"

One just never knows. The tin violin music was being bounced from "D" layer to "E" layer all around the globe and back again. Eight whole minutes lumbered past. The violin was replaced by a fair piano concerto, maybe an opus? Tick-tock, tick-tock – the wall clock began to drown out the on-hold music, my damned ear buzzing returned, and I thought, gee, I hadn't talked to Eunice in over a year.

"Eunice North, how may I help you?"

Electricity ran through my body. It was Eunice all right. Her voice seemed raspy, far away, but she sounded good, sexual. Hey, I hadn't talked to a woman in months – she sounded terrific.

"Hi Eunice, it's me, Jim Morgan." I was speaking fast, too fast, I could hear my own voice and became aware, self-conscious – of a need, a need to say so many, many things, and to say them all, all at once.

"James, it's so nice of you to return my call. It's only been four days since I left word for you to call me. Are you well? Were you sick or something?"

"Well. You know, babe. There aren't a lot of phone booths north of the Arctic Circle."

Was I being *too* flippant? Was the silence in the headset a – disconnect? Perhaps she was actually considering how many phones there really are at an Ice Hole. I broke the silence.

"Are you still as good looking as when I saw you last?"

I could visualize her mouth puckering up on the right side of her face. She loves flattery and the pucker is a way of accepting it. She could pucker and keep on doing business, it helped her achieve, over achieve, and never have to say, "Thank you, I do appreciate the compliment." But, that's her way. I continued.

"What's it been now, a year, two, since we've spoken?"

"It's been awhile, James. I must say it's nice to hear your spunky, sarcastic voice again."

She sounded sincere. She sounded happy. She sounded as if there weren't any hate left in her heart; at least, there didn't seem to be any latent hate in her phone voice. She continued.

"I'm looking for an Engineer to enhance my staff, Jim." She paused. I waited for her to elaborate. She always elaborates.

"I'm making you an offer. Interested? That is, if you can get away for awhile?"

"Oh, ...I could probably take a walk. It wouldn't look good on my next resume. I'm also making a few grand a month up here, playing poker. How big a salary you offering?" Yeah, I lied about poker – it was a whim of the moment, a bluff. After all, she did say, "I'm making you an offer." Didn't she?

Yeah, the cards were coming fast, and if I knew Eunice, she'd have a card or two up her silk sleeve. She said, "I need an Engineer." Not,

"I need *you*. I need your love. I want you. Come back to me." No. What she said was, "I need an Engineer to enhance my staff." And that! *That* – would cost her dearly.

She elaborated, "I'll match your current salary plus ten percent. I'll give you a thousand dollar sign-on bonus; and, if I know you like I think I do, you'll need that grand to pay off your gambling debts. Right?"

The offer was sweet. I was mentally packing my suitcase as soon as I heard, "...match your current salary." I was ready to leave Hell Hole Thirteen for half my salary. Yet, I still needed to know how badly she wanted, *me*. You know, male ego and that sort of thing.

I countered, "Well, last night wasn't my best night on the green felt; but I'm far from being in debt, Eun. However, I will need a bit of relocation money. Say, three grand..."

"Okay. That sounds fair to me. I need you here in four days. I have a lot of nasty deadlines to meet."

"I need a week. And – one more perk."

"Ah... What's that? What perk?" Eunice rarely uses, "Ah." She was mentally running through her cited offer assessing what it was that she had forgotten, what option had she *inadvertently* failed to mention?

"I get to use you on weekends, dates and stuff."

There was a long pause – a terribly long pause. It was an embarrassing moment. My face flushed and I sorely regretted saying, "...use you." Yeah, I thought, I had blown one super fine offer, let alone my chance of leaving the bustling arctic wastelands. And then I heard her sweetly proclaim the following magic.

"I'd have sworn that I had mentioned that, Jim. When we were talking about bonuses? Didn't I?"

The ace of hearts slid out of her sleeve. The cards were all in play. One of us was going to loose their shirt. – I deftly called her hand.

"I'll be there in a week. By the way, how am I going to be used to enhance your staff, Eun?"

"For starters, you're going to run down a rare tortoise for me – a *Malagasy* Tortoise."

•   •   •

"Break, break. Hello Americanos. Want to chat, amigos?"

Our connection was broken. I set down the headphones while the Latino's plea to chat crackled on. And I thought, "Yeah, I can run down a tortoise." And then I thought deeper, about the fable...

Chapter Three

In a quickly drafted letter of resignation, I placed Sparks in charge of Ice Hole Number 13. My little joke on the oil industry, and began packing some bare essentials: toothpaste, clean underwear, sunglasses, a picture of mom and dad on their sailboat, calculator, pens and pencils, alarm clock, and my gold on blue Purdue pennant. I stuffed this all into an overnight bag, took one last look around my room, shook my head in disbelief, and pulled the door shut on an era of self-imposed prison. I had made a lot of money during my stay, but it was time to move on.

Circling the Ice Hole in the site's Cessna erased all doubts I may have subconsciously held about leaving the oil fields. I dipped my wings left and right in a grand adios to my cheering friends and fellow workers. Some of them I'd recall often, some of them would never again creep into my consciousness. I placed the nose cowl on the distant southern horizon and headed for Kotzebue forevermore away from the icy, barren Brooks Range.

Refueled and fed, I climbed out of Kotzebue to cross the Arctic Circle and the Seward Peninsula to Nome, a mere two hundred nautical miles away. For companionship I listened to some old Beatles' tapes on an early Sony Walkman.

This helped me to not think or worry about what I was doing. Technically, I had stolen the Cessna. Although, no one ever said I couldn't use it. And no, Virginia, I didn't have a pilot's license. And, after all was said and done, the three-hour flight was quite uneventful. Which just goes to show that even adventures have their lulls.

I did miss Nome by a few miles to the west, about thirty; but was able to follow the coast eastward until I saw some vivid signs of life. My navigational skills are weak and confined to the cardinal points of a compass. I landed without radioing in, as I didn't know what frequency Nome used, or how to set it if I did. There are three things that I need to study before applying for my pilot's license, radio operation, navigation and meteorology. Luckily, I had some nice weather, a true rarity anywhere near the Seward Peninsula.

Tony, a genuine bush pilot who works for Wein Airline, came out of his office and pointed out a spot for me to park the oil company's plane. It was Tony who taught me to fly. Together, we raised a lot of husky fur whenever I had cause to be in Nome, which was often.

Once, when he was too drunk to fly a DEW line mail run, I offered to steer his plane – so he could sleep. The jaunt went well and ever since then, Tony has given me free flying lessons.

Tony helped schedule me out to Seattle via a DC-10 that was departing within minutes of my arrival in Nome. The Golden Nugget pilot, a friend of Tony's, let me fly free as a parting gift from the land of gold and frozen honey.

I entrusted the Cessna key to Tony who promised to keep it from my boss, Bob Carpenter, until I received my last paycheck. Tony hates Bob – over some girl – and I will be quite surprised if that Cessna is ever seen again, at least in one piece.

I waved my good-byes from the vibrating steps of the DC-10 and hurriedly boarded. Twelve hours later I was in a taxicab fighting the rush hour traffic into downtown Seattle.

●   ●   ●

The young desk clerk at the Westin Hotel excused himself and returned with a sophisticated and very starched manager whose face flushed as he asked me whether or not I had reservations. It seemed that I was somewhat miscast for a stay with the Westin's normally opulent clientele. My beard was shabby, there was mud on my mukluks, my parka was lightly coated with Alaskan crude, and its fur hood was splotched with gobs of drill-bit grease. I may have had an odor problem too, but – a crisp one hundred dollar bill made me an instant red carpet guest without further fanfare or ado.

As I signed the guest register, I told the young desk clerk to get a big, fat, medium-rare steak sent up to my room by a naked woman. He said, "Oh my gosh." And went off to fetch Mister Starch for a second time. This time I had to modify my order, a six-pack of beer would replace my desire for a hostess 'd au natural. I tipped the kid a twenty and headed for the elevators. The plush lobby was scattered with a handful of beautiful women and I soon caught myself staring. I really had been gone – *too* long. Yeah, it was a wonderful feeling to be back in civilization and to discover that the libido was still functioning on all five, or six senses. I saw a cute blond – damn: Then, a big brunette. And then another one clad in a mini-skirt. And I saw yet another, with legs all the way up to her waist – busty, and smiling – in that order.

The elevator arrived and I watched a group of even longer legs exit the car. Did I die and go to heaven? I entered the mirrored car and watched myself rubbing the whiskers of a neo-barbarian, me. And my mind began to race, I'd shave, I'd bathe, I'd – purchase a suit, I'd – I'd… Damn. I *had* been away too long. I decided there and then that I'd "chill out."

While waiting for room service to bring up my dinner I made a few phone calls. The first one went to Bob Carpenter who was in Dallas, Texas for the week. I told him that I quit. That it was a simple case of cabin fever, that I was seeing naked girls running through the trees that surrounded Ice Hole 13 and that every time I caught one she'd be too skinny for my liking.

He wasn't amused. I told him he could pick up the Cessna in Nome, from Tony, and that I loved him like an only brother.

Bob thanked me for letting him know where the Cessna was and then, in the same breath, added, "I'll see that your final pay check goes to a worthy charity, Jim."

I could only say, "Fair is fair, Bob. By the way, I put Sparks in charge of 13, gave him a hundred dollar a week pay raise and – the keys to the liquor room."

My second call went to an FTD florist. I sent Eunice a dozen white roses with a note that read, "With Love, Your Latest Staff Enhancement."

The third call went to American Air Lines where I booked a dinner flight to Chicago for the following evening. I wanted to treat myself to a first class seat but had to settle for coach, a small concession for such short notice. My last call was that inevitable call home.

Room service arrived at the same time that mom answered the phone. "Hold on, ma. Someone's at the door."

"Jimmy? Jimmy? Is that you, dear?"

"Yeah ma, it's me. Hold on a minute, okay?"

I over tipped the waiter, popped the tab on a beer and began undressing all the while explaining to mom why I was coming home to visit. She was excited. I could hear it in her voice. She said that she was writing me a letter when the phone rang, "…what a coincidence."

"Hold on while I get your papa, Jimmy." The line went dead while she went off to find dad. That's my mom, totally dependent upon dad. I popped open a second beer and peeked at the steak under its silver domed serving tray. I was just about to hang up the phone when mom returned.

"Daddy says we'll pick you up at the airport. What time will you get in? Oh my, I'll have to get your room ready. Will you be here for dinner? What can I make for you? Oh, I know, your favorite, spaghetti. Are you bringing a guest?"

I cut her short. She was being the exemplary mom, covering all the bases and playing outfield as well. "Hey. Hey, mom. I'll be in late tomorrow. I'll call you when I get in. I must go now. See you tomorrow. Love you, and say `Hi' to dad for me."

I cradled the phone, devoured the steak, and took a thirty-five minute shower. Yeah, it would be nice to visit my parents again, especially since it would be a short visit, one day, two at most. Any longer then that would be madness. Yeah, their little boy is grown now. One day they will discover this fact of life and our relationship will be much, much sweeter. Until then, it's home tonight and gone tomorrow; at least, as long as I can afford such luxury.

The last Coors deadened my racing mind. I pulled the thick hotel blanket up over my head and slept deep into the following afternoon. My adventure was gaining momentum.

Chapter Four

Snow obscured my view as the big 747 vibrated down onto O'Hare's complex and crowded runway system. The huge moist flakes melted as quickly as they platted down on the taxiway; but, in the lower, cooler, dormant grass fringe areas there remained spotty patches of neo-accumulations. These blotches stated, "Hey, it *isn't* quite spring. No, not yet, not here, not here in the Windy City of Chicago."

My female cabby, a flirtatious college student, yakked on and on about Chicago's nightlife. "Ever been here? Ever been there? Ever been? Ever been?"

"No. Not recently. No. Not since the mid-eighties. No. Never heard of that club. No. I'm not married. No, I'm not gay. No, I haven't been exposed to the AIDS virus. Yes, it is nice to meet someone who's independent and has her own apartment. And no, I don't like steamed clams on the half shell."

When we pulled up in front of my house, mom and dad were both peering out of the front window. They were like a pair of old pumpkins still flickering in expectation of at least one more late trick-or-treater to come rapping at their polished mahogany doors. I tipped the hot little cabby-student a twenty, and for a second I thought that she was going to kiss my hand, or something. But, she was just giving me a low oriental bow, a show of tip appreciation. I wondered what she would have done for a fifty as I walked up the drive and into the open, loving arms of my dear old mom.

We sat up until sunrise chatting and solidifying our family bonds. We shared some warm smiles and much laughter, something that comes easy when one is comfortable and at ease with one's own parents. Yeah, mom was mom and dad was dad, and I, I am their only child. As long as I followed their script, fulfilled their parental expectations, and played the role of needful, loving child, their world was mine and I was prince and heir to all their worldly treasures.

In motherly efficiency, mom had all the family news prepared for narration in chronological order. Dad, not to be outdone, had all of his latest innovations laid out on the living room floor for my personal viewing and inspection. His tool and die shop had been very productive over the last few years. He boasted of seven new patents, which I must admit, was very impressive. His latest innovation, a brass coil wrapped around a glass jug, "...will revolutionize the soft water industry." Or so dad claimed, with flailing arms and animated gestures of universal magnitude, that bespoke of a totally unique, uncompromising, consumer necessity (...why I'll be damned, dad. Sell me ten of them there suckers, right here, right now – cash money.).

And then came his inevitable pitch, "Join the business, son. Share the glory (But, what about money, dad?). Your talents wouldn't go to waste around here, son. No-sir-re-bob. We could use that education of yours to expand (But, what about money, dad?). It would be fun, Jimbo. We could work side-by-side, twelve hours a day, seven days a week, 365 days a year, (But what about money, dad?).

Inevitably I'd ask, "What about money, dad?"

"Oh, the money will come, Jimbo. Of course, I can't pay you a fat salary like the oil industry. But, we'd work something out. After all, the business will all be yours, one day. That's something to consider, eh Jimbo?"

Dad couldn't come close to matching Eunice's lucrative offer. And we both knew, I wouldn't last under his iron fisted, mad managerial dictatorship. But, I do have fun fending off his partnership offers. He expects it, and he no more wants me under his wing than I want to be there. We remain friends this way and I love him dearly for knowing and understanding how things "really" are. Which, I think he does. But then again, maybe he doesn't? Yeah, life can be confusing, especially when dealing with parents.

We slept in until two. Mom started her spaghetti while dad helped me uncover the Austin 3000, vintage 1963. Rebuilding and restoring the Austin was my pet project, but dad soon insisted on doing everything. I was literally reduced to spectator and gofer. Dad made many of the parts from scratch right there in his shop. Once, he shut down his production line for two days while he molded a pair of rocker panels for the undercarriage. As shop owner and managerial tyrant he gets away with such nonsense, but – that's another story.

When I announced that I was taking the Austin to Washington, dad became ill. "No-no-no, son. You take my Volvo, it's much safer and you'll be more comfortable on the road." This was said with absolute "parental" authority.

I didn't argue. I knew better. I simply dropped the subject and began to plan accordingly. I'd have to *steal* my own car.

It felt great to be back behind the wheel, the oak wheel, of my honey. I headed for the bank, growled to the bank, as the old Austin responded to the road like the tiger she was designed to be. If it weren't for the residual slush I'd have put the top down; but slush is slush and the top stayed up.

At the bank and not needing a loan was quite the novelty for yours truly. Although it felt odd, I found myself asking, "How much is my *portfolio* worth?" I knew it would be considerable, and it was, as a matter of fact, it was down right significant. Dad would surely be impressed, hell – I was impressed. Yeah, I had arrived at that point in one's life when one has to incorporate, or "get married."

Not-wanting to get married, I ordered all of my stocks to be sold and the monies to be converted into safe Treasury Bills. My thinking was thus, "Avoid wedlock." With all of my finances tied up in T-bills, I'd be safe. After all, who in their right mind would cash in a Treasury bill just to get married, right?

I purred up and down Michigan Avenue in a lightheaded, early spring daze. I had become a relatively rich guy, and it had come way, "way" before its time. It was time to enjoy my fortune. I went window-shopping the mini-skirts, revving the 3000 at anything wearing nylon, but I could only see my beloved Eunice.

Did I really love her that much? I swung the tigress onto Lake Shore Drive and headed home. It was getting dark, the city lights were coming to life as Chicago transformed from business Mecca of the mid-west to entertainment heaven. I could have hung around and played but hey! Mom was making spaghetti, what can I say?

That last night of my stay was sheer delight. We sat around, relaxed, watching carousel upon carousel of slides. Slides of dad sitting on the Austin, dad polishing the Austin, dad working under the hood of the Austin, dad in the driver's seat of the Austin, dad sitting on the Austin's fenders, and there was even one of mom working in her flower garden. We snacked late on leftovers and washed it all down with a homemade apple pie, alamode.

It was midnight when I crawled into my comfy teenage bed. Mom hadn't changed my room one bit since my college days. It was much cleaner, my poster of Janis Joplin had disappeared, and it didn't smell like a pile of old gym socks. My collection of baseball cards was still boxed right where I had left them. Yeah, it was comforting to be home, to languor in old memories, to be cared for. I flipped off the light and let the darkness clear my head of old, youthful times. It seemed like an eternity before I finally fell asleep, but I did, and I dreamt.

Eunice was in Chicago. She was auditing my bank. She was yelling out some terribly vicious nonsense. "Sell that stupid old sports car. Grow up. Settle down. Marry me, you – you goof-off, take the plunge."

She picked up a stack of papers and waved them in my face, all the while continuing her angry tirade. Crumpling the papers in her fist, she thrust them toward me, shaking them vigorously, furiously, "And this? This really takes the cake of all things – T Bills. Don't you know there's a stiff penalty for cashing one of these before their time? – You make me sick, Jimbo."

She finally threw the papers into my face. "You're not coming into my bed with thoughts of an early withdrawal, you – you, financial philanderer."

Mom entered the dream. Her soft, gentle voice purred out from the deep recesses of a shiny, but cob webbed, bank vault that was emitting a soft yellow incandescent glow, "Eunice is right, Jimmy. Treasury Bills suck. Now be a good boy, and put your money back into IBM, Microsoft, and Pepsi Cola like you did before. T Bills are so democratic – so wasteful, and so downright bureaucratic they actually turn my stomach, Jimmy. And, I do so want to be a grand-mother, didn't you know?"

A halo formed above her head, a halo that was inset with ABC blocks. Yeah, it was my mom okay, the saintly nun of procreation making her pitch for grandmother hood – from inside a bank vault.

Dad entered, wringing his hands in a greedy-lawyer gesture, say-ing, "Don't you worry son, I'll take that old Austin off your hands. That way, you can be matured, boy. You know? Pleasing our women folk is a real damned important part of business. And, there's noth-ing wrong with driving an Edsel – err, I mean the Volvo. So, act like a real grownup, mature adults drive Junkers all the time."

Dad's grin expanded, "After all, *we* all have to mature. And, soon-er or later, I will, too."

That's when dad became soulful, morbid – he began to weep – "I want your Austin, Jimbo." He fell to his knees. "I want that Austin.

I want *my* Austin." He turned into a two year old and went into a tantrum, kicking, spitting. He began throwing toy Volvos everywhere, in what one could only describe as nightmarish, vehement anger.

And I woke, fumbled around for a cigarette, lit one, and then tried to dissect my nightmare.

I couldn't understand Eunice's anger. Mom, in her halo of ABC blocks, well, she's a sweetie. Dad? Well, dad will get over my taking the Austin. After all, it is *my* car.

It was six AM. I dressed and packed silently in an extreme effort to not wake my parents. I didn't take many clothes, as nothing seemed to fit anymore. And, what I had, wouldn't be adequate in Eunice's world anyway, at least, not in her public world.

I had just loaded my golf clubs and tennis racquets into the passenger's seat of the 3000 and was trying to figure out how to fit in my fishing tackle when mom startled me.

"Your father's getting dressed. He's come to terms about you taking the Austin. Can I make you some breakfast, honey?"

Dad poked his head up above mom's shoulder like a Jack-in-the-box, "Don't forget, she red lines at 7000, Jim. She doesn't leak oil, but she does burn a little, check it every now and then. And the carbs, they're set for winter, they'll need adjusting when it gets a little warmer, okay? Well, drive defensively, Jimbo. You would have been *safer* in the Volvo. It has air bags and…

Thank the almighty gods that dad volunteered to answer the ringing phone. I kissed mom on the cheek and told her not to worry about dad's Austin, it was insured. She smiled like an all-knowing sage away from Tibet, and then a tear let loose and oozed down her maternal cheek.

I waved to them both – dad had returned and was hugging mom around the waist – as I pulled out of the driveway. It's a sad happiness to leave home. I'd miss them both terribly – for two minutes.

I growled down Maple Street for three whole blocks in first gear, reminiscing my visit, and wondering how long it would be before I'd return home again. And then, I began thinking about Eunice and the Austin came alive and began to roar. It had turned into the MGM lion itself, personified and unchained, free to venture where it will. And I thought, next stop, INTUIT U., Eunice's arms, and hopefully – all her charms.

Chapter Five

It takes twelve hours to drive to Washington, D.C., gas, oil and comfort stops included. This trip required two additional, unscheduled delays. The first was in Indiana near the University of Notre Dame. I knew it was Notre Dame because I could see the golden dome above the budding trees south of the toll road. This is where an ugly, burly state trooper wrote me out a sixty-two dollar speeding ticket. I'm sure this was an act of god or something. Because, if I hadn't been stopped, I'd have missed seeing the cathedral's golden dome, and "Oh Boy," that would have been a huge loss, right?

The second stop was in Pennsylvania where I was clocked on a fancy state of the art radar gun while doing eighty-one miles per hour. This time, I didn't see any golden domes. I couldn't blame that ticket on anyone other than myself. Yeah, I'd have to slow it down. The patrolman said so. Lucky for me, the cop had a sense of humor.

After ticketing me, he says, "Okay Anthony, keep old' Cleopatra here under control. We don't post these-here speed limits for our health, you know?"

I must have been searching for golden domes or cursing the toll road gods, at any rate, I didn't openly respond to his wit, and he added, gruffly, "Hey, got the message, Bud?"

Shaking my head yes in brash acknowledgement, I climbed back into "Cleo" thinking, "Bud? Yeah, right. What a dickhead."

I phoned Eunice from Hagerstown and was surprised to hear her personally answer, "I know it's you. How may I help?"

As soon as she recognized me as the caller, she went into an apologetic tirade over the way she had answered the call. No doubt, she was expecting a call from one of her mind readers, some student, or a politician. Then, when she finished raving on about her white roses, she promised to meet me at the institute's gatehouse, "...around eightish."

Yeah, I was getting close to Washington. "Eightish," gave me time for coffee, time to sightsee, time to contemplate existence and all the vagrancies of simply being. I threw in a Deep Purple tape and cranked the volume up into the 100-decibel range. During their version of

"Hey Joe," I pondered away on such mundane thoughts as, "How many lovers had Eunice taken since we split." And, "Did she wonder the same thought?" I concluded that it didn't matter as I crossed the bridge into D.C., noting that it was almost "eightish."

Traffic was light and I made the gate at eight sharp. Eunice was there ahead of me. She was out of her limo chatting with the young uniformed sentry. She looked radiant, poised, and obviously out of place alongside the overweight Rent-a-Cop.

Our reunion was somewhat awkward, neither of us spoke for a moment, we just smiled, one on the other – in reminiscence of what once was – and, in consideration of what might yet develop. She broke the reverie, "It's been a while, hasn't it?"

"Yeah. Too long." And I thought, "Damn, she looks good."

She nodded out a slow agreement, then said, "Follow me in, it's not far." She made a head motion, a point, "I'm just up the road."

I followed the institute's limo, a huge dark-gray stretch, up a gently winding road where we turned into a circular red bricked drive which fronts her residence, a huge English Tudor. Eunice bounded out of the limo and motioned for me to park near the door. As I turned off the key I noticed that the limo had left – to wherever it is that limo's go. Later, I learned that the institute owns four of them, but I still don't know where they're kept.

As I stepped from the Austin I couldn't help but notice the appearance of a huge black woman who literally dwarfed Eunice, me, and the 3000. This endomorphic pudge ball turned out to be none other than, Mureatha, Eunice's servant. She smiled at me as if we were long lost friends showing a gold tooth and open warmth that one usually reserves for one's lover. And I smiled back, openly, thinking, "Yeah, ...we'd been lovers – in some previous life."

Eunice was half way to the door yelling for me to follow her, "Leave your things. Mureatha will get them." And I thought, so much for introductions. Perhaps, it's not proper to introduce your domestic? I said, to Mureatha, "Nice meeting you." Then I headed after my beckoning employer, and – hopefully – soon to be lover.

Entering the massive foyer was an experience in itself. The floor was done in a white slate surrounding a circular reflection pool that boasted a brass cherub pissing into it from a small and underdeveloped penis. The walls were done in a textured plaster and were inlaid with large rough-hewn wooden beams that immediately awed one's senses with their bold and pseudo-western ruggedness. Eunice confided in me later that the effect was designed to evoke a sense of femininity in a masculine world. Then added, "...every time I come in this door I want to run up stairs and put on a pair of Levis. I think the architect blew it."

A white deep pile carpet covers the double set of stairs that lead up to a balconied second story. How Mureatha kept this area clean is way beyond my imagination. And, it was always kept spotless.

Eunice held out her arms, for what turned out to be a platonic hug. She whispered, "Welcome to first class, Mister Morgan."

Yeah, she had gone big-time, no doubt. She was a big-league, up-town, big shot, and she knew it. As I took a second astonished look around her designer cavern, I had to ask, "Where do I register?"

Eunice missed the one-liner. The poor creature had educated herself clear out of simple jocularity. Her seersucker suit and her dumbfounded stare were a major tip-off. I looked at her with apathy expecting her to say something like, "Wait here, I have to run upstairs and put my hair into a bun, read a few classics, and then we'll have a spot of tea and nibble at an itsy-bitsy crumpet."

Instead she says, "It's all a bunch of foofaraw, Jim. All show." She waved her arm in a grandeur sweep, "Although, it does demand a sense of propriety, don't you agree?"

I did agree, and in my best Clark Gable, I said, "Frankly my dear, I give a damn."

Mureatha burst through the front doors. She was carrying all three of my suitcases, the golf clubs, and tennis rackets and – by mistake – the Austin's passenger seat. Noisily she plodded across the slate and waddled determinedly up the stairs, first leaning deeply right, and then almost losing her balance in a lean to her left. Stabilizing her load at the halfway landing she took a noticeably deep breath and then sprinted up the last ten stairs. At the top, she uttered a loud grunt that sounded like, "Humph." As if to announce an effortless climb which really wasn't.

Eunice grabbed my arm and with a light tug led me off to her den. The den is not a working space in the true sense of labor. It was designed to host social gatherings for an intellectual few; and, could easily be mistaken for a library, tavern, meeting room, or a recreation salon. Everything is done in soft green leather and polished woods accented with a lot of brass. The entire east wall was windowed with small-pane glasswork that offers one a peek-a-boo view of the pool and patio, which was closed for the winter. A gas-log hearth made the room seem cozy and homey in spite of its vast dimensions.

Eunice moved behind the bar and dimmed the lights while asking if I still cut my Scotch with water. I nodded while studying the brush strokes on an original Monet that was lighted and on display between two neatly aligned bookshelves.

"It's on loan, the Monet." Eunice was enjoying my sincere show of wonderment. "Next month we're getting a Picasso."

I sat across from her on one of the ten bar stools. She threw a few toggle switches and the patio lit up casting a mellow glow throughout the den. A white neon light flickered once before announcing the bar to be open.

"The pool is heated, it'll be set up and running by the first of May." Boast. Boast. "There's an exercise room and sauna off the south deck." She pointed. "We have a live-in fitness-trainer who takes care of it through October." She elaborated, "It was a bit much for Mureatha to cook, clean, and maintain a pool. The trainer will move in when the pool opens. You'll like her. She's from India. She's into yoga and practices a lot of meditation..."

As Eunice continued I couldn't help but notice her radiance – she belonged. She fit the décor and added to its ambiance. I put my arms on the bar and pulled my drink and monogrammed napkin to the rail. Momentarily, I fixated on my watch, my Rolex fit in, and I felt an instant relief – actually, more of a self-esteem boost. Yeah, it was a certainty – I fit her mosaic, I "belonged," too.

"...She doesn't speak very good English, I think it's a defense mechanism." Eunice stopped her prattling, intuitively aware that I was tired from driving and not giving her one hundred percent of my attention.

"Mureatha will be down in a minute. She'll show you to your room. I've had her draw you a bath. Are you hungry?" This was all said in one breath, business like, it had to be said and so it was.

Although I wasn't paying full attention, I did hear the "are you hungry" part. I smiled away my inattentiveness and said, "You look beautiful, Eunice." Her eyes sparkled blue ice, her lower lip curled into a playful, "I know" grin and then we locked eyes, one onto each other, searching, searching for clues, for some wee subliminal nuance that would erase all the hours since we last contemplated *each* the other. It was an awkward moment, a weird moment and it lacked something, something mortally essential, and I concluded, it was intimacy.

I reached my drink and presented her a toast, "To the boss."

"Oh no-no-no." She softly protested, smiling, hefting her gin and tonic, "To my latest corporate acquisition, *you* – James P. Morgan."

And there it was, was she "only" the boss? Was I "only" her latest "Corporate Acquisition?" I had to find out – quickly.

"Yes, a hot bath sounds terrific. And yes, I am a little horny... err, ah, hungry."

Her ice blues twinkled mischievously, "If I didn't know you better, I'd have believed that to be a genuine Freudian slip, Jimbo."

I changed the subject nodding my head backward toward the lobby, I asked, "Is that troglodyte your maid, Mureatha?"

"Mureatha's an excellent maid, Jim. She's also an excellent cook. Good help is scarce here in Washington. You treat her nice – for my sake, okay?" Smiling, I nodded. She continued, pleaded, "I wouldn't know what to do without her. She's really good, promise me, Jim. Promise."

"I swear. I promise not to tease the help – Scout's honor." Then quickly added, "But if I know you, you'll wait on her and she'll be telling me how I should be nice to you before the day's over, right?"

Right on cue Mureatha entered, "Your bath's done been draught, sir." She spoke this with laughter in her voice. Then looked to Eunice for approval, getting the nod, she waddled off.

I mouthed silently to Eunice, "...done been draught?"

"She's Cajun. I think you'll like her, Jim. Just give her a chance. She's quite amazing. You'll see." Then, raising a chastising, motherly finger to me, she concluded, "Be nice."

"Hey, I'm only an employee, write it into my job description." And there it was, the flippancy, the arrogance, and the wit that Eunice abhors. And, as usual, I didn't catch myself before it was too late. I smiled quickly, quick enough that she had to take my remark in a humorous vein, which she did. Her mouth curled, she stretched, and she'd opted to ignore me – this time.

Rounding out from behind the bar, she announced, "I'm going up for a quick shower and slip into something more comfortable. We'll eat here at nine. Mureatha will be back to show you to your room." As she crossed the room she added, "Enjoy your bath, ta-ta."

It had been two years since I had asked Eunice to marry me. She was still the same Eunice that I had fallen in love with, but, somehow, much different. Yeah, the "ta-ta" was new, as were her seersucker wool suits, and her lavish environment. Yet, there was something else different, aloofness, and a somewhat mysterious quality that I couldn't quite pin down. Or, maybe, an old quirk was missing. Whatever it was? I couldn't put my finger on it. But then again she was still the same old Eunice, prim, self-confident, poised, controlled, on top of everything – ready for anything.

Mureatha, the Alley Oop mistress of the Potomac Riverfront, returned to announce, "I'll shows you to da rooms now, Mister Mogins."

I corrected her, "Morgan, Mor-gan. Not, Mo-gins, okay?" After all, I hadn't seen my job description, not yet, and until I did, I'd at least have some say on how Oop would pronounce my name. "That's M-O-R-G-A-N, better yet, just call me, Jim."

"Yes sir, Mister Mogins. Whatever you likes, sir."

Again, there was that laughter in her voice. I said – "That's better." Resigned, I followed her, mimicking her waddle, a small rebuff for bastardizing my name.

My rooms were on the second floor facing the Potomac River. The suite has three rooms and a huge bath. Everything bespoke of quality, plush quality. When Eunice said, "Welcome to first class..." She wasn't blowing smoke. Actually, she had understated the castle's opulence – ten fold.

Mureatha stood at the door with her hand out, palm up. I had seen this gesture a million times before by bellhops, waiters, and valet parking attendants from New York City to the icy shores of Nome. I pulled out a small clip of bills and removed a five-spot. It was automatic – tip the help.

Mureatha jumped back a full two feet. "No sir. No sir. I jus' want your keys, Mister Mogins. Can't be taken' no tips round here, sir. Miss North payin' me plenty 'nuff dat I ain't taken' no tips from da guests, sir. I jus' needs to move da car to da back, sir. Back to da garage." She was pointing east, to a wall, to let me know in what direction my car would be stowed. It was an awkward moment, I put away the fin and handed her my keys, asking, with reluctance, "Can you drive a five-speed?"

"Yes sir, yes sir. I can drive an eighteen-wheeler, sir. – Longs I got dem keys."

And to myself, I thought, "Yeah, and I bet you do windows, too."

She had turned and was moving out the door, then – as if she had read my thought – she says, "Yes sir, longs I got dem keys."

Let me express a bit of reality, "Mureatha didn't need the keys." No, she is physically capable of carrying the Austin out to the garage – on her back. As I watched her descend the stairs I came to a further conclusion: In actuality, she is a "Jell-o." She had been molded into her humanoid figure by an evil fifth dimensional entity that uses parallel worlds for its sick moments of levity and extraterrestrial entertainments. And as she reached the last stair and began to ooze onto the slate vestibule I had yet one more fleeting thought, "How in the hell was she going to get her big fat ass behind the wheel of ol' Cleo?"

Contemplatively, I closed the door and began surveying my new home. The spacious three-room suite boasts a large bedroom with a walkout lanai. A small but adequately equipped office, PC, laser printer, and enough power software to choke the most avid hacker sit off the main TV/sitting room. This big room has an excellent film library and presumptuously shelves enough books to satisfy the needs of any intellectual pursuit. There is even a kid section that offers some talking books. It had been a long time since I had last read, "Chicken Little." The fox button intrigued me to no end. Ah, such a literary marvel.

The suite proved out to be most functional yet very, very gracious. Eventually, I did add a coffee pot, two ashtrays and a three-way bulb to the bed lamp. Aside from those modifications I found everything quite luxurious and exceptionally comfortable.

Everything was unpacked and neatly organized into a master, walk-in closet. Fresh towels, oversized and fluffy, were laid out on the tiled bathroom vanity. The bath was designed for masculine efficiency, not necessarily the whirlpool sunken tub that measured seven by seven baker's feet, but by the quick shower that has a surround spray similar to that found in a drive through car wash, replete with an after-shower blow dry hair-system. The mirrors are wired not to fog and the shower doubles into a dry heat sauna. I am still impressed, and very much spoiled by the suite's ultra techno-bath.

The walls are tiled light gray with random Revolutionary War scenes staggered around all four walls. The room literally says, "Wake up." And yet, it can relax one to a fault. Two wall hampers, one marked "Laundry" and one labeled "Dry Clean Only" disappear to some mysterious and unseen world somewhere below the suite. Over night, hamper deposits are returned to the suite's door – crispy clean – and, without a bill.

I stripped and entered the churning whirlpool bath. A Celsius thermometer announced the water to be 40 degrees. As I sat there enjoying the sensation of twelve water jets massaging my flesh, I did a mental calculation to convert Celsius to Fahrenheit. Forty degrees times 1.8 equals 72 degrees, then add 32. The water was a tepid 104 degrees Fahrenheit. And I thought of Eunice. Imagined her in her own shower and wondered if she needed me as badly as I desired her.

And I looked at my watch and it was nearly nine. Twenty whole minutes had raced away since dunking my toes to test the warmth of Eunice's roiling waters. And it was with great reluctance that I cautiously stepped from the tubs caressing heat to towel, blow dry my mane, and dress for a late night dinner, and hopefully, much more.

I put on a new white shirt and pair of black slacks, then opted for a summer tan sport coat. Eunice would call me on the black slacks, but – hell, it was Friday and late. I left my top two shirt buttons opened and put on a gold chain that I had purchased in Fairbanks – it matched my Rolex. When I stepped back from the mirror and looked at myself, I felt good – macho, and caught myself in a soft whistle, an 1814 battle hymn.

It was a few minutes past nine when I walked out the door and bounded down the staircase. My stomach rumbled with hunger as I crossed the slate to enter Eunice's multiple-function den. Yeah, it was indeed time, time to strap on that old feed bag, and – much, *much* more.

Chapter Six

Eunice was standing at the bar preoccupied with a stack of classical CD's, many of them still sealed in their original cellophane wrapping. She was wearing a white blouse; seductively open to expose a most sensuous bit of cleavage. A snap glance lower disclosed the absence of a bra and when I let my eyes roam even lower I was treated to a view of tight-fitting Levis. Levis cut to enhance her figure and to openly emphasize her model's butt, small, and yet, so playfully proportionate.

Yeah, she was "Miss Erotica," youthful, seductive and totally aware of the look she affected. And, it wasn't a look affected to do institute business. However, it *was* intuitive – at least in my mind.

Without looking up, she says, "What do you want to hear, Jim? Piano? Violins?"

As romantically as I could, I answered, "How about your heart beating against my ear?"

"Is that like rap or heavy metal? I haven't heard... Here we go – this will set a nice mood." She slid a silvery-gold disk into a stereo component, punched a few buttons, and tiny green lights flickered across the system's face and the whole room filled with the sound of exotic bells tinkling out in what one could only describe as quadphonic bliss. She had selected some new wave, Enigma, soft – yet pounding and mystical.

She lowered the lights to let a pair of translucent candles flicker up warm dancing shadows throughout the den. It was eerie, romantic and sexual, – an immediate sensation of blatant seduction permeated my being, titillated my very soul. She came to me, she in a quintessential smile of unspoken need touched me, and neared yet closer. Then spoke, soft, close to whispered, "I see that you're still dressing like a pimp, Jimbo."

"And you my sweet, just where have you hidden your scarlet letter? Surely it's not sewn into your bra." I had gently reached out cupping her left breast with a wanton sexual caress – ready for rebuff, yet praying for a positive, non-response.

"Ah, what's this? No bra? My, my, such a flagrant dress-code violation for a woman of stature." And our eyes locked; hazed in that reckless abandon that transcends emotional restriction. We were already making love – spiritually banging one the other without so much as lowering one's zipper or lifting one's skirt.

A leaden silence ensued, the moment, the music – the entire atmosphere was threatening to explode, to disintegrate from idle tit-for-tatting on each the other's dress. The passion, the frolic of non-sensical social intercourse was about to go "poof." And, I didn't want that to happen. – "No." Not then, not on *that* night.

In placation I whispered, "Isn't time supposed to cure old wounds, Eunice?"

She countered, sardonically, "Time cures broken bones, Jim – *nothing* cures a broken heart."

And then she changed, her eyes sparkled and a weak smile over-took her exposed negative countenance as if she had caught herself being too open, too honest, and was innately compelled to cover up the heavy, close to dramatic, emphasis that she had overtly placed on the word *nothing*.

An icy chill shot up my spine lingering momentarily along the nape of my neck. Something was amiss. Maybe it was the music – Enigma, the bells, the erotic symbols, the chants, that ethereal chant-ing and its' suggestive, mystical taunts. – No. Something was afoot, a devious switch had been made, a hate filled statement was being shrugged off with a pacifying, smirk smile that belied a smoldering vengeance, one that *time* would never, ever, begin to quell... And then, as quick as the insight had flashed into being, it was gone, evap-orated by that lovely, lovely heat of passion.

Our lips came together, hungry, warm and slightly trembling with that cosmic need to commingle, to fulfill the need of becoming one with the essence of the other's being. It was a precursor, an open promise to fulfill an obsession, and that – would *not* be denied, no – not by a mere broken heart, and surely not by...

Mureatha floated in like an over-gassed zeppelin carrying two sil-ver covered plates of what turned out to be red snapper garnished with a pile of crisp, steamy asparagus spears. The hypnotic spell, our momentary know-nothing trance was shattered like so many of a man's capricious dreams. Yeah, Mureatha entered like the subservient blast of one's trusted alarm clock when it dutifully screams out, "It's reality time – wake up."

And how did she know? What was her cue? Who directed her untimely entrance, and just who is it that orders asparagus spears for a man? – Surely not me, a macho knight fresh off the Alaskan oil frontier – no, not me. The blimp hovered, scanning her placement of silverware and now uncovered plates. Content that everything was proper and that no demands or complaints were forthcoming she vanished, like the metallic soul of a long dead and forevermore deflated dirigible, oxidized into some ethereal dimension.

Eunice did give Mureatha a slight nod of approval before she departed, a deft dip of her head, a nod that directed that everything was going in accordance with her wishes. It said, "You're excused, dear. I'll ring if I need you. Now leave us. I, the white queen, have my male opponent in check – my pawns are no longer needed. You are simple fodder littering my game board and may impede my cry of mate. If I screw this one up I will need more than you, my maid – a mere servant, to reclaim my superiority. See? So go. You're bid a hale and hearty goodnight, and beware, don't let the oaken door hit you in the ass, amen." Yeah, it was a small nod all right, a real oratory venture in silence.

Were Eunice a lesser soul she would have simply waved Mureatha off, the way one waves off a pesky fly. But no, not Eunice, she had to tell her everything, and her perfected nod had said it all.

Eunice, using her index finger, began a contemplative poke at the buttered asparagus. Lifting one from her plate she poised it near her lower lip, then spoke, with a deliberately malicious stare focused dead-eyed into my corneas, "Do you really want to sleep with me, Jim?"

The stare held, unblinking, cold, shark-eyed; then, tapping the spear to her lip, not sexually, but contemplatively, and not so much as waiting for, or wanting my *positive* reply, she bites off the butter-dripping tip. Then – and this really boggled my mind – she threw the remaining sprig to her plate with a show of flared-nostril feminine vehemence.

The stare continued, a searching stare. She was looking for something, something that only she would recognize if, and only if, *she* were able to see it.

I must say that this display for the dramatic had made me feel very, very uncomfortable to say the least. I actually felt that I was dining with a bona fide fruitcake that was exhibiting a poorly played role in an Alfred Hitchcock-type psychodrama. But then again, this was Eunice, the intellectual madam of intuitiveness. My supposition is that intellectuals just do these sorts of things on occasion. Don't they?

Deep down, I knew what she was looking for. It was no big secret, no mystery. Yeah, I did want to sleep with her. And yes, I'd allow her a moment of temporary madness if that's what it would take for her to clear away the stormy clouds that she had churned up above our, once upon a time, "dynamic" relationship. Yeah, even though her moment was somewhat bizarre and borderline schizoid – I loved her, and most certainly *desired* her.

I pleaded, "I really have changed, Eunice – I really have. Why, I've even put all of my money into Treasury Bills." And there it was, I had bared my heart and opened up my soul – the rest was up to her.

Coldly, she says, "We'll see, Jim. We'll see." Then pushed her plate to the center of the bar. Apparently her appetite for the dramatic excluded Mureatha's red snapper.

Still operating in a mode near melancholy, she popped the cork on a fine wine that dated back into the mid-30's and with a distant look, a look of remorse, filled our crystal flutes with a golden nectar that was fit for the finest of fine wine connoisseurs.

With all the sincerity that a beggar could muster, I hefted my glass in a toast to new beginnings, "To a fresh start, Eun."

To which she added, in a cool somberness, "We'll see, Jim. We'll see."

The red snapper was delicious; however, I did think the asparagus a bit stringy and way over-seasoned. But the wine, the wine was a gift from Bacchus the ultimate god of all worldly pleasures. The music drifted into a slow-tempo saxophone that cried out in a nonverbal language that spoke of impetuous lust. Yeah, things had mellowed nicely since our "new beginnings" toast. Eunice's eyes hazed with sexual anticipation. Our human needs, our sapient desires were now, mutually understood, impending, explosive, and demanding righteous fulfillment.

And I woke, the next morning, contented.

Eunice, warm in my arms, looking at me in a half-awake sleepy grin, asking, "How do you like working for me *now*, James Morgan?"

• • •

Two years earlier, almost to the day, I had asked Eunice to marry me. It was on April first, All Fool's Day. I gave her a plastic ring, and – she promptly told me where I could put it, and it wasn't on her finger. Later that same evening, at a ritzy Hollywood restaurant, I paid a violinist to approach our table and play "If I Were a Rich Man" from "Fiddler on the Roof" as I presented her with a flawless one carat diamond. She calmly said, "No way. Daddy thinks you're a bum."

The violinist hit a sour note, eeeeeee. The other diners who sat around us stopped chatting, a horrendous silence overtook our entire section of tables, heads turned toward us, questioning eyes demanded to know what was going on. And I thought about her words, "...Daddy thinks you're a bum." "No way. Daddy thinks..." And as my face paled and I honestly considered crawling under the rug, she smiles and says, "April fool, Jim."

A slow but rising applause from our neighboring diners soon confirmed her acceptance of engagement. Nice champagne was sent to our table and the violinist turned happy hillbilly and fiddled up a lively reel. Eunice, beside herself, left her seat to show off her ring to anyone and everyone who'd care to look. More wine arrived, I stood and toasted, "To my love and future bride." It was fun, we were an instant hit, and some unknown benefactor paid our bill and a third magnum of champagne came bucketed in ice to extend our blissful happiness. Yeah, our reckless spontaneity earned us a free meal and way too much bubbly for a weekday evening.

Later that night, on my way home, Eunice had to return to Stanford where she was lecturing the following morning, I was overcome with a need to express my excitement – yeah, I needed to shout it from a rooftop, paint it on a billboard. I rolled down my window – shouting my joy to the world, "She said, Yes!"

I pulled into a roadhouse called, "Rascals Only." As it turned out, "Rascals Only" was a topless dance club. The dancers were hot and the beer was cold, and Bunny... Wow, she was so happy to hear about my engagement that... One thing led to another and. I don't know how such a thing could have happened but... Bunny accompanied me home and into my bed.

Eunice, elated from good fortune, decided to cancel her early classes and surprise me with her presence. After all, she did have a key to my apartment. It was a beautiful idea...

Eunice let herself in. Stripped naked. Then tiptoed silently into my bedroom where she quietly slipped under the covers – right next to my fluffy little friend, Bunny.

Ever hear the word "Pandemonium?" It's a word used by the great philosopher Milton to describe the capital of hell. My apartment, my den of inequity, exploded with foul expletives and a rapid round of fisticuffs that left one blond hare lumped limp in my lap. The champagne, the beer, the gin, the toasted shots of Old Grand Dad, all the booze hefted to celebrate my future marital bliss came out, the same way that most of it had entered, quickly. Although it wasn't quite as liquefied as it once was... Is there no nice way to say vomit? I know I was ill – groaning, regurgitating, the dizziness... Yeah, it was an earthquake; the San Andres fault had opened up and swallowed me whole, casting me straight down to middle earth and Milton's nightmare – Main Street, Hell.

I still have a vague recollection of Eunice walking stoically toward her car, naked, clutching her clothes. And, snippets of Bunny, whimpering, wiping puked-up lobster bits from her small (but well formed) breasts. Her cute little face all smeared in blood – Eunice had broken her nose. And, occasionally, I get this blurry flashback of myself, I'm hugging this cold white porcelain bowl, it's huge and a big whirlpool keeps trying to suck me into its depths but it only gets my guts because I hold on so tightly.

And I recall waking on the bathroom floor, cold and very near that descriptive state of cadaver, awaiting burial. I hear someone sardonically say, "He's alive." It's a cop, I see his shoes and hear a radio crackling off his shoulder... Yeah, I was still alive, but I didn't care to be – it was that bad.

After weeks of trying to patch things up, I came to the realization that I was beating my head against a brick wall and threw in the towel. She was scorned. She was through with me – forever. She built a moat of hatred around her soul, a moat so deep and vast that a whole fleet of aircraft carriers couldn't cross it, let alone costly flowers, and *actually* begging on bent knee.

Yeah, it was over. The band had packed, ticket stubs were reduced to so much chafe in the wind, the spotlights were off and the stage was being dismantled. Did I *once* get a sign of hope? – A flickering spark? – Some inkling or *hint* at forgiveness? No! Nada. None.

My job in the aerospace industry began to suffer badly from my loss of love. I picked up two written reprimands for gazing out a window while the landing gear of the X-8-94S Super Condor, the project that I was working on, collapsed on its first experimental takeoff – as if it were my fault or something just because I had worked out the strut's stress analysis. Yeah, the handwriting was on the wall – the axe would fall, soon. Life had become a nightmare and I didn't know how to wake myself out of it.

I called a college buddy whose father happened to be "in" on the Texas oil industry. They were looking for an Engineer to do field exploration around Brooks Range up in Alaska, could I get away? I could and I did. One week later I entered Ice Hole No. 13.

Apparently, my self-imposed exile made a positive impression upon Eunice. After all, I was back in her bed, life was once again beautiful, love was love not lust, and I had made a lot of money in the interim. Now, back to the adventure.

• • •

Over breakfast, Eunice delineated her expectations of me as her newest staff acquisition. My first assignment would be to guide and support a group of twelve scientists down to Madagascar, a large island off the southeastern coast of Africa. I'd be the advance man; I'd fly down, set up a tent camp and make everything as "easy" as possible for the following expedition. I'd be given a hefty expense account and be authorized to use it as best as I saw fit, to ensure that everyone came back happy.

To quote Eunice, "If you have to kiss some ass, pay off an official, or bribe someone – just do it."

"No." She wouldn't put it in writing. And, "No." It would *not* be written into my Job Description. After composing herself, she added, "Look, I need someone on this project that I can trust implicitly. That's why I've brought you here."

She moved to the window and continued talking. Her back was to me; I think she was fixated on a tugboat that I could see beyond her that was chugging slow against the Potomac current. "The CIA has contacted me, Jim. They believe that an international spy is monitoring my expedition. They also believe that this spy will try to steal the tortoise – once we find one."

She turned away from the window and moved back to the table, she was being cautious about what she was saying, choosing her words carefully with an open deliberation as to what she'd divulge or not divulge to the one whom she needed to trust, "implicitly."

"I'm sure this all sounds a bit cloak and daggerish, Jim. But, should this tortoise turn out to be genuine, it would be a very significant find. Not only to us, but to the entire free world as a whole."

She sat down; she looked drained, limp, "Just trust me on this, Jim. This tortoise is really important."

So I asked, "Just what's so important about this turtle, Eun?"

"Tortoise, Jim. Tortoise. Remember, tortoise on land. Turtle at sea. Turtles are amphibious, tortoises aren't." She caught herself over-explaining, her voice had risen, and she was on the verge of anger. Catching herself, she smiled and slowed her verbal chastisement. Collected, she continued.

"...It has to do with evolution or something. This particular tortoise, the Malagasy Rex (rex is Latin for king) is believed to possess a chemical that may heighten one's intuitive senses, namely, the *sixth* sense, ESP. We believe this chemical may be the trigger, the catalyst that causes an electro-chemical reaction in the brain's neuron system. We think that dendrites can control the super string vibrations surrounding particle physics..."

She paused, looking at me quizzically – did I understand what she was saying? She must have felt that I was in tune to what she had said – because she continued.

Summarizing, she concluded, "Our theory is tenth dimensional, it should work, it will open a lot of technological doors if we are right and the tortoise is real."

I challenged, "Do you believe this?"

"Yes. There's too much smoke, too much technological, tangible, data has surfaced from our anthropological studies to simply ignore. There's a fire in this tortoise, Jim. We've got to find it and harness its' power. That is, if we can?"

She paused, lowered her voice, she was excited, she was getting emotional then caught herself, "The problem is, the Rex may be extinct. The natives on Madagascar may have used them all up, right into extinction."

Yeah. She believed it. One could tell by the excitement in her voice. And, she'd find one – if indeed, one did exist.

She continued, "We believe that one may have been found only one week ago; but, we couldn't confirm it."

She went silent, contemplative, picking through her thoughts, organizing just how much she would, or could, tell me. Maybe she was waiting for me to ask, why not? So, I asked, "Why not?"

She slowly elaborated, "About a year ago, an anthropologist was doing field work in Madagascar. He was specifically studying the old shaman ways of inter-island communication, namely, thought transference. He published an article on old tribal ceremonies and named a Malagasy Rex - extract as the opiate used by the shaman to perform their silent communication from one end of the island to the other."

I interjected, "I thought they used drums?"

"Will you let me finish, please?" She continued, irritated, intent to emphasize her sincerity and the import of what she was relating, she stared me down before continuing. "I called him – the anthropologist, I invited him here to the institute (I wondered – by phone?). After picking his brain, I was convinced that the Rex was real and that they still existed. I hired him right on the spot to return to Madagascar, find a Malagasy Rex and bring it back, here – to the institute.

He called me from the airport in Madagascar. He was excited; he believed he had found a Rex. He was all set to take the next flight out..."

She stared down at the table with a pained look, not seeing the table, but distantly collecting dim thoughts. So, I prompted her, "*And?*"

"He was murdered."

It was my turn to study the table and to distantly collect my own thoughts; murder is a topic for the ten o'clock news. It is not a good subject for an Engineer getting a rundown on his employment expectations. Yeah, the word *murdered* hung in the air like a big red balloon, a balloon filled with poisonous arachnids, ones that hadn't been fed in six weeks, and, it was about to burst, and, wouldn't you just know? I really, *really* hate spiders. But, before I could orally vent my feelings, Eunice continued.

"The CIA thinks he was killed for the tortoise. But, the Malagasy Police think it was a simple hold-up, for his wallet. Not, for the tortoise. An off duty policeman was at the airport and saw the whole thing. He chased the robber and killed him in a shootout. It was an opened and closed case of mugging – as far as the Malagasy government is concerned. An airport janitor swept up the tortoise like so much trash and dumped it into an incinerator."

This expanded story made me feel a little better.

Then, she elaborated this, "The CIA is convinced that there was more to it. The robber turned out to be an old-school Russian spy who had defected to an African safe-haven that caters to terrorists. He had been inactive for several years, but they still monitored his whereabouts as he had caused Russia's new order some significant resistance. He has been linked to an organization known as the Recheeka, a bunch of die-hard anarchists and out and out terrorists."

And then she abruptly stopped. In response to her pause, I prompted, "And?"

"That's all. I need an Engineer. I picked you. This expedition has been in the mill for some six months. It begins in a very few days, and I fully intend to use it to find a Rex. The CIA has promised to protect us. As soon as we find one, *you'll* bring it back. And, of course, you'll be fully escorted by the Secret Service. I do think it's an unnecessary precaution, but the CIA insists. You're not afraid are you?"

I answered the ragged gauntlet that was cheaply slapped against my face, "Nope." And smiled, because I was thinking, "just cautiously apprehensive."

She must have read the false bravado in my flippant, "Nope." She rapidly shot back, "Well, it sounds easy enough to me. All I'm asking you to do is to bring me back a little ol' tortoise, that's all I'm asking. – Jimbo."

Her use of "Jimbo" after she was finished was a subtle key to the onset of a sexual interlude. That, and the way she rubbed her collarbone just above her cleavage. She does this when business is concluded. The nuance says, "I'm thinking of me now, I like me, and I'll stroke myself while I mentally withdraw from the dominant position of being a female corporate director."

Yeah, Eunice can say, "Jimbo," with twenty-four distinct and separate meanings. This "Jimbo" was totally sexual – no doubt. Smiling coyly, she says, "This wears me out, Jimbo. I'm going up for a nap. Want to join me?"

I looked at my Rolex. It was only nine. What can I say? I was just as tired as she was – or wasn't.

Chapter Seven

Eunice's suite, like mine, is comprised of three rooms. Her rooms are somewhat larger and there's a 1,400 square foot walk out garden-patio that overhangs the pool area. A spiral staircase descends artistically to a flagstone patio deck that extends outward from the den. A huge oak limb spreads out and across one corner of the lofted garden which gives the terrace a genuine, flavored dose of Frank Lloyd Wright's ideal of splashing bits of nature throughout one's masonry. Eunice has shown me a blueprint plan, her own design, to enclose the garden. She concedes that it's a conditional plan, qualified with, "...if my fiscal budget passes."

We frolicked and napped naked in her Swedish down feather bed for over two hours, then bathed together in her sunken six foot by eight foot Jacuzzi bathtub for another luxurious hour or, maybe, much longer. Ah, time, it becomes so fleeting when one finds one's self so totally immersed in such a sensuous activity.

Yeah, we were having fun. Eunice was being fun, her environment was fun – it was high-tech high-jinx and very exciting. I was in love with the boss and the boss was in love with me. Life was indeed grand, and I was getting paid handsomely to endure such joyful exuberance.

Eunice has a business laugh that sounds like, "tee-heeee." It's soft, yet penetrating, and demands one to ask, "What's so funny?"

And I did ask.

"Oh," she says, "I was just thinking. I need to give you a title, something with dignity and an air of authority. I want people to recognize your position, your abilities, upon casual introduction. You do need to sound important if you're going to accomplish anything, especially here, in Washington. I was thinking, Field Research Engineer, or Senior Vice President of Global Field Expeditions. But the only title that comes to mind is, Resident Dick." She began to flail wildly in a frenzy of splashing, sloshing water everywhere. She was five, maybe six years old and acting her age. She had gone stupid, and I allowed her, her moment of obstinate abuse. Obviously even a highly cultured psychoanalyst has periods of blatant hysteria.

Resident Dick indeed. Ha, ha...

Later, we lolled around her sitting room wearing fat robes and discussed her latest manuscript on ESP. Mureatha catered in a pot of fresh brewed coffee while I tried to appear interested as Eunice ranted on about super string physics unifying the quantum fields with the theory of relativity, "...the brain's dendrites go somewhere, Jim. Particle physics may hold the answer. Blah, blah, blah..." She may as well have told the walls for all that I could understand of what she was saying.

Eventually, she began to outline my duties with the institute, that is, aside from my "resident" duties.

"Next Wednesday, you'll meet with the CIA agent who will accompany you down to Madagascar. You'll be immunized, get a passport, receive a crash course on the Malagasy language, learn the customs and courtesies of Embassy protocol and go through a small arms training class."

"Small arms training?"

She waved her hand in dismissal, "It's a package deal." She didn't elaborate and she wasn't going to, the subject was closed.

She continued, "I've made reservations for you at the Hilton in downtown Antananarivo. That's the capital of Madagascar. It's pronounced, An-tan-an-a-ree-vo. It's a mouthful even for the locals who have shortened it to Tanan. You'll arrive there a full week before the scientists."

My duties sounded fairly easy, I'd set up a tent camp, make arrangements for food and sundry supplies, employ a local cook, and do everything necessary to ensure the success of Eunice's tortoise expedition.

The CIA agent would act as our political emissary. Mr. Agent Au Secret would be traveling under the guise of Personal Assistant to the Expeditionary Overseer – me. In essence, I would have a personal bodyguard.

Eunice gave me a fat portfolio on tortoises and an even fatter one on the island of Madagascar. She told me to, "Study them well. You are going to be my field expert while you're down there." She added something about, "...being way overpaid to sit around a Hilton..." But I think she was talking to herself, making a mental note for future reference.

We spent the remainder of the weekend rekindling old love, touring the institute, strolling about the grounds and meeting a few of the resident professionals. We dined in on Mureatha's excellent cooking, and even found the time for a cutthroat game of Scrabble.

Yeah, we're fanatics when it comes to scrabble. We use chess clocks (one hour limit), and keep each other honest with the latest edition of "The Official Scrabble Player's Dictionary." Eunice, the writer, usually creams me with seven letter words. She was ahead by sixty points by the third play. By the time the tile-bag was empty we each had seven tiles left on our rack, she was ahead 390 to my sorry 311.

Eunice, because she counts all the letters, knew that I was stuck with three tiles of the letter i, and one letter u. She had thought the game was won and had begun to talk some trash, "Come on, Jimbo, play your four pointer, bite the bullet – play."

And play I did, I laid down all seven letters to spell out the word, "IRIDIUM." The final score, after a formal challenge to the play, 413 to 390, a come from behind last play victory.

Eunice became silent, then, nonchalantly, knocked the board over onto the floor. She stood and walked haughtily toward the door. Without looking back, she stated, "My newest employee will clean up. I have work to do."

Yeah, Engineers play wild Scrabble. And Psychologists? Well, they're just wild. Eunice refused my offer of a rematch several times over the next few days. For all her refinement and highbrow mannerisms she still chortles out with trash, like, "Up my ass." And, "Iridium, it's a *suck* word." So. – Back to the adventure.

By Monday, I was beginning to feel at home in my new environment. I slept late and took long hot whirlpool baths. I had Mureatha bring me in gallons of coffee. After all, I *was* working. As an immediate task, I was given twelve dossiers on the scientists who would be hunting the tortoise. I was intent on being a good employee and attacked the dossiers with a keen sense of propriety.

The individual folders were neatly organized and the format was identical on all twelve scientists. Page one was an application form and attached to each was a check for $2,500.00; it was costing the scientificoes to hunt the elusive tortoise. Below the checks were resumes, biographies, and a 5 x 7 color photograph of the applicant. Under these were big fat red envelopes all marked with big, bold, black lettering, "CONFIDENTIAL."

I called Eunice to ensure that I was supposed to read through these. She told me that they were Expanded Background Investigations called, "EBI's," and that I should read through them. She added, "You have a *Need to Know* security clearance, Jim. It's a specific type of clearance that has been given to you by the CIA."

And that was that. I'd tell you what they contained, but as of this writing I have been told that they haven't been declassified and that they probably won't be, at least, not in "my" lifetime.

All twelve of these scientists could literally walk on water. They could reasonably argue amongst themselves as to which one of them ought to get the next Nobel Prize. These twelve men and women held more degrees and certificates than there are marks on a Kelvin thermometer, not to mention their distinctive merit awards. I had read Journal this and Journal that until I was blue in the face and ready to puke.

One of these intellectuals, Dr. Altie, worked part-time as a lexicographer for Webster's' International. As soon as I read this, I went and unpacked my Scrabble set. I'm good, but why tempt fate?

I finished the portfolios early on Tuesday afternoon and decided to do some sightseeing. Eunice had left me a message that said she'd be in late because she was, "On the hill," or something until seven that evening. I translated this message to read, "Keep yourself busy, Jim. I'm going up to Congress. I've got to do a little soft-shoe shuffle on top the old pork barrels. See you at dinner." And that translates into, "Confidential."

I rang Mureatha and asked for the Austin to be, "brought around to the front." Affluence has some silly rules at the top, having one's car brought around front is one of them. I went to the window and watched for her arrival, wondering what would have happened if I had gone down and got the car myself. Hell, I didn't even know where the garage was; let alone where the keys were kept. I heard the Austin before I saw it. Mureatha ran through the gears like she was playing a cello at the Met. Yeah, she had a knack for the mechanical. I found myself smiling; the old broad had some spunk and a playfulness that she kept well hidden.

The near seventy-degree temperature dictated that the top was coming down. Mureatha studied every move I made, watched me undo every snap; make every fold of the top. She was a medical student doing her residency, readying herself for orals, no – for practicals. She helped button down the boot without directive, the Austin now belonged to her, and it was her responsibility. I would only drive it occasionally. The car had obviously been washed, and – I'll be damned if it hadn't just been waxed, too.

She produced a bottle of window cleaner and began to spot clean the chrome as I climbed in behind the wheel. She smiled big, knowingly that it was *her* car. Her lone gold tooth gleamed out in a hearty farewell as I lumbered, easy, down and out of the laced-brick drive.

Washington, D.C. is a great place to cruise. It gives one a great sense of history, and – the women, Washington women are surely one of America's greatest assets, no pun intended. It was grand to see so many mini-skirts. I believe there's a symbiotic relationship between long legs and politics, at least, in and around Washington. It was a difficult task keeping my eyes on the leggy traffic and driving safely all at the same time. I had to slow Cleo down from a guttural roar to a playful purr. I did this in the name of practicing safe sex.

A white Corvette fell in behind me, which also had its top down to expose two blond, sightseeing, locals. I slowed a bit further in an attempt to get them to pass me; I wanted to check them out – to see what they looked like. But they slowed, too. It was simply too nice a day to speed along and miss the sights.

I turned into a parking lot reserved for Washington Monument visitors and slid Cleo into an open slot. The lot was practically empty as it was early spring and kids were still in school, where they belong. The girls followed me into the lot but didn't park near me. As they passed I had noticed their license plate, which read – "TA TA"

I had this thought, "Ha, they must be friends of Eunice."

The girls pulled into a space near the main path leading to the monument. I backed out and eased over to an empty spot next to the "TA TA" kids. It was such a nice day, what harm could a little friendly flirtation do?

The girls had already opened their trunk and were in the process of removing some expensive looking camera equipment that included 200mm lenses and a tripod. I immediately pegged them to be professional photographers. I pulled my, by comparison, junky old 35mm camera out from under the seat and held it up, while asking, "Do you girls happen to know if there's a film stand at the monument?" They didn't know. But, it did open the door for some lively camera discussion.

We concluded that mine needed replacement. The girls sincerely enjoyed showing off all the auto-this and auto-that features of their equipment. They were both "very" cute and we spent the next two hours taking photos of each other. Yeah, it was a nice interlude from the humdrum of historical sightseeing. I happily posed for them, on the Austin, on their Corvette, in front of the monument, sitting on the Austin with both girls (by tripod), at the "TA TA" tags, and rolling in the grass where we had mock wrestled for the un-disputed crown of "Monument Wrestle Mania Number One." All in all, we had taken some seventy-five odd photographs – some of them, after dark.

The taller blond, Sophie, was really cute. Her friend, Bess, was a mite standoffish and seemed to be deeply introverted, but that seems to be a trait of serious artists and photographers. We had fun. It was innocent. It was spontaneous social intercourse of the highest order and I had enjoyed myself tremendously.

Sophie wrote down my address at the institute and promised to send me copies of the pictures that we had taken. I had to beg off meeting with them on the following day due to my CIA briefing. But I did promise to call them, as soon as I returned from Madagascar and the foibles of dealing with international spies. Sophie gave me her home phone number, saying, "I'm mostly free. Maybe we can get together and have dinner when you return. I'd really like to hear more about your trip. It sounds so exciting, so mysterious, promise you'll call, okay?"

I wholeheartedly agreed. But alas, we had to go our separate ways. Me, I'd go back to Eunice. And Sophie, well, being mostly free – left a lot of room for speculation.

It was dark and chilly when I entered the Institute's gate. Mureatha met me at the front door, she looked tired, drained, it was almost as if she were angry with me. And I thought, "Maybe one isn't supposed to stay out after dark in D.C.?"

She had her hand out for the keys and I handed them to her as she said, morosely, "You's late for dinner, sir. Miss North waitin' on you. You best hurry on in, sir."

Hell, something was amiss. I wasn't *that* late. Kidding, I said, "Don't forget to check the oil, babe."

Mumbling, but coherent, she answered, "Yes sir. Dinner's done been served, sir."

Eunice was eating soup when I entered, she stopped and asked, "...and did you have a nice day, James?"

"Yeah, babe. Washington is a neat city, and this weather, it's something else, especially for someone fresh out of Alaska, eh?"

She snapped her spoon down "hard" on the table. Her face became ridged, "Did anything *interesting* happen while you were out this evening?" There was a distinct edge in her voice, a cutting edge, a bitter "castrating" edge. Her tongue was a well-honed sword and it was at the ready for verbal combat.

With trepidation, I said, "Nooo. Why do you ask, Euni?"

As soon as I finished the word, *Euni*, a term of endearment, I was overwhelmed with a bad feeling, a guilt feeling, a masculine, gut, guilt feeling – one that can cause nausea in a two count. Somehow, I intuitively knew, Sophie and Bess had become a major problem.

Honesty is always a good policy, especially when one is on the spot and suffering from irrational guilt feelings. I volunteered, "I did meet a couple of cute blonds at the Washington Monument. I asked them back here for dinner and sex, but – they refused. Aside from that ...just plain old sightseeing."

"Those *blonds* were CIA agents." She looked hurt, she sounded hurt. She stared at me a long time exhuming her pain and open disgust. I was in big trouble, and – when one is in big trouble, one should forget honesty and rely on silence, at least – until one confers with his attorney. I kept silent and tried to look innocent, which was really hard because I felt so guilty.

"I have been advised (deliberate pause), by a top CIA directorate, to keep you on a short leash." She reached her spoon and began to idly stir her soup. Nothing else was said. We ate in total silence. Oh, there was an occasional tinkling of China, and my napkin fell to the floor once – with a horrendous thud, but – all in all, it was a very quiet meal. I may be understating this, but – Eunice was pissed.

Mureatha came in and cleared the table without looking at anyone. The grandfather clock ticked into the silence from a whole room away. That was when Eunice cocked her head slightly, still not looking up from the table, and demanded my attention, "Jim?"

Looking up from my own mental preoccupation – I was rolling a pea back and forth on the table linen – our eyes locked and she says, "I'm only going to say this once and you had better listen, and listen well."

"I'm listening, Babe." I was sincere, and I was sure that Eunice recognized my sincerity. She continued. "This tortoise, this expedition, is really important to a lot of people. Two human beings have already died..."

Her tirade continued for a full twenty minutes. I was humbled down to the bone. I "was" truly sorry. I pledged a whole new allegiance to flag, country, Eunice May North, and the entire free world, to include mom, apple pie, Fords and '55 Chevy convertibles. I really wanted her to believe in me, I even gave her the Boy Scout's salute. But, as usual, I was sounding like an ass.

On the bottom line, I didn't get fired. Between the lines, I was almost fired. And, "on the line" was my love, Eunice. "Not to mention the adventure." As a ramification, I had to sleep alone that night. Eunice was not a happy Institute Director and had developed one of her infamous migraine headaches.

That night, I lay awake a long time contemplating my own personal stupidity. Had the two blonds been Libyan sympathizers or Iraqi spies, the expedition would have been jeopardized, to say the least. I contemplated how the blonds, just kids, could be involved with the CIA, and be – secret agents? Yeah, it was beyond my comprehension. They should have been cheerleaders for the Washington Redskins, *not*, CIA spooks.

It was way past midnight when I finally fell into a restless, nightmare filled sleep.

And I dreamt – of CIA blonds.

Sophie and Bess were two spiders webbing up and down the Washington monument. They scurried up one side, then – conferring at the eye, they'd point and nod and then dance down a web stream as if in a race, or – after the certain capture of some snared and helpless prey. Their moves were quick, deliberate, but once they arrived – there was no game, no food to feed their mechanical and hungered lust. They'd look upon each other in surprise, then shrug in a dumbfounded confirmation that they had accomplished – nothing.

Then off they'd prance, awkward-looking, sixteen legs moving in harmony, yet, ten of them never touched the pink silk threads of their own device, 'round and 'round they'd go, up and up, until, back at the eye, a new conference, animated pointing, directives issued – then pounce. And again – they accomplished nothing; there was nothing there.

I moved to the base of the obelisk and shouted at them, "Hold still! Hold still. I want to take your picture so I can show it to Eunice, so hold still, okay?"

The cute one, the one named Sophie, paused and – smirking – called down, "Call me for dinner, soon. I'm mostly free, and always hungry." And she added, "Bring your shit camera. I could use a good laugh, you, you, Bimbo Jimbo." Then scurried up and into the eye.

Bess called down, "I'm cute, too." A tear formed in her spider eye as she backed into the monument's window emitting a low hiss that was out of context with my personal knowledge of arachnids and then – I called out to her, smugly, "Ha, ha, ta, ta – spiders don't hiss.

Eunice tapped me on the shoulder startling me into a chill and giving me goose flesh and – I thought *she* was a spider. I spun around while screaming and found myself looking at an angry woman. Her hands were on her hips, her teeth were clenched, her eyes narrowed and she spoke, "You're supposed to be the Resident Dick, not the *Residential* Dick."

I pointed up at the monument, "Look Eun, they're not blonds after all, they're just spiders, see?"

I turned back toward Eunice, and when I did I was hit full in the forehead with a carrot that knocked me backward a good three feet.

Stunned, I could only watch as she began to throw carrot after carrot into my face. I fended them off as long as I could with my hands and arms, but soon, I was inundated, buried up to my neck in red-orange tubers, many of them tied into seven strand bunches.

All the while, Eunice was screaming, "Take this and this and this... Share them with your fluffy little bunny bitches you, you – damned to all hell, Bunny Monger."

"Eun, they aren't bunnies – they're spiders. Spiders don't eat carrots." It was a useless plea. The carrots kept coming. I was buried. All sound became muffled, everything became blackness and my body became ridged, I couldn't move.

I wasn't afraid – I was actually content with the tranquility that the blanket of tubers supplied. My thoughts focused on Eunice and I wondered why she couldn't tell the difference between a spider and a rabbit. Yeah, she really had "over" educated herself. I tried to push myself out of the carrots but it was useless. I was doomed. I was going to suffocate. I made a small listless plea for help, "Help." And as soon as I did, I began to laugh. Everything had become clear, I was experiencing this tremendous clarity of thought "Eunice was a jealous person."

I began to wiggle my head back and forth trying vainly to get my head above the carrots. I needed to share my new insight with Eunice. I had to tell her. Yeah, she'd see the error of her ways and stop her dang-blasted carrot barrage. Everything was going to be fine.

I woke to the sound of a foghorn blasting on the Potomac. It was probably a foggy morning. I lie awake recalling my dream and found that I held a vivid recollection of its detail. I lit a Camel and watched the smoke waif through a dim beam of light that was entering the room from between the curtains. I decided there and then to share my dream with Eunice. I'd ask her to analyze it for me, she thrives on analysis, she thinks she knows it all, and – maybe she does. Yeah, I'd wait until breakfast, or lunch, and ask her for a scholarly opinion.

I put out the cigarette and slept until the clock rang. Upon reawakening the dream had lost its backbone, the clarity of subconscious reasoning was muddied up into oblivion by the droning on buzzer of the radio alarm clock.

I showered and dressed conservatively. Hell, I had serious business to do. Yeah, I was to meet with the CIA. My adventure was culminating, and soon I'd receive my, "Small Arms Training."

Culminating? Hmmm, more like – *snowballing*.

Chapter Eight

My indoctrination into the covert dealings of the CIA was canceled. According to Eunice, "The CIA doesn't want you anywhere near their headquarters." Then capped her statement with an emphatic, "Jimbo." This ugly and highly derogatory use of my name immediately perked up my ears, as it was meant to do. Normally, I'd challenge such obstinate name abuse. But, I was compelled to allow her this gross name bastardization because I deserved it.

Yeah, I was the victim of my own stupidity. And now, like it or not, and I didn't, I allowed Eunice her open show of self-righteous employer indignation. It was in consideration of, or in condensation of, maintaining our happy and workable employee/employer sexual/financial relationship.

So, instead of a trip to Langley, I did an abbreviated orientation at the nearby, Andrews Air Force Base. The briefings took place that very morning. I was to meet a CIA agent at the main gate to the base, supposedly, the very agent who would accompany me down to Madagascar. He would "personally" escort me around the military complex to insure that I minded my p's and q's.

Eunice walked me out to the waiting Austin, Mureatha was not to be seen, and gave me a cool peck on the cheek as I slunk in behind the reverberating wheel. She bent down to the window while advising me to, "...act professional, and please, take these briefings seriously." Then, trying to placate me with some humor, she says, "By the way, Jim. When are you going to get a real car?"

When I arrived at the base, I immediately began looking for the white Corvette with the "TA TA" tags. After all, it was a beautiful morning, a daydreaming morning, and I gave it some time for the memory of my spy, Sophie. Yeah, it was just a pleasant thinking day.

What I did find waiting for me was a young male Naval Cadet on loan from Annapolis. He was sitting at attention in a gray sedan with a government motor pool tag-plate that boasted, TAX EXEMPT.

After locking the Austin, I climbed into the gray, drab and very mysterious world of our seldom-exposed CIA circles.

By nine-thirty that morning I had undergone a complete physical exam, received an armful of international immunizations, underwent a dental exam, experienced a plastic-gloved finger probe for hemor-rhoids, and had an ugly Physician's Assistant hold my testicles while I coughed. She said she was, hernia hunting.

By eleven I had visited Mr. Phlebotomist who had drawn way too much blood for a simple physical. I think it was a test to see how much blood can be taken from an individual before that individual faints. Or, maybe I was being used as a secret donor for some covert military test project. Thanking me, as if I had a choice, the phle-botomist took my, now his, bucket of blood and left me sitting there in his five-foot square cubicle.

A long time passed before the starched cadet poked his head in and asked if I was okay. He was slightly grinning. Whatever it was that was going on he was obviously in on it. He directed me onward by pointing down the hall, "Optometrist Clinic – three doors down on the left. Knock twice and wait. Someone will let you in." His direc-tions were curt and matter of fact followed by another tawny grin.

He must have read my apprehensive impatience as he gently added, "As soon as you're through there. We go to lunch."

I nodded approval and headed weakly down the hall and knocked lightly on the unmarked optometry door. A balding man in his early fifties opened the door and bid me to enter, "Here, here, take a seat, here." He had a German accent but looked to be more Oriental than European. Three more Orientals entered from a side door and aligned themselves in a semi-circle around my chair. They all wore horned rimmed glasses and matching white lab coats, no one talked, they all seemed to be waiting for me to say something first.

So I asked, "Is this optometry? I am in the right place, aren't I?"

"Ah, yes-yes. Please make yourself comfortable. This will not take long." Then, in pecking order from left to right beginning with Adolph Bruce Lee, they each took a look into my eyes. Each in turn made an audible, "Hmmm." Then stepped back to their respective position in the semi-circle.

A large machine, one that resembled an armless robot was wheeled in and placed flush up against face. My head was then strapped taut against its cold metal eye-fittings. The eyepieces gave me a yellow-lit view of several, small, numbered targets. I was asked to rotate my eyes clockwise from one target to the next as rapidly as possible. I did this for several minutes, and then, "Zap," a bright flash of white light totally blinded me. I felt the straps being undone and old Adolph was saying, "All done, Mister Morgan. Your eyes are very healthy. When your temporary blindness passes you will notice a fresh clarity of color in your surroundings. This will only last a few minutes before your normal vision returns."

As all I could see was a yellow-orange nothingness. I reached up to rub my eyes but was scolded sternly to not touch them. This temporary vision loss was deeply unsettling to me and I voiced my alarm, "I think you should have prepared me for this blindness, don't you think, Doc?"

"One needs to be relaxed for these tests, please forgive us for your discomfort. As soon as you can see, you may leave. Good luck to you, Mister Morgan."

The door opened, and then closed, I was left alone, blind, and feeling quite helpless. It didn't take long for my sight to return. And, as the optometrist had warned, I did experience a heightened visual acuity that lasted for several enjoyable minutes before my normal vision settled back in. Crying, I stood and left to find my cadet. He did promise me lunch and I was ready.

On our way to the "O" Club, which stands for Officer's Club, we made a short stop in a room entitled, Pass and ID. I was guided to a chair and photographed three, maybe four times. The entire photo session lasted two minutes and we were off to lunch not waiting for the photographs to be developed.

After a very good steak and some excellent coffee we returned to the Pass and ID room. By the way, someone picked up the tab for our lunch and it wasn't the cadet. We simply sat down, ate, and then left. Our conversation at lunch was sparse, "Pass the salt, please." And, "Delicious steak, eh?" To which the cadet responded, with as much starch as there is in a sack of potatoes, "Yes, sir."

When we entered Pass and ID a young airman, a "one-striper," said, "Here you go, sir." And handed me a freshly printed, visa stamped, passport. And, it even had my real name on it, James P. Morgan, just waiting for my signature. I think I had expected it to read, "John Q. Smith," or "John Doe." But, there it was, "James P. Morgan," bigger than life itself. I signed it and placed it in my inside jacket pocket. I think this was somewhat of a disappointment. I wasn't to be a spy after all. I was destined to be *me* – my passport said so.

We moved to a basement room, a classroom that was replete with desks and a "green" blackboard. I was directed to sit in a chair at the side of the teacher's desk and told to wait, "...a language specialist is on the way over. I'll wait for you outside."

As soon as the door banged closed, an elderly woman re-opened it. She had an armload of multi-colored folders. She clopped across the room and slammed down the pile of papers. "Going to Madagascar are we?" Each syllable was emphasized similar to the voice of a badly programmed speaking robot. There was no intonation and no inflection whatsoever in her vocal structure, and I couldn't help but wonder, just "where" in the world does our government find these people? Surely they had to move a hefty rock and do some very serious digging to expose this one – my *language* instructor.

I kept a straight face and answered her question, parroting her monotone, "Yes we are."

We babbled along in French for a good twenty minutes. I had not used my French since satisfying my foreign language requirement in my freshman year at college. I was really struggling to understand her, and likewise, her me. Finally, we decided that I'd get along just fine. That is – if I could get by on eating ham and eggs three times a day.

The ten pounds of paper she carried in were tutorial aids for me to study – at my leisure. Somehow I had misplaced them prior to leaving the base.

And then it was back to the health clinic. A Chinese, Doc Ho, entered, bowed deep, and then smiled a most toothy smile to no one in particular. After a brief pause to read his notes, he says, "Ah. Hue smokes too much – the cigarettes. Hue *muss* do it more exercise. Hue uses too much the sauce. Cut down. Hokay?"

Emphatically and as Chinese as I could, including a slight bow of my head, I promised, "Hokay, Doc."

And so it went, one farce after another. Our next stop was at base headquarters. It was just after twelve o'clock – high noon. The purpose of this stop was for me to meet with one of the Ambassadors from Madagascar. We entered a sparsely decorated briefing room and waited at a podium facing a huge table that could easily sit twenty or more people. Within two minutes, several bird colonels escorted in our Malagasy Ambassador. I shook a cool, damp hand, never aware of him being formally introduced. He said, in essence, "Welcome to my country. I am confused here, at times. Now, I must go."

Yeah, it was international protocol at its finest. I never did catch his name, and I have never seen him since. My cadet, who had stood at attention and didn't breathe during the entire one-minute visit, said, after the small group had hurriedly departed, "He's quite a nice fellow once you get to know him." And, I'm sure he is.

At twelve-thirty we entered the base theater. The place was empty except for an unseen projectionist and us. We took seats in the middle section halfway to the screen. The lights went off and the cadet excused himself, saying, "I've got to make a few phone calls. I won't be long."

I asked him to bring back some popcorn. He said, "I'm sorry, sir. I'm not authorized to... Bla-bla-bla..."

And there I sat, semi-oblivious to the WW-II, black and white, and very tattered celluloid movie on the island-life of Madagascar. The narrator told of its' military significance, of abundant crops, of vast forests, mineral wealth, and exotic ores and, not once did the movie mention, or show, a tortoise.

The movie ended in under an hour. My cadet returned just as the lights were being switched on. We walked in silence to the gray sedan and he drove me to the main gate. He gave me a brisk academy salute and offered, "Good luck on you trip, Mister Morgan, I hope we meet again some day."

My guess, at the time, was that nobody had informed him yet that he was to be my escort down to Madagascar. I saluted him back while saying, "Yeah, sooner than you'd ever think possible."

Yeah, I was a cattle. Prodded here and prodded there all morning. The Army is like that. But, I now had indoctrination. And, for what all that is worth, I do not know.

On my drive back to the institute I found myself constantly checking the rear view mirror. I was watching for a tail. I was also experiencing a new sensation, namely, *paranoia*. Yeah, I knew that I was being watched, if not by Sophie and Bess, then by some other spy hidden behind the lens of a 200mm telescopic camera.

As I turned onto the road leading up to the Institute's gate house, I couldn't help but laugh at the antics of my day of indoctrination. Hell, I already knew that I shouldn't smoke. And, one knows when one has hemorrhoids, right? And, what did he say? "...Lay off the sauce." Yeah, like this is just what a guy needs, a guilt trip. At least he didn't say, "Lay off Scotch."

Later that evening, Eunice, ever the patriot, pointed out the value of my trip to Andrews Air Force Base, "If you had failed your physical I'd be hunting for a new Engineer, Jimbo."

"Oh no. Does this mean that I have to quit smoking?"

"A smart person would heed his doctor's advice, Jimbo."

"Yeah, but tell me, Eun. What's a guy supposed to do after sex?"

She shook her head in bewilderment, saying, "You're hopeless." Then added, "Maybe I can help you, Jimbo." These were all good Jimbos.

Reluctantly, I asked, "How are you going to do that, Eun?"

She offered, "The next time we make love, I'll pin you down until you fall asleep, hence – you won't be *able* to smoke."

"Yeah, right. You and your maid as a backup."

She glared at me, narrow eyed, defiant, "I bet I can."

"Nah, no way. You're the weaker sex you'd never be able to keep me down. I'm not some little rag-doll that you can throw around at will. I've got forty pounds on you, Eun."

She boasted, "I'll have you to know, Mister Big Shot, that I've been taking self-defense classes. You're going to be in for one hell of a big surprise if you try lighting a cigarette tonight, Buster."

"Oh yeah?"

"Yeah."

"Well, give it your best shot, Eun."

Her eyes softened into a narrow playfulness, a romantic readiness – a readiness to prove me wrong. It was a tit-for-tat non-verbalized come on. It was time for sport, time for testing the proverbial pudding.

So I had to gloat, "You might, and I stress the might, be able to keep me down for ten seconds, tops. That is – if you're not passed out from ecstasy."

Eunice stood and moved sexually toward the stairs, without looking back at me she wiggled her index finger for me to follow her. The time for talk was over. It was good old Missouri show me time. And I followed most willingly. After all, I had an image to maintain, I was the Resident Dick, and, "...if one talks the talk one had better be ready to walk the walk."

Eunice's clock rang at precisely five a.m. I threw her off and lit a Camel. Now I ask you. Who won?

Chapter Nine

On Thursday, Eunice and I visited an L.L. Bean specialty shop to purchase a few expeditionary items. This shopping stint turned out to be quite an adventure, in and of its self. We even purchased an English pith helmet. It was great fun and we shared some deep chuckles buying up all the various field gear. It was an insane spending spree, and to this day, I have never worn that English pith helmet – except to get a belly laugh out of Eunice.

My expeditionary wardrobe, which was all charged to the institute, cost $4,279.19 plus tax. One of the items that we had purchased that day was a Swiss Army knife, which I still have. It has proved itself over and over again, as a bottle opener, and most often as an excellent fingernail trimmer. Everything else purchased that day was for the sole purpose of appeasing Eunice's sense of propriety. Yeah, her vision as to how an employee should dress to lead an expedition into the wilds of Madagascar was somewhat irrational. When all was said and done, we could have saved about $4,000.00.

We finished shopping around noon. As we waited for the limo-driver to load our packages, Eunice announced that we were lunching at the infamous Watergate Hotel with Senator Alberquist. According to Eunice, "...a major Midwestern political genus." He also has a paid seat on the Institute's Board of Directors.

"Be extra nice to him, Jim. He always votes in my direction."

Senator Alberquist turned out to be a most affable personality. My negative expectations of dining with the hierarchy, an image of boredom and stuffy political rhetoric, fell over the transom as Alberquist told story after story on how to get a soy bean to vote Republican.

Yeah, he's getting my vote, and I've never even set foot in Iowa. The eloquent Senator also has a gifted knack for listening. We talked on and on about such mundane, but virtuous, subjects as the owning and driving of a classic vehicle, namely, an Austin 3000. It never dawned on me at the time how he knew that I drove an Austin, but he did. I was much too busy relating how a 3000 roars, how it draws attention to its' driver, and how invigorating it is to weave in and out of slower, heavy traffic. That, taking the wheel of my Austin was akin to taking up the reins of a full-bred, full-blooded racehorse.

Eunice, who appeared "out of the loop" joined into the conversation nicely with a bit of highbrow humor, "The only thing that I have to handle is my chauffeur." And the Senator roared in with a very appropriate laughter, it was an oral art form that only a few distinguished personalities ever attain. Then, not to be out done, he closed Eunice out with a Ford and Chevy story that had left her red faced and excusing herself from the table. The lively conversation was pointed and bawdy, he was master and he knew it, let there be no doubt about it.

Eunice left us, and as to where she went? I neither knew, nor did I ever ask. On hindsight, it was a planned excursion, a disappearance that allowed her men a bit of mental intimacy, a male to male bonding that seems so important in and around our nation's capital and among the mover's and shaker's who legislate industry and direct – however subtle – its fortunes. Yeah, the Senator picked my mind with the crass expertise of a migrant farm laborer, quick and dirty. My mind was gleaned clean right down to my innermost thoughts and my deepest preservation motivations.

Fraternity, sports, achievements, affiliations, and even religion went ping-pong across the green linen tablecloth. I was interviewed, scrutinized and analyzed all in one fell swoop. And – it was fun. After all, I do consider myself to be an *entity*, and one with nothing to hide, at that.

Eunice returned, as if on cue, to hear the good Senator, stand and say, "I do need to leave. It has been a most rewarding afternoon." We shook firm hands as Eunice told me to take care of the check. She was going to walk the Senator out to his chauffeured pick-up truck. The fertilizer magnate laughed heartily at her joke as they locked arms and left.

Yeah, there I sat, high from fine wine and fine conversation. I left a tip as hearty as Alberquist's laugh and headed for our own limo. Life was grand and Washington was becoming fun. I'd even have something to inflate on my first Expense Account. What more can life offer, eh?

Eunice met me as I was leaving and we sat back down. "Senator Alberquist likes you, Jim." She was jubilant, on the verge of laughter. She needed to be asked, "What's so funny?" And I did ask.

"Oh, it's Alberquist. He really does like you. He only likes people who he can manipulate, control with an iron hand. If he didn't think he could dominate you, use you, he wouldn't have said that he likes you."

"Does he like you, Eun?"

"Oh, heavens yes. I'd do anything for that man. He's a great and honorable person, Jim. When he uses someone, it's only in a most noble and constructive manner. People literally prosper under his guidance and paternal leadership. His integrity around here, around Washington, is so well known and highly respected, that it's practically legendary. His friendship is something to be very, very proud of, don't take it lightly."

On our way out, I physically bumped into the (then) Speaker of the House who gave me a horrid angry glare. Instead of apologizing, or saying, "It's okay, I'm a friend of Alberquist." I found myself saying, "Wow, it's you." Not, "Oh, how clumsy of me, Mister Speaker." No, it was – "Wow, it's you."

Eunice ran out the door. She didn't see, or didn't want to see, what did or would happen. On my way to catch up with her, I decided that she didn't see, and to leave the incident behind and to just not mention it, due to my own personal embarrassment.

Later, nearing INTUIT U., Eunice asked me to please work on my social clumsiness. To which I could only answer, "Hell, Eun, I'm clumsy enough without working at it." I had said this humbly and the issue was very discretely dropped.

Back at the Institute, Eunice went to work at her big, campus office. I busied myself packing the L.L. Bean wear into ten matching brown leather suitcases. I have always looked upon packing as a ghoulish nightmare. Inevitably, I'd forget something. Or, I'd run out of packing space. Like on my trip from Chicago, I forgot underwear. And when packing the car – I had no room for my fishing tackle.

This time things would be different. Eunice was totally thorough. Nothing would be overlooked on this trip. She even purchased handkerchiefs. Yeah buddy, hankies would have been right at the top of my list, yes-er-ree-bob, right along with that English pith helmet. Everything went well and I even wound up with some room left over, room for returning, and for souvenirs.

Eunice returned from her business by four-thirty and announced that, "I've ordered the tennis nets to be put up." This was said with a hint of challenge in her voice. Tennis *is* Eunice's number one love, and, "love," is her normal score. She doesn't play well at all but she loves the clothes, especially her white tutus.

The first modification to the Institute of Intuitive Thought under the North regime was to have tennis courts installed behind the Tudor. They are totally fenced in and lighted for extended evening play. A practice-ball cannon, which I have never seen uncovered, sits between the two separate courts. The courts are open to the university residents on a first come, first serve (no pun intended) basis.

Eunice boasts that she can find herself a match at almost any hour of the day or night. Her tennis mania is well known around the campus, but alas – so are her skills.

"Sounds like a challenge, Eun?"

"Get your racket, and your wallet, Jimbo. First one on court wins serve."

We grinned at each other sizing up the competition. Me, knowing that Eunice has never beat me a full set, saw dollar signs etched on her forehead. And her, she was oddly looking at my waist... The race was on, the race for first service, like a pair of teenagers we bounded up the stairs for our rackets, pushing and shoving, as if there was only one more life-boat to be had before our ship sank.

Eunice yelled out, "Whites only, Jim. And don't forget your Camels, Chubby."

"Chubby? You'll see Chubby, Eun. That's what you'll call my wallet when the match is over."

I threw my clothes off in front of a full-length mirror and indeed I had grown a small set of love handles. The passive years on the Alaskan frontier had taken its toll. I grabbed a handful of flesh, fat, and pondered the meaning of love handles as I pulled on a ten-year-old Rod Laver tennis shirt. Chubby? Oh boy, I'd give her Chubby. "Chubby aces." Yeah, I did need to trim myself down, tone up the old muscle mass. I vowed then and there to begin a strict exercise program – as soon as I got down to Madagascar. I grabbed up my rackets, not bothering to tie my shoes, and headed for the courts. Chubby or not, I could still get myself ready faster than any woman alive, right?

I was first on court and did some stretching warm-ups, and then began a slow jog around the asphalt. I was making the third round when Eunice made her entrance. She wore her tutu whites with a matching headband. She carried a small cooler, some over sized towels and a white leather tennis bag that held multiple rackets. If nothing else, she looked good. She looked like a pro. And, if I hadn't known her better, I'd have been quite intimidated by her appearance.

The court lights came on. It was sixty-two degrees – perfect. The match was on. Eunice threw me three monogrammed white tennis balls. In script below her initials, the balls were effeminately embossed with, NUMBER ONE. I was impressed. I didn't know that white tennis balls were still being manufactured, and – it was the first time that I had ever seen one monogrammed.

She had moved into the green, two feet in, knees slightly bent as her body swayed tentatively right and left, she hadn't warmed up, but – she was ready. It had been a full two years since I had last swung a racket. I needed to warm up a little, hit a few, and get a feel for the court's surface. So I asked, "Want to hit a few, Eun?"

"No, no way. I'm ready, serve." She was out for blood.

I taunted her, "Did you bring your purse, Priss?" To which she nodded in the affirmative, a very confidant and cocky, "I did."

I added, "Name your poison, Sweetness."

Without hesitation she called out, "Best three out of five – a hundred each game and a hundred each set. And, a hundred on the match." This was all said with a cold finality. There was no room for negotiating, no hedging in her voice, no hint of backing off, or – backing out. The terms were her's and they were etched in stone. Her confidence was stoic.

I began to worry. This was really high stakes. Just what was she up to? I could hardly back down. I answered, "You're on."

Yeah, my confidence *was* rattled. A terrible thought raced through my mind, "Had she been taking lessons?" So, I asked, "Hey Eun, what makes you think you're going to win? Been taking lessons? What?"

She answered, "A few, now serve." And there it was. I was being hustled.

I moved to the line and served up an ace to her backhand. It was pure luck; I was aiming for her forehand. I was in big trouble, big time. Somehow, I managed to win the first game and that gave me a wholly renewed confidence.

We switched sides and she came after me with a terrific top-spinner that forced me out of court. She had learned her lessons well; she was playing great tennis – for a girl. She held serve and the set went six all. I won the set in sudden death. She accused me of a bad line call, which gave her a double fault, and gave me the set win. She bitched and moaned actually "pleaded" with me to take her serve over, but – I stuck to my call. If, she would have resorted to crying I might have, *might* have, relented. I lit a cigarette in a stupid show of bravado, a victory thumb of the nose. My pretty, my cute little opponent, was looking somewhat disheveled and slightly worried, but, not quite ready, yet, to call it quits.

As we passed, to change sides, she verbally noted, "Why, James, I've never known you to sweat so profusely, is that your stamina I hear faltering, or is it just your *heart* about to explode?"

Yeah, I was sweating profusely, my stamina was faltering, and indeed my heart was racing. But I was the one who was up a hundred bucks and wanted more. Eunice's second set has always been her strongest. She played the set well and edged me out with really bad, flagrant, line calls. I *knew* they were bad calls – she even questioned me as to why I *wasn't* arguing them, and I said, "I trust you, Eun. Just call 'em like you see 'em, Babe." And, her calls got cleaner.

Yeah, if she were a man – I'd have punched her out.

She won the second set, six - four. She was up two hundred and began to gloat. But I knew I had her. Eunice had never beaten me at third set. It was money in the bank. And it was, I trounced her 6-2 and it felt good. I had no guilt, nor did I feel a need to show her mercy, no – none whatever. I was up 300 biggies.

The fourth and final set was cruel. Eunice was complaining to be cold. The temperature had dipped to fifty, comfortable to me, devastating to her. I killed her, six - love.

Throwing her racket toward the cooler and heading quickly off court, she called back, "I'll pay you in the tub. If you can make it up the stairs – Chubby?"

Once again, the new employee – me, was left to clean up. I gathered up our props and headed for her tub and the earned payoff. On my way up the stairs, I momentarily considered *not* taking her money – for about ten seconds. Yeah, if she had won, she would have demanded to be paid right then and there, on the spot, gloating and smirking, no doubt.

Her tub was steaming and it had hundred dollar bills floating all about the surface. I couldn't help but smile over her creativeness to pay up. Then, in a last ditch effort at poor sportsmanship; she turned on the Jacuzzi jets to launder my court windfall. The bills dipped and churned in a mad chaotic turmoil. Yeah, it was a simple show of capitalistic reality, money, no matter how much of it one has it's still hard for one to part with it and – more often than not – much, much "harder" to *grasp*.

Chapter Ten

After diving for dollars, we dined late on a stuffed Cajun chicken, an ancestral specialty, ala Mureatha. Afterwards, we moved to the bar and sipped on an excellent brandy. Eunice prattled on about the expedition: "Be nice to him. Be extra nice to her. Ensure this. Ensure that. Don't screw the women. Don't gamble with the men. Stay sober. Be subservient. And – blah, blah, blah."

I finally had to say, "For Christ's sake, Eunice. I'm not a little boy. You're beginning to sound like an overly protective mother."

"Oh – I know, Jim. It's just – you tend to fuck off so much. I just want this project to go as smoothly as humanly possible. I've gotten so close to it that I can't help but worry about every little detail."

Reassuringly, I advised, "Relax, Babe. What can go wrong?" I placed a comforting hand on her thigh, which instantly brought a thin smile to her face, or maybe it was a grimace, because it was accompanied by a soft noise that sounded like, "Humph." She then added, in a gently moronic tirade, "Everything goes wrong that can go wrong. It's a law – Murphy's' Law."

She scooped up her snifter and downed the remaining brandy in one huge unfeminine gulp. Then elaborated, "Okay, Jimbo." – This was very near a sexual Jimbo. "Like they say in football, you got the ball, don't *bumble* it."

I didn't correct her fumble on bumble – I thought it was cute. Raising my glass of nasty tasting, but expensive, brandy, I saluted her. "To your sensible capitulation of control."

This time it was a real grimace. She was still reluctant. She couldn't let it go, power, control, and authority, are three terribly hard things to surrender, especially, when one felt as strongly as Eunice did about finding herself a Malagasy Tortoise."

So I added, "And to a safe and bountiful turtle hunt."

"Tortoise." She corrected, and the grimace departed, she was still able to correct me, and one could surely see the import of that, right? Yeah, it was just another deft upper-cut to one's chin, another outward show that she controlled her environment, it was autonomy on the edge of sublimating into a wisp of sub-microscopic invisibility, and then, she was saved by a bell, she knew, she'd always have "some" control, at least, as long as she was the one who signed my monthly paychecks.

"Yeah, yeah." I agreed. "To the elusive *tortoise.*" I then threw down the fiery turpentine in a big brash swallow. My eyes watered, my throat contracted, and I could barely add – but did, "To serious business, no screwing off, no fucking around, and – all work and no play."

Eunice grimaced again, and then began to fidget with her collarbone, the "finished with business" fidget. The *probe* into her deepest latent sexual needs. As a read of holistic body language, I knew that a sexual encounter was about to unfold, no, *erupt.*

Then she stopped, just short of piercing her cleavage line, and made an abrupt return to a piece of unfinished expeditionary business, "Oh, Jim. I'd almost forgotten. Tomorrow you're to meet with the CIA agent who's going with you."

"Oh yeah, I thought we'd met already, at the Washington Monument. What's that blonde's name, Sophie?" I was being playful, Eunice wasn't.

"Our government doesn't send attractive blonds half way around the world into a jungle just to titillate the likes of you, James Morgan." She squiggled up her nose while giving me a snooty glare, and then mumbled, "At least I wont have *that* to worry about."

"Ah. Do I detect a bit of jealousy?"

She responded with a pointed, "Yes." Then, under her breath, added, "Love *is* a bitch. Isn't it?"

Eunice was on the verge of melancholy. I changed the subject, "So, Eun, where do I meet this spook? Down some dark alley off Pennsylvania Avenue?"

"No, Jim. We're meeting here, on the veranda. I've planned a barbecue for noon. Mureatha is marinating ribs right now. I thought it would be fun. There's a chance of showers but they shouldn't hit until evening. It'll be fun. Don't you think?"

"Yeah, fun. I hope this agent of yours is more fun than that cadet I met at Andrews. One more hour with that piece of starch and I'd be howling expletives at the moon, Eun."

"Come on, Jim, be nice. I know you can be – if you try."

"Yeah, okay. So, what's this spy like? I'm sure you've got a fifty-page top secret file on him, right?"

"No, I don't. The only thing I know is his code name, Kidd. Spelled with two ds. I swear, Jim. That's all I know."

She paused, contemplating, searching through her mind as to why she didn't know more about this Kidd, other then how his name was spelled. My guess was that she felt snubbed, or – she really did know more than she was swearing to. She continued.

"We can pick his brain tomorrow. Just remember, be nice. Whether you like it or not, I do have to work with these people."

"I'll put on my *kid* gloves, Eun. I Promise." I then crossed my throat, swearing, "Cross my throat and hope to choke, I'll be nice to the kid from the CIA who spells his name with a double D, so help me God, amen."

A brief silence ensued as Eunice weighed the sincerity of my oath. Her scrutiny was deepening – too deep, I had to break her trance, and "Do you think he'll wear a disguise, Eun?" She shook her head in the negative, saying, "You're hopeless, Jim. Simply hopeless."

•   •   •

Later, while Eunice held me in her "Lotus-No-Smokus" karate hold, I asked, "Would I be missed if I were to play a round of golf in the morning?"

"No. Just be back here by noon."

Yeah, Eunice is my kind of boss. I asked my lovely, "Is there an easy course near by?"

She pondered this, trance like, and then placing her nose flush against my own, said, "Yes." Our eyes were but an inch apart; "I have a friend at East Potomac Park. It's just down the road. I'm sure he can get you on. I'll call him first thing in the morning. I think he can arrange a match for you. If you'd like?"

"I'd like. You'd better let your friend know that I haven't played in over two years, and – my handicap is a nineteen."

Eunice went into hysteria, "Nineteen? You have a *nineteen*-stroke handicap? Ha, I thought you were a good golfer, Jimbo?"

"I am, around the handicap set."

I needed a cigarette bad, real bad. I tickled her ribs and she dove away to protect herself. Before she could recover, I had my Camels out and was lighting up. So much for her karate junk, eh?

Eunice was up and in the shower by five. I scooped up my clothes and, naked, slipped into my own room and the luxury of a steamy hot shower. I shaved while playing golf in my mind. I was getting par after par and kept hitting the flag with my chip shots.

I dressed in yellow golf pants and a V-neck golf sweater that mom knitted for me back when I was in college, it was my "lucky" sweater. I got a par on the first hole that I ever wore it on. I pulled out my bag and checked my shoes, everything was on the up and up, I had a lot of balls – golf balls, and plenty of tees. The only thing I needed was a tee time.

I went to the desk and worked on the financial kit that Eunice had assembled for the expedition. I'd have an "emergency" credit line of 100,000.00 dollars, American, at the Chase Manhattan Bank of New York City, New York, USA. And that converted into, a "whole bunch" of Malagasy Francs.

Mureatha catered in a pot of coffee and a homemade strudel. At ten after seven Eunice called with a seven-thirty tee time. I rang Mureatha and asked for my car to be brought around front. She advised me that, "Miss North requested you a limo, sir. Do you still wants your little one?"

I opted for the Austin and I could hear an excitement in her voice when I did. She'd get to play with her new toy, which would make her day. Yeah, I'm just not a limo person. What can I say?

Mureatha had put the top down – the slave was a free spirit at heart, no matter the fifty-degree temperature. As I pulled out across the bricks, she yelled out to me, "Don't yous be late for my ribs now. Hear?"

I waved out in acknowledgment and headed for Potomac Park. It was early in the season and I was surprised to see so many golfers lined up at the first tee. I pulled into an open slot and, as soon as I stepped out of my door, a golf cart hummed up behind me.

"Good morning, Mister Morgan. My name is Tim. Here, let me get those clubs for you, sir."

Yeah, Eunice did have some pull around Washington. As soon as my clubs were strapped in, Tim says, "I've arranged a match for you, Mister Morgan. His name is Al and he has an eighteen-stroke handicap. He's waiting for you on the back nine. Your fees have been taken care of. If you'd like to go right out, just follow the cart path and stay to your left."

I tipped him a twenty, put on my golf shoes and headed for the tenth tee.

Al, an ex-clubhouse pro, extended his deeply wrinkled, eighty-year old hand, and asked, "Want to play for skins?"

"Yeah. I can use the lessons. Name your poison, Al."

We agreed on ten dollars a hole. We also agreed to discard our handicaps. Al took honors, based on age, and the match began.

Al shot par on the first hole and made me pay the ten skins, up front, before leaving the green. And so it went, ten after ten. We finished the back nine by nine-fifteen. Al was up by a hundred and twenty-five bucks, counting some foolish side bets, like longest drive, longest putt, and closest ball to the flag on the par 3, fifteenth hole.

Al, the big spender, insisted on buying coffee – laced with rum – between the nines. He said, "Your money's no good in here, Morgan. My treat."

Yeah. The old fuck had a way of making one feel special, all the way to *his* bank.

Al also had a penchant for telling great golf stories. Like the one he told me about Ben Hogan, how, "...he could kick a golf-ball farther than any man alive." And about how, "...the last time that I played with Arnold I had to spot him three strokes." But, now that I think about it, he never did say "Palmer."

I did decline his offer to, "...double the skins..." on the front nine. Fun is fun, but "stupidity," well – that's something else.

Al uncovered his, "Big Bertha" and strode out onto the first tee. He bent over to tee up his ball. And then, kept going down until he had crumpled all the way over on top of it – dead. He had a stroke, a brain aneurysm. Our match was over. Al had lost the entire front nine with a single stroke. Yeah, he's probably happy wherever he is; after all, how many golfers can ace an entire nine. "Way to go, Al"

Yeah, it was so quick, so sudden, and so very, very final. I drove back to the clubhouse leaving Al where he had fallen. This was my first experience with real death. Oh, I had been to a few funerals and such, seen it on TV enough, but, this was different. I felt so "helpless."

I sat in the clubhouse bar and narrated my story to a local cop. Tim, whose official title was Golf Pro, left a bottle of J&B Scotch at our table. It turned out that I had inadvertently notified Al's next of kin – as Tim was Al's son. I have deliberately omitted the use of Al's last name in this writing. His son is now playing on the PGA tour and has asked Eunice to ask me not to use it. And, so be it. "Good luck to you and yours, Tim."

After a short while I found myself quite alone in a most somber clubhouse. I had an overwhelming need to call home and talk to my mom, "Hi mom. I just called to say, Hi. Someone just died on me, mom. And, I just wanted to ask, how come, why? What's your thoughts on an afterlife, mom? And, by the way, how's dad?"

The J&B was gone. I stood and reeled to the door just in time to watch the silenced ambulance haul away Al – and my 125 dollars. It was almost one o'clock. Damn, Eunice *was* going to be pissed. I flopped into the Austin and zigzagged off toward the Institute. Yeah, the barbecue was going to be awkward, the double D Kidd would surely get the wrong opinion of yours truly, me. What was it that the CIA had told Eunice, "Keep me on a short leash?" Ha. I laughed, things weren't going well, no – not well at all.

"Extenuating circumstances? Is that all you have to say for yourself, *extenuating* circumstances?" As an understatement, Eunice was furious. Her face was red and she looked very similar to a hungry timber wolf, a rabid lobo ready to tear into the fur of some unwary baby chipmunk.

Then she softened, suddenly. Her voice took on a personal calm-hurt tone. "How could you do this to me, Jim?"

Yeah, she was on the periphery of tears.

"I've only had a few Scotches, Eun."

It hadn't dawned on me to tell her about Al's demise, and – for sure, I shouldn't have used the endearment, Eun. I should have said "Madam" or "Doctor," anything but, "Eun." Yeah, *Commandant*, Stalag 13, would have been quite appropriate.

I turned my back on her and walked up the stairs and into the revolutionary bathroom. Eunice hung on my heels expelling a mouthful of enlisted sailor expletives. Wherever had she learned such obscene language? For sure, it *wasn't* at a nunnery. She was coming up with some dandy shit, mostly directed at my manhood. I kept my back to her, undressed, and entered the shower.

She left, slamming the door. It didn't shut and she returned to slam it again – harder. But not before yelling in, "The only expedition you're going on is one to the blank-ity-blank Unemployment Office." Slam! And then another, slam! And then she was off.

The silence inside the shower was wonderful. I turned up the heat and the room filled with steam. I stood there for the better part of an hour contemplating life and all its situational foibles. My inner vision had me shooting a hole-in-one at the Master's Tournament down in Augusta. I was smiling, and modeling my green blazer to a CNN camera crew.

I pondered Al's claim of an eighteen-stroke handicap – he had shot par on the back nine. What did he say? "He was having a lucky day." Yeah, something like that.

And I wondered just how far one *could* actually kick a golf ball?

I seriously wondered where all the hot water was coming from and how long it would be before it was exhausted?

I thought about life – working for dad, and *that* was a sobering thought. And then, I thought about Eunice. Just where in the world was I going to find another woman as bright and as childish as her?

And then this angelic voice pierces the steam, "Jim, honey, I'm so sorry. Can you ever forgive me? I, I hope you're all right in there? – Jim? Are you feeling better?"

"Yeah, yeah. I'm feeling just wonderful, Miss North."

"I was just informed about your golf match. Tim called me. He wanted to know if you were all right. You should have told me, Jim."

"Tell me something, Eun. How big is your hot water heater?"

"I don't know – it runs on solar power or something." She paused, and then asked, "Want to talk about it, Jim?"

"No, not really. I'll look it up on a heating schematic when I find some time."

"I meant, about Tim's father?"

"Not much to talk about, Eun. The old guy cheated me out of a hundred and twenty-five bucks, and then fell dead before I had a chance to get even. Technically, I beat him by one stroke on the front nine. He owes me ten dollars. Not much else to say about it, Babe."

"Want a woman to wash your back, Jimbo?"

"You offering?"

"Yes."

Eunice slipped into the shower fully dressed, saying, "This place does have a lot of hot water, doesn't it?"

Chapter Eleven

Yeah, being in "hot water" by one's own inadvertent device can be quite chilling. I shouldn't have thrown down so many doubles. Hands down, I was still, somewhat, "under the influence" as I towel dried and began to dress for the barbecue. Perhaps I would have worn something a step nicer than a half-sleeve Purdue sweatshirt, Levis, and a pair of overused Docksides if I were thinking a little more sensibly. But I wasn't, and I didn't. I wobbled and did a slight reel as I reached for my Rolex, saying, out loud, "Easy does it there, Sparks." I blew dry my hair, put out the lights, and headed out the door.

Halfway down the stairs I had to pause and lean against the wall in an open effort to steady myself. I couldn't help but wonder what happened to the *old* Jim Morgan, the one who could party all night and still balance an assembly line when the eight o'clock whistle blew. Out loud, but to myself, I concluded, "I'm never going to drink again as long as I live, so help me G..."

But, I never got to finish my oath. Eunice was bounding down the stairs behind me, asking, "Who on earth are you talking to, Jim?"

Eunice had changed into a stunning, form fitting, jump suit. She stopped abruptly on the stair just above me to wait for an answer. Which was, "Myself."

Hell, there wasn't anyone else in foyer, who else "could" it have been?

Her eyes rolled upward in a show of disgust and asked further, "I suppose you're answering yourself, too. Huh?"

"Yes, yes I am."

She put on her psychoanalytic face, a forced-seriousness face, and said, in a bad German accent, "Dis is not goot, Herr Morgan."

"Yeah? Well, too bad, Freud. Look, when this barbecue is over you can put me down on your couch and screw around with my head. Until then, if you want something to analyze? I've got some racing forms for you to study, okay?"

I don't usually mind her analyzing me; actually, I rather enjoy it. Most often, I simply tell her to get off my back as I have a life to live, and that I don't give a damn if I don't meet her own ethnocentric views of existence. Nine out of ten times she'll back off and cheerfully change the subject.

She smiled at my chastising vituperation (verbal tirade), and offered, "*We* have a label for the likes of you, Jimbo. You're eccentric." She stepped down to my stair and took me by the arm while adding, "Ready to party?"

We had crossed the den and were about to exit the patio doors when Eunice says, "Oh, I've got a big surprise for you, Jimbo."

Eunice threw open the door and there, sipping a lemonade, dressed in an all white sun dress and a broad rimmed society floppy hat, sat a smiling and most dazzling *spook*, Sophie.

She says, sweeter than a fifth of Southern Comfort, "Hi, Jim. All packed? Ready for our trip to Madagascar?"

"No. Not quite. I... I still need film for my camera."

Chapter Twelve

By three o'clock that afternoon, our clandestine barbecue was forced indoors by a dense black line of ominous looking thunderstorm clouds that had rolled in on us from the western side of the Potomac River. We had watched the cumulonimbus build as we dined. They started out as small white puffs of fair weather cumulus off in the distance and then built and built, rolling higher and ever more massive until lightening bolts fingered out below their pinkish-green, slowly undulating, and continuously lowering bases.

Although the storm was accurately forecasted, we hoped for it to stay west and to allow us our early outdoor venture, at least, into the evening. But, it was not to be. One humongous thunderclap and a series of bolted spherics sent us scurrying across the patio and into the safe haven of the Tudor's interior. No sooner had we closed the veranda doors than a howling wind blew down to rattle each of the many little den windows. The institute's very foundation seemed to tremble from the din of continuous thunder.

The frequency of high voltage lightening strikes had multiplied until it appeared that the Tudor was being subjected to an exterior strobe light, which, indeed, it was. It was eerie, and I couldn't help but think of the storm as an evil omen, a negative portent of doom to our up and coming tortoise expedition.

We huddled together at the bar sipping on Harvey Wall Bangers. Sophie commanded the conversation with a rundown of her latest intelligence reports, reports that she had obtained only minutes before leaving her Langley office that very morning.

"A French Linguist had been kidnapped while photographing the Leaning Tower of Pisa on Monday. On Wednesday, the linguist was found floating, face down, below the Bridge of Sighs in Venice."

"Whoa." I had to interject. "Just what does a French language specialist have to do with us?"

Sophie was looking into her Wall Banger when she continued, "His language specialty was Malagasy, the official language on Madagascar. However, that in and of itself is not the problem. The real problem is an ex-Russian spy who goes by the name of

Margolova. This Margolova, a genuine bitch, was spotted at the Tower of Pisa only minutes before the linguist disappeared."

She took a deep draw on her Banger, for effect (?), and then continued, still looking into her umbrella-clad tumbler. "As of last night, Margolova has been seen in Venice, a mere two canals over from the Bridge of Sighs."

An extraordinarily loud peal of thunder rattled the ice in our drinks. It had also rattled everyone's nerves; we had all fidgeted in unison to the reverberating drum of the angry meteorological gods. Eunice uttered, "Holy shit," with an emphatic stress on each of the orated syllables. Her remark may have been directed at the thunder, or at Sophie's insight on the bitch, Margolova, or both.

With goose flesh prickling both my arms, I questioned, "Why doesn't someone arrest her, or – shoot her. You say everything like she's the kingpin behind it all. So why do you allow her to continue? It seems like a bunch of nonsense. Just – *stop* her?"

"It's not that easy, Mister Morgan. We don't have any proof that Margolova is involved with this kidnap-murder. There's no motive either, only coincidence and proximity. Personally, it's a *smoking gun* case to me as I've been tracking her for years. I'm absolutely positive that she's involved – but that's all.

We have the Italian government watching her. Their police are calling the linguist's death an *accidental drowning*. Our hands are tied. The only thing we can do is to watch her, follow her, document her moves, and *hope* that she makes a mistake. Besides that there's nothing else that we can do."

A long continuous thunder roll had forced Sophie to pause. We all looked at one another with furtive glances, again, not knowing if the looks were for the thunder or for the intelligence that was being dumped on us so openly. A deluge of rain washed against the windows as Sophie continued.

"Margolova has been exceptionally shrewd. She has a genuine knack for avoiding the law. She – well, she's living every day with a noose around her neck. We're going to get her, soon. She's been getting sloppy; it's a simple combination of over-confidence and advancing age. Wherever she goes these days, she just – well, stands out, like a flashing red light. She's doomed; and, the scary part is we think she knows it and simply doesn't give a damn. Her acts of violence have been getting bolder and more vicious by leaps and bounds, she's begging to be stopped."

Eunice began shaking her head, "This whole program has gotten way out of hand. I'm going to stop it, right here and now. I'm canceling the expedition."

Sophie and I glanced at each other not saying anything.

Eunice lowered her head still shaking it in a slow negative, saying, "Three deaths, three people have died over this tortoise and we don't even know if one actually exists. It's – unbelievable."

We all went silent. It was a weird silence. The storm relented, too. It was as if the storm abated just to acknowledge Eunice's interjected decision.

No one spoke for a full minute. A few dim flashes of lightening lit up the windows. A glowing reminder that a storm *was* still present – the brunt of it had passed, but indeed, the atmosphere was still in a chaotic and volatile state and was predicted to remain so throughout the evening.

My mind went into a vivid recall of Al crumpling over his golf ball only a few brief hours earlier. His death was much closer to home, for me personally. The other three, the linguist, the anthropologist, and the expatriated Russian mugger, well, they had all died in direct association with the expedition, true – but so had Al. I was about to point this out to Eunice, the fourth death, but Sophie spoke out ahead of me making a prudent plea for Eunice to reconsider her snap and emotionally laced decision.

"You know, if the tortoise falls into the wrong hands... a whole lot of people are going to suffer terribly. We can't just back off and let her have it. It would be irresponsible, and, probably criminal, too. No, you can't cancel, not now. Too much is at stake, Miss North. – Way too much."

"Oh, I know you're right. It's just that everything's going so crazy. Murder..." Eunice let the word "murder" hang in the air.

She looked at me and asked, "What do you think, Jim?"

I decided not to mention Al; I also decided "not" to mention how pleased I was to be going on an expedition with Sophie. I wanted to go. I said, "I'd like to go. I've never been south of the equator; besides, I don't want to unpack."

Humorously, I added, "If we don't go, I'm going to look awfully funny walking around Washington in my pith helmet."

Eunice laughed, and then said to Sophie, "I'm surprised that you still want to go, Miss Kidd, especially since meeting my Field Engineer, Mister Morgan."

"Ha, ha, Eun. Very funny."

Sophie and Eunice were clicking; somehow they had found a moment to be hilarious. It was one of those times when, "You *had to be there* to appreciate it." Actually, it was more of a "tension release" than anything else, a "Thank you Harvey Wall Banger moment."

Sophie excused herself to the bathroom. I had moved to the windows to allow them some giggle space. I was noting some open patches of blue sky when Eunice came up behind me and placed her hand on my shoulder startling me.

"I'm sorry for getting you involved in all of this, Jim."

"Oh, don't be silly, Eun. How often does a guy get to lead an expedition, have foreign spies chase him and all the while have a beautiful blond tagging along as his personal bodyguard?"

"Well, Sophie's right – we can't quit. The tortoise "is" important. I just want you to know that I'm having terrible guilt feelings over your being involved, I mean... I've *really* turned apprehensive about all this, Jim."

"Aaaa – how guilty are you, Eun?"

"Very. I've got you hanging out on a precipice, Jim. I had no idea how dangerous this project was going to become, I feel terrible."

"Well, I think it's fun being out on a precipice. I'm enjoying the intensity, Eun. Deep down – I'm chomping at the bit to get going."

Eunice sighed, making a slight frown, "I've sensed this all along, Jim. I must confess. I was hoping that this project would burn out some of your wanderlust and maybe settle you down. But now, I'm just scared. This spy, Margolova, she sounds like a real psychopath. And, well – I do love you, you know?"

"Well, I've been thinking, Eun." I paused until she prompted me to continue, "This *is* a great time to ask you for a pay raise."

She backed up a step and slugged me on the arm – hard. I screamed out, "Hey, that really hurt." And, I wasn't pretending.

Sophie had returned, "Wow, how many rounds did I miss?"

"Ah ha. – You saw it all. You can be my witness. This is a blatant case of employee abuse. I'm going to sue."

From the bar, Sophie called out, "I didn't see a thing. What on earth is he talking about, Eunice?"

Eunice whispered into my ear, "I have never denied an employee a raise for *thinking* about it. I just *ignore* their thinking."

Then, lowering her whispers another octave, "I'll personally see to your raise later, Jimbo."

Undeniably, this was a clear-cut case of sexual harassment – on the job. It was great!

Sophie, now caught up in the awkward position of a whispered conversation, openly asked, "Should I come back after the final bell?"

"No, no." Eunice comforted, "The masculine element has been clearly subordinated, the issue will be put to bed – later." And again, the girlish giggles rekindled as Eunice joined Sophie at the bar. It was Eunice's time to establish her role of dominance over me in the eyes of Sophie, the Kidd. And most likely, it would be a role of sexual dominance – no doubt.

I excused myself and went outside to enjoy a moment of fresh air and to blast myself a cigarette. The storm had passed. Birds were chirping and a rainbow, a very faint and dissipating one, spanned out above the eastern tree line. I walked back to the tennis court fence and was delighted to see that the courts didn't puddle. Beyond the courts I noticed a downed tree limb. It looked to be wind damaged but it may have been downed by a lightening strike. I didn't go closer as the ground was wet and soggy. I took a final puff on my cigarette and flipped it out on the sprawling well-manicured lawn. I watched it smolder for a minute feeling guilty at having marred the pristine landscape with such a brash and obtrusive discard.

On my way back to the den, I recollected my visit to the Washington Monument. I vividly recalled Sophie's come-on, "Call me for dinner sometime, I'm mostly free." And I couldn't help but say out loud, "Yeah, right." And then I smiled to myself as I recalled a quotation by Sigmund Freud about women in general, "...they are like a black forest." And again – but I can't recall the exact context – "...they are all members of a dark continent."

Smiling, I reentered their den.

The two clams observed my approach up to them, they had obviously been discussing me, or some female subject, else they would have been openly jibber jabbing as I came in. Sophie pulled me into their conversation with, "How did you do at the small arms training class, Mister Morgan?"

"It must have been canceled. Maybe they just forgot about it. There wasn't one." I did an exaggerated shoulder shrug, "I just didn't have any..."

"Have you ever fired a weapon, Jim?" This was the first time that Sophie had ever called me, Jim – in front of Eunice.

"Yeah, sure – lots of times. A friend of mine, up in Alaska, had this .357 Magnum which was a lot of fun. We'd build a few snowmen and then use them for target practice. It was easy."

Sophie prompted, "Ever shoot anything that was alive? Birds? Animals? Humans?"

"No." But then, speaking reflectively, "When I was a kid – with one D, we'd go out to my uncle's golf course and shoot crows. Does that count?"

Eunice butted in, "You have an uncle who owns a golf course?"

"Yeah. My uncle Louis."

"Then how come you only have a nineteen-stroke handicap?" This childhood fact had struck Eunice as being *terribly* funny. Cracking up, she had to leave the room. As to where she went I never asked; but I do recall that I was glad to see her leave.

Sophie, smiling, continued her probing interview, "Have you ever fired a shotgun, rifle, bow and arrow, ever throw a hand-grenade?"

"No. I stayed out of the army; I disguised myself as a student. I'm actually a pacifist."

"I've read that in your file. Weren't you a member of a radical group or something? While at Purdue?"

"Yeah, the Peace Doves. But we were hardly radical. The only weapons we used were flowers. I was actually arrested once for throwing a daffodil on the hood of a campus police car, but the cop was a member of the Doves, the arrest was staged for the sole purpose of getting some press."

Sophie expressed an obvious let down, "Oh."

I asked, "So, just how much do you know about me from your little files?" I wanted to know, too. Fair is fair, right?

She smiled, "Enough. I think." Her smile was more on the line of a grin, as if she were hiding something, something that amused her.

She demurred, "Let's see... Here's what I know, according to my file. You goof off, a lot. Don't go to church on Sunday. Fly planes without a license. Sailed a 30-foot sloop to Hawaii, solo. You drink J&B Scotch Whiskey often, and at times to excess. You write poetry. You are an over-achiever with nearly a million dollars invested on the New York Stock Exchange."

I stopped her short, "Wrong. Wrong, wrong, wrong. I've just put all of my money into Treasury Bills."

She cocked her head at this, slightly, as if in disbelief or as if to say, "So what?" Then continued.

"Oh, I almost forgot. You've got a yellow butterfly tattooed on the inside of your right thigh, or is it your left?"

Yeah, Sophie knew a lot more about me than I would have ever guessed. I would have bet big bucks that only Eunice and Bunny knew about the butterfly. And, on hindsight, Bunny was so drunk that she wouldn't have known if I had legs let alone a tattoo.

Sophie was waiting for confirmation with raised eyebrows, it was a question that she knew I couldn't deny, if her file was right then she was privy to some highly personal information.

I asked her, brashly, "So? What do you want? A personal showing?"

Eunice returned, "Have I missed anything?"

"Yeah. Soph here can't remember which leg my tattoo is on."

"The left." Eunice said. Then continued with, "I guess that to mean that I haven't missed anything of significance, eh?"

Sophie said, "I was just telling Mister Morgan about the file we have on him. It lists distinguishing marks, but I couldn't recall which thigh the butterfly had landed on, the right or the left."

"Well, he'd have probably shown you if I hadn't returned." Eunice had caught herself in an ill attempt at humor. Her remark had made her sound like a jealous teenager due to the inflection of her voice.

Sophie looked to me for help. Startled, she was helplessly taken off guard by Eunice's seemingly terse statement. The *faux pas* intensified, the feminine gamesmanship was shutting down, I offered, with a shrug of my shoulders, "Hey, it's only a butterfly."

We all laughed. Eunice gave me a cornball look, one that I could not put into perspective, and the party, nee barbecue, came to a congenial end. Eunice and Sophie seemed content with their working/social relationship. They had formed a hug and kiss bond from this day of companionship, they had become friends. Eunice invited Soph to remain for dinner but the offer was declined.

"...I've a ton of packing to do, and I must return to Langley for my final briefings, and blah, blah, blah..."

We walked her to her *TA TA* Corvette and waved her a fond

farewell. Eunice commented, "She's a really nice kid." And added, "You watch out for her down there, Jimbo."

I promised Eunice that I wouldn't take my eyes off of her, not for a second. And for that, I had to endure a solid blow to the upper arm, which I might add, left a major bruise. She then took me by the arm suggesting that we discuss my raise. I told her that she needed to check on which thigh my butterfly was on, as it constantly "flutters" whenever I'm near her, and it does, and she did.

Chapter Thirteen

Making love with Eunice has always been a unique experience. It was always fun and it specifically lacked of any preconceived expectation other than total gratification. One time, she'd be demanding and selfish to the point of being dictatorial. And at other times, she'd shyly request passivity and let me control the pace and tone of our recreational commingling as if she were nothing more than a sexual tool, one that needed manipulation and forceful handling to achieve one's individual satisfaction.

However, giving, taking, and in general, sharing ourselves, each unto the other, was always paramount to our time and seemingly insatiable need.

This time was no different. Other than an open awareness of a ticking clock that limited our bout, demanding that we make a timely arrival at our eight o'clock dinner. Albeit, even that, added to our mad and impassioned joy. Our early evening romp concluded in a most orgasmic effort followed by a hectic race to the prearranged dinner table.

We dined on a Creole trout wrapped in a thin cabbage shell. A meal guaranteed to maintain Eunice's slim physique and to leave her male counterpart, me, in search of second helpings. Which, was served up faster than a French SST takeoff. Mureatha had second-guessed my need for seconds, bless her heart, and it was served with the biggest smile that ever graced the face of an out-to-please servant, indeed.

Mureatha returned with a "petite" slice of almond cheesecake for Eunice and a slab of the same for me. She gave me a wicked look before excusing herself for the evening. Eunice nodded once and the old workhorse, laden with all the earlier dinnerware, went her cheerful way.

And I wondered, and asked, "How much do you have to pay a maid these days, Eun?"

And she answered, "Not enough, Jim. Not enough."

Yeah, it was a vague answer. Eunice was tired or mentally preoccupied. I made a feeble attempt to discuss the expeditionary finances but that had failed to hold her interest. She was giving me short yes-no answers with a nonchalance normally reserved for a child going through its "why" stage of development. It was making me sleepy and I yawned openly in a deliberate show of boredom directed at her blatant show of abject inattentiveness to my needs.

Although it was mundane detail-insecurity talk, it still had to be taken care of. We needed to have a meeting of the minds, "I" needed to know how much I could get away with, etc., etc. And it just wasn't going well, not at all.

Eunice yawned openly, stood, and announced, "If you have any problems, call me. I'm sure there'll be a phone somewhere, even there, in the jungle." This was said with a staid finality and our conference was over.

Suddenly, she perked up. It was as if standing had cleared away her cobwebs and given her a whole new field of energy. It was strange and totally unexpected. She was as hopped-up as a junkie laced with speed. Agitatedly, and with an abnormal display of physical emphasis, she bombards me with, "Oh, that reminds me, Sophie will be taking along a two-way radio." Then, without giving me time to respond, she says, "I want to inspect your packing, Jim. Let's go. It's getting late." And yet again, without waiting for me to respond she heads for the stairs, still talking, "After all, you are staying at a Hilton. I can't very well have my representative going around looking like a cheep motel-vagabond. Can I?"

Dumbfounded, I followed. My thoughts raced from: "She's gone mad, crazy. All the way to making an inane guess that she was just horny and was looking for a reason to get into my suite, and ulti-mately – my bed. When I entered the door, after her, she was already going through a big suitcase. I leaned up against the wall and watched, deciding that she was, indeed, a nut case.

Four minutes into the seventh bag, she blurts out, "Where are your rubbers? I know we bought rubbers."

"They're in my wallet."

"Cute, Jim. Make sure they stay there."

"When you find the handkerchiefs – you'll find the booties."

And so it went and, until this day, I still wonder what it was that she was so diligently looking for.

The Inspector General finished her luggage tour with an animat-ed plop to the suite's sofa. She looked disappointed; her surge of power had waned dramatically. She yawned, saying, "You did a fine packing job, Jim. I'm proud of you."

The day was ended. Yeah, it was a hectic day. A day of death and spies and too much cheesecake, it had worn us out. We hugged and kissed in a Platonic show of affection. It was late. It was time for rest. We yawned in tandem and Eunice, my nutty little inspector, went her way.

I killed the lights and stepped out onto the balcony. The skies had cleared and the air seemed clean and crisp. I took in a few deep breaths of our Capitol's air and just stood there, thoughtless and feeling somewhat drained. So much had happened, so fast. I felt tired, a very sudden tired. I went back in leaving both doors open and sat on the bed, contemplating a cigarette. With an effort, I undressed and crawled under the fat imported down comforter, and pulled a fluffy pillow up and over my head. And I dreamt.

• • •

Sophie was there. We were together in an igloo that was lit by a lone wax candle. She was in a crib, a huge oversized crib, and this amused me. She was so out of place. I began to laugh, an inner silent laugh. I tried to go to her. I was moving, but I wasn't going anywhere, I just couldn't get any closer.

A figure appeared above the crib. It was Eunice. I stopped my advance to watch and listen. Eunice was saying something in baby talk, talking down to Sophie, soothing her. "Coo-chi-coo my baby, my honey. Coo-chi-coo my sweet little CIA spy, my CIA friendly. Mama's here, mama's here. Coo-chi-coo, coo-chi-coo, my darling."

And then her voice changed, it became ugly, taunting, "Coo-chi-coo, you – you little slut."

Eunice began shaking something at Sophie, something plastic, it was a baby toy, a baby rattle. I moved closer and indeed it was a rattle. The rattle end of a Texas Diamond Back Rattlesnake still attached to its four-foot host, its body twisting rapidly in Eunice's manicured hand. I stepped back, but didn't really move. Sophie's face puckered. She was on the verge of crying. She reached out a chubby baby hand. It was holding the snakes head, a comic laughing head, the snake says, "Goo-goo, ta-ta, ma-ma." Then laughed, enjoying its' capacity to produce nightmarish fear in my soul.

Then I heard drums, hundreds of drums. I dropped to my knees and crawled into the igloo's exterior opening. There, ahead of me, were thousands of snowmen, all dressed alike in black top hats and red scarves, and – they had guns. They appeared to be moving, but I couldn't tell, not for sure. I yelled back to Eunice, "They're coming, Babe, I can see the blacks of their eyes."

She looked angry. She threw the wiggling snake into Sophie's crib and yelled out, "Damn." She moved toward me, huffing, saying, "Blast them, Jim. Blast them all into hell."

"Here, use this." She handed me a revolver. "You can't get a pay raise for just thinking about one, you know? So start shooting."

I felt cold, naked. I was naked.

Eunice pointed down at the igloo's exit tunnel, "Go."

I took the pistol and entered the tunnel. Taking aim at the nearest snowman, one with a really twisted carrot nose, I pulled the trigger, while shouting, "Take this you ugly sack of ice."

The gun jerked in my hand, slightly, ever so slightly, and a stick popped out of the barrel, seven inches, and dropped out a plastic flag that read, "BANG."

The snowman grabbed his coal-buttoned chest with a puffy snow-hand and began to melt while making a "hooo-zeee" noise, then – vanished.

I reloaded and fired again, and again, and again. Over and over, I kept slaughtering them; no sooner had one melted than another one would attack. It was madness and it was relentless. The fields ran red with hand knitted scarves – it was sickening.

Finally, after days and days of non-stop flag popping, exhausted and ready for a break I came to realize that there was only one snow-man left. It was big ugly wet sucker with the meanest looking row of black teeth that ever snarled at anyone, ever. Yeah, this one was bad, real sinister looking even his carrot was shoved on backward showing a greenish circle where the leaves had been removed. I loaded the flag and sighted in on him just above his unwashed carrot and fired. Nothing happened. My pistola was hopelessly jammed. Eunice, who never left my side, my backside, handed me a new weapon, a big gun, a heavy thing that must have weighed ten pounds, easy. I had to hold it with both hands.

Re-aiming, I pointed the small cannon to the snowman's central belly coal and squeezed. The bullet came out slow, similar to a torpedo moving through water, but it was moving true, right for its target, the snowman's gut.

Frosty saw it coming but there wasn't anything he could do. He froze... He may have made a last-ditch effort to jump aside but – I couldn't tell. At any rate, he was too late. The shell plunged into his gut and exploded sending a white bird-shit looking goop flying out in all directions everywhere. His top hat hung in mid-air for the briefest part of a second and then plopped to the icy tundra, spinning once on its brim and then coming to a silent, solemn halt. Then, the dream got weird. The hat changed into a crow. The big torpedo pistola transformed into a .22 single shot rifle and I heard Al yelling, "Fore!" I couldn't see him, unless, he had been reincarnated and was now the crow. Eunice was yelling at me to shoot, "...with a 19 stroke handicap you're use to a lot of shooting, now shoot."

I shot. The old crow did a comic somersault and fell on its' back with its' legs pointing straight up in the air, it groaned once and then said, in a dying agony, "N i c e... Shot..."

Eunice was screaming, "Did you get it? Was it a birdie? An eagle? What?"

"No, Eun. It was a crow."

"A crow? What in the hell is a crow?" Eunice was furious.

I answered, "It's one stroke on the whole nine holes."

The crow began to vibrate and then began to hop up and down on its' back, still dead. Then it grew, its' anatomic structure changed into a dark metallic roaring machine, it became a Mig-29 with flames blasting out of its' engines that made the earth tremble and shake sending bits of igloo ice down onto my nakedness.

Eunice was yelling viciously, "You're making way too much noise, Jim. Can't you see? Sophie is trying to sleep."

I looked at her. She was scanning my nudity while saying, "And for Pete's sake, cover up that butterfly before them crows see it."

As calmly as I could, I explained, "Them ain't crows, Eun. Them, is Mig-29s."

She ripped the rifle away from me, angry, telling me to move away, that, she'd handle it. We changed positions. She calls out to me over her shoulder, "It's hats. Top hats. That's all that I see, Jimbo." She aimed the .22 and said, "Pow. Pow. Pow."

I asked her, "Are you getting any of them, Eun?"

"Just the stupid ones. The ones who surrendered their common sense to intellectual pursuits." She paused and looked at me, grinning, said, "You didn't expect me to just say "yes" did you?"

"No." I had to agree. "I guess not."

She returned to her work, "Pow. Pow." She would pretend to recoil after every volley, and she was quite good. Very animated, she was really getting into it, "Pow, pow, pow."

I moved to the crib in an effort to sooth Sophie, who was crying – well, "whimpering in her youth," would be more exact.

"It's okay, Honey. Those old crows are just hats. Eunice is blasting them all into hell. Everything is going to be fine, real soon."

That's when my mother entered. She moved me forcibly away from Sophie, screaming wildly, "Why aren't you helping Eunice? Here, let me take care of this precious little kid. You get yourself over there with Eunice and kill some hats while you're still young. Now scoot."

Reluctantly, I demurred, "Okay. But, before I go, I want you to know something; I've never killed a hat before. I mean...can you, like, give me some insight or something? You know, Ma, like, is it morally acceptable, is it politically correct?"

She grabbed up a broom and began jabbing it at me, saying, "Shoo now, you get going. Be a man, you – you rascal."

I sidled up alongside Eunice, "How's it going, Babe?"

"Great. Have a look for yourself, Jim." – Which I did.

It was gruesome. There was black silk and shards of hat brim scattered everywhere. And damn... there was much, much, more than top hat material strewn about, there was rabbit fur flying everywhere, bales of it.

"Shit, Eun. You're shooting bunny rabbits, Babe."

"Yes, isn't it marvelous? I'm going to kill every damned one of them, Jim."

She leveled her .357 Magnum and pulled down on the trigger, yelling, "Bang, bang, bang, Ka-pow."

It was terrible. I couldn't watch. I crawled back to the crib to check on mom and the kid Sophie. That's when everything turned horrid. Soph and mom had turned into bunny rabbits. I stood in front of the crib, wide eyed, and mystified, and in stark amazement, blurted out, "Damn."

It was mom and Sophie, no doubt. Mom's curls were a little straight, but her apron was a dead giveaway. Sophie – oh, she was still as cute as a button (I must confess, I have argued with myself over this "cute as a button" cliché. Personally, I think a button is nothing more than a functional adjunct to a man's coat sleeve, very similar to the "n" in "Damn." There is, most probably, some phobia for people who think that buttons are cute. I have made a note to question Eunice on this, one day.), her blue eyes gave her away instantly. It was – by the way they radiated.

Instinctively, I called out to Eunice, "Eunice! Eunice. Come here, quick. Look what's happened to Sophie and my mother. They've both turned into bunnies."

I watched her crawl back into the igloo, stand, and begin a forceful rush toward the crib while leveling the .357 at mom and Sophie, growling ugly, "Adios, my fluffy little friends."

I shouted, "No! No. These aren't *evil* bunnies, Eun. Eun?"

• • •

I opened my eyes. Eunice was standing over me with a genuine concern written all over her face, saying, "Having nightmares are we, Jimbo?"

"Yeah, yeah." I was panting, "You, you were going to shoot them."

"Who? Shoot whom? What are you talking about?"

"Sophie, you were..."

"Sophie? Sophie, I'll give you Sophie." She picked up a pillow and began to beat me with it, savagely.

There comes a time in every man's life when he ought to keep his mouth shut. Especially, when he wakes up disoriented from a dream about another woman. This! This was one of those times.

Mureatha carried down my bags at exactly nine a.m., she was excited to come get them, to corner me, and tell me that she was going to personally take care of the Austin during my absence. And once again, I had the urge to tip her. I think it's the way that she stands, palm extended, up-turned, itching, and waiting for recognition. I whispered into her ear, "Thanks, Love. Just keep it under a hundred. Okay?"

In a hearty voice, she bellowed, "Shore-nuff, Mister Mogins. Shore-nuff."

At the limo, Eunice gave me a Platonic nip on the cheek. She has this thing about displaying one's affections in public. And I respect her sense of business propriety. I was quite pleased with her addition of, "Chow." It said, "I'll miss you." What more can a man ask for, eh?

My baggage overflowed the trunk and some of it had to be put in the passenger's compartment. Sam, the uniformed driver, guided me to the front seat, suggesting that I'd be more comfortable up front, "It's not that far, Mister Morgan."

And I thought, "Yeah, the honeymoon is over." And indeed, it was.

Just as we were exiting the Institute, from *North* Avenue, the limo's cellular phone buzzed. It was for me, it was Eunice.

"Tell Sam to take you to Andrews Air Force Base. Your itinerary has been changed. Sophie will meet you at the main gate. Do you understand, Jim?"

"Well, I don't understand but I'll do as you say, Babe."

"Good. And don't forget, I want daily reports. No excuses."

"No problem, Eun. Anything else?"

"Yes, I love you. Be careful."

"Yeah. Ah, I love you, too, Eun. I'll see you in a month or so."

I gave the phone back to Sam and told him about our change in plan. He nodded a limo driver's nod of acknowledgement, and then made a clarification statement, "Goodbye Dulles, hello Andrews."

Sophie was at the main gate as promised. She was sitting in her TA TA Vette with the top down and had her emergency flashers, flashing. When she saw us coming she stood up and began to wave her arms in a frantic effort to ensure that we wouldn't miss her. As if we could, I mean, a beautiful blond in a white Corvette doesn't need to stand up and wave her arms to get noticed, right?

We pulled up directly behind her. She jumped out and ran back to Sam's opened window. In total control, she ordered Sam, "Follow me, and stay close. We're cleared to speed, can you handle it?"

Sam gave her a thumbs up sign and a "Can do" grin. Soph made a similar, acknowledging, smirk and then raced back to her idling Corvette, a ready and chomping at the bit, Corvette. She leapt into its' seat, not opening the door, and tires began squealing. An airman with three stripes had stopped all gate traffic allowing us to pass. Sophie gave him a crisp salute as she flew past him and entered the base. The heavy Cadillac didn't exactly peel-out, but the quick acceleration was enough to throw me back in my seat. Soph was already a good hundred yards ahead of us. I looked at the speedometer and from where I sat it had already passed the seventy MPH marker. Blue military trucks had stopped all cross traffic allowing us to run wide open.

Sam was quite impressed one could see it on his red face and hey, so was I. Sam asked, "Just out of curiosity. What's in all those bags, Mister Morgan?"

"Sam, believe me – you wouldn't believe it."

Sophie hit her brakes, and so did Sam. We were two blocks behind her when she turned onto the Andrews' runway and it took us the whole two blocks to slow down and make the turn. Even then we had skidded around the corner fishtailing momentarily before Sam regained full control. Re-accelerating, Sam says, "I'd believe you – believe me."

Sam was looking at me, waiting for an answer, when Sophie hit her brakes again. I pointed, yelling, "Sam."

Soph had slowed dramatically and was easing up to a helicopter that was already running, waiting for takeoff. We pulled up behind her and stopped. Soph was motioning for me to go to the helicopter from a standing position inside her Vette. An orange suited officer came up to the limo door and opened it. "Mister Morgan?"

I nodded, "Yes."

"Follow me, sir. Your baggage will be taken care of by Miss Kidd."

I grabbed my briefcase and topcoat, and thanked Sam. I threw my head back toward the luggage, and having to shout, yelled out, "Just clothes." Sam acknowledged my disclosure with a nod and a tight-lipped grin. He gave me a thumb up sign and called after us, "Good luck to you, Mister Morgan."

The captain guided me under the rotating blades and into the door of the giant chopper. The noise and wind were horrendous and I was very surprised at the relative quietness once we were inside and the door was closed. As I buckled myself in the chopper began its' accent. Obviously, all the red lights and speeding was on my behalf. I must say I felt like quite a big shot. But, deep down, I knew this, "I didn't know what was happening," and that, was somewhat scary.

I smoothed back my hair as best I could (I don't carry a comb) and tried to make myself as presentable as possible. I then asked a blue-suited lieutenant sitting across from me if we were going all the way to Madagascar "...in this thing?"

Smiling, he said no, "...we're only going to Dover Air Force Base in Delaware. We'll be there in just under forty minutes."

Hell, I didn't even know where the state of Delaware was; let alone where Dover Air Force Base was. I wondered if I'd be met when we landed. I wondered how long it would be before I'd get to see Sophie again. And then I decided not to think, at least, for the next forty minutes. I opened my briefcase and read a pamphlet on the Malagasy language. Deciding that I could order myself a Scotch and water in their twisted French. I put the booklet away and spent the rest of the flight sightseeing.

We landed without it being announced. The rotor blades hummed down into a dead silence, the lieutenant across from me said, "Welcome to Dover," as he unbuckled and moved to the opening door. I followed and was given a hand down by the orange suited Captain who directed me to a blue school bus that was parked some hundred yards from us. He pointed, saying, "That's your ride, ah, Morgan, isn't it? I hope you enjoyed your flight."

So, I headed for the bus. My ears were ringing and my body was tingling from the chopper's vibrations. It felt good, walking; it was a cool morning, brisk.

Yeah, I felt invigorated, and under all that invigoration, I felt lost.

The old bus driver asked if I was, "Morgan." I nodded and he motioned for me to get in. At least I was in the right place; the bus driver knew my name and that in and of itself was a comfort. I asked him, the bus driver, about my luggage.

"Don't know about luggage. It's not part of my job. I just pick 'em up and drop 'em off. That's all I get paid for. Want to know about luggage? You go to Base Ops."

We moved slowly between rows of huge aircraft, planes that the bus driver called, "Cee Fives." I was just about to ask where we were going when he stopped. "Here we are, Captain."

As soon as I stepped from the bus, it departed. And there I stood, dwarfed below the nose of the world's largest cargo jet, a C-5 Hercules, Jumbo Jet. I had read about them, had even seen a movie on them when I worked in Los Angeles, but the size... It was simply awesome.

"Hey. Are you, Morgan?" The one striped airman appeared from out of nowhere. Well, at least I didn't see where he came from.

"Yeah, that's me, Morgan."

"Come with me, sir. I'll show you to your quarters."

"Quarters?" I questioned.

"Yes, sir." He came closer, "Can I take your bag, sir?"

I said, "Nah, it's only a briefcase. Lead the way, Sarge."

I followed him up a metal ramp and into the darkened bowels of the C-Five's massive gut. We wound around several rows of wooden crates and padded boxes. Twice, I heard my guide say, "We're almost there. You still with me?"

There were lights on ahead of us. I could now see the airman in front of me, up until then, I could only hear him and barely discern his movement. If someone were to have yelled, "Fire," I'd have had one hell of a time finding my way out.

Then I hear this airman say, "Here he is, Kidd. He's all yours now."

Chapter Fourteen

Sophie has one undeniable character trait: She is cute. Aside from being intelligent, outgoing and vivacious, she has a way of exuding her cuteness. Yeah, she uses it in the same way that a surgeon uses a finely sharpened scalpel during a brain surgery, deftly, delicately, and all but unseen by his attendants. And, like an excellent surgeon, she's aware of her talent and spends a lot of time capitalizing on it. Not so much for dollars, but for the loftier pleasure of living in the state of self-actualization.

For Sophie "*not* to be cute," well – that would be like a surgeon who operates without assistants, it could be done, but it just wouldn't be much fun, especially for the patient.

Soph was wearing an Air Force blue baseball cap with golden letters stitched across its peak that read, RANK. Her jacket, also Air Force blue, subtly stated her CIA code name, Kidd, which was done in very effeminate gold script embroidery. So, there she was, running around an Air Force Base with the vested power of some Major General, presenting herself as one, RANK KIDD.

This is the type of cuteness that Sophie thrives on; it's that feminine kind of cutesy hardball that only a few innately beautiful women can ever hope to play. Yeah, Sophie is Major League, and she knows she's made the All Stars. So, watch out for the curves.

When she turned to lead me ever deeper into the C-Five A's massive belly, I couldn't help but notice the golden script that was so emphatically laced across her back, which read, "RELAX."

After weaving through a short maze of yet more crates, ones that rose all the way up to heaven, we came to the front door of a huge thirty-two foot, self-contained, camper van. Sophie, with one foot in the door, turned and pointed to a "Welcome" mat that was thrown down below the step, saying, "Wipe your feet, James. We're home now, at least, for the next day and a half." I wiped them with an exaggerated vigor and entered the covert luxury of our CIA's ultra mobile hideout. Hell, we could fly, we could drive, and I just knew that somewhere, probably in the crates we had passed, there had to be a cabin cruiser, or an atomic submarine. Yeah, there was probably a whole team of Navy Seals, up in front of us, somewhere, standing at attention, waiting for Soph to snap her fingers and point them toward an objective.

The first thing I noticed upon entering was my luggage. It was stacked neatly up to the ceiling in an aluminum bar rack. I was truly surprised, and had to ask, "How in the hell – how did you get all of this here, ahead of me? I was only on that chopper for forty minutes, tops." Smiling, she says, "Lear jet. There wasn't room for you because of all the baggage. So I put you on the shuttle. I hope it wasn't too inconvenient, it was the best I could do."

"No. I didn't mind, not at all. Actually, I got some work done on the way over." Which was a mildly facetious white lie.

Sophie began a grand tour and as she pointed things out – various pieces of the van's equipment – it became self-evident that we were in a self-contained eavesdropping device. Proudly, she boasted, "We can pick up any radio or TV frequency in the world." Then, pointing to a leather headset, said, "With these, we can hear an ant fart at four hundred yards."

Sophie had either worked with the van previously, or had done her homework well. She even knew how to contact the President, "...if we need to." She said, trailing off her intense and most knowledgeable spy-van indoctrination lecture (This section has been edited by the State Department and I cannot describe any more of the technological amenities that the van had actually contained.).

Which was impressive to say the very least, allowable.

The van has a kitchenette with a thirty-day canned food supply and a 200-gallon water tank. Sophie advised, "...shower quick, 200 gallons doesn't give you much time for singing."

Personally, I was thinking, "200 gallons is a lot of water, from an Engineering perspective." But I didn't challenger her. She was on a roll and I didn't wish to disturb her "niceties spiel."

The van was designed to sleep six people. There were two bedrooms, both to the rear. The forward one had two bunk beds and the aft compartment, the master suite, had a full-size bed. The built-in storage bins, probably designed for clothing, were mostly filled with an assortment of electronics and miscellaneous test equipment.

We would be living out of our suitcases as was depicted by Sophie's mess in the bunk-bed room. She had her baggage scattered – some opened, on three of the four cots. She would sleep on the fourth. I was allowed the master suite, and, sternly told, "Don't mess with the gizmos, Jim. When you need to sleep, sleep. Then get out. Okay?" To which, I nodded out an agreement while feeling somewhat chastised – way before my time.

The bathroom was small but complete with a four-foot tub and shower. A ten-gallon electric hot water heater was a much better water conservation tool than Sophie's no singing warning. A community hair blower was mounted next to the mirror and full compliments of disposable toiletries were stored in a quick-lock bin alongside the standard sized stool. There were enough towels, all color coordinated, to dry several elephants. The bathroom didn't have a window, but there was an exhaust fan that sported a penciled note, which read, "Please use when showering, THX." I have never figured out what "THX" was, unless it was the author's initials? Oh! I was just told – "Thanks."

"How much does a thing like this cost?" I asked. Sophie, looking disappointed, answered, "A lot." But, I can't get anyone to tell me how much "a lot" is. My guess is, since it's a specialty, government design, it was – a *lot.*"

She led me up to the captain's chair, the driver's seat, and showed me some more gadgetry. One of the things that I had personally enjoyed was the heated back massager and the unlimited positions that the seats could be put into by servomotors.

She pointed out an intercom device, reverting to her serious teacher's voice, "Pay attention, Jim. If the pilot calls us, it's probably important. Okay?"

I nodded, I understood.

"You have to hold down this button while you're talking or they won't hear you. Okay?"

I nodded, I understood.

"If we need to call them? We are asked to allow them 30 seconds to respond to our call. They are busy up there and we are listed as a very low priority, this trip."

I nodded. I understood. "Okay." Yeah, it all seemed easy enough. The crash course was going well. Sophie was an excellent teacher. Then, as she physically hovered over me to differentiate a color-coded set of switches, I was struck with her scent. It was a very pleasant odor, soft, delicate and sensuous, yet youthful.

Immediately I knew. I had developed an instant crush on the

teacher. And I wondered if could she tell? Did she know? Was she deliberately leading me on? And I thought, "No." No, it's just *me* – I was falling in love. Or, Cupid had shot me in the ass with an errant "lust" arrow. Catching myself, I redirected my thoughts to the business at hand. I questioned her on a small red light aglow on the dashboard.

"Oh, that. That's the whore's light. When it's red, it's daytime. When it's green, it's night." She paused, reflectively, and then added, more to herself than to me, "I don't know why it's called a whore's light." And then, speaking to her self, "Oh, I bet those guys were just hitting on me." Then trailed off her thought in an obviously "happy" recollection.

Then, redirecting her *own* thoughts to the business at hand, she points to another red light, "This light is the... ah, intercourse light. It...ah, tells us when we're plugged into the... ah, aircraft's generator."

Sophie had openly blushed. She was caught up in the argot of male misnomers. She quickly moved her pastel fingernail to another bank of lights. And started to say, "This is..." When the lights that she had fingered, lit. Announcing, "FASTEN SEAT BELTS." And continued her lecture, "...the fasten your seat belt light." Then, smiling big, she added, "How timely."

Soph slid into the passenger's seat and buckled in, cutely saying, "Buckle up, James. This "could" turn into one *hell* of a ride."

That's when I began to blush. We both went silent. The giant engines came to life, they were audible, but not too very loud. The van itself began to vibrate ever so slightly; it was enough to announce that we were a part of the plane. We finally looked at each other in some comic understanding. Soph, smiling, threw off her seat belt, saying, "I better check and see that everything's secure." She put a hand on my shoulder, adding, and "Don't fly off without me." And she was gone.

The intercom came to life, "This is your Captain speaking. Welcome aboard, CIA. We'll be taking off in about five minutes. We're clear all the way to England. Is everyone cozy back there?"

I hit the send button, and answered, "Ten-four – over."

Soph returned a quick moment later. I told her about the Captain's announcement, "We are taking off in five minutes and we are going to England."

She climbed into her seat and began to buckle in, "I'm really excited, Jim. Aren't you?"

"Yeah, I've never been to England before. Especially by camper."

The aircraft began to roll; all of the normal takeoff sensations were present. I could feel our speed building and the cabin pressure beginning to stabilize. I caught myself stretching my jaw to pop my ears and noticed that Sophie was doing the same.

Sophie advised, "The cargo bay is pressurized, Jim. So is the van. If we loose pressure we have our own oxygen in the ceiling." She was pointing to two little doors above our heads.

I asked, "Where's the vomit bags?"

My question took Sophie by surprise. She immediately looked ill. "Are you going to be sick?"

"No. I just didn't see any. I was wondering where you kept them?" She breathed a sigh of relief. Earlier, she had announced herself to be the maid, cook, and chief bottle washer. Airsickness must have been one of her clean-up duties, based on her open sigh of relief.

The FASTEN SEAT BELT light went blank. With renewed spirits, Sophie offered, "How about some lunch, Mister Morgan?"

Over sandwiches and mugs of powdered milk, Sophie outlined our passage to Madagascar. After refueling in England, we'd make a short stop in Madrid, Spain. From there we'd wing down below the equator into Africa. We'd land in Asmara, Ethiopia and transfer to a commercial airliner that would take us across the Mozambique Channel to Antananarivo's International airport. The entire trip would take us thirty-six hours, give or take a few, either side of the equatorial divide.

I asked her if she had been there before, and she answered, "No." But like myself, she had attended a French class and had seen the same 1940's wartime movie that had been dumped on me. Consolingly, she added, "My French is fair, we'll be alright." Then asked me, "How about you, Jim? Ever been there?"

"No. I've never left America." – Basically, this was true. But, I felt that I should clarify myself, "Well, I've sailed to Oahu once. And I flew a Cessna over to a little Russian island in the Bering Straits. I've hit the Mexican border towns, Juarez and Tijuana; and, I've been up to Toronto, Canada, but I don't count those."

Soph looked at me quizzically, then questioned me, "What were you doing on the Diomede Islands, Jim? You're supposed to have diplomatic permission to visit them, aren't you?"

"Oh, we were just goofing off one day. A friend of mine, the guy I told you about – the guy with the .357 Magnum – well, he wanted to go bear hunting from the Cessna. I agreed to take him up. Eventually, we scared one out onto the ice pack. A big old brown bear." I paused to see if Sophie was listening.

"Go on." She prompted, "I really want to hear this."

"Doyle, my friend, used up a whole box of bullets shootin' at the sucker. I don't think he ever hit it. But it was fun just watchin' the bear run. We could have run it to death. At least – Doyle *thought* we could. He wanted to."

Sophie looked intent – perhaps, she was sorry for the bear.

I continued, "Well, to make a long story short, it was a beautiful day and the islands were right there. – It was something to do. The Cessna was equipped with skis and I set it down on the beach. We got out, took a piss, got back in and took off. End of story."

But I didn't tell Sophie the whole story. I didn't tell her about all the "Piss on Russia" jokes that we generated. Or how we tied the four hundred pound bear to the skies of the Cessna right after taking our piss. Or how we almost crashed because of the bear's bulky carcass coming loose, how it dangled by one paw in a port to starboard sway that threatened to rip apart our landing gear, or how Doyle had to climb down and cut it loose when we were back at the Ice Hole, 200 feet AGL, and how it exploded like a water filled balloon when it hit the icy tundra after being cut loose. No. I didn't tell her that. After all, Sophie was a Federal Agent. So, I kept some of the story under my illegal huntsman's hat. Besides, it was my friend Doyle that did it. "Not me."

Sophie said, "You know that I'll have to put a note in your file about your going over to Russia? Don't you, Jim?"

•   •   •

We played gin rummy for the next several hours. We played for a penny a point. I wound up kicking her butt for thirty dollars. That's when I found out that she was an extremely poor loser. She tried to be cute about it, but had failed miserably, pouting, she said, "You'll get your money when we get to Asmara. I'll pay you in beads. I believe that's an acceptable currency there."

Yeah – ha ha, on me. I wonder what she would have done if the wheels of fortune had stopped at her purse instead of mine?

Sophie (stormed) went to the bedroom door advising me that she hadn't slept the night before, adding, "Wake me if you're bored."

Then (slammed) pulled the door snugly shut once she was inside.

I contemplated her remark "Wake me if you're bored." I could only conclude that her statement was "asexual," and that my boredom would only earn me some more Ethiopian beads. However, I did let my thoughts linger, irrational thoughts, sexually pleasing thoughts. But they were only thoughts. Ah, such problems, those of a virile male.

I went to the Captain's chair and played with the multi-band radio that was built into the dashboard, snacking on roasted peanuts and a brand name cola. After awhile, I went to the VCR and played a John Candy movie. After a few minutes of that, it became snooze-a-roo time and I dozed off on the bolted down green leather sofa.

My repose was cut short by the cheery voice of our captain, "Sugar Plum to Baby." Then again, "Sugar Plum to Baby." Pause, "We'll be landing in twenty minutes, that's T-Minus-Two-Zero." Pause, "Hope you've enjoyed the flight. Over."

"Sugar Plum to Baby." I wonder who thought that one up? I hit the send button, "Copy – Sugar Plum." I couldn't bring myself to say, Baby. I did add, "Over and out."

The "Whore" light was green. It was dark out. I went to Sophie's door and knocked, saying, "Sugar plum to baby – we're landing in twenty minutes."

"Thanks, Jim. How did we get here so fast?" She sounded groggy but awake.

I couldn't help but answer her, "We flew." Well, it amused me... I then went to the bathroom, shaved, brushed my teeth, and – was about to put a hot towel on my face when Sophie calls through the door, mumbling, "Hey, what ever happened to ladies first?"

I opened the door and there she stood, eyes half-closed, her toothbrush hanging from her mouth, hair all tangled, wearing a red nightshirt that ended at the knees – she was beautiful. After sizing her up, I offered, "Sorry, Priss. Want some coffee?"

Through her toothbrush, she says, "Make it a gallon, will ya?"

The coffee had just begun to perk when the FASTEN SEAT

BELTS sign came on. Sophie bubbled out of the bathroom. She was wearing a Miami Dolphin sweatshirt and a pair of snug white shorts. She was animated, cute, saying, "That coffee sure smells delicious, Jim."

Then said (ordered), "Go up and buckle in. I'll get the coffee. It's in my contract."

The landing was smooth and uneventful. The big engines whined down and left us sitting in a *dead* silence. Sophie tuned into the BBC radio station and we listened to an early morning news program while waiting for the seat belt lights to extinguish. The English accented newsman was the only real clue that we were actually in England – aside from the fact that we were told so by Sugar Plum.

He had called us to say, "We'll be on the ground for three hours." He went on to say that the crew was going onto the base to eat. That we could leave the plane to stretch, but added, "We're parked in a quarantine area – the perimeter is guarded by vicious dogs, so – don't wander off, Kids."

Sugar Plum did ask if he could bring us anything. Baby asked for, "Fish and Chips." Sugar asked, "White sauce or red?" Baby looked to me for a preference, I said, "White." Baby answered, "Both." Plum said, "Copy." Click, "Out." Baby said, "In." Click, "Out."

I guess they tired of their code-word game, the Captain said, "I've got that data you asked me for, Soph. Are you ready to copy? She responded, "Fire away, Chuck."

Sophie spent the next five minutes scribbling down numbers that defined the "D" and "E" layers of our atmosphere, along with an ionization message from some solar observatory in Australia. It was all in numerical code but was key stuff for Sophie to know while working her radio. Chuck finished with, "That's it, Kidd." Soph said, "Got it, Chuck." And that was it. No "over." No "out." Nothing!

Sophie shoved the pad and pencil to a flat spot on the dash, then – in an exaggerated English Accent – asked, "How about a stroll on English soil, James?"

Agreeing with a, "Pip, pip, me lady." We were off.

The entire airplane – and most of England – was shrouded in a dense fog. It was so thick that we had to bend over to see the cement that we were standing on. And it was cold, a damp, penetrating, maritime cold, that hovered near the forty degree mark.

Sophie immediately entered into a warmth dance, hugging

herself snugly with both arms. Her teeth began to chatter and she mumble-shuddered something, like, "F f-fa, f -uck this, I - I'm ow -out ta, – here."

I remember teasing her, "What's the matter, Priss? Too cold for your little short-shorts?"

She sort of answered, while heading for the stairs, "Haa-hup your-zz – Mmm-Mor-gin." Then disappeared into the misty, misty mist-mush. So ended our picturesque stroll around merry old England.

I heard her race up the metal stairs. Then stop, when an unknown voice beckoned out to her, "Hey, Kidd. The generators are up. You're cleared for power."

She called out, "Thanks, wherever you are." Then called out to me, "You coming, Jimbo?"

"Yeah, yeah. I just want one last quick look at England, first. Okay?"

She didn't answer. I did hear her clank up into the aircraft. I bent down and looked closely at the cement, I could only see about a fifteen-inch circle. I reached out and touched the moist surface. It was real cement all right, and I wondered, if, the rest of England was as hard and as cold as the spot that I was, then and there, standing on.

I fumbled around for the stairs and then ran up into the cargo door. Sophie was huddled there, waiting, shivering. I looked back and down the steps that disappeared into the swirling fog. It was weird, the day's events raced through my mind, the limo ride, the chopper, the bus, the enormity of the C-5 A and the CIA camper van. It was all surrealistic, fake, all a dream. Yeah, I was in the twilight zone between that which is real and that, which is not. I think I may have been entering a vertigo trance.

Sophie spoke, "I'm going in." And for the briefest instant I thought that she meant, "jump into the mist."

I turned and followed her shorts through the boxes. We were nothing more than a pair of rats locked in a winding complicated maze. But we knew this, it was warm in the camper and fish and chips were on their way. What more could two CIA rats wish for on a cold and foggy night in England, eh?

Sophie began to set up her radio as soon as we had entered the van. She told me she'd be using a satellite link to Langley. I watched her intently, not to learn, but to take her in, to enjoy her every move. She was a show, an act that needed an audience, someone to admire her dexterity and her innate tenacity. It was fun and somehow extremely fulfilling. She would explain things as she worked: "This is a frequency modulator, it does blah, blah, blah. This is a microchip relay distortion thing-a-ma-jig and it does blah, blah, blah. This is a voice scrambler and it..."

"Oh, I read about those in a spy book by, somebody."

Sophie looked at me, shook her head, said, "Not like this, this is state of the art, actually, it's still experimental."

"Well, how does it work?"

"It's really easy, and virtually impossible to hack, think of our radio signal as coil spring being pulled in and out at ultra random lengths in micro seconds. It becomes a bunch of noise. The receiver controls the sender's pattern by a random segment of pi. It's all digital, literally foolproof."

I listened in as Sophie made her call to Langley. They didn't use fancy call handles like, Sugar Plum and Baby, no, it was just like a normal phone call. It reminded me of calling home from college when I needed money.

"Hi Mom. How's Dad? How's the dog? Why am I calling? Oh, I was wondering if you could spare an extra fifty bucks? Gee thanks, Mom. Yeah, I love you too, Mom. Bye."

Yeah, just an ordinary conversation, a little small talk, a few pleasantries, and, "Bang." Here comes the check, nice, neat and all so very casual.

It was obvious that Sophie knew the person behind the voice at her headquarters; it was a man she called, "Handsome."

"Hi, Handsome, haven't heard your voice since the Christmas party. What have you been doing with yourself?"

Handsome whined on about his wife being pregnant, "again." And that this one, "...had *better* be a boy." He went on to say, "A man just ain't designed to live under the same roof with five women. Know what I mean, Kidd? Why, just yesterday, I come in from work and the girls had the whole living room painted pink. So, I go out to the fridge and get myself a beer, come back and sit down in my TV chair and what do you think I find? – Lace doilies on the armrests. Why, pretty soon, they're going to have me puttin' my beer on lace coasters. Don't get me wrong, Kidd, I love them girls dearly as sin. I just want a boy this time, know what I mean, Kidd?"

The small talk was winding down; it was time to ask for the

money. Sophie asked, "What's with all this fog, Handsome? Are we going to get stranded here?"

"Nope." Said Handsome. "There's a cold front moving in on you right now. You'll have clear skies in an hour. At least by sunrise your time."

Sophie's voice took on a more serious tone, "Anything new on our friend, Margolova?"

"Yep." Snapped Handsome. "She's left Venice. The local police dropped in on her just to see how she was doing. You know, check her passport for visas or maybe kick her ass. Anyway, nobody answers. So they break down the door. And what do they find? A corpse. The corpse, before he died, he'd spent the last two years down in Madagascar, studying ocean life. You know, like seashells and turtles. The boss says it's a direct link to your operation, Kidd."

"How was he killed, Allen? Did they say?"

So, "Handsome" had a name, Allen. Ah ha, Sophie hits on married men, or at least she's not above flirting with her fellow workers, as long as they're handsome. Alan paused, researching his reply if he had one, "Yep." He paused, as if he were studying a report, "Here it is, Kidd. She beat the guy to death. It says here that he was tortured. He had multiple stab wounds, but... cause of death, says, blows to the head. Want me to fax you a copy, Kidd?"

"No." Sophie sounded drained, reluctant, "Anything from the boss, Allen?"

"Nope."

"Has my car been picked up from Andrews?"

"Yep. I saw it on my way in this afternoon, ...ah, how did the top get torn, Kidd?"

"You're kidding?"

"Yep."

"Damn you, Allen. You'd *better* be kidding." Sophie was perking up, handsome, Allen, did have a way with women, no doubt. Sophie added, "I'll be calling again tomorrow, you working?"

"Nope. It's Betty Boop's gig. Are you still going to call?"

"Yes, Allen. But thanks for the warning."

Sophie began stowing her radio gear, letting out a dramatic, and romantic sigh, "That Allen, he's every woman's dream."

"Yeah? Sounds like every man's dream, living with five women."

"Oh?" Sophie teased. "Most men I know can't keep one woman

happy, let alone five."

"Well... not to change the subject or anything, but, who is Betty Boop? And, just how big a threat is this Margolova?"

"Betty Boop is my roommate. Her real name is Sally Wonderful. And no, I'm not kidding, it really is, Sally Wonderful. She's a natural born cynic, and, I believe she's written the book on sarcasm. Most people can't stand her for more than five minutes, but she keeps me in stitches. She's very self-righteous, too. Last week she began to wash our paper plates, a frugality thing."

Soph began laughing, "That's not the bad part. The bad part is that she dries them in the microwave.

"When I first met her, I thought it was all a big put-on. You know, anything to get a laugh. But, over time, it became quite clear that she was just being herself. Since then, I've taken her under my wing. She's hopeless, but I love her dearly."

A sharp rap on the door ended Sophie's narration. It was time for fish and chips, English style. Which by the way was delicious. As we sat down to eat our jet-lag breakfast-dinner, Sophie told me more about the bad bitch, Margolova.

"She's bad news, Jim. She's a real psychopath. She was born to an old WW-I Russian Field Marshal who eventually built the USSR's Air Force. Later, he was instrumental in developing their space program. Margolova became a test pilot, of sorts, and today, she claims to have been a cosmonaut. She also claims to have been the first woman in space, but, our sources, the people who should know, totally deny her allegations."

I interrupted, "How old is this bitch?"

"Again, we're not sure. We think, between fifty and sixty. I've seen photos of her that were taken about a year ago and she could easily pass for thirty. She has a penchant for younger men, your age, Jim."

"Yeah? Likes them in their prime, eh?"

"Ummm." Sophie gave me a smug look, "You don't even want to think about messing with her, Jim. Her last six lover's all turned up dead. Their deaths all coincided with the advent of a new flame in her life. It seems that she lives the old adage, love 'em and leave 'em – dead."

She paused and look at me quizzically, said, "Men aren't very bright, are they?"

I gave her a cutesy smile. She continued, "Margolova had a lot going for her in the late sixties, prominent husband, car, an apartment in Moscow, and a ton of political friends. Then, she was in a plane crash. It ruined her inner ear. She was ousted from the test pilot pool and given a disability stipend from the space agency. She still has trouble with her balance. It's known that she occasionally falls down from it, just plop, and she's down." Soph paused, sifting through her Margo knowledge.

"Her husband made arrangements for her to live out her life in a convent, an alternative to divorce. That lasted for about three months. She slipped away one night and nobody sees her again for two years. Her reappearance is suspiciously timed with her husband's demise, he's murdered on the very day she emerges from seclusion and begins a teaching post at the Moscow University. She becomes a regular figure around the Kremlin and is known to date everyone of importance within the KGB. This scenario continues for several years; then, a sex scandal erupts at the university. Miss Margolova is named kingpin and gets the axe. The KGB takes her in, makes her an international courier, i.e., spy.

After a short time she is given free rein, full autonomy, to collect information any way that she sees fit. The KGB liked her style, especially the way she had of seducing Engineers."

Sophie had stopped her narration and was eyeing me like some little boy caught with his fingers in a cookie jar. Then continued, "Especially those Engineers working within the Aerospace Industry."

Soph had emphasized the word "Engineer" as if it were synonymous with the Black Plague. And it made me think, "All Engineers can't be as stupid as I was during my meeting with Sophie and Bess back at the Washington Monument, could they?"

She went on, "Margolova showed up everywhere where work was being done in Aerospace. We'd scare her out of Huntsville, Alabama on a Tuesday, and by that Friday she'd be wooing an Engineer on the outskirts of White Sands, New Mexico. Shoo her out of the desert and she shows up on the West Coast dining with a Titan III fuels expert. We chased her around relentlessly for four whole years."

"Why didn't you guys just throw her in jail?"

"Believe me, we wanted to... We *simply* couldn't catch her. Every time the FBI moved in on her she'd vanish. It seemed that she had an inside informant, a mole, or a double agent was helping her from within the FBI, or the CIA. Then, in 1979, a very special agent, known as the "Sandman," was put on the case. He was supposed to stop her, with finality."

Sophie looked at me to see if I understood the gravity of what she had said; or maybe, in a moment of hindsight, to see if I concurred with a *finality* undertaking. Which "did" seem reasonable to me, at the time. Hell, if the bitch was stealing our national secrets, then she ought to pay the consequences. It just seems to come with the territory, doesn't it? I motioned for her to continue with a gesture of, "Oh well, that's the way the old ball bounces." And she continued.

"Sandman followed her down to M.I.T., she was screwing a top-notch computer professor who was designing access codes for the Pentagon's war systems." She paused for effect, a good narrator's trick, and it worked. She slowly continued.

"The very next day, Margolova is spotted up in Canada. She was seen boarding an Aeroflot destined for Russia. Eight days later, this same computer professor reports a foul smell emanating from his attic. He calls his landlord and they go up to investigate the odor. It was Sandman, or, at least what was left of him. He was decapitated and dismembered and his parts were strewn all over the attic. Except his head, which is still missing."

I threw down the steamy piece of cod that I was just about to savor and began to idly look around the camper, not seeing anything in particular, but looking for something that was sane, something that would help me to regain my sense of rationality. And guess what? There wasn't anything.

"There's more." She continued, "A few years pass and there's no word on her. We believed that she was murdered, imprisoned or remarried. Her file became inactive. She was only being mentioned when people talked about some of the old-time "bad ones." Then, two years ago, she surfaces in France. In just two short weeks, Margo is placed at the scene, or very near the scene, of twenty-two murders. They were all college students, all of them exceptionally bright political science students who were about to graduate. Each of them was destined to fast-track it up into France's political elite."

I questioned this, "Political *student* assassinations?"

"Yes. Actually, it's much worse than that. The Russian's refuse to acknowledge her as one of theirs. They insist that she is acting on her own. They believe that she's trying to propagate old school Communism. Our inside sources confirm the Kremlin's statements and have insured us that she *is* acting as a lone wolf, a rebel with a cause – the rebirth of Marxist's Communism."

"She sounds more like a serial killer to me."

Sophie looked confused by my statement. "Well, yes and no."

She began to talk slower and picked her words, "There is a political underground in the new Russian breakup. It's run by some hard-core old time Marxists who would still like to rule the world under their form of Communism. This sub-power group was once known as the Cheeka. Today, they call themselves the Neo-Cheekovites. They are extremely secretive and we can only compare them to something like the Mafia. Everyone knows they're there, but nobody quite knows where or who "they" are. Although, "they" have a way of evoking fear and terror all through the new political structure."

"Technically, the Neo-Cheekovites *don't* exist. They don't have offices and they don't keep records. Nobody has ever claimed leadership let alone membership. It exists, but it doesn't."

This is where Margolova comes in. We believe that the Neo-Cheeka controls her. They're the ones who are paying her way and have been ordering her to make the assassinations. We just don't know how, or, how to prove it. It's Marx's "specter," and it's spread all around the world, not just over Europe."

I commented, "This is some deep shit, isn't it?"

"Yes." She said. Then stared out of the van window facing a crate marked in black letters, "THIS END UP."

To break her trance, I said, "Hey, we're in England, let's give James Bond a call, let him handle it."

Without breaking her stare she stated, in a matter-of-fact, certainty, "It's been tried."

Then looked at me, serious, breaking her boxed-in gaze, she says, "Not by Ian Fleming's Bond, or that new guy, Gardner, but by some of England's best."

"Oh yeah?"

"Yeah." She mimicked me, she was angry, said, "Their bodies have been strewn all across Europe. It's almost as if she enjoys being hunted, she wants us to chase her, it gives her something to kill, agents. I guess it keeps her attentive."

I seriously asked, "I didn't know that "00" agents really existed, Soph?"

"Well, they're not called double "0" agents, if that's what you mean?"

"Yeah, that's what I meant. So, what are they called?"

She looked back to the crate, "I'm not at liberty to discuss that." Her attitude had become prissy and it was ticking me off. Maybe, I was getting scared. I didn't know. Or, maybe, I was just tired. I knew this, I was mad. We had discussed murder upon murder and now, she was going to withhold the "00" stuff.

I snapped at her, "Yeah, right. I'm in this up to my ass and you're not at liberty to discuss James Bond. Well, screw you and the CIA high horse that you're riding on."

She turned and gave me a look of incredulity, her jaw hung open, as I continued, "Just how much *don't* I know about this whole damned setup?"

There was an awkward silence. I prompted, "Well?"

"Actually, you know just about everything. Margolova has been my specialty ever since I joined the CIA over five years ago. As of right now, I'm considered to be the world's foremost authority on her – excluding her mother Russia."

"I've been totally open with you, Mister Morgan. Everything that I've related to you is classified "Eyes only," and I surely didn't have to tell you as much as I did. You've been cleared on a "Need to Know" basis, and, I thought, that, well, if you were to meet up with her. This information *might* help you."

"Well. Thank you very much, Miss Uncle Sam. Just when do I start collecting myself some hazardous duty pay for hunting down spies?"

Sophie was shaking her head in a slow negative, "Eunice was right. You can be a real pain in the ass, can't you?" I should have listened to her warnings much closer, she really "does" have you pegged, Jimbo."

"And don't call me, Jimbo." I said this as nice as I could – under the idiotic circumstances of our ego dominance struggle.

"Sorry, Jim. ...James? Mister Morgan?"

And there it was, her cuteness. Sophie could get away with a whole lot of shit, and, she knew it. She could just jut out her well formed breasts in a female taunt, "Don't forget, I'm a girl, see? And I'm cute, too. So, back off, while the going's good, got it?"

I was still angry, internally. I answered her, "Just Jim, is fine. And, by the way, is your name really, Sophie D. D. Kidd?"

"Just call me, Soph. That's my *real* name. I'll tell you all about the

"D.D. Kidd" when I get back."

She had stood while talking all the while moving toward the innards of the camper, "Want some coffee?" As if nothing had happened, nothing more than a few grand hallelujahs at a Sunday morning prayer meeting. Mea culpa, mea culpa, I had seen the light and the only thing that I could really do was hit the old dimmer switch. Amen. I say unto you, amen.

"Yes, please. Two sugars."

Chapter Fifteen

While Sophie made coffee, I busied myself at cleaning up our fish and chips breakfast, wondering, "... just what kind of fish had we actually eaten. It was very tasty when we first began to dine, but then, the more we discussed Margolova, every bite became less and less enjoyable." As I stuffed the odoriferous remains into the trash I concluded that it was either shark or barracuda. I had double-checked the lid to insure that the odors would remain confined, and, with a clean slate, returned to my seat.

Cuteness followed close behind with steaming mugs of a tasty Belgian coffee. Still standing, she began her personal biography.

"Sophie was my grandmother's name on my father's side."

Again, she looked at me checking for attentiveness over the rim of her coffee mug, and then went on. "My other grandmother was named Agnes. Sophie was chosen as the lesser of two evils, according to my dad." She set down her mug, while continuing.

"Sophie D. Kidd is my CIA moniker. I use it when I'm out in the field; it's my code name. Actually, everyone seems to prefer it over my real name." She contemplated this a moment before continuing. "When I first hired into the CIA I was assigned to the Internal Affairs Department. In the field, Internal Affairs is known as the, Death Division. A lot of our older agents work there. It's a "last stop" before retirement, and one is considered to be "retired in residence" when one transfers there.

So, the old timers began calling me Kid from day one, and it stuck. Soon, people from outside the department began calling me, "D. Deadly Kidd." And now – I'm stuck with it.

Around the office I'm called Dee-Dee, for D. Deadly, and in the field, I'm just called, D. Kidd, or Kidd. A lot of people think it's my real name and actually call me, Sophie D. Deadly. And my boss, well, he just calls me, Soph.

When I hear my real name, which is, Sophie Marie Alberquist, I know that it's my parents, or that someone from payroll has a check for me."

"Did you say, Alberquist?"

"Yes. Sophie Marie Alberquist."

"I just had lunch with a Senator named Alberquist. Are you related?"

She smiled proudly, "Yes, he's my father. That luncheon was set up so that you two could meet. To quote dad, "No daughter of mine is going half way around the world with some big jerk who owns an old sports car and flies around in an airplane without a pilot's license, unless I meet him first, face to face."

Immediately I recollected our meeting. "So, that's how he knew I had an Austin."

"What?" Soph questioned, "What are you talking about?"

"The Senator... your dad, he knew that I owned an Austin, that's all." And, I couldn't help but wonder to myself just what else did he know?

In a smiled blush, a blush laced with humor, Sophie cooed, "Daddy likes you." And there it was, no doubt about it, a deep and hearty sexual innuendo, a blatant tease that bespoke of sexual conquest with direct, parental approval.

And it made me angry. "Oh fine, daddy likes me. Maybe we should get married? Or at least be engaged before we fly south of the equator, you know, anything to keep daddy happy, right?

Yeah, anything to protect his little baby's virtue and all that other happy horse shit. I was sarcastically treading on her father's openly protective nature, and Sophie was enjoying every blasphemous word of it. So much so, that she entered into a hysterical laughter, a contagious laughter, and soon, we were both in stitches. And when we questioned ourselves as to what was so funny, we laughed even harder. We no longer knew, and no longer cared, as a stifling tension had come to an abrupt end. Yeah, we had become comrades in idiocy, and daddy, love him dearly, had unwittingly surrendered his parental bondage, evermore.

In an effort to regain our composure and our individual sense of decorum, we had to stop and empty our bladders. While doing so, the airplane's jets whined to life and shortly thereafter the red FAS-TEN SEAT BELT sign announced that, soon, the bulbous eagle would make its' run down the cold English runway and begin its next scream, southward, down and into Spain's own coveted airdrome.

Ah, the land of conquistadors, bullfights, castanets and olive skinned beauties dancing away in their brightly colored, red and orange ruffled cottons. And I hoped that our view of Spanish soil would be better than that of our stint on the beautiful British Isles.

The whore light went red; daylight had dawned on the eastern European shores. I yawned openly. It was time for owls, vampires, and spy Engineers to get some serious sleep. I stretched while announcing my intention to hit the sack.

"Enjoy your view, Deadly. I'm turning in – for the day."

In a coy and seductive tease, I assumed the tease, Sophie asked, "Want me to tuck you in, Jimbo?"

I answered with adamant, "No." Adding, "And don't call me, Jimbo."

In an effort to provoke me yet deeper, she adds, "Sweet dreams my lovely... I mean, James. Jim? ...Mister Morgan?" And then sat there looking at me with her sparkling blue eyes, eyes that danced brightly above a playfully sexual grin. Yeah, she was pushing her cuteness to the limit, and it worked. And I knew then why her colleagues and co-workers called her "Deadly." And, believe me, it had nothing to do at all with the department that she was assigned to, no sir, not at all.

As I pulled the covers up over my head, I couldn't shake the recurrent thought, "Daddy likes you." And I lay there thinking, "Did *Eunice's* daddy like me?" And I didn't know. Then I thought about Sophie, about making love to her, and I recalled her last words, "Sweet dreams *my* lovely." And indeed, they were.

Soph woke me just before we descended into Madrid. She said that it was almost noon and that we'd be there for three hours due to a maintenance glitch. She added, "The pilot said we could dine at the O Club, the Officer's Club. Interested?"

"Sure. Are you buying?"

"I never ask a man to lunch unless I know that I can foot the bill, Mister Morgan. Besides, I'm on an expense account."

"Ah, Soph, you're my kind of woman. Let's get married."

She backed herself out the door, saying, "Yeah, right. I'll go call Eunice and ask for her blessing." She pulled the door shut with a brisk snap. Through the closed door she continued, "She'd make a wonderful maid-of-honor, don't you think, Jimbo?"

I yelled, "I think you had better quit calling me, Jimbo!"

The shower stall was cramped, but adequate. Although I had hurried my shower routine, I found that one uses ten gallons of hot water quite rapidly. I blew dry my hair and dressed in under ten minutes. I dressed casually in tan slacks and a short sleeve Polo shirt. I felt fresh and clean as I passed through Sophie's bedroom, a room that looked like someone had dynamited their luggage open instead of unpacking it. Sophie, underneath all her cuteness, is not a neat nick. I couldn't help but think, "Kid, with one d."

Soph was waiting at the door. She scanned me from head to toe and gave me a nod of approval. Then came another nod one that meant for me to follow her, and I did.

When I found my way out, Sophie had already descended the aluminum stairs and was chatting with Sugar Plum. A bright Spanish sun blasted me in the face, as did a rush of hot stagnant runway air. Madrid was having an early spring heat wave. The concrete was sending up convective heat thermals, big puffs of super heated air, which are not un-similar to a bubble rising in a pot of boiling water.

By the time I put on my sunglasses and made the bottom step, I was sweating. Sugar Plum had broke off his chat to talk with a mechanic. Sophie came up to me and whispered, "You look like a spy, Jim. Take those silly things off, will ya?"

"Oh yeah? Well, I am. Aren't I? A spy. I'm just getting into the role, Deadly." And for that, I was called an "asshole."

A dark blue, air-conditioned, staff-car pulled up to us and its' driver asked if we were the ones going to the "O" Club. We rode in silence and I *kept* my sunglasses on. The air-conditioning gave me a chill and I rolled my window down. The blast of outside heat was too hot, and I rolled my window back up. I couldn't find a happy medium and rolled it halfway down a moment later.

Sophie, agitated, said, "Having fun with the window, Mister Bond?" It was most amusing.

I egged her on, "Holy shit!"

"What?"

"I left my Flash Gordon decoder ring back in Washington."

She could only say, "Oh boy." And all the while shook her head in a bewildered gesture.

Sophie had dressed smartly in a white cotton shift with red trim and accented earrings. Except for the blond hair, she looked very Spanish. Heads turned as we moved through the club and into a small alcove off the main dining room. It was a non-officer nook designed to segregate visiting civilians from the jet-jockeys. At least, that was my thinking.

Sophie, on the other hand, suggested that the nook was there for the privacy of Generals and other, visiting "dignitaries." And, she was probably right.

The little room was dominated by a giant oil painting of Don Quixote. The artist depicted Don Q. riding his ass toward an old monstrous windmill with his wooden lance projecting outward along his feeble forearm. Yeah, it was good, the sick idealist venturing out naively onward and upward to slay his phantom enemies. I looked closer and decided it was done in oils. The frame and its' red felt brocade was a bit much, but – we *were* in Spain.

A red rose complimented our table. The silverware included salad forks, too. Salad forks are one of the subtle traits of fine dining. Soft, indirect lighting gave the table a highly romantic atmosphere. Ah, it was so Spanish – so subliminally sexual.

We dined on a Spanish rice smothered in steak bits and mushroom sauce. Sophie ordered a Portuguese white wine that was very sweet, but soon melded nicely with the spicy, peppered, sauces. It was a delicious fare served elegantly in a solidly built den.

The "O" club was earthy, rugged, it spoke out, "Enjoy this "terra firma." The adobe plastered walls and its wooden arches bespoke of earth and not of air, a safe cradle where airmen, once extricated from the fragile bonds of space and fluid vapors, could enjoy their "natural" ties to mother earth herself. And, when that last tasty bite of an overly rich desert settled home, one knew, innately, earth and sky were sublimely opposite, yet one, in the grand ebullience of God's natural order. Yeah, the environment, the meal, the totality of where we were was adventurous, yet it was a haven, a haven for genuine adventurers.

And then, Sophie shattered the moment in a pointed stab, she asked, "Are you really going to marry Eunice?"

Have you ever seen a romantic bubble pop? Her question had taken me by surprise. It was a sudden reality check. A check that one shouldn't have to endure during a fine repast, especially when one's only focal escape is a giant picture of Don Quixote wrestling with irrationality.

"I've already asked her to marry me, two years ago. She accepted, but things didn't work out so well at the time."

"Oh?" Soph needled. "What happened?"

"It's a long story." I waved my hand to dismiss the subject. "I don't want to talk about it right now." I didn't want to tell her how stupid a guy could get when he's confronted with a cute pair of teats in a topless roadhouse. Right?

"We've got a lot of time, Mister Morgan, ah ...Jim. I'd like to hear about it, really."

She was taunting me and I knew it. Yet, she seemed so sincere. She placed her elbows on the table cradling her chin in the palms of her hands and began to tap her lips with her fingers in a show of impatience, said, "Come on, Jim. I'm waiting."

"Well, we had a misunderstanding..." I started to recant, but Sophie broke in, in mid-sentence, "Ohhh, I bet it was over that topless dancer, Bunny." This was said as, "Eureka!" It was uninhibited spontaneity, a brash display of, "Ha! You really got yours, didn't you, Jimbo? Boy oh boy – you sure were *stupid*."

I looked off, away from her excitement, and found myself once again fixated on the Don Q. painting. Only this time, I focused in on the dark roiling clouds above the pewter colored helmet of Don Q's unpolished armor, at least he had some protection from his phantoms, some skimpy metal defense, whereas I had nothing. I sat there naked in front of my adversary, the "deadly" Kidd, and it pissed me off.

"Isn't there anything about me that you *don't* know?"

"I'm sorry, Jim, ...Mister Morgan, I read about you and the Bunny in Eunice's file." She was attempting pacification, but her mind and body were out of step with each other, verbally she was sorry, physically, she was cracking up, amused to no end.

I had raised my voice somewhat in anger, "Well, isn't this all just fine and dandy. Just when in the hell am I going to get to read *your* files, Miss Comedienne?"

Our waiter appeared, "Is everything satisfactory, sir?"

"No." I said, standing. "Everything here is not satisfactory." I handed my red napkin to the waiter while pointing to the table, and said, coolly, "Miss Deadly will *pay* for this. Please excuse me." And without further ado, I headed for the door.

Yeah, I sorely needed some space, some room to gather my thoughts and to put the whole spy scenario into some sort of "manageable" perspective. Once outside, I found the heat oppressive, the wind was calm and there weren't any clouds to shield me from the sun's radiant power. I scanned the base for signs of reality. It was ultra clean like every other base that I had ever been on. I watched a one striped airman driving a gang-mower tractor through an empty field and I felt stupid, dumb, I simply wasn't in the know.

It was true. I didn't know what was going on. Out loud, to myself, I said, "You're just not cut out for the spy business, Jim Morgan. You'd best let it go." And I did. And I instantly felt better. I forced myself to relax, I stretched, and even the heat felt welcome, it had become sensual, caressing and – comforting.

It was the second time in a week that I had experienced a bout of paranoia. Just a moment ago I was questioning the fact that we were indeed dining in Madrid, Spain. I walked over to an olive tree and placed my hand on its' smooth bark. I had never seen a real olive tree before and as far as I knew, it *was a* fake. My hands felt cold against the bark. Was it from the air-conditioning? And as quickly as my panic attack came, it disappeared. My anger had miraculously dissipated. I took a deep drag on my cigarette and heard an inner voice say, "Nobody's twisting your arm to be here, Jim Morgan." And after that, my mind was simply blank. I don't know how long I stood there but it was quite a good while.

I was lighting a third cigarette when Sophie exited the club. She stood under the red door's awning and lit a cigarette herself. She was looking toward me but made no attempt to approach me or to converse. I didn't know she smoked. She looked dumb with a cigarette dangling from her lips. There was a good forty, fifty feet separating us. I yelled over to her, not with anger, but so as to be heard, "Those are bad for your health, you know?"

"Yes, I know." Then she added, in a soft monotone, "So is working for the CIA." The latter part was said more for her own benefit, not necessarily for mine.

I guessed that she had wanted to continue on, as if nothing had happened. After all, we did have a moment to collect ourselves and rethink the issues.

She called out, "I haven't had a cigarette in over a year." She held the butt in her fingertips and stared at the fiery tip, the same way a child would hold a dried out cattail on a summer evening – letting it smolder and smoke to keep away mosquitoes.

I asked, "Is that in your file?"

With abject resignation, she answered, "Probably."

Chapter Sixteen

We climbed out of Madrid with our compass needle pointed due south toward the equator – where beyond lay the southern hemisphere. This, in and of itself, should have been total excitement, but it wasn't. The Air Force jumbo jet now hosted two upset and grumpy adventurers. And there we sat, together, in silence, each contemplating our individual misfortunes.

Mine were, "What am I doing here?" And, "Did I really love Eunice?" Both questions were ill defined and far from being totally inclusive. To make the situation worse, my thinking was severely clouded by a simple fact, "I had fallen in love, or *lust*, with a very deadly kid whose Senatorial sire, "Liked me."

Sophie's were ...I *didn't* know. Surely Margolova. And me the malcontent, pseudo-spy, whom she had probably guessed was in love with her, or worse – lusting her. No, I couldn't read her withdrawal, but whatever it was that she was contemplating, it was deep. She was in her own world, seeking, pondering paradoxes or something. Whatever? Perhaps Asmara? Which was our next stop, the old and impoverished capital of the Ethiopian empire.

Ethiopia is often argued to be the seat of *all* civilization. It is a land of undeveloped mineral wealth, coffee, cotton, sand and date palms. Its' official language is Amharic, which is very old and very guttural. English is the primary second language and is spoken by most educated Ethiopians.

Sugar Plum advised Baby that we would land about sunset, Asmara time. That's about twelve hours ahead of Eunice's time back in Washington, D.C.; this particular time concept always amazes me. Had I actually traveled forward in time? Hey! Hands down, I was now a full twelve hours ahead of Eunice.

I excused myself, announcing, "I'm going to rack out, Kidd. The view (I pointed to the crates) isn't moving my soul at the moment. I need a power nap."

She gave me a nod that barely broke her revelry and I left her to her clandestine CIA thoughts, if indeed that's what they were.

The camper bed felt exceptionally comfortable and to my own

surprise, I slept the entire way. Soph pounded on the door, and then yelled in, "Pack it up, Mister Morgan. We land in fifteen minutes." This was an "all business" announcement, and with a fifteen-minute warning, it was obvious that she wasn't ready for a bit of idle chitchat over a mug of Belgian coffee. In fact, it was downright mean.

I did manage to pack, clean up, dress, and had just begun to fasten down my seat belt when we went into a mad, bumpy roll down an unseen runway. It was the first time that I actually needed a seat belt, it was that rough. And I couldn't help but think, "Welcome to the third world, eh?"

Three crew members showed up, one of them was an officer, and in no less than five minutes our baggage was off-loaded and stacked neatly on the gravel runway, just off the port wing tip of the Herc (a nickname for the C-5?). No one talked and the engines were kept running. The door closed and the captain, Sugar Plum, gave us a snappy salute from his cockpit window. The behemoth engines whined loudly as the over-fed condor inched away from us creating a mammoth cloud of Ethiopian dust. Thankfully, a light breeze kept the dirt and debris east of us, away from our open and totally exposed drop-off point.

And there we stood. We were on an auxiliary airfield, a flat cut in the earth's rocky crust some twenty odd miles from Asmara. It was not an airport. There were no buildings, no fences, no windsocks, no lights, no nothing – excepting a few weeds, and even those appeared to be dormant, or dead.

Later, when I researched the exact location of the landing strip, I found out that the airfield was an Italian creation that was made during WW-II. A lone bulldozer cut a level path through the yellow stone and the King of Ethiopia pronounced it a landing site for all allied air forces. So.

There we stood, hands on our hips, watching the C-5A whine out of Asmara. It slid over a rock mound and disappeared leaving us in a total and deafening silence that made my ears ring. I looked at Soph and asked, "What now, Priss?"

"We wait."

We were waiting for the arrival of a CIA "chartered" aircraft, a "B-25" bomber that was converted to haul beans out of Madagascar. The twin engine Mitchell was built in 1940, and according to Soph, who had seen a picture of one, "...it's a really neat looking airplane."

And I thought, "Yeah, right. It's probably in as good of shape as the gravel field that we were standing on." And for an instant, I thought about digging out the pith helmet. Needless to say, I was somewhat apprehensive about the last leg of our trip, in a 1940 "anything," let alone an aircraft that should have been recycled years and years ago. But, there we were.

Sophie was properly dressed for her African debut, Eunice would have been proud of her. She was wearing a tan safari outfit replete with a zebra banded Australian field hat. Under her left arm she wore a snub-nosed .38 detective special in a brown leather, wool lined, shoulder holster. It went well with the epaulets on her designer field jacket.

Yeah, Sophie fit the African scenario. And me? Well, I looked like a young Engineer that was kicked out of his first-class seat on a Pan Am flight to give a quick look-see as what could be done to modernize an old abandoned airfield on the out, out-skirts of Ethiopian antiquity. I recall patting my breast pocket to ensure that I was carrying two pens, the cardinal badge of any worthy Engineer, and, when I found the esteemed personality extensions in their proper position, I felt most secure in my hostile East African environment. Sophie told me that we were off loaded at the auxiliary airstrip due to the B-25 connection. "The pilot has been banned from landing in Asmara." She said this without a hint as to why.

"The Air Force agreed to bring us this far just to give the pilot a chance to use this auxiliary field, it'll go down in the books as a training sortie. It'll save the taxpayers a bundle of money, combining business with pleasure. Don't you think?"

"Yeah, pleasure." I sat down on the suitcases and lit a cigarette. I thought, "Yeah, I'm getting one hell of a snow job, here, in the desert. Next thing, she'll be telling me that we have to row a leaky boat across the Mozambique Channel, to combine business with sadism."

Sophie continued, defensively, "It *is* a valuable exercise for the pilots, Mister Morgan, and only a small inconvenience for us."

I did a deliberate scan around the desolate area, and then asked, "What if your B-25 doesn't show? What then?"

"It'll be here, Mister Morgan. We've used this route before, it's more punctual than most of the major airlines."

Right then, as if on cue, the B-25 appeared on the clear and night-darkening southern horizon. We watched it approach and in a very few minutes it looked to be coming straight at our heads, and it did, buzzing us at about ten feet off the ground. I knew a few pilots up in Alaska who were nuts, but this breed of African hellcat was unbelievable.

The pilot banked off to the west with his wing tip so close to the ground that I'm sure he had left an etching in the gravel. I could only think that this guy was very, very good, or very, *very* crazy. The bomber continued its pirouette through 270 degrees. It then leveled, and touched down in a landing roll directed right at us, and our neatly stacked luggage. He was going to land perpendicular to the runway. So much for the Italian's labor on a north to south airstrip, eh?

The antique propellers stopped spinning some forty yards in front of us but the silent monster continued rolling, right up to us. We were both frozen in awe at the unorthodox arrival of our timely CIA charter. The plane did a slight nose dip when the brakes were applied, some "few inches" away from running right over us. I felt that we had held our ground just to test the pilot's skill, but, maybe not. At any rate, we stood our ground. Once it had completely stopped, I reached up and touched the plastic nose, it was that close.

We stepped off to the side in hopes of seeing the African cowboy who'd pilot us into Madagascar, but the windows were blackened with a one-way sunscreen that blocked our chance to view him.

Stenciled below the cockpit was the pilot's calling card: "Cool Hand Luke, NASA Reject, 1969"

A thick wooden ladder dropped down from the open belly of the ex-bomber and dug itself into the rocky soil. Following quickly down on its oak rungs came a huge black man who had to weigh 400 pounds, give or take a few biscuits. Actually, he waddled down, shifting his weight from side to side until he hit ground. Then he threw up his arms and did an exaggerated yawn, sucking in enough air to fill up a small life raft. Then, while exhaling, says, "Hello."

Sophie approached him with her hand held out to shake hands, asking, "Cool Hand Luke?"

He was young, maybe twenty – twenty-two at tops. He wouldn't take her hand, just shook his head no. Then said, "No. Cool Hand Luke is too drunk to come down now. Him's sleeping. I'll wake him up when I get this loaded." He was nodding toward our luggage, being serious, intent.

"I'm Abdul Amin. I'm Luke's best worker."

I asked, "If Luke's sleeping? Who was flying?" I had pointed my thumb toward the cockpit.

Abdul Amin was astonished, he said, "Luke." And it was said in such a manner that it meant, "Hey, don't you know? Only Luke can fly this airplane, how could you be so stupid?"

After an awkward moment, Abdul added, "Luke only fly, drink, and sleep. Now he sleeps. After I load you – he fly."

Sophie jumped in, "When does he drink?"

Abdul smiled, "Ah, miss, him drinks all the time. Him the best drinking man in all of Tanan."

Sophie and I exchanged looks of apprehension – shock, would be a better expression. Soph shrugged, saying, in Luke's defense, "Well, he's on time."

Abdul, who insisted that we call him "Abby," loaded all our baggage, one bag at a time. He jabbered out that he was paid by the hour. He added, "Besides, the boss needs some rest, we've been working for twenty-four hours now. We made many trips to Tanan since yesterday. Boss says, "Busy, busy bees, is we. Him's a hard working man."

With the last of our bags loaded, Abby motioned us up the home-made ladder with a wave of his huge, flabby, baby-fatted arm. We sat on a two by ten board that acted as passenger seat. Our seat belt, singular, was a one-inch thick rope that was latched across our laps, very loosely. Our feet rested two inches from the opened bomb-bay doors. Actually – there weren't any doors. They had been removed to control the odor incurred during "hog and pig" loads between the larger cities. That's when I became vocal about our seating arrangements.

Sophie expressed herself thus, "Calm down, Mister Morgan, it will be fun, especially after riding in that cooped up camper all day and night."

Abby pulled up the ladder and tied it firmly to the magnesium framework that acted as a rib to the B-25's chest. He picked up a funnel, inserted it into a rubber hose and spoke into it, – loud enough that we could hear him say, "Hey Boss. Wake up, Boss. We all loaded now, Boss."

The engines sputtered into life with visible puffs of a gray-white JP-4 fuel smoke and then began a purr, a purr like that of a panther out for an evening prowl in search of red meat. And just that fast the ground began to slide past the floor opening, faster and faster, until the gravel blurred into a cement and we began our rise out of nothingness, and then up, up over more, nothingness. The ground changed to patchy clumps of bush haphazardly strewn out and about a barren semi-desert of rocky dusty wasteland and the bleak East African topography became even bleaker as we raced eastward into the colorless hue of a darkening equatorial twilight. Sophie had put her arm across my back looping her hand through a crate wire. Her eyes were closed and she stayed in that immobile position throughout the entire flight. Abdul, on the other hand, stood the entire trip in a three-foot square. He was not tethered to the aircraft or its load in any way, yet seemed quite at ease and totally in balance with the swaying craft, no small feat for such a rotund ball of African baby fat.

Stacked behind him were a dozen crates of small reddish-green apples. After watching him eat his forty-third apple, including the cores, I had to conclude that the apples were his lunch and not a part of Luke's cargo. Never once did he offer us one, but he did smile with utter contentment after each apple was swallowed. I'm not sure if he knew it, but he had put on quite an amusing show. Bravo!

I had poked Soph a few times to get her attention but she was deep in meditation, Nirvana – or somewhere. Wherever she was, it was beyond worldly contact. It was useless to attempt conversation due to the noise level, which was horrendous, but I did wish her to see the apple swallowing antics of our pseudo-flight attendant. It was a happening, a pure marvel.

Luke flew low over the Mozambique Channel; my guess was 200 feet, which I based on the size of the waves. Yeah, we were that low as we dashed across the tropical ebony waters. Sea soon gave way to land and I thanked the gods to be, for a safe dry crossing. Even though I consider myself to be a fair swimmer, I do believe this: "Every sport has a practical limit and swimming the Mozambique Channel at night is one of them."

We began to climb higher; ear popping was the clue to our elevation change. That, and an obvious upward tilt of the aircraft's straw lined floor. Abby sat down on his three-foot square and let his feet dangle in the wind that rushed past the fuselage. He had no show of fear and several times he leaned forward to peer sideways under the plane, probably looking for familiar landmarks. He was scaring me terribly and I couldn't help but wonder if he knew so, and just what kind of rush it had given him to flirt with instant death. Surely he couldn't have been simply *that* stupid, could he?

After about twenty minutes of his antics, he stood and grabbed the wooden ladder and held it down into the rushing wind. The B-25 had made yet another successful sortie up to Antananarivo. Before the wheels touched pavement the engines were cut. We glided in, smoother than a loose goose's feather. We did a silent bump and roll and gently rumbled into a full stop that took no more than twenty short seconds.

Abby positioned the ladder and tested its set on the tarmac. Sophie went down first, saying, "Miracle of miracles, there really is a God."

I followed her down echoing her witticism – from my heart. Abby unloaded our baggage, carrying one bag at a time down the big ladder. It felt extra special to be on firm ground – no, it felt great, wonderful, to be alive, and to be done with Luke's flying circus, err. Service.

Sophie announced that she was going to find a taxi and left. I called after her, "You had better get two with all this luggage." She had said something in response, but I didn't hear her.

Abby carried down the last bag and stacked it neatly on top of the others. He reached into his pocket and withdrew a piece of paper, then pushed it toward me, saying, "Luke say for you to sign this, in triplicate."

I took the paper and read the letterhead, Luke's Bar & Grill, and below that, in pencil, East Coast Air Service. And below that, scrawled out in a sloppy hand-written up-sloping line, "Two bods to Tanan two grand."

There was only one page of paper. I signed it three times and handed it back to Abdul. He never looked at it, just took it and stuffed it back into his shirt pocket.

I said, "Thanks for the ride, Pal. It's been fun."

Abdul "Abby" Amin smiled big, said, "No one ever thanked me for the ride before. They always sick. You two are my best passengers, ever." He kept smiling as he backed up to his ladder, climbed up and withdrew the steps. His head popped down from the bomb-bay opening. He looked at me, said, "Bye." And then he was gone.

The B-25 fired up its engines and was in a roll back toward the runway before the start-up smoke had time to clear its cowlings.

At a thousand dollars a head, the mysterious Luke was probably going back to Asmara, for more CIA *bods*.

I sat down on an American Tourister "Pullman" bag that belonged to Sophie and lit a cigarette. I strained my eyes looking for an oncoming taxi, but there was no movement, no sign of life, whatsoever, anywhere, around the international terminal. And I could only wonder if it was closed for the night?

And so I began my first night below the equator. Suddenly, I felt all alone, which indeed I was, but it was a "lonely" aloneness. Something that I had never before experienced, not ever, throughout all of my distant and varied travels. It was an unsettling feeling, one that foretold of gloom and doom, and a loss, a loss of environmental control. I couldn't snap my fingers and summon three uniformed waiters – know what I mean?

I turned my attention to the sky and focused in on the Southern Cross. Even the stars were strange. Absent were the dippers, that phenomenal mainstay of our northern hemisphere. And I had envisioned myself standing on the earth, upside down. And, indeed I was. I lit another cigarette. The adventure was culminating. Soon, I'd be in a hot shower at a Hilton and my sense of reality *would* return.

Chapter Seventeen

Antananarivo is one of the world's largest "mile high" cities. Its' elevation is 5,000 feet above sea level on one end and climbs to over 6,000 feet on the other. Consequently, I found myself breathing with some difficulty; however, this may have been psychosomatic. I had read that air is thinner at higher elevations and was consciously reacting to my low oxygen knowledge. The air also felt chilly; but then again, it should have been due to the higher altitude. I threw down my third Camel and immediately took out another one. Lit it. And then watched it to see if it burned slower. I couldn't tell. Then I thought, "What a way to make one's living."

Sophie returned, a mere seven cigarettes later, in style. She arrived in an old Reo flatbed pickup truck. The driver, a young Malagasy kid, was obviously into bodybuilding, his biceps were the size of basketballs. His name was Juan. Juan was barefoot and wore a tank top and cut-off jeans. His hair was tied back in a Wall Street type ponytail. Hands down he was an Adonis, and he knew it. One could tell by the way he strutted. Yeah, he was half peacock, and half Mount Everest.

Without introduction Juan began loading our bags by physically throwing them, in six-foot arcs, onto the flatbed. Soph came over to me and began to explain that Juan was the best transportation she could find. Just then, I saw young Hercules pick up my 300-dollar briefcase.

"Whoa there, Pal. Let me take that one, if you don't mind? Compren-day?"

Juan stopped, looked at me weirdly and handed me the briefcase while saying, "Sure, Mack. No problem."

It was after nine when we arrived at the Hilton. And lucky *me* got to ride with the baggage. Juan made short work of unloading. Of course, there was no respect for our bags or their contents, didn't he know, "Arrow shirts break?"

When Juan finished, he did a beautifully executed back flip with a half-twist, from the edge of the flatbed down to the parking lot. Grinning, he went to Sophie; pushing away the twenty-dollar bill she was holding, takes her hand and kisses it, saying, "Your suitcases were my pleasure, totally."

Soph was sucking this up, big time. I thought, "Yeah, right. The day baggage becomes pleasure a whole lot of bellhops will be lined up to receive their welfare checks."

The Hilton's doorman, reminiscent of my recent stay at the Westin in Seattle, came up and asked if we had reservations. I ensured him that we did with a twenty-dollar tip. He bowed reverently promising to see to all of our bags, personally. He picked a piece of straw from my lapel, which earned him a second twenty.

Our reservations were in order. We'd have adjoining suites. Eunice had made the reservations. And to have a whole suite was a very pleasant perk, indeed. Yeah, it was time to relax and enjoy the "Hospitality Plus" regal Hilton atmosphere. We ordered dinner to be served in, in Sophie's suite.

Later, over a tasty lamb stew, I told Sophie that I was going to put down a hundred dollars for limo service to the hotel on my expense account. Then asked her, "What are you going to claim?"

With a big smile she declared, "I'm not keeping an expense account this trip, Jim. I was told that all my out of pocket money would be paid by you. I'm supposed to just give you a receipt and you're supposed to pay me, on the spot." She stood and retrieved her purse, opened it, took out a scrap of paper and handed it to me. It read, $150.00 for truck rental.

She quickly added, "I offered him a tip, but he refused."

"One-hundred and fifty bucks for that old pile of junk? You've got to be kidding?" And I thought, "What ever happened to the old days when a guy could pad his expense account and make a couple extra, few, dollars?"

Still smiling, she says, "I know it's only a scrap of paper, but that guy wasn't a regular limo service. Is this going to be a problem?"

"No. It's okay. Just, ah, don't mention that he refused the tip, okay?"

Seriously, she asks, "Why not, Jim?"

I put up my hand to cut her off, "Just let me handle the finances, okay?"

Sophie gave me a look of genuine surprise, "Oh, you're going to inflate your travel voucher. Aren't you?"

So, Sophie was the new saint of travel voucher accuracy, or maybe, and I must stress the *maybe*, she was gullible enough to be honest on her own expense account. I asked her, "How old are you, Kidd?"

"Twenty-seven."

"Yeah? Well, where has the CIA been hiding you, in an air-tight vault?"

She looked at me with a coy grin, "You are going to pay me, aren't you?" And then added a cutesy, "Please?"

Right then and there, I was hit in the ass with a bolt of genuine insight. I was suddenly in the position of paying someone else's "inflated" expenses, and – I didn't like it. It just wasn't the same.

Since she was begging, I had to answer, "Yeah, sure. Just make sure you get receipts, okay?"

I was thinking that I had been, *had*. But, maybe not! I gave her the one-fifty and buried my suspicions. I was also thinking, "Eunice will shit a brick when she sees a $200 notation for a limo-truck. But then again, maybe not?"

After dinner, after room service removed the roll-in table and empty wine bucket – we didn't order wine, but it came along as a package deal with fresh-cut flowers and candle light (I kept the tip at 15% as Eunice is a stickler when it comes to over-tipping, the tip came to $27.20 and wouldn't show up on my personal account any-way, but it would be itemized on the hotel receipt.). Sophie announced that she was going to call Langley and invited me to lis-ten in while we had drinks from the in-room bar. To which I had readily agreed.

I made the drinks while she set up the scrambler. When the inter-national overseas operator connected her with Langley, she put the receiver into a box, the scrambler, and we listened in on a small room-speaker equipped with a send/receive switch.

Sophie talked with a woman named, Dawn. Dawn's voice was very maternal. Dawn knew Sophie well enough to inquire about her sex life, too, which Sophie openly responded.

"Well Dawn, I had a taxi driver put his hand on my thigh this evening. Does that count?"

"Oh good gracious, Kidd. That would be good enough for me, especially at my age. Why, I'm beginning to breathe hard just think-ing about it, Sweetie."

"Well, I'm sorry to say, that was the extent of it – a hand on the thigh. The guy just didn't have the balls to go further. I guess he had a thigh fetish. What's a woman to do, Dawn?"

During this feminine tête-à-tête Sophie threw me a sly wink, or – perhaps, she had something in *her* eye? No, it was a wink. It was a deft wink. And she was smiling, too. Yeah, it was downright, "flirtatious."

Dawn chided back, "You crack me up, Kidd."

Their small talk trickled into a narration of our B-25 bomber ride and the mysterious pilot, Cool Hand Luke. As I listened, I came to the conclusion that we flew over in a 747, first class, with an in-flight movie and unlimited flutes of complimentary champagne. Yeah, I couldn't help but wonder where Sophie was when the Mozambique Channel came splashing up through the missing bomb-bay doors. I concluded that she was a die-hard stoic – or a sadist.

Sophie tired of their chitchat, "So, what's the latest on our sweetheart, Margolova?"

Dawn became more maternal, "Damndest thing, Kidd. She flew out of Turkey early this morning, filed a flight plan to Madrid, but never showed up. The bigwigs think she's on her way to visit you, Honey. Does this surprise you, Kidd?"

Sophie cleared her throat, she was thinking. Dawn broke the short silence, "You are expecting her, aren't you, Kidd?"

Sophie answered, "Oh, yes." Which was said with so much ice that it had given me an instant chill. Then she asked, "Any messages from the boss?"

"No, Honey. You're doing fine, you're still on your own."

After some girly good-byes, Soph began to stow her equipment. She was being methodical, working slowly. It was obvious that she was deep in thought, probably digesting her, Margolova news. I didn't break her reverie, as it was pleasant to me just watching her move. When she had finished she moved toward her bedroom, handing me her glass as she passed, saying, "Stiffen this up for me, Jim. I'm going to freshen up, be back in a sec." And she was gone.

We were drinking J&B softened with locally distilled water. Soph had already had two, and myself – three. Suddenly, I felt loose and knew that the earlier drinks had suddenly hit home. It had been a long day and I had truly felt like the proverbial weary traveler. I poured out two stiff nightcaps and moved to the sofa, setting our drinks on a mahogany coffee table. The sofa was soft and plush, and, I thought about how easy it would be to fall asleep, right where I sat. And I thought about the expense of renting suites, and, if Eunice knew that the suites were adjoining?

And then, I thought about Sophie's call to Dawn, "...the guy didn't have any balls, Dawn." And, "He must have had a thigh fetish, Dawn." "Does that count, Dawn?"

I sipped my drink and wondered what it would be like to make it with Sophie, and, just how much balls does a guy have to have to hit on a Senator's daughter? I was just about to answer myself when Sophie exited the bedroom.

And there she stood, poised – ready for bed. She had on a pale yellow teddy that was designed to – not hide, her matching bikini bottom. I held forth my glass in a toast, "Ahhh, to my favorite color, baby chick yellow."

The Deadly Kidd crossed the suite turning off lights as she went until we were consumed in a total darkness. No doubt, it was lights out in Antananarivo, the mile high capital of the Malagasy Republic and all civilized Madagascar. She moved deftly to the balcony curtains behind me and opened them filling the room with silvery, iridescent, southern hemispherical starlight. Then stood there, a sumptuously juxtaposed silhouette that enhanced the grand firmament of all heaven above, and – of all hell below.

• • •

Over the years, Eunice and I have had many discussions and in-depth conversations on the many and varied vagaries of intuitiveness. Eunice tends to evoke a hocus-pocus mystical shroud around the seemingly elusive facts of intuitive reasoning. She perceives these supposedly subconscious insights as being way beyond the norm of any mere cognizant ideal or reality applicable to man's material existence.

At times, I am inclined to agree with her, namely because she is the foremost paranormal expert in this field which is still in its Parapsychological infancy, and albeit the world. However, my own personal experiences tend to support my own novice arguments that everyone leaves a subconscious trail that exposes one's innermost wants and desires that have been socially repressed by ethical self-righteousness. We simply have no known conscious way of interpreting these subliminal and minute eccentricities. Yet, when one is deluged, bombarded, with enough of these clues, we tend to cry out, "Eureka!"

So, speaking of intuitiveness, be it normal or paranormal – I *knew* this, "On that early spring, star studded morning in the Hilton Hotel, a mile above sea level, with a J&B Scotch in my hand, no lights, and a genuine babe, star gazing the heavens in a pale yellow, brushed cotton teddy, baby-fat oozing from her snug fit bikini bottom... "Yeah! "I *intuitively* knew."

•   •   •

Sophie lit a cigarette with what sounded like a Zippo lighter. This was only the second time that I had seen her smoke, and I knew this, too, that the nicotine was probably knocking her silly, as one knows when one only smokes one cigarette a day. I had found this out while working in the oil fields. I'd go all day without a cigarette and then, "Kapow." – What a rush!

I lit a Camel testing for the rush, but it didn't appear. I guess I was living the sustained nicotine high and could no longer tell if I was getting buzzed or not. Yeah, I've argued my addiction, whether it was nicotine or a psychological type of addiction. For me, the truth lies somewhere in between. For Soph, well, she blasted for the high, at least that was *my* thinking.

I broke the silence, "Those are bad for your health, Kidd?"

"Yeah." She said. Adding, "So's the Scotch, isn't it great?"

She moved away from the window, slow and graceful, moved to the sofa and sat down next to me, close. She smelled sweet like a bouquet of fresh flowers, flowers that were dipped in vanilla and then dusted lightly with Johnson and Johnson's baby powder. A scent that said, "Hey! I'm very clean. Smell me. Touch me. I've done this just for you. Now enjoy me."

I reached out and touched her knee. It was soft and cool to my hand. I moved my fingers easily up her thigh and she felt even smoother, softer. I heard her breathe, a gentle and relaxed purr that acknowledged a reckless abandon of whys and wherefores of the sensations at hand, a green light to foster her deeper emotions and arouse further her pre-surrendered needs to frolic in a teasing and playful surge toward finer passions, namely erotic and soulful sexual experimentation and I moved a bit higher...

Sophie reached her drink and set it on the back of my roving hand, the game was on hold. I halted my caress. She spoke softly, sexually,

"Just *where is* that butterfly of yours, Jimbo?"

I raised my hand slightly for her to remove her drink. She did, and I moved my fingers up her thigh until they abutted her panty line, saying, "About here." Then began making a small circular movement with my index finger about the size of a quarter. In response to this playful advance came an involuntary muscle spasm followed by an almost inaudible, "Ummmm."

"Actually, Kidd, it's slightly higher." I said this with as much non-chalance as humanly possible in an effort to remain disarming, and yet remain informative. I paused briefly, then, with a magician's deftness slid my hand to the precise location of my own fluttery tattoo just under her soft bikini brief.

"Here." I whispered. Then delineated it's fifty-cent piece size with a gentle circular massage. I noted that she was breathing in short, shallow breaths not wanting to expose any hint of excitement, yet she was calmly vibrant and I could sense her growing desire, her need – to commingle. She was too silent, too passive.

She moved out from under my caressing hand, set down her drink and stood, facing me, she bent down to where the cut of her teddy exposed her breast right at my eye level, then took my face in her warm hands and looked directly into my soul, saying – softly, sweetly..."You know I'm going to see it, don't you?" And she did.

Chapter Eighteen

The twelve scientists, the expeditionary flesh, would arrive in one week. They would be coming in on a corporate jet on loan from a wealthy toy manufacturer, Kids First, Inc., Camden, NJ. It would go down as a noble gesture right into the heart of their ledger book. One major industrial tax write-off! Unknown to the petri dish dozen, was the who, that pulled the CIA thread that weaves its way around and through the fabric of our industrial complex that made their trip affordable from its very earliest clandestine inception.

Eunice May North, under the Intuit U. letterhead, had promised the tortoise probers, testers and measurers, transportation, a tent, three meals a day, a lab with electricity, and enough running water to keep their hands and faces free of bacteria. These contractual promises, according to Eunice, were my "written" job description. And, hey – what could be easier?

The next morning, the morning after the night before which was a pleasurable eve, was Monday. It was time to crack the whip and get things rolling. Yeah, I had a lot of things to take care of. Much more than met the casual observer's eye.

One of the first things on my list was tent inspection. Fourteen tents, on loan from the Peace Corps, were stacked neatly in the hotel lobby awaiting our use. When I located them, I was quite surprised by their weight. They weighed 203 pounds – each. I wrestled one onto a brass baggage cart and brought it to my suite.

Undaunted, I pulled out the directions and went to work. By ten o'clock, I decided to hire an assistant, specifically, a tent expert. I rang the concierge for help.

"No, not escort service. I need a Field Assistant. Someone who can help me set up a few tents, run errands, and cook."

The knowledgeable concierge said that he knew the right person to fill my needs and that he would send him around, "...within the hour." I couldn't help but smile. – Yeah, this was what being a Field Engineer was all about, "Getting the job done."

Not more than five minutes had passed when a knock sounded at the door. I looked through the peephole expecting housekeeping and was surprised by a familiar face, the face of a smiling, Abdul "Abby" Amin. I opened the door and greeted him, "Hi, how may I help you, Mister Amin?"

The big Ugandan stood there like a fat lump on a log. His smile vanished quickly making him look, startled. He said, "Oh, it's you, Boss."

On a humorous note, I teased, "What's wrong, Big Guy? Did I sign the wrong travel voucher?"

Abby laughed, "Ha haaa, Boss. No, you signed good, Boss." Then he just stood there, looking big.

"Well?" I prompted, "What? What do you want?"

"Ha, Boss. Uncle Bobby says you want hard workingman for your fields. He say you a rich bastard, Boss. He says you got plenty of hard work for Abdul. He says that you can pay through your nose, Boss. How can you do that, Boss?"

"Yeah? He said all that, did he?"

"Yes, Boss. Uncle Bobby the smartest man in all of Tanan."

"Well... Can you put up a tent?"

"Yes sir, Boss."

"Well... Okay. Come on in." I motioned for him to sit on the couch, which he did, taking up a full two-thirds of its area.

I asked, "How come you're not up flying with Luke Skywalker?"

"Ha-ha, Boss. That from *Star Wars.*"

I clarified myself, "Yeah, you're right. How come you're not working with Cool Hand Luke?"

"Oh. Him's dead, Boss."

"Dead?"

"Sure is, Boss."

"What happened, Abby?"

"Oh, Luke went drinking in Tanan last night. He went to Sal's, a very bad whorehouse. Police say it all a big mistake. Very big accident, Boss."

"Hold up a second, Abby. I'd like Miss Kidd to hear this, okay? She's just next door." I pointed to the adjoining room-door and started for it. Abby nodded that it was okay to get her.

I knocked loudly, and then yelled through the door, "Hey Soph, can you come in here for a minute? I really *need* you Kidd, hurry up."

She called out, "Okay, Mister Insatiable. I'll be there in a sec. Men..."

I didn't hear her last few words. I went over to Abdul and asked him how the concierge knew that he was out of work.

"Oh, him's my uncle, Uncle Bobby. Him knows everything." I said, "I see." But, I didn't.

Out of the blue, without my asking, Abdul began to elaborate, "When I hear about Cool Hand Luke, I run right over here and tell Uncle Bobby. Uncle Bobby wants to know everything that happen in Tanan, Boss." Then, as an afterthought, he added, "Bobby always need a good bellhop, Boss. That what I am now, bellhop."

Sophie entered, "naked." She saw Abdul, said, "Shit." And then, crumpled back through her open door and into the sanctity of her own suite. Her entire appearance couldn't have lasted more than a two count. One, two – shame on you. Now, if I had been alone, I would have been elated.

Abdul said, "Wow, she got nice teats, Boss."

I told Abdul that we had better keep quiet about Miss Kidd's unexpected nakedness, man to man. He agreed, smiling out his oath of silence.

Sophie knocked on the door and I let her in. She was wearing jeans and a red flannel shirt. Her blush matched her shirt as she asked for permission to enter. In an effort to put her at ease, I said, "You should have been her a minute ago, a streaker visited us, ran through here naked as a jay bird."

Abby, quick on the uptake, said, "She didn't look like you, Miss Kidd."

Sophie was had and she knew it. She handled herself with dignity and grace, picking up on my lead, she said, "Oh, darn. I miss out on all the fun." Then looked me in the eye and added, "Don't I?"

I called room service for a pot of coffee and doughnuts. Soph sat down across from Abdul and began to grill him on Luke's demise. She was good. She asked all the right questions, like "Who killed him? Who witnessed it? What were the circumstances? What was he doing in a whorehouse? When did it happen? Where did it happen? And her last question, the why question, remained unanswered. Abby didn't know *why?*"

Soph excused herself, saying, "I have to make a phone call. I'll be back in a minute." Then left.

In my heart, I felt that Luke's death was directly linked to our arrival, or the arrival of, Margolova. Openly to Abdul, I stated that death was a major pitfall of too much drinking. With his head lowered, he nodded out an agreement. Of course, I didn't know what happened and was just guessing. But, I knew that Sophie would find out everything. Of that, I was sure.

I finished interviewing Abdul and hired him on the spot as field consultant, cook, and personal assistant. He had happily agreed to a hundred dollars a day, plus room and board while in the field. He would be paid daily, and it was understood that the job was only temporary. Hey, he did state that he could put up a tent, cook, and that he knew Madagascar as well as he knew his own backyard, Uganda. What could go wrong?

I told Abby to meet us in the hotel lobby at eight a.m., and to be ready for a full day's work. He agreed, all grins, saying, "Luke only pay me fifty cents an hour, Boss. Uncle Bobby right! You a rich bastard, Boss."

I rationalized to him, "Well, Ab old sport, I'm being subsidized by my own rich uncle, Uncle Sam. We can afford to pay you a little bit better than Luke." Then I showed him to the door with a stern warning, "Eight a.m., sharp."

I watched him skip down the hall toward the stairwell, yelling out, "Uncle Bobby, Uncle Bobby, I got the job. Uncle Bobby." I closed the door wondering if I had done the right thing, that of including meals for Abby while out in the field. I crossed the room to Sophie's door and entered without knocking – hell, I was fully clothed.

Soph was stowing away her radio gear when I entered. She must have heard me enter, as she said, without looking around, "I've got good news and bad news, which do you want to hear first?"

"Ah, give me the bad news. Then cheer me up with some good stuff."

"Margolova is in Madagascar. She's staying at a villa on the west end of town. An old Turkish gunsmith owns the place. As far as we know, the Turk is a solid and respected citizen of Madagascar. He makes hefty political contributions to all the right candidates and always pays in gold rands, minted by the Republic of South Africa. In return for his financial support he's left alone to enjoy a life of isolation in his fortified villa."

Soph paused a moment, then added, "He practices some old Hindu cult religion that demands silence. It's rumored that he hasn't cut his hair or fingernails since he settled here, some twenty odd years ago." She paused again frozen in some deep recollection. "Oh, I mustn't forget, he keeps a staff of servants, and, they have to wait on him in the buff. Kinky, huh?" And then added yet more, "Oh. She arrived with two Iraqi toughs, the same two that accompanied her in Venice. We don't have anything on them, yet. But Washington is working on it."

I asked, "What about the pilot, Cool Hand Luke?"

"That's the good news. He was killed almost two hours before Margolova landed. A local hooker transmitted Luke the AIDS virus. When he got the diagnosis, apparently last night, he went looking for her. He found her, pulled out a razor blade and proceeded to carve the word AIDS across her chest. When the police arrived, he attacked them with the same bloody razor. The cops had to shoot him, in self-defense – 28 times."

"That's the good news?"

"Well, at least we know that it wasn't Margolova who killed the pilot."

Soph added, for her own benefit as well as mine, "She won't bother us until *after* we find the tortoise, Jim. Of that, I'm almost certain."

With split second spontaneity, I offered, "Yeah, that is good news. All we have to do now, is to not find the Malagasy Rex, and, we'll be home free."

Ignoring my sentiment, Sophie continued, "Once we find the tortoise she'll come in like a pack of gangbusters. But don't worry, Jim. I'm well prepared to handle anything she can throw at us."

"Us?"

"Yes. Us." Sophie was adamant.

I clarified my position, "I'm working under the impression that if, or when, we find one, it's you who will return it to Washington, Soph. At least, that's what Eunice led me to believe back at the Institute."

"No, no, no." She said, while shaking her head emphatically.

"When we find this turtle, *you* take the turtle back to the Institute. My job, is to see that you get it there."

"Yeah? Well, just how confident are you that I'll make it back, Miss Deadly?"

With a coy snickering smile, she says, "I'm betting your life on it, Mister Morgan."

Chapter Nineteen

The remainder of that Monday was spent with a phone glued to my ear. I ordered rental cars, contacted local suppliers for electrical equipment, groceries and toiletries, made arrangements with the local hospital for emergency medical treatment, and established a line of credit with the, "First Bank of Madagascar."

This was actually handled by the Institute before our arrival, but I wanted to know my financial operating parameters, up front, and voice to voice with at least "one" Assistant Manager. The expedition could, under my signature alone, spend up to $100,000.00, American, without notifying Eunice.

The local oil company, who had leased us Shell Camp, gave me a genuine runaround, transferring me from one department to another in an effort to find the camp's keys. After one whole hour, I was finally told this, "...ain't no keys to Shell Camp, it's abandoned. Ain't nothin' out there, 'cept shells. The last guy out there retired – six, seven years ago. Ain't nobody been out there since, least that I know of anyway." And, that was that.

Shell Camp was named for all the shells that litter the ground in and around the campsite, and I'm not talking about seashells, either. We're talking tortoise shells. Thousands and thousands of them! Big ones and little ones, literally, tons and tons of tortoise shard lay everywhere.

The map I had, which was supplied to me by Eunice, placed the camp some sixty miles west of Tanan, as the crow flies. It sits on a creek that was formed from mountain runoff water, and is aptly named, Travelle Creek. There is a road on my map that leads up to the camp, labeled in with pencil, Shell Camp Road. When I looked closer at the map I discovered that the road was also drawn in by hand, and I couldn't help but think, "Oh boy!"

Tortoises are protected by the Malagasy Republic, they are an endangered species and it is against the law to remove one from the island. However, Eunice had obtained permission for the expedition to remove one, and only one, Malagasy Rex, if found. Aside from that we were only approved for field study, period.

Sophie spent the afternoon studying recon photos, cleaning her snub-nosed .38, and a pair of fancy hunting rifles. She was very "antsy." One minute she'd turn on the TV and a minute later turn it off. A few times, at least eleven, she'd come around jutting out her chest in an open suggestion for me to take a break and play house, or something. The only thing I could do was to turn my back on her antics and continue working, after all, I did have work to do. After awhile, she gave it up and fell asleep on my couch. I enjoyed her presence, even in sleep. She was doing her thing and I was doing mine. We were very comfortable with each other, which made the day quite functional, and I knew, the oncoming evening promised to be just as cohesive.

By six o'clock I became confident that everything would work according to plan. I was in control and knew that nothing serious blocked our way. The expedition was *on*.

I took out some Hilton stationary and wrote Eunice my first "daily" report. As I contemplated what to say, I came to realize that it was already our third day out.

Dear Ms North,

All suppliers contacted. Cook/Field Consultant hired at $100 day, plus tent and board. Sophie is working a lot of overtime – no complaints. We will inspect camp tomorrow.

I signed it, J.P. Morgan, R.D., sealed it, and threw it in my briefcase. My business day was done.

I called room service and ordered steak dinners to be served in Sophie's suite, along with flowers and wine. If my "bodyguard" was going to work overtime, it was the least I could do, right?

I woke Soph, she was sleeping hard, she came awake slow, dazed and disoriented. She said, blabbered, "We ought to ...ah, dine in today, Jim. Ah, Margolova might be, will be watching us, maybe. If she hasn't started already, okay? Would you mind?"

"How about a T-bone steak, baked potato and a tossed salad?"

"You guys from the Institute really can read minds, can't you? Make mine medium rare. And, you forgot to say apple pie. I'm craving it, Jim. Oh gads, I hope I'm not pregnant!" Then smiles, "Just kidding."

I went back to the phone and ordered a whole pie. At the same time, I ordered a picnic lunch for six plus a cooler of lemonade to be ready by eight a.m., sharp.

Sophie went off to bathe, leaving her door open. It crossed my mind to join her, but opted for a quick shower in my own suite. My thinking was thus, "Why hurry a good thing, we'd have plenty of time to snuggle after dinner." Besides, I didn't want to come across as being over-sexed or "pushy." So, I stayed in my suite and watched the Malagasy news.

There was no mention of a police shootout with Luke, but coffee prices were down, oil prices were up, the president's son was returning home for the Easter break from Citadel, a military academy located on the Southeastern coast of the United States; and, NASA was installing a new, 28 foot, parabolic dish antenna atop some mountain north of the Tanan. There was no mention of an American tortoise expedition, and no mention of Margolova's arrival with two henchmen, nor was there any mention of Turkish villas swarming with naked slaves.

The weather lady, an animated teacher with a slight mustache, showed how the winds were going to cause clouds above the city due to an orographic wind flow up the western mountain sides. It would be hot and there was a slight chance of a sprinkle in the afternoon.

Dinner arrived while Sophie was blow-drying her hair. I excused the uniformed waiter and lit the dinner candles myself. Peeking at the steaks made my mouth water, and I yelled at Sophie, "If you're not in here in ten seconds, I'm going to eat your pie, Priss."

While we ate, I told Soph about my plans for the following day, namely, to survey Shell Camp. She said that she'd help in any way that she could, once the camp was secure. I genuinely and most readily accepted her most gracious offer.

Sophie then turned teacher and presented me with a handful of CIA rules that I was expected to follow "religiously." The one I remember most vividly was, "Don't wander off by yourself." Of which I had no intention of doing anyway. Hey, when a man has a bodyguard, *needs* a bodyguard, why in the hell would he go wandering off by himself? She had added, as my body protectorate, "The penalty for being stupid could well be death."

I said, seriously, "Don't use the word *death*. Okay Soph?"

"Oookay." She mused. But couldn't let it go, she added, "Then don't wander off under threat of castration. Is that better?"

"Look Kidd. Fifty lashes with a wet noodle is threat enough for me. I won't wander off. I promise."

"Kinky." She then says, "We should try that sometime."

"What? Castration or Flagellation?"

"Noodles, silly. Castration wouldn't do *me* any good. Would it?"

And then I regretfully asked, "I wonder what penalty Eunice would give me if she knew that I was relieving my tensions in your lap, Soph?"

She said, "Is that *all* you're doing – *relieving* your tensions?"

I stared into my pie as if it were a crystal ball, poked it with my fork, not wanting to answer her, not then. I simply couldn't bring myself to answer her. Everything that had happened between us had happened, too quickly. I didn't want a showdown, not then, not before I got to know her better, much better. I looked up at her ready to bare my confused soul – to explain my deepest self. Our eyes met, she began to speak with a frivolous smile on her slightly blushed, angelic face, "If my boss knew about last night I'd be back in my father's office begging constituents for campaign contributions... burrrr, gives me chills just thinking about it. I swear! I never want to lick another campaign envelope as long as I live, so help me."

I stood, saying, "I can certainly put those sumptuous lips of yours to a much better use than that of envelope licking, *that* I can guarantee." I blew out the candles casting the room into a shadowy darkness, a covert shroud for the illicit moves of an unfolding love scene, or at best, a covert attempt to hide our individual needs for a reckless sexual indulgence. Ah, such flagrant lust, so physical, so passionate.

Sophie challenged, softly, "Your bed or mine?"

"Yours first. It's closer. Mine later."

Chapter Twenty

Our rental cars, two huge Ford station wagons, were parked in front of the hotel, gassed and ready to roll, at eight a.m. as promised. Abdul was ready, too. He was asleep, but I could tell, he was ready. The desk clerk told me that he had been there all night, waiting. I woke him, showed him the tents, and then directed him to load them into the matching wagons. He smiled and yawned while shaking his head in a positive acknowledgement of what he was asked to do.

Soph and I threw down a pauper's breakfast while allowing the big Ugandan ample time to complete his task. Sophie made a staunch suggestion that I closely supervise my new employee. I told her, "He's my responsibility, Soph. I want to give him every chance to fail, and if he does, then I'll know exactly how much supervision he's going to need. That's right out of Supervision 301, a core requirement for an Engineering degree."

"Well, excuse me Professor Morgan, I was just trying to be helpful."

Yeah, she got snooty. I guess it's true; no one likes to get chastised, especially when they're trying to be helpful.

The tarmac highway, a deeply rutted back road that leads out of Tanan toward Shell Camp Road hadn't seen any repair work since WW-II. At one spot, only a few miles out of town, a ten-foot tree had grown smack dab in the middle it. I didn't give a shit about the wear and tear on the rental cars but I did slow things down for our own safety and comfort.

The penciled in road was easier to find then I had earlier imagined. A big red sign with a yellow arrow pointed it out to us. It was a good thing, too, because it wasn't much of a road, not at all. It was mostly loose gravel, fairly straight, but terribly dusty.

Three hours later – we arrived.

Sophie, who drove behind me, was the first one out of the car and made an impassioned strut directly to a half-mooned outhouse. Abby, more attuned to the natural wonders of the wilderness, began relieving himself on the gravel, which created a whole new creek, pictorially, "Ol' Steamy Yellow."

Shell Camp has four buildings – five, counting the privy. After being told that there was nothing there, and that no one had been out there for six years, I was quite surprised to find everything in such "workable" repair. The largest building, a kitchen and dining hall, is large enough to house the entire expedition to a sit down dinner. A propane tank fueled the stove, empty, but serviceable. Unfortunately, there weren't any freezers or cooking gear. The sink had a faucet, but nothing happened when I turned it on. Yeah, it was obvious, very soon I'd be wearing my plumber's hat, indeed.

The smallest building, aside from the toilet, was an eight by ten cement block generator room located right behind the kitchen's back door. I poked around the twin diesel power plant long enough to convince myself that they'd still run. They had been left in immaculate condition. The last operator had done his job well, he must have had a genuine love of the mechanical as everything was left in pristine, long term, storage condition.

The other two buildings were identical twins, from the outside. Both are the size of a small two-car garage. One is north of the dining hall and the other is south of it. The north one was a bunkhouse designed to sleep eight people. The beds were still there and made. Amazingly the camp had not been vandalized or molested in any way, at all. No locks, no fences and – no ransacking? Weird. There was a three-foot by three-foot shower in the bunkhouse and again there was no water when I tried the faucet. An old potbelly stove dominated the room. The place smelled dusty – it *was* dusty. The old but intact window panes were dirty, but... Right then and there, I commandeered it as my personal Site-Residence and Camp Engineering office. Being on the advance team had its rewards, eh?

The south building was used as a storage-utility wing and was cluttered to the ceiling with oilrig junk. Much of it was items that I wish I'd have had while up on the Brooks Range. Yeah, one man's garbage is always someone else's treasure. The storage bin would be easy to convert into a field laboratory. Everything was coming up aces. I returned to the bunkhouse feeling a bit giddy, our good fortune was simply unbelievable.

I had just started to trace the water lines when Soph entered. She was carrying a rifle slung over her shoulder with a large scope affixed to the top of its barrel. She looked authoritative, like a top-notch guide about to lead off a hunting safari. In this real bossy voice, she says, "I'm going out to insure that the site is secure. Don't wander off." I thought she was being a bit dramatic. Considering where we were and all, but she was security – love her dearly.

Abdul had followed Sophie in and was sitting on a bunk waiting for direction. I told him to take one of the beds and set it up for himself in the kitchen. As site cook, he could sleep there, at least, until someone complained.

"When you finish that, make a list of supplies, we'll need to feed fifteen people for thirty days. You're now in charge of the kitchen, Pal. You're our Chef."

Abby was all smiles, "I make good beans, Boss. But I can't write."

"Wow." I said. "What a bummer, Pal. Tell you what, you get the bunk moved then I'll put you to work setting up tents. How does that sound, Ab?"

He grinned openly with abject approval. I turned and left to find Sophie. But, I didn't get very far. I had to look back to where my employee was making a horrendous racket. Abdul had hefted the entire bed and was forcing it through the door without having disassembled it. I stood there for two whole minutes watching him. It was most amazing. Yeah, I thought that I had hired a strong back, but, in essence, I had hired myself a comedian."

I found Sophie west of the camp standing up on a huge boulder some 200 yards away. She was motioning for me to join her, which I did. As I neared, I could see that she had her rifle out and was sighting in on something, something that she wanted me to see. I hurried, but running in the soft shell and earth was tedious. The field was large and I wondered if it was ever used as an airstrip or a helicopter pad. About fifty feet from Soph's granite boulder I began to see a few shells, some of them as big as football helmets. The ground turned to all shell bits and I was making a noisy crunching sound on them as I came up to the base of her rock, "What's up, Kidd? Besides you?"

"I can see the Mozambique Channel. Come on up."

With some difficulty, I managed to climb the massive stone; it wasn't easy as the sides were very smooth. When I reached her, she handed me the rifle with a pathetic warning, "It's loaded, Jim. Be careful."

I put the scope to my eye and scanned the vast, rugged landscape. It was awesome. It had a beautiful strangeness about it. A foreboding beauty, that says, "You can't know me, not ever."

The coast is 150 miles away. I was unable to discern the channel, with any certainty. I locked in on a pair of long legged egrets gliding gentle above the forest's sprawling canopy. I followed them for the longest time moving the cross hairs from one to the other wondering what it would feel like to pull in on the trigger and drop one. In my mind's eye, I did. The egret's feathers exploded as my bullet slapped into its sleek white back sending it into a rolling, downward death plunge into the tree tops, and then, I watched it smack through branches, cart wheeling end over end until it slapped the forest floor, lifting a shattered wing in a brief, from the grave, salute to his unseen assassin. Its mate, oblivious to my shot soared on. The wind racing over her own forward flight blocked her lover's plea, "...to wait. No more.

And I felt small for having advanced my thoughts to its mate. Where I only felt remorse for the widow and that, only as a vague afterthought to my own insensitivity with such a glorious natural wonder.

I lowered the rifle and panned the scenery with my naked eye. The egrets were both swallowed up by the whole, as if they had never existed. And for an instant, I felt the whole. I felt that it wanted to consume me, too – just as it had the egrets.

Who knew? Who cared, where I was at that particular moment in time and space – just who?

Sophie put her hand on my hip, "It's beautiful, isn't it?"

"Yeah, it's overwhelming." And to the monster, the pure immensity that stood before me, I mentally said, "I'll contemplate you later – when I find time."

Sophie was talking, "...this place should be crawling all over with tourists, Jim."

"Yeah." I said. "There are tortoises everywhere."

"Tourists, Jim. *Tourists.*"

"Oh, sorry. I'm a bit overwhelmed, Soph. I think it's the altitude. I've never liked heights."

"Here, give me that Browning before you hurt yourself."

Her rifle was light, much lighter than any weapon I had ever handled. It was a fancy piece, designed for a woman. As I handed it to her, I asked, "I'll bet you'd like to see Margolova in that sight, eh Kidd?"

With her back to me she answered, "Yes. I would." Then she leapt to the ground, a good twelve-feet below, landing firm on both feet and began a forced march back toward the camp proper, without so much as once looking back. No doubt, she had her nemesis, Margolova, mentally sighted, ugly, in her precision Lancia Marksman scope, arguably, the best scope manufactured anywhere in the whole free world.

I watched her all the way to the kitchen, and then duplicated her leap from the rock. When I hit ground, I rolled forward into the shell fragments, dirt, and gravel. It was a stupid feat of nonsense and I paid the piper for my grand show of ignorance. I felt like my legs were broken and my hands were both bleeding. I ripped my pant knee and I could feel blood oozing down my right leg. Yeah, I felt the fool. As I hobbled in, limping like a three legged dog; I felt a most horrid pain – that excruciating pain of total embarrassment.

The first thing that I noticed when I entered the kitchen was the open picnic basket. The next was Abby's bed. He did manage to get a bed into the kitchen, but it was only so much trash heaped up against the wall. Sophie and Abdul were sitting in the dining room making up a grocery list. As I passed them, I said, "Put down a First Aid kit, Soph." She nodded, never looking up from her tablet. Abby was engrossed with four sandwiches and the whole jug of lemonade. No one noticed my bloody entrance. I said, "I'll be out back. By the creek." Again, no one noticed my bloody departure.

I followed the half-buried copper pipe right into Travelle Creek where it disappeared under the clear, rapidly flowing water. The water system was beautifully simple, self-priming, and fully gravitational. I reached into the cold water, cleared the pipe end and happily watched a whirlpool form on the creek's surface. Very soon, the site would have water.

Sophie burst out the kitchen door, screaming, "We've got water, Jim. What should I do?"

I yelled back, "Let it run. It'll clean out the system." She waved that she understood and went back in.

I sat down on the grassy bank and began cleaning my wounds. I was still bleeding in a few spots but concluded that I wouldn't need stitches. Yeah, getting that water to run was a tremendous ego boost. Now, if the generators fired... But that was getting ahead of things, like fuel and oil. Yet, my vigor was renewed. I strode back toward camp to attack my own nemesis, the tents.

I handed Sophie the tent manual and told Abby to follow her directions, "I'm going out back to fire up the generators. If you need me I'll be in the generator room."

Sophie's jaw was stunned open and about ready to hit the floor as I turned and slipped out the back door. I did hear her say in a childish, snooty parody, "Aye, aye, Captain Big Shot."

Technically, Soph could have told me to, "Screw off." But she didn't, and as soon as I cleared the door, I let out a sincere, "Thank you, God." And slipped silently into the mechanical world of grease and, soon to be heard, thundering horsepower.

The grand old ladies were drained of their oil, their fuel lines were disconnected; and, their batteries – well, they were nowhere to be found. After a quick put-together, it only took me twenty-minutes, I knew that the twin madams would fire as soon as some JP-4 fuel hit their copper veins. Yeah, they'd sing all right, a lot louder then those fat Old Italian opera singers, and I'd take side bets on it, too.

My work in the generator room was finished until I could get fuel. I smeared a bit of grease on my hands and made sure to brush some against my cheek, then went to join my tent-erecting crew.

One tent was up, which *genuinely* impressed me. Sophie looked disgusted, and Abby, I found out later, "Don't like working for, or with, women." It was unnatural and contrary to his concept of Ugandan masculinity."

Yeah, like I said earlier, Sophie could have done her own thing, stood guard, slept in the car, picked wild flowers, or just stood around looking cute, but she didn't. I told them to keep up the good work and that I'd be back to help them, as soon as they heard the generators start. Armed with a cup of lemonade and two chicken sandwiches, I returned to a nice cool, quiet corner of the generator shack.

I contemplated Sophie's energetic nature while I blasted half a pack of cigarettes. After a short while, a heavy guilt set upon me. Philosophers can sit around their ivory towers and contemplate the universe, but Engineers have to earn their keep. Reluctantly, I moseyed into the storage building for a look-see, as to what it would take, effort-wise, to clean up the clutter and get rid of the aged cobwebs. As I entered, a broom fell away from the wall and literally hit me in the ass. The omen startled me, I was doomed to work and, I couldn't help but wonder, which Malagasy God had

I unknowingly offended?

I spent the whole afternoon cleaning out the lab, diligently, enjoying my physical marriage to the mystery broom. Under some dusty boards I found a case of 10-w-30, BP motor oil, which I quickly fed to my two powerhouse beauties. Aside from that, everything else was just trash and I stacked it all up behind the building, neatly, out of eyesight. I had finished my chores simultaneously with Sophie's completion of Tent City, Shell Camp's newest suburb. I was sore and tired, as was my crew. The sun was setting into the African distance. It lit the sky in a reddish-orange hue. Soft pinkish tints bathed the camp with a warm rinse of pastel shadows, a mellow close to a very constructive day. We stood by the station wagons content with our individual efforts and knew that the hard part of setting up camp was over. From that moment on, it would all be fun and games. Well, almost.

The three-hour drive back was exhausting. Abby rode with me and slept all the way. Soph drove alone, saying, "It's correct CIA procedure..." But the real reason was Abdul. Sophie was at her wit's end with his laments for food. The big guy was hungry and was letting her know it in no uncertain terms. He had even complained that she ate too many sandwiches, for a girl. Personally, I thought it was all playful teasing. Soph, on the other hand, was demanding his dismissal.

We dined at a small diner on the outskirts of town. I thought the food was terrible, but my crew ate heartily, oblivious to the fly and bug infested environment. Ab, on his third piece of pie, chortled out, "This is the best place to eat in all of Tanan, Boss." If I'm not mistaken, the diner was named, "La Trough," or "La Peig Sty." However, they did serve a delicious cup of local coffee with a bean in the cup.

Back at the hotel, I paid Abdul his 100 dollars and advised him to be ready for work by sunrise the next morning. He said that he would be there, and then, he was gone. Sophie announced that she was going to soak in her tub until midnight. Then added, "I'm going to call Langley first. You're welcome to listen in, Jim?"

Desiring a hot bath myself, I begged off, saying, "I've got to make a report myself, Kidd. Then I've got to make a list of hardware for the lab." But added, "Give me an hour. We'll have a drink or two and you can fill me in, okay?"

"Sounds good." She sounded spunky, sexual, and added, "My door is always open to you, Mister Morgan."

"One hour, tops." I promised, acknowledging her superbly orchestrated innuendo.

I kept my daily report as short as possible:

Re: Ms North,
Tents up. Water running. Please send Sophie's boss a letter of appreciation for her un-tiring erection efforts.
J.P. Morgan, R.D.

Upon rereading my report I noticed that I had omitted the word "tent" before the word "erection." Eunice would probably get a kick out of the blooper, so I let it alone. I sealed the report and threw it on top of the first one.

I then made a thorough read of Soph's shopping list and added a few things that she had omitted: 200 gallons of fuel oil, a radio and a television, flashlights, batteries, extension cords, blankets, and a case of Scotch whiskey. And below that, I wrote, "Portable-Potties," in red.

With this done, I hit the shower. "Thank you, Mr. Hilton. Thank you for the unlimited hot water and plush, plush towels."

It was nearing midnight when I tapped lightly on Deadly's inner sanctum. She must have been dozing, as she sounded startled, "Jim? It's open..."

I really did want to know the latest news out of Langley and let myself in. Soph lay sprawled on the sofa wearing her white fluffy Hilton bathrobe. It became her, added to her cuteness, her sexuality.

She yawned openly, saying, "How about a rain-check on those drinks, Jimbo?"

"Oh, sure, Kidd. You look beat. How about a back rub, while you fill me in on your call to Washington?"

Suddenly, she was excited, "Oh, Jim. Would you? You're such a darling." She stood and moved gracefully toward her bedroom disrobing as she walked. I followed her. I heard her jump on the bed. She was ready. I groped for her in the darkness. I found her – then straddled her soft baby flesh, positioning myself to be as comfortable as possible as I played the role of masseur. She was relaxed, totally relaxed, as I placed my hands against her sumptuous body and began a slow methodical manipulation of her cool, pliant flesh.

She went into an *ooh* and *ahhh* narration of her communiqué with Langley and didn't stop relating until she had completely finished. Actually, she may have deliberately dragged things out in an effort to extend her massage.

"Nothing new on ...*ahhh*, Margolova. Abdul is – *ohhh*, clear to work for you. We're getting a – *oooh Jim*, special box to return the tortoise in. It'll arrive – *ahhhaaa*, by an Embassy Courier in the – *oooh*, morning. It's – *ohhhyeaah*, called a "D.L.I.D.S." – *ahhh*, box."

I stopped massaging, resting my hand on her taut buttocks and asked, "What in the hell is a D.L.I.D.S. box?"

"Continue my back rub – a little lower, and I'll tell you all about them, Mister Hands."

"Okay, I've been bribed before. You talk, I'll rub."

"Ahhh, myyy, goood-ness. D.L.I.D.S box is – ohhh Jimmy, a dioptic light intercepting diode, sensitive – ohhh soooo sensitive, security box. Ohhhh, wow, Jim, don't stop, ever. The box is built like a safe. It can only be opened when it reads "your" irises. Ummm! Jimmmm. Mmmmmm. If – ummmm, anyone tries to open it besides you. – Oh boy, Jim. Ummm. A toxic acid will release and destroy the content of the box."

Stopping my caresses, I questioned, "So, if I'm captured or something, I'll be tortured until I open the box, right?"

Sophie rolled over, "No, we don't think that will happen. The Russian's, including Margolova, know all about the D-lid boxes. We leaked them the secret years ago just to be sure they wouldn't mess with them. They're foolproof, Jim. Even you couldn't open it unless you were totally relaxed and wanted it opened."

"What if they kill me? I'd certainly be relaxed then, wouldn't I?"

"It doesn't quite work like that, Mister Morgan. However, if you were to get killed the CIA has a videotape of your irises, that's how they set the lock in the first place. The tape was made during your eye exam at Andrew's Air Force Base. We could still open the box with your video tape."

I placed my hand on her tummy and began to make small circular movements while contemplating the D-lids box. I asked, "What's to keep her from killing me, then destroying the box? That way, no one would get the tortoise. Right?"

"Ohhhh, Jim!

My circular movements had moved somewhat lower, I prompted, "Right?"

"Ohhhh my gooood-ness, if she wants it, she'll wait until she can steal it, later, from the, oh sweet jeeeezes, the institute."

Sophie stiffened in a moment of personal satisfaction. Then, a split second later, oblivious to our business discussion, she entered into a highly angelic, feminine snore. Our meeting was over. I softly covered her with a sheet and quietly returned to my own bed.

I lay awake contemplating D.L.I.D.S. boxes, iris sensors, and the softness of Sophie's flesh. I concluded that there might be a ramification, or two, associated with the carrying of a D-lids box. I pondered the technology behind iris reading. And then, I thought about Sophie, how she let me fondle her so unabashedly, something that Eunice would never let happen. Because, she'd have to surrender all control for a moment and that simply wasn't her way. And, when I switched off the lights, noticing that it was almost three am, I pondered myself right to sleep, wondering, just when *does* the Malagasy sun rise?

Chapter Twenty-One

Sophie woke me at 6:15 to announce that coffee was on its way. She had already dressed and was antsy to work, right then. So I sent her off to get a five-ton truck, "...and take Abdul with you. I'll meet you downstairs in an hour." Then buried my head under the covers to await the coffee.

By noon our shopping spree was finished. It was not an easy task considering the bulk of foodstuff we had purchased, which included pots, pans, silverware, mixers, and light-fixtures for every tent. This was a fun morning, according to Sophie. And it was a real back-breaker for Abdul – who had to load all those things into the truck all by himself. And he did an excellent job, too. Loading a truck was not much different than him loading Luke's aircraft. The best I could do for freezers and refrigerators was to rent some antique restaurant fixtures at exuberant prices. The charge for their delivery was down-right, ludicrous. I think our Uncle Bobby called everyone in Tanan and told them to jack up their fees for the rich American, who, "...pays through his nose." We did manage a timely delivery date – for that very afternoon.

Our luck paled when we ordered the fuel oil. Normally, a few greenbacks can get the attention of a service-orientated business, normally. However, the best I could do with our fuel dealer was a fol-lowing day delivery. And that was *only* because I knew, Uncle Bobby. Bobby's cousin did lend me, free of charge, four five-gallon gas cans. Yeah, it was enough to get us started, and it did last us until his tank truck made it out on Thursday.

It was pushing five o'clock when we pulled into camp, the "Bilk-Um-Dry," Appliance Co. was already there awaiting our arrival with a five man crew, an exemplary example of human dexterity and show of mass-attack efficiency. They unloaded their wares in a lightning four-minute barrage, synchronized blur of human beings, and then they left. It was a no nonsense slam-bam thank-you-man event, "Any problems? Call da boss."

Soph and Abdul unloaded our own wares while I went and fired up the power sisters. They ran like a pair of bitches in heat, sang like a pair of soprano hairdressers off the back streets of Seville, and I knew as soon as I heard them fire up that life at Shell Camp would indeed be a glowing success, at least, in the electrical output department.

I strung the cable for tent lighting and insured that everything cleared my ohmmeter, the way a good Engineer should. Everything was done that could be done, by sunset. Yeah, Shell Camp was now alive.

I placed Abby in charge of the camp. He would spend the night being our night watchman. Actually, I needed him to be there for the fuel delivery next morning. It would also give him time to make up his bed, and to organize himself into his "Chef" duties. Abby was excited over, "being in charge." It was the first time that he had ever been in charge, of anything. Or so he said, "...except, when I was a boy, I was in charge of our dog Mammou. She runs away all the time. My mamma would beat Mammou, and me too. Mamma said we were both nuts, Boss."

As we gathered up our things to leave, Abby took out a five-pound canned ham and was preparing to make sandwiches. He told us that he was going to practice cooking. Yeah, it was a scary notion, leaving him with all that food, but what harm could he really do? As we walked out the door he yelled out a smiling good-bye, Boss. He was so intent with his cooking that he never looked up.

Sophie suggested that we leave him a gun. To which, I had to protest openly, "No way, Soph. He'd eat it!"

We left the station wagon and drove back in the van. We'd exchange it for another wagon in the morning. Soph slept the entire way back. Which, considering the bumpy roads, was quite a feat.

Back at the Hilton, Sophie begged off dinner. She said she was, "Done in." Actually, I felt the same and hit the showers, it was a quick rinse and lights out.

Over breakfast, in Sophie's room, we decided to move ourselves into Shell Camp. We packed, checked out, and headed for the U.S. Embassy to pick up the DLIDS box. Hopefully, we wouldn't need to return until Sunday when the scientists would arrive. We traded in the truck for another wagon and were at the consulate's office by ten. While Soph went in, I strolled around the beautiful grounds. The American Embassy is a very modern looking facility, it probably cost us, us tax payers, an arm and two-legs to hoist our flag above the rugged Malagasy soil, but it sure did give me a sense of pride, and a sense of welcome, knowing that the old red white and blue was waving briskly in the wind above my head. Yeah, it spoke to me, it said, "It's okay that you're here, this country accepts your presence."

Soph slept against the DLIDS box all the way to camp, the wagon was that full – top to bottom. We arrived shortly after one, just in time for lunch, ham sandwiches. Chef Abdul had created 25 pounds of ham sandwiches. He then packed them all into the refrigerator so solidly that we had to pry them loose with a spoon. Our proud Chef announced, "I was going to make more but the box is full up, see. No more room, Boss."

The fuel truck had come and gone. Abby said that he fed the driver a few sandwiches, the ones that wouldn't fit in the icebox. He added, "I put my X on his papers. Was that okay, Boss?"

"Yeah, Ab. That was good. You did right, Pal."

I looked at Soph, "Anyone ready for a sandwich?"

"Sounds great, make mine ham." And to Ab she asked, "You going to eat with us, Chef?"

Ab said, "I don't want one right now. I'm full." Grabbing his belly, then looking at it, says, with a note of reluctance, "Well, maybe just a few."

After lunch, we organized the bunkhouse. I walled the room off into three sections, using old Malagasy army blankets hung by electrical cord. Soph took the south end to include the old Franklin stove. I had the north end and the shower stall, a 3x3 tin closet hung with a plastic tablecloth that acted as a shower curtain. We had a ten-gallon water heater, but no drain. The water ran outside via a chiseled notch in the cement floor. The middle section was designated, Camp Office. A card table served as the office desk and my briefcase served as the in/out basket.

I wondered how long it would take for the scientists to complain about us having the heated building and shower, while they rolled around in their sleeping bags.

Sophie began setting up her equipment as fast as Abby could carry it in. There was a lot of it, too. I was already thinking about changing my handmade sign from Camp Office, to CIA Headquarters. She set up a portable dish antenna and locked it in on a geo-stationary satellite located north of the island. Instantly, we had a "universal" communication system. According to Sophie, "... we could call the

North Pole on this if there was a phone there, absolutely free. Want to call your mom and dad?"

"No. But I've got the number of a good bookie in Chicago."

Soph looked at me quizzically or momentarily dumbfounded, "Why would you want to call a bookie, Jim?" To that, I refused her an answer.

Ah, it was going to be great, three whole days of backwoods bliss. There wasn't much to do until the scientificoes made their entrance on Sunday. Yeah, sit back and relax. Keep Abby out of mischief, eat a few thousand ham sandwiches, watch some Malagasy sub-titled TV, sip a little Scotch, enjoy the deadly charms of Miss Deadly, and – "order a Porta-Potty." Damn, I had almost forgotten, I reached into my briefcase and made a big note in red ink, "Porta-Potty, ASAP." I took it and nailed it to the inside of the bunkhouse door. My work for that day was officially done, spelled, D.O.N.E.

Chapter Twenty-Two

That night, after a ham sandwich supper, Sophie made her report to Washington via satellite. Dawn, the CIA matriarch, was at the helm. As they prattled, hopefully through her scrambler, the pseudo-mother/daughter team giggled skillfully around a touchy subject, namely *my* sex life. Now I know why "talking around" is a breach of security when it involves classified material. Any halfway bright hacker would quickly discern that an Engineer while confined to a work camp by a flippant mother named Dawn was laying some Kidd.

I had blushed twice before Sophie asked, "What's the latest on Margo-bitcho, Dawn?"

Dawn remained lighthearted but did interject a more serious tone into their conversation. "Oh Honey, the bigwigs here, the ivory tower think-tankers, are trying to convince the director that she's down there to commit a political assassination, her target... is the president's son. The kid is a definite heir to the Malagasy Republic, Honey. He's home now, spring break for two weeks, starting today. He's been attending Citadel, a military college in South Carolina; I think it's in Charleston. The kid is pro-capitalist and is an outspoken critic of Communism, especially the old school Lenin stuff. He's exactly the type of target that would make Margolova's mouth water. It's the same target she hit in France a few years back. Remember?"

"Yes. The Political Science students." Sophie's voice became somber, her face paled as Dawn continued. Hands down, the covert narration I was listening to was dark and sinister. I think my own face paled.

"There's a note here, it says that you two have met during an assignment two years ago. Remember that, Kidd?"

"Yes. He was seventeen. Too young for me, Dawn, a nice looking kid, a heartthrob off campus. Citadel is an all male school. I had a lot of fun there. That was my first real field-assignment."

Dawn interjected, "If they're in college, Soph. They're old enough. Eh, Kidd?"

Dawn continued when Soph didn't answer, "Ah... Me. So Kidd, it looks like you're off the hook this trip, at least as far as the think-tankers think. Looks like you're on a paid vacation, Honey."

"Any word from the boss, Dawn?"

"No. He was down a little while ago, listened to your last tape. He got a kick about your knee-fetish friend, your limo-truck driver. First time I've seen him laugh in six weeks. Last thing in your log is date, time, and his John Hancock, Honey. You're still on your own, Kidd."

While Soph stowed the radio, I asked, "Doesn't anyone complain about the way you girls carry on. I mean, all the sex talk...?"

"Well, when things get serious we *do* drop the small talk. We are professionals. You know? But, then again, we are also human. The boss spent twenty years in the field – he's very understanding. Actually, it's encouraged to be open and candid when we report in. If a field agent gets too stressed out, starts to loose it, go wacky, the command post is trained to pick up on it. The agent will get some R and R, or worse, given a desk job. It's a known program."

"Sounds like something Eunice would come up with."

"Oh, I thought you knew. Eunice *did* write the program. As a matter of fact, she trains the entire communications department, on site, at Langley."

"No. I didn't know that. And there you go divulging state secrets again."

"Oh, sorry. Well, you've got a clearance, you've got a need to know, just don't repeat anything I say and you'll be fine."

"Yeah, right."

And I began to wonder if I was indeed a part of a Eunice North research project? Eunice wasn't above such treachery; she was probably listening to Sophie's taped record of our sexual exploits right now. And I thought yet more, and concluded, "Damn."

Sophie elaborated, "Yes. She's been working with our radio people for over a year now. At first everyone thought it was all a big joke. Then, nice things happened, and everyone jumped on the bandwagon, including me. Eunice's efforts are making life a whole lot better for the stressed out or overworked agent."

"Well, I'll be darn. Eunice never once mentioned any of this to me."

"Well Jim, our programs are classified, she doesn't have a legal right to discuss them with just anybody. At least..."

She trailed off her comment and went into a deep thought, probably back to our original discussion. "Ah, well, I just don't think she should have told you."

"She didn't."

I changed the subject, "Hey, I'm going out to those rocks and blast a few cigarettes. Want to join me?"

"Sure. Let me get my gun and a jacket. Let Abby know where we'll be. I'll meet you behind the kitchen in a sec."

Grabbing my own jacket I headed for the kitchen. Abby was at the stove. He was practicing the art of omelet preparation. The kitchen was a mess – as was the Chef. I looked into his pot and was forced to inquire, "What in the hell is this?"

"Omelets, Boss."

"Oh. I thought it was egg soup." I suggested, "Try a little less milk, Sport. It'll thicken things up a whole lot faster."

"Ha-ha, Boss. We don't have any milk. Miss Soph said it would spoil out here. This just water and flour, Boss."

I made a mental note to have the Big Guy dig a deep, deep garbage pit first thing in the morning. Shell Camp was going to need one, soon. I let Abby know where we'd be and headed for the door with a genuine queasiness rising in my stomach.

Ducking into the generator room, I did a quick check on the pulse of the online power plant. She was running at a smooth 60 cycles/second insuring a clean voltage output. Her oil level remained constant, and as clean, as when I filled it the previous day. I left her with a confident air that she'd run all week without as much as skipping a heartbeat. Ah, she was doing me proud, and I knew her beautiful backup sister was equally capable.

Soph beat me out to the granite outcropping. She was wearing her RELAX jacket and a ball cap. She was sitting cross-legged on a blanket and had brought along a bottle of J&B Scotch, two glasses filled with ice and a bag of salted peanuts – what a woman!

"Isn't this beautiful, Jim?"

"Yes, it is." And that was a gross understatement. The sky was literally dancing with starlight. A shooting star broke madly across the twinkling firmament adding yet a further stroke of majestic paint to the already regal masterpiece of a silver studded semi-gloss blackness.

Soph cried out emotionally, the way one discovers a kitten in a pet shop window, "Oh, Jim. This – its just, *unbelievable.*"

I took a stab at some wry humor, "Did you bring your umbrella, Soph?"

"Umbrella? Why? There's not a cloud in the sky, Jim Morgan."

The southern hemisphere was experiencing a meteor shower. My reference was to the numerous shooting stars that we had witnessed. Obviously, Sophie was not in tune to my wit.

She moved her face within an inch of my own and asked, "Why would we need an umbrella on a night like this?"

I answered, "Oh, I thought we could do a few Mary Poppin-leaps off these rocks...you know, be kinky, or something."

"Here." She said, handing me a drink. "I think you need this." Oh well, so much for *my* humor.

Then she asked, "By the way, did you bring your screwdriver, Mister Engineer?"

"Screwdriver? What do we need a screwdriver for, Soph?"

She put the back of her hand against her forehead in a mock appeal of shock, "Oh my goodness. You didn't bring your screwdriver, and here I was, beginning to believe that you only asked me out here to screw around."

Sophie enjoyed her joke. I had been had. I deserved the soft retort after the umbrella bit. I said, "Okay, I've been had, but it is nice to know that my woman has a sense of humor."

"And that's not all I have. I've also got the hots for you, James Morgan."

She put her hand inside of my shirt and began to rub my chest.

I whispered to her, "For someone professing to be hot I find your hands awfully cold, Deadly."

"Deadly? Here's deadly." She grabbed a handful of my chest hair and pulled viciously.

It was a totally insensitive onslaught. The harder I tried to escape the harder she would pull. Finally, I did wrench myself free. Soph held up her hand. "Oh, look. You're losing your hair, Jim." She was laughing hysterically.

I grabbed her by her shoulders, knocking over our drinks and the bottle of J&B. "Do you know what a man does to a woman who pulls out his chest hair, Miss Deadly?"

"No. What is it that he *thinks* will happen?" She was laughing uncontrollably.

Aggressively, I said, "The girl winds up with a big fat hickey sucked into her prissy little neck." And I tried desperately to pin her down and carry out my childish but heated threat.

Then her voice changed, it became serious, authoritative, "Wait Jim, stop! Look. There's a car coming. Damn it. Get up."

I looked and sure enough a car *was* coming. It was still a mile, maybe two, down the road, but it was the only road into Shell Camp and it dead-ended right smack-dab in front of the bunkhouse door. And, we weren't expecting company.

Sophie stood. The vehicle's lights went dead. I said, "Oh shit." And before I had finished, Soph had already leapt off the boulder and was in a full-out sprint towards the kitchen. I eased myself to the ground and followed her at a moderate jog. By the time I had covered twenty yards Soph had entered the kitchen and I watched the camp lights extinguish one by one as I pounded ever closer to the back door, thinking, "I'm never going to light another cigarette as long as I'm in the spy business."

Upon entering the kitchen, lit only by the propane flame under Ab's bubbling omelets, Abdul advised, "Miss Soph said for you to stay here, Boss. What's going on, Boss?"

Huffing, trying to catch my breath, I started to tell Abdul what I knew, but before I could catch my wind, Soph burst through the front screen diverting my attention. She was carrying the rifle with the scope in her left hand and had changed her top for a black sweater. In her right hand she held a .357 Magnum which she held out to me grip first. "Here, Jim."

Our eyes met and locked onto each other for the briefest part of a second. It was a chilling instant, her eyes were those of the already dead, cold, and distant – not giving any hint or clue as to the machinations building or already built behind their deep blue, dilated, frigid depths. She broke the contact. She knew... She said, in no uncertain terms, "It's loaded. Be careful." She never questioned the fact that I would indeed accept it, it was just, "Here, Jim. It's loaded. Be Careful." And, there was absolutely no "emphasis" on the phrase, "Be careful." It was a computerized voice command; it was oatmeal time at the orphanage – again.

The weapon was heavy in my hand. I glanced down at the oiled piece; it was identical to the one I had fired up on the North Slope while in Alaska. In the blue glimmer of the stove burner I read an epitaph to my recent thoughts, it was etched into the .357 with artistic scrolls and loops, but in a highly legible script, "Be careful. Love Dad." My heart was still racing from my run to camp. Things were happening quick, too quickly.

Soph called out from the front door, "Stay put, guys. I'm going out to see what our visitor wants." She turned to leave, then paused in an afterthought, adding, "And please, Jim, don't shoot me by accident on my way back in – I'd still like to get laid tonight." And then she was gone.

Ab said, "I'm scared, Boss."

"Well, it's probably nothing, Ab – just a car coming down the road. Sophie will check it out just to be safe." I didn't tell him that the driver had suspiciously shut off the headlights, or that Soph was a CIA agent, or that I was scared, too. After all, what good would that do? And no, I didn't tell the big guy about our international spy and political assassin, Margolova.

However, I did ask, "Can you handle a gun, Ab?"

"Sure, Boss. Luke taught me to shoot his Uzi lots of times."

"An Uzi? What were you guys doing with an Uzi?"

"Luke says we need to be prepared, Boss. He said that we were good Boy Scouts, Boss."

"Okay. Come on. I'm going to get you a gun."

We went out the back door and slipped into the bunkhouse. I found the Colt .45 that Soph kept in a box under her bed. She said it was a big piece of junk, "...always jambs on the fourth round." I handed it to Abby and was about to show him how the safety worked when he cleared the magazine, tested the spring, jammed the clip back in, pulled back the slide and had it ready to fire before I got my finger pointed. Abby knew *all* about a Colt .45 army issue sidearm. The gun looked tiny in his huge hand. He whispered, "I'm not scared now, Boss."

We stood by the window and watched – for anything. Shadows danced around the surrounding fields. Everywhere I looked I saw movement, a light mountain wind was rustling every bush and shrub just enough to alert the hair on one's neck to stand on end. Every triangle palm, every polka dot plant, every stubby old butterfly palm had a spy lurking behind its fronds. They were out there okay, just waiting, watching us. Phantoms were everywhere. The silvery starlight cast an eerie glow to the Malagasy soil and scrap grass that peppered the grounds. My hands were sweating. I heard my watch tick. The intensity of cowering in the dark from an unseen enemy was bewildering.

Abby began to hiccup, "Sorry, Boss."

After a few, very noisy, hiccups I decided to scare them out of the big Ugandan. "I hear that your girlfriend is pregnant, Abdul?"

"Yes, Boss. That why I working for Cool Hand Luke, Boss."

Ab's hiccups intensified. My own fears began to subside. It was quite obvious that the big guy's problems were much, much more serious than the problem lurking outside of Shell Camp.

I told Ab to stay put. I needed to turn off the stove before his eggs burned and to get him a glass of water for his hiccups. He was driving me nuts. I had to do something. "And, don't shoot me when I come back. Okay?"

"Okay, Boss. Why can't I come with you?"

I didn't have a good answer for him. I said, "Someone has to guard the Scotch."

Once outside the bunkhouse, I flattened myself against the wood shingled wall and listened for unusual sounds. The only thing I heard was Ab's, hic hics. Mimicking James Bond, I edged around to the rear kitchen door with the .357 raised in the ready. It was an exhilarating experience, I really didn't know what I'd do if I were to come face to face with Margolova. I decided that I'd yell, "Freeze." Then, when she raised her hands, I'd... I'd... Well, I wasn't quite sure as to what I'd do next. I'd play it by ear and see what happened. I said a few quick prayers and they did help – the kitchen was empty.

Ab's goo was bubbling and smelled terrible. I shut off the gas and placed a lid over the stench pot. I filled a quart pitcher with creek water and hurried out the door. In a low stooping run I made it back, round trip, in less than two minutes. At the door I called out in a loud whisper, "Ab? It's me. Don't shoot, Pal."

He answered, "Is that you, Boss?"

"Yes. I'm coming in. Don't shoot."

"Okay, Boss."

The water worked wonders. Ab's hiccups vanished. We sat in silence for the next thirty minutes watching, waiting, and praying.

"Jim?" It was Sophie. "Guys? It's all clear. I'm coming in. Don't shoot me. Okay?"

I couldn't see her but yelled back, "What's the password?"

"A stiff shot and a hot shower." She had already came up to the door without me seeing her – she was grinning, "Anyone shit in their pants?"

Over a neat Scotch in the dining hall, Soph gave us a full-blown narration of her encounter with our intruders.

"I jogged out to them along the side of the road until I saw the car. I watched them through the scope, two of them. They were spying. They both had binoculars and were watching the camp. I slipped around and got behind them. I listened to see if they were talking, but they were quiet. So, I pull out the .38 and walk up to the open window. I put it right into the driver's face and asked him, "Having car trouble this nice evening?"

The driver, a real ugly kid, says, "Oh, we were just wondering what all the lights were doing on at the camp. We thought it was closed down."

He spoke in English. I didn't believe a word he'd said. I told him that the camp was under lease, and that I was a part of the "armed guard" hired to protect the camp. I then asked them to leave, pointing out that they were trespassing and subject to a citizen's arrest.

The passenger, I think they were brothers, started to say that they were lost, and could they use our phone? But, I cut him off and told him that we don't allow visitors and that there was only one way out, the way they came in. Then told them to get moving while they still could. Then they left. The passenger was pissed. They'll probably be in trouble for letting themselves get caught."

I sincerely asked, "Were you afraid, Soph?"

"Why no, silly. Protecting you is my job. This is what I get paid for. And, I'll have you know, I'm damn good at what I do, too. Handling a couple of punk bozos like those two is a piece of cake."

Abby said, "That my nickname, Boss."

"What's that, Ab? What nickname?"

"Bozo. That my nickname in Uganda, Boss."

I didn't respond, but looked at Soph for her response. She refused to respond, also. She changed the subject.

"They won't bother us again. They'll report that armed guards patrol the grounds. Margolova will come by herself the next time. She won't trust those two again." Soph was talking to herself now. The narration of her exploits was over. She threw down the remaining Scotch. Set the glass down toward the center of the table and announced, "That's the end of my partying, at least, for the time being."

Sophie D. Deadly had entered her own world. If one could read her mind at that particular moment, one would surely see images of her nemesis, Margolova. Indeed, very "bloody" images at that. And on that I'd have bet my whole next paycheck.

Chapter Twenty-Three

The next morning, after a ham sandwich breakfast, I put Chef Abdul to work digging a camp garbage pit. I was homing in on the Ugandan's finer talents, namely, his use of a pickaxe and spade. After watching him for fifteen minutes, I made a mental note to put him in for a significant pay raise, he was *that* good.

Sophie volunteered to clean up the kitchen. Our cook, Chef Abdul, was not quite as adept at cleaning up his messes as he was at making them. Personally, I hate kitchen work. After all, it's woman's work, isn't it? Before checking on her progress, I made a stop in the generator room to insure that my hands were good and dirty. I learned this tactic in Supervision 101 back at Purdue; it makes your crew *think* that you're actually doing something.

Entering the kitchen, asking for some soap, I elicited the following comment from Sophie, the maid, "Wow, looks like you're earning your pay today, Jim."

"Ah yes. From sun to sun an Engineer's work is never done." Then added, "How's things going in here? Need a hand?"

"Well, I could use a little help, but I can see that you're busy. I'll manage."

"Yeah, you look like you've got a handle on things, Kidd. I still need to connect a fleutimizer into the rig's galloping housing. It has to be done. I'd sure hate to see the whole thing blow up on us."

Sophie was intent, "Sounds serious, Jim. Do *you* need a hand? I'd be more than glad to help you."

"No, no. The kitchen is just as important as the generators. And believe me, Soph, I really do appreciate all the work you're doing in here." I patted her on the ass in a physical show of lust – I mean, love and appreciation. Then headed for the generator room to blast a few cigarettes and enjoy its shade.

Yeah, I didn't spend five years in college to stand around washing dishes. And I thought, "Sophie sure does look good in an apron." And, that stack of pots and pans would definitely keep her out of trouble. Wasn't domestic work designed for the health of the feminine soul? I'm sure I had read that somewhere, probably in

Philosophy 469. Besides, women *like* that sort of work.

After over-rationalizing this subject, I began to ponder whether *Sophie* had been to college. I didn't know. Then I thought, "Damn! If she had been then I had better get in there and give her a hand – she'd need it."

When I returned Soph was putting away the last of the camp silverware into a serving rack. "I'm all finished with the motors. Need a hand?"

"No. I'm finished, too. What I need now is a cigarette and some coffee. How about you, Jim?"

We sat in the dining room and discussed what we needed to do before the scientists arrived on Sunday. I needed to make at least one more trip into Tanan. I wanted some more cable and some better light fixtures for the lab. Abby requested more eggs, and Sophie wanted to get her hair done. And, I still hadn't ordered the Porta-Potties. It was becoming an eleventh-hour issue and it needed to be taken care of as soon as possible, at least before Monday.

Sophie still needed to scout out the creek. She said it had to be done. It was *her* highest priority and it was decided that we would do it that very morning while Ab was doing his digging. I had invited myself along, suggesting that we make a picnic of it. "I'll throw together some ham sandwiches and get my screwdriver."

"What do you need a screw...driver, for..." Then she laughed, recalling her own wit.

Shell Camp sits on a small plateau that slants downward to the west. There's thirty miles of dense foliage and forest canopy that descends gradually into a semi-arid desert area that tapers on down to the Mozambique Channel. To the north is a craggy mass of peaks that stuns one's senses with their majesty. And there are deep valleys all around us that have never been entered into by any human being.

To the east lies Antananarivo, our nearest city. Clouds usually cover the mountaintops and keep the camp in shade until mid-morning, then, when the sun breaks out, Shell Camp heats up like an oven. This was one of the reasons why Sophie wanted to finish her scouting early, to beat the heat.

We headed up the access road retracing Sophie's route on the previous evening. It was too brisk a pace for my liking but I did manage to keep up with her simply to show that I could. I was huffing and puffing hard by the time we reached the spot where the two Turks were caught spying, which was a good mile from camp.

Sophie gave me her binoculars so that I could survey the camp from the perspective of Margolova's henchmen. They had picked a good spot. Our entire site was wide open for monitoring. I scanned out back where Ab was diligently digging his pit. He was working slow, but steady. It appeared that he was doing well, considering that he was alone and unsupervised.

Sophie led me up the road another hundred yards to a spot that didn't overlook the camp. She unloaded her backpack that was full of electronic gadgetry. I watched her uncoil a wire and peg it out across the width of the road, then, without narrating her moves, she connected it to a small black box. She put the unused items back into her bag, stood, and announced, "We now have a doorbell, Mister Morgan. It's really sensitive. We'll probably have a false alarm or two, but it's the best I can do for now."

It sounded good to me. I for one didn't want to be surprised by any international spies – especially our *friend*, Margo-Bitcho.

We stomped through tall grasses and thick foliage for another hour. Soph set a few more wire traps at places she believed to be advantageous to a – as she put it, "nosey enemy."

We worked our way back to the kitchen and took a coffee break with Abby, who was soaked to the bone by his own sweat. The sun had come out and the temperature shot into the mid-eighties. Yeah, it was too hot for digging garbage pits. Abby and I sat around and kept cool while watching Sophie connect up her alarm system.

"There." She announced, "All we need now is an intruder."

It was time to test the pudding. Soph showed us how to turn off the alarm then headed for the car and drove out to deliberately trip the wires. It took her four minutes to hit the wire and activate the alarm. The siren was maddening. I went outside to see how well it could be heard from the courtyard and it remained a clear and distinctive piercing sound. I waited outside for Soph to return. When we went in to shut off the alarm Abby was sitting with his hands up covering his ears.

Soph was proud of her work; she was strutting, grinning from ear to ear and teasing Abby. "Listen to that, Abdul. Ever heard a prettier song?" Ab wouldn't be goaded. He just closed his eyes and kept his hands up to protect his ears. Finally she shut it down content with the knowledge that we were all safer now due to her techno-doorbell.

Soph was hyped up and ready for more work, "Okay, Jim Morgan. Go get your screwdriver. We've got a lot of ground to cover before sunset. I'll get the sandwiches. Meet me at the creek in five minutes."

I put Abby in charge of the camp. I told him to have lunch, take a nap, and to let the digging go until it got cooler. He liked being in charge. He's what one would call managerial material. I grabbed up a blanket and clipped on an electrician's adjusting screwdriver to my shirt pocket. Hey, every good humorist has his props, just like every good Engineer has a viable plan. Yeah, that's why I grabbed a blanket, too.

Soph was at the creek when I got there. She said we would be walking the bank for at least two miles each way. "If we need to run out of here on foot we'll at least know what we'll be running into." Which made sense to me. After all, we did have the blanket.

Travelle Creek is a shallow mountain-water runoff. It winds down from the granite peaks of central Madagascar and ends at an estuary that opens up into the Mozambique Channel. The creek rarely goes deeper than a few feet; although it does have a few pools below a few waterfalls where the depths have never been measured. The water is pure and drinkable especially at the higher elevations.

Soph gave me a map to look at. It was a photo-recon map shot in the early sixties by the U.S. Air Force. The entire creek was visible as a tiny ribbon zigzagging down to the coast. There was a small village at the estuary labeled Pimakeel Bay. If not for the label, one couldn't tell that a village was actually there. I wondered how much things had changed since the U-2 recon aircraft took the picture over thirty-years earlier. The road to Shell Camp showed up as vague and indistinct line. It ended about where we were but there weren't any buildings visible, nor was the site labeled.

We headed south, and west, moving down the creek. The walk was fun and most invigorating. Occasionally, we had to wade in the creek itself to maneuver around a thick growth of deep green vegetation. The ground sloped downward at a five-degree descent. Yeah, it was easy going, a real nature hike.

Then we turned around. Suddenly, every step was an uphill battle, literally. Five degrees downhill is bliss, five degrees up is the tenth circle of hell itself. Sophie, the CIA gazelle and two-thirds mountain goat left me behind, panting, in an oozing rush of salty sweat. I felt like a marathon runner, I was on the twenty-sixth mile pushing the mental wall and this madman jumps out from the crowd of cheering well-wishers and begins to beat my legs with an solid steel baseball bat autographed by Al Capone.

I went mad. I yelled out into the shrubbery, "I hate nature, I hate creek-beds, I hate mountains, I hate hiking." I threw away the blanket. I swore off cigarettes, then sat down and tried to light one – only to find that the pack was soaked into a mushy ick. And I swore, "I'll never, never, start out on a hike that begins downhill."

An hour later I came parallel to Shell Camp. Soph was lying in a fat tuft of grass watching my approach. I tossed the screwdriver at her, "Here. Have a ball, Kidd. I'm going in. It's nap time."

Laughing, Sophie stood, shook her head and said, "You're going to miss all the fun, Jim."

"Yeah? Well, it's going to take a lot more than a promise of sexual promiscuity to get me up a creek without a battle." I waved her a sincere farewell gesture and dragged my body toward the Absteer, who had returned to his pit-digging duties.

I limped right past the big guy, saying as I passed, "Knock off whenever you're ready, Pal. I'm going in for a siesta."

Ab threw down the shovel, saying, "I'm hungry too, Boss. What are siestas, Boss?" He was at my side in a two count.

"You can't eat a siesta, Ab. It's a nap."

"We don't got that word around here, Boss."

As we walked, hobbled to the kitchen, I wondered how many languages Abdul spoke or understood. I asked him.

"I don't know, Boss. Around here, everything sounds about the same. In Uganda, I can understand everyone, except a few Bushmen. They don't make regular words when they talk. They say, oo-daba, daba, ooota, and make many grunts, like ug, ug, and ug. They point a lot. I can't understand the Bushmen, Boss."

I slapped Ab on the back, it squashed from his sweat, "Maybe they're all politicians, eh Ab?"

I left the big guy digging sandwiches out of the fridge, announcing my intention to sleep until Soph returned. Ab nodded and I headed for the bunkhouse to test out the shower and to soak my throbbing leg muscles.

The ten-gallon electric water heater gave me a three-minute rinse of steaming hot creek water before it petered out. It was hot, then instantly cold, there was no in-between. The water slow drained into the courtyard. As I toweled off I looked out to see what kind of mess I was making as the tents were set up only a few feet from the drain hole. Indeed, the water began to puddle and was seeping toward the tents. This was a new problem and it needed an immediate resolve. A three-foot French drain would do the trick. I'd put Ab to the task – first thing next morning. I lay down on my bunk to visualize the future drain and fell right into an afternoon snooze.

And I dreamt a very wet dream.

Shell Camp was flooded. The tents were floating around the bunkhouse in a slow, circular motion. One of the tents, a pink tent, drifted up in front of me. Eunice was standing between the canvas door flaps shaking her head in a show of disgust, or – a show of incredible disbelief, something negative. She was dressed in a black draping gown, a Victorian mourning gown, replete with bustle and a throw back tear-veil. And I called out to her, "Hey Eun, who died?"

A bald headed scientist swam out from behind Eunice's tent. He swam strong and sure right up to the bunkhouse door, and then began a dog paddle at my feet, saying, "Pull the plug, Morgan. We're all out here drowning in your shower water, and you – you, why – you just languor around in there waiting for more, and yet more, hot water. It's disgusting, sick. Can't you fix anything?"

Twin shark fins darted in from behind the generator shed fast and efficient. It was a one-two count and they were at the bald scientist pulling him here and there as he screamed out in an unbelievably shrill cry of, "Hellll..." before he was dragged into the swillish depths of the murky putrid shower waters.

And then he was gone. I was sure he had tried to say, "Help," but, maybe not. Maybe he was saying or just going to say, "Hell." Or, "Hello." I couldn't figure this out – not positively. Bloody bubbles, tiny uppervessant bubbles, like those in a fine champagne rose to the surface where the scientifico had gone down. I yelled into the agitated tomato-sauce eddy, "Pull your own plug you stupid ol' bastard."

Abdul came up beside me from inside the bunkhouse. He held a four-foot spear in his left hand and was pumping it up and down; in his right hand he held a fat ham sandwich. He was saying, "Ug, ug, ug, oooa, abba-abba, I want to be elected, me make um big time politician, ug, ug, eh Boss?"

Sophie squeezed in between me and the Ab, she had just come out of the shower, she was holding a submachine gun tight to her waste, she began shooting into the water, yelling, "Don't worry, Jim. I'm trained for this. I can handle this rising tide of public opinion, see?"

The pink tent, *Eunice's* tent, made a full circle around the camp. Eunice began screaming at Sophie, "You bitch. You damned bunny bitch, you, you couldn't recognize public opinion if it bit you on the ass."

Soph began throwing sticks and stones at Eunice. They were in a ruthless, biting, shouting match, "Intellectual rhetorical bitch. Intellectual bullshit that's *all* you know. You're nothing but a rhetorical scum sucking slut, Eunice."

Soph turned, dropped her cut-off jeans and shot Eunice the moon, pointing to her ass while chortling, "Right here, Bitch. Right here."

Enraged, Eunice dove out of the tent headlong into the churning waters and began swimming toward the bunkhouse, gurgling, "I'm going to rip that bunny fur right off your CIA butt you fuckin' bunny bitch."

Sophie started crying. She began pleading with me, "Mister Morgan, how can you let that whore talk to me that way? Do something, Jimbo. Hurry, she's getting closer, can't you do something? Aren't you going to help me?"

I was confused, my allegiances were bi-polared, I needed to mediate, stall for time, but there wasn't any. Eunice was almost on us. I called out to her, "Eun. Hey Eun. It's really okay, Eun. Abby is going to dig a drain, Babe. See? He's got his spear. He's ready. See? Now go back. All right? You're going to catch a cold, Babe. Now go back. Please!"

Eunice stopped swimming. She stood. The water was only up to her ankles, "How could you, Jim? How could you?" Then she began crying.

"How could I what, Eun? What are you talking about?" I was more confused than ever. "What? What did I do now, Eun?"

Sophie pulled up her jeans. She grabbed me by the shoulders and began shaking me violently, "Wake up! Wake up. Wake up you idiot, can't you see what's going on?"

"What's going on? Where? What are you talking about?"

She put her face tight up against my nose and yelled even louder. "Wake up! Wake up."

And I did wake up. Sophie was standing over me smelling musty and sweaty. She was smiling. She asked, "Having nice dreams, Mister Morgan?" She shut her eyes, pretending sleep, "Euuunnniee. Euuunn-eee. Euuuuun-eeee. Hunn-eeee. Baay-beee. Hunn-eeeeeeee. Euuunn-eee."

I grabbed up my pillow and swung it at her hard hitting her flush in her closed eyed face. "Fa-whoosh!"

And then an amazing thing happened. Soph, out of well-honed reflexes, somersaulted into a karate stance while emitting a horrific karate yell, "Hieeee." It was blood curdling, and it gave me instant goose flesh. She was in full stance, ready, ready to strike or defend in an instant's notice, tensed, the way a cobra arches its head just before spitting its deadly venom.

Sophie offered, "Sorry, Jim. Reflexes." She instantly dropped her guard; her body almost appeared to go limp. Then she continued as if nothing had happened, "What were you having, Jim? A nightmare?"

"Yeah. Actually, it was, a, more of a, wet dream, than anything else. Hey, do you really know all of that karate stuff, Kidd?"

"Yes. I started when I was five. Now, it's a healthy way to stay healthy, especially in my line of business."

"So," I asked, "What are you? One of them black-belts or something?"

She smiled, her sly smile, "Well, I was a black belt at the age of ten. Today, well, let's just say, I'm considered a Master, okay?"

"Okay with me. I wouldn't know what you'd be talking about anyway, I never got into that self-defense stuff."

With an air of justified arrogance, Sophie began to tell me of her many awards and national titles. Her list was quite impressive and, I was quite impressed. It was comforting to know that she was *that* good, that she was a "Master." – Na, nah, nah, take that, Margolova!

I asked, "Hey, Babe? How about you head out to the kitchen and chop us up some salad." And for that snide remark I had to swallow my entire pillow, whole.

Chapter Twenty-Four

That night when Sophie made her routine satellite report back to Washington I listened in, by invitation. Soph's roommate was manning the communication center when she made contact. The alias, Betty Boop, whose real name is Sally Wonderful, presented herself in a highly professional manner. I kept my ear tuned to pick up on the cynical qualities that Soph had mentioned earlier back on the C5-A aircraft. If Soph's pal were indeed a bona fide cynic she was keeping that side of her work-personality well hidden, or else I had a personal misunderstanding of the word cynic.

Soph: "Hi Sally, it's so wonderful to hear your voice, sweetheart. How's everything around the apartment?"

Sal: "Oh Sophie. Everything's fine. Neat as a pin."

(Long Pause)

Sal: "A.L.E.X. calls every day. Says he misses you terribly. You must call him as soon as you get back. And, T.E.D.D.Y. has sent you flowers. They're little ones. Where does he work, at a funeral home? Or what?"

(Long Pause)

Sal: "You got some calls from that hunk, P.H.I.L. Remember him, the guy from FBI? He asks too many questions for his own good, Kidd. You'd think he was a cop or something. You know? Stuff like: Where are you? When are you coming back? I swear, Kidd. The guy is falling in love. What do you think, Soph?"

Soph: "I think they're all in love, Sal. We'd better start up the herpes rumor again. Tell them that I'll be back in town as soon as my simplex goes dormant. Except for P.H.I.L., he has too many friends around Langley. Tell him I'm off to Iraq on a secret mission. He'll quit asking so many questions. He gets scared shitless when he thinks he knows something that he shouldn't know. If his brain were as big as his biceps I'd consider marrying the jerk. He *is* nice, just a little weak in the brain department. What do you think, Sal?"

(Long Pause)

An aside: During this long pause Soph was looking at me in a funny way. It was almost as if she were talking about me instead of, P.H.I.L., whom I instantly hated. Was she pointing out my short-comings? Oh, oh. I was confused – was I falling in *love?* I had jumped into her charms with both feet. Damn! I was doomed.

Soph: "Just handle it, Sal. I need a break in the dating game. Know what I mean, Sally?"

Sal: "Sounds like you've met one of them Malagasy hunks, Kidd."

Soph: "Well, Sal, I'm living under that old adage, ...when in Rome... Avoid the church."

(Laughter)

Soph: "Oh Sal, this is too much. We'd better get down to business.

Sal: "I'm sure you've got an old adage for that one too, Kidd."

Soph: "Yes. Get things done quick. Then, you've got more time to screw around."

(Long Pause)

Sal: "Well?"

Soph: "Here goes. The camp is secure. We can walk out down the creek if we need be. And – I need a MAV-861, use a justification code of 329-13. If the boss should balk, try using Code 329-21. That's his favorite code when he wants things done his way. Ah... That's all. All done."

Sal: "If you get a MAV-861, Kidd. I'll kiss your ass in front of the White House and give you five minutes to draw a crowd."

(Laughter)

Soph: "It never hurts to ask, Sal. Besides, it would be a blast."

Sal: "Which one? The MAV? Or getting your ass kissed?"

(Feminine snickering, a couple of nasal hog snorts)

Soph: "What's the latest on Margolova, Sal?"

Sal: "The Malagasy Army is tracking her. They've put a young major on her tail. A... Major LaCruel. Word is that he'll take her out, unofficially, if she gets within a hundred yards of the president or any of his family. I read his file this morning. It sounds like he's trying to live up to his name, *La-Cruel*. That's the latest, Kidd."

Soph: "Has he been briefed on our operation, Sal?"

Sal: "He knows that you're there and that you're CIA. He's been told that the scientists are on a genuine expedition to study tortoises. He's smart, Kidd. He's probably derived more then we've told him. What do you think, Kidd?"

Soph: "I haven't seen the file on LaCruel. You'd better give me a quick rundown on him. What do you have, Sal?"

Sal: "No photograph. He's a native Malagasy. Thirty years old. He has a twitch in his right eye. He rubs it and it's listed as a distinguishing mark, red swollen right eye. Also he has a missing pinky finger, right hand. He's five foot and eleven inches. 140 pounds. Wears a pencil-thin mustache.

(Pause)

Oh, here's something interesting. He's a karate expert. And get this, Kidd. This is a footnote. He lost his pinky on a *live* TV show. He was giving a demonstration of his karate skills. Tried to break a sword – edge up, with a karate chop to the blade. This doesn't sound like a very bright person to me, Kidd. What do you think?"

Soph: "I've heard that it could be done. *I'm* not that advanced. I'll stick to bricks. Anything else?"

Sal: "There's a pencil entry by the boss saying that LaCruel is the best that their army has."

Soph: "Any orders from the boss?"

Sal: "No. But Papa is watching. I have to call him as soon as I pass you the LaCruel junk, which I just did. Is there anything else I can do for you, Roomy?"

Soph: "No. That does it, Sal. Give my love to the Iron Man. Oh, don't forget to water the flytrap. Okay?"

(Giggling)

That ended their conference. Soph began stowing her equipment. I had a lot of questions for her, "What is a MAV-861?"
"Oh, that. It's a military assault vehicle. Model 861. It's new. It's still in the experimental stage. It's an ultra-light dirt bike. It's an army thing, but really cool. They won't be available until the year 2003, but we have a prototype for field-testing. I was assigned to ride it to see if a woman could handle it. This would be a great place to really test it, down along the creek."
"Do you think you'll get it? We *are* in Madagascar you know?"
She shrugged her shoulders. "Maybe."
From an Engineering perspective, it would be dumb to send a dirt bike all the way down to Madagascar so that Ms. Deadly could ride it through a creek. However, aside from this Engineering perspective, I'd sure like to be there if her roomy had to kiss her ass out on the White House lawn.
Soph added, "Some politician, from New England, says that the

windshield is too heavy for a woman. His argument is that by the year 2010 the army will be mostly women. Now, because of his foresight on past issues, everyone thinks that the bulletproof glass is too heavy. It's unreasonable, I can lift the whole thing, glass and all with one hand."

"What about this guy LaCruel? Think he'd really kill her, Margolova, if she gets near the President?"

"Sounds like it. When Sally said, "...take him out," she didn't mean for a candlelight dinner and ballroom dancing."

"And what's so funny about feeding your Venus Fly Trap? You sounded like you were going to feed your boss to it."

Soph was all smiles, "Oh that. Sal and I have been teasing the boss about our flytrap for over a year. We told him that we were having trouble finding enough flies to keep it healthy, as a joke. Then one day, he brings us a fly. Pretty soon, he's bringing us an envelope full of flies every day. The real kicker is we don't really have one. Now, we're afraid to tell him. We don't want to hurt his feelings."

"Boy, you spies really are sinister. Aren't you?"

"We like a good joke as much as the next guy." Then she smirked, weird, "We *love* for a good laugh." Then she assaulted me in a tickling frenzy. "Especially, when it's an Engineer that does *all* the laughing."

Chapter Twenty-Five

After a good laugh, one that turned into an excellent one-hour love feast, we turned in. And to my surprise, Sophie snored. Goddesses aren't supposed to do such things, are they? On hindsight, it wasn't such a terrible snore. It was more of a cute snore. And, if it weren't for the fact that we were sharing a twin bed, I'd have been oblivious to her throaty hum. Ah, her satin flesh cuddled close to mine made up for so many, many of her other feminine short-falls, to include, angelic snoring. We slept all that night, cozy. Until the harsh buzzer of my alarm clock spat out its unwelcome message that the sun would soon rise, "Hey! It's five a.m., Friday morning, up and at it. – Now!"

Speaking of snoring, when we entered the dining hall we came to believe that we were in Manhattan, in fog, listening to a tramp steamer announcing its position by an air-blasted foghorn. Abdul, buried under five wool blankets, was shaking the very foundation of the Shell Camp kitchen. Yeah, if the Olympics had a snoring competition, Abdul Amin from Uganda would surely win the gold.

I banged around the kitchen making fried eggs and toast while singing out a haughty version of the "Mule Skinner Blues" sung in my deepest bass baritone. This finally roused Luke's sidekick to sit up and ask, with his head covered in a blanket like a monk, "What that you cooking there, Boss?"

"Eggs, Ab. Would you like to have some?"

Abdul, still swaddled in blankets, edged up to the stove, "Ha-ha, Boss. You need a bigger pan, Boss." He moved to the fridge and withdrew two dozen eggs while saying, "You're kind of singing make me real hungry, Boss."

Soph volunteered to clean up the dishes while I took Abby out front and showed him where to dig the French drain. I told him to take his time, take lots of breaks, even to take a nap if he wanted, but to have the drain dug by the time Soph and I returned from Tanan. I put him in charge of the camp and insured him that we'd return by sunset.

Sophie came out with her .45 and handed it to Abby, "Keep this nearby in case a wild animal wanders in." Then she told him how to handle an intruder. "Be nice, but be firm. Tell them that you have a lot of work to do before your boss returns then ask them to leave. If you point it out that they are trespassing, they'll leave."

"What should I do if they don't go away, Miss Soph?"

"Yeah." I added. And I really wanted to know, "What if they *don't* just go away, Soph?"

Obviously, Sophie didn't like the dual questions. Adamantly, authoritatively, she hedged, "Don't worry. They will. Believe me guys. They'll leave."

Deliberately, I pressed the issue, "Well, what if they don't?" After all, I was Ab's boss. My employee had a right to know how much authority he was being given, didn't he?

Soph threw her hands up in the air. She was becoming quite perturbed. "If they don't leave. Take out the forty-five and shoot them."

She caught herself, she recognized her own anger, "Look, you guys are making a mountain out of a mole hill. This is all very simple. If someone should come along that doesn't belong here – just ask them to leave. If they refuse – get your gun. You have the right to protect yourself. If they still come at you or start breaking in – *shoot* 'em."

Soph was serious, dead serious. She asked, "Any questions?"

Abby, kicking his toe in the dirt, squeaked, "No, Miss Soph."

Realizing that she was intent, I said, "If my new employee is happy, then I'm happy. Now let's get out of here so that we can get back before sunset."

The drive into Antananarivo was quiet, almost sullen. Our first stop was at the Hilton to insure everything was ready for the expedition's arrival. The bus I rented was already in the parking lot awaiting our use. Sophie made an appointment to have her hair, "...cut and fluffed," right after lunch by the Hilton's duty hairdresser. Things were going well – too well.

When I tracked down the concierge, Uncle Bobby, I was disappointed to find out that Madagascar did not have a portable potty service. "This is an amusing concept, no? I know of no one who would deal in such an item as this, Mon Cher." He looked at the ceiling, searching his wit for – ? Then he pops his lips with a three-finger pop, "Mon Dieu (which means, "My God!")!" How very foolish of me. I have almost forgotten my brother, the contractor. Surely,

Mon Cher, *he* can make anything desired from a mere scrap of old timber. Sit. Sit. I'll bring him to you with a quick telephone call, no?" And he was off. No doubt to aid and abet the bilking of the rich bastard recently in from America – me.

We sat in the large and empty lounge where Sophie chastised me over and over for stating to Uncle Bobby that, "...money was no object." And, that I should quit *pretending* to be so rich.

Thirty dreadful nagging minutes later, Uncle Bobby returned shoving ahead of him a stout cigar-puffing Malagasy contractor who indeed looked to be Uncle Bobby's brother, chubbier, unkempt and somewhat odoriferous, but most assuredly his brother.

Over stiff drinks, I penciled out a rough draft of my dream toilet. Without adding dimensions, I drew an oblong floor plan that showed four stools, four sinks and two showers with one side labeled men and the other half labeled women. Each side showed a separate entry. Below that, in block letters, I printed the following list:

Four lights and two electrical outlets/both sides.

Two exterior door lights.

Two sixty-gallon water heaters/one each side.

Mirrors over the sinks/all sinks.

Water pump and water line from creek.

Cesspool adequate for 15 people.

I handed the sketch to Bobby's brother. In my best French, I said, "It must be completed by ten o'clock on this coming Monday morning. How much?"

He sat and studied the sketch for a solid ten minutes. Once, his cigar ash dropped onto the sketch – he didn't remove it.

Then, in perfect English, he looks at me and says, "Twenty-two grand, American."

I figured he had doubled his estimate at Bobby's suggestion, he looked to be an honest man, so I countered with, "$14,000.00 American, half now and half on completion – and no bullshit."

He turned beet-red but was smiling big, displaying a mouth inlaid with black and rotting teeth. He stood and extended his hand to close the deal. We shook firm and hard – the deal was closed.

Bobby ran to the table with a phone, "To transfer to our bank your American funds, Mon Cher."

The bank president was on the line, on hold. The banking transaction took all of twenty seconds. We stood and left. The contractor had already gone. Uncle Bobby was coiling the phone line neatly around the phone base while inching backward to his office. I stopped and gave Uncle Bobby a hundred dollar tip for aiding our business deal.

Gaily he asked about his cousin, Abdul. I thought this was a ploy to filch a larger tip. I pulled out a five-dollar bill and held it out to Uncle Bobby. Looking at the amount, Uncle Bobby chuckled, "No, no, Mon Cher. Your hiring of my cousin needs no reward, praise Allah."

We finalized our shopping by one o'clock and returned to the Hilton in plenty of time for Sophie's beautification program. We made a plan to dine in the lounge. Soph went her way and I headed for the bar.

Upon entering the lounge I was met by a standing Uncle Bobby and a uniformed Malagasy policeman.

"Do not be alarmed, Mister Morgan." Offered the starched and polished officer. "May I see your passport, sir?"

I produced the passport with reluctance; no one had ever checked us into Madagascar, officially. I said, "Sure, sure, most certainly." I was being the most condescending American to ever set foot on his Malagasy soil.

The clean-cut officer paged through the passport pausing momentarily on my photo, saying, "Everything seems to be in order, Mister Morgan. Would you be so kind as to join the Chief of Police for a social brandy, Mister Morgan?"

I nodded courteously, "I'd be most delighted to..." And I strained my neck to look around the duo and spot the Chief who I thought would be sitting in the lounge.

The officer offered, "The Chief is at headquarters, Mister Morgan."

I said, "Oh, please call me Jim. And your name is...?"

"Rudy, Rudolphus Marian Neville. Just call me Rudy." He extended his hand for a hearty, solid, political handshake. The Chief had sent his best. Rudy was a professional emissary and probably heir to the Malagasy Police Chief's throne. And probably his most trusted henchman.

"May I inform my assistant as to my whereabouts, Rudy? It'll only take a minute."

"Most assuredly, Mister Morgan. I have a car waiting outside. I'll wait for you there." He excused himself and moved toward the lobby. Then, over his shoulder, he yells, "Thanks, Uncle Bobby."

Sophie's hair was being washed when I entered the beauty shop. The beautician went away when I came up to the sink and got Soph's attention. I quickly told her what had happened and asked her if there was anything I should "avoid" talking about. "Oh dear heaven, yes. Do *not* mention the CIA. Remember, I'm your camp security and assistant, I work for Eunice, and, be dumb, act like you really *are* an Engineer. Do you think you can handle it, Jim?"

"Well, acting like an Engineer is going to be tough. But what if they ask me something easy. Like, how come your passport isn't stamped? Or, who's Margolova?"

"Just tell them the truth. Nobody *checked* our passports. Let them worry about it."

"And Margolova?"

Soph grabbed up a towel and began drying her hair, "I'm going with you."

"No, no." I said. "I'll be fine. This is my chance to be a real spy. I want to do it. You stay here and get pretty. I'll be fine. Honest."

She relented. She sat down looking like a whipped puppy just in from the rain. She looked at me, serious. Then gave me one of her boss's best lines, "Okay Jim. *You're on your own.* Be careful. Watch what you say. Promise?"

"I'll be back for lunch. By the way, that beautician is working wonders with your hair. That wet bubbly look is kind of neat, it makes you look, *deadly.*" I turned to leave and "Wop!" She hit me square in the back of my head with a wet towel. Some people simply can't stand a compliment and Sophie is one of them.

When I turned, she asked, "Can I tip the beautician, Jimbo?"

"Just get a receipt, Soph. Get a receipt. And don't call me Jimbo, Deadly."

The Chief of the Malagasy Police is an old, old man. He is heavily age spotted and very thin, sunken featured, and his uniform looked to be three sizes to big for his frame. There's no way he could reach 100 pounds on a bathroom scale – he looked pathetic. Death was surely high on his list of life's priorities.

He has a small unkempt tuft of pure white hair and his matching mad eyebrows gave him a more Russian appearance than the island or Polynesian look. When we shook hands I had the impression that I had grasped a rubber glove – one filled with brittle sticks and an icy gelatin. He had the weakest handshake that I had ever experienced. It was "nothing." I may as well have shook hands with a cadaver. And his eyes, they were huge in proportion to the rest of his facial features. They were glazed with a milky film, a mucus that needed to be wiped, and under that mucus were the definite signs that can only be attributed to one's being a lifetime alcoholic, the red imbedded lines often referred to as being chronically bloodshot. Yeah, for all practical purposes the Chief was already dead.

Nor did he smile. More than likely he couldn't. However, he did speak. He ordered me, in a raspy nasal whine, "Take a seat, Mister Morgan." And yet, somehow, he did maintain his air of earned authority. I was compelled to sit and I did.

Motionless in his leather chair, he continued, "I'm to understand that you're here to head a biological study of our tortoise population. Is that correct?'

"Yes sir. That's correct." The old buzzard was making me extremely nervous and he knew it.

"Can you speak the Malagasy language, Mister Morgan?"

"No. I know a little French, and that's been getting me by, so far. Your fellow countrymen have been very tolerant of my ignorance." To which I received a slow-motioned, short nod, one of universal understanding and multi-world problem acknowledgement.

He reached into an opened desk drawer and removed a bottle of cognac. One could actually see a layer of dust on the bottle's curvature. He set it down on the desk with effort then returned to the drawer and pulled out two tumblers that hadn't been used in some time. The Chief produced a green rag and wiped the insides of both glasses. He was definitely arthritic. It took him several minutes to complete his wiping ritual. Undaunted by his own ineptitude, he shakily poured the cognac into the still dirty and grease-smeared glasses.

He pushed one a few inches toward me, but I couldn't reach it from where I sat. I stood to reach the drink. I held it up to the old codger and toasted him, "To all your fond memories, Chief."

In a slow unison we emptied the heavy glasses. The cognac was fire, silk and mothers milk all mixed together and swallowed in one ostentatious gulp. I set the glass down and eased back into the guest's chair. The chief took the glasses and returned them to the desk drawer, then replaced the cognac bottle making no effort to conceal his secret bar.

He studied me for a moment, and then said, "Should you encounter any problems while visiting our village, Mister Morgan, you will call me." He made a deft motion for me to leave with his crinkled fingers.

I stood. I was going to thank him for his courteous offer of assistance while in his village. But by the time I was upright Rudy had entered to announce, "I'll return you to the hotel now, Mister Morgan."

We drove back to the Hilton in silence. I'm sure that Rudy was aware of the twilight zone atmosphere that I had just left. It was respectful of him not to make anything of it. At the hotel, as I stepped out of the cruiser, Rudy tipped his hat with his index finger, saying, "I am at your service, Mister Morgan." Then drove away, probably to make funeral arrangements for his mentor.

I felt that I had made two sincere allies in Madagascar, its Chief of Police, and its "Future" Chief of Police.

Chapter Twenty-Six

Sophie was waiting for me inside the front door. I asked her, "Pardon me Miss, have you seen a drab, dish-water blonde loitering around in wait of a handsome American Engineer?"

Quick on the uptake, she answered, "I did see someone who'd fit that description, about an hour ago. She was kitchen help, a mere domestic. She's cleaning the guest rooms right now. Since she's busy, how about buying a cute blond a nice big, fat, juicy steak, Big Boy?"

Women never look their best when they just walk out of their hairdresser's chair. But a man can't tell them this, no way. We have to lie through our teeth like I did on that Friday afternoon, "It would be my life's pleasure to dine with such a wonderful piece of hair."

Sophie, like every woman, sucked this up. Hey! "I had noticed." She was pleased with my lie, one could tell. With a happy smile she hooked my arm and we strolled into the restaurant for steak and an assortment of Malagasy greens.

I gave Soph a full narration of my visit with the Chief while we waited for our meal. Soph confided in me that she was really getting worried. She said that she was on the verge of calling the American Embassy to have them free me from the pokey.

"Pokey?" I asked, "What's a pokey, Soph?"

"Oh, you know, the slammer, jail, the hoosegow."

"Oh." I said, "I've never been in one. Your CIA argot throws me every now and then."

"Sorry." She said this while fluffing her new hair. "When one is as pretty as me, one can get away with a little argot, and a whole lot more. Don't you agree, Jim?"

Yeah, I had to agree. If Soph talked like one of Abdul's bushman pals, she could probably get more votes for a Senate job than her own father, based on looks alone.

I asked, "Soph, how come your not in the movies?"

Her facial muscles went limp and her smiling, vivacious, cheerfulness vanished, she was now going to take my frivolous question quite seriously. She began slowly, contemplatively, "I'm not real sure, Jim. When I was younger, ten, twelve years old, that's all I ever dreamed of, being an actress, like most girls at that age. Mom supported my dream..."

Sophie trailed off her narration after the word dream. I had to prod her to continue, "You've got me on the edge of my seat, Soph. What happened?"

Slowly, she continued, "I started high school. We had this actor's group and I joined up first day without hesitation, it was exactly what I wanted to be doing. But, I found out real quick that I couldn't memorize lines. Every time I was cued – I'd ad lib and improvise.

Actually, it was really funny. Only thing – I was witty. Othello isn't. Soon, I was reduced to a stage prop, a tree, a walk-on, or a wait-in-the-wings third-in-line understudy for a supporting role. The high school stars were all a bunch of monkeys, at least – that's what I thought back then.

So, I threw myself into politics. Dad made the leap easy. I entered college, my heart set on a Jurist Prudence degree..."

Again she trailed off. Again, I prompted her along, "Don't stop now. Come on. I really want to hear this."

"Not much more to tell, Jim. I was fun. I'm pretty. I'm a party girl, and my grades suffered the consequences. I was placed on academic probation. I panicked. I transferred to the Social Sciences. I was still fun, still pretty and partied even harder. I lost my scholarship, dad cut me off and I hired into the CIA, looking for adventure. The end. Here I am."

"I would hardly call this the end, Soph. How old are you? Twenty-seven?"

"About that."

"Well, come on." I gave her a challenge; "You can ride off into the Malagasy sunset with an old Engineer who really likes your ass."

I stood, waved my arm toward the door, "Exit, stage right."

Sophie stood, "Speaking of ass, Mister Morgan, I need to pick up some feminine napkins, before, we ride off into that glorious sunset of yours."

Sophie was right, she couldn't follow a script worth a damn, her ad lib *was* witty, but once again, she had reduced herself to a mere stage prop.

It was after four o'clock by the time we gassed the wagon and picked up Sophie's monthly essentials. I put on my spy sunglasses and headed the big Ford into the setting sun. After two miles, Soph demanded to drive, she said, "I don't want to ride into the sunset, Jim. Not as long as I can drive." Hey, argue with that one.

All in all, we had had a most constructive day.

Chapter Twenty-Seven

The Seventy-three odd miles to Shell Camp gives one some of the world's most breath taking views, from waterfalls to sprawling vistas, the mind is constantly in a state of awe, at least for the passenger. For the driver it's a somewhat different perspective. The driver must focus entirely on driving and one's awe is derived from the numerous pits and crevices that one must dodge to safely maneuver the two-thousand-foot descent to Shell Camp Road.

The last ten percent of the drive is over loose stone. A rut cut into the earth by an old steam driven bulldozer. The one lane path becomes downright treacherous because of non-use. One minute you're on the road, the next, you're skidding off into a weed field and left wondering, "Whoa, where did the road go?"

Yeah, I was happy to have Sophie behind the wheel. It was nice to sit back and enjoy the view.

Every few minutes or so, Sophie would point out a dense growth of palms, a jutting rock formation, or a bend in the road where we had to slow to under five miles per hour. According to Soph, these areas were all potential ambush spots.

By the time we reached the camp access road, I had slunk way down in my seat in an effort to avoid being hit by an incoming sniper's bullet. Soph looked at me and asked, "What's the matter with you, Jim?"

"Just trying to get comfortable, Babe."

"Humph." She snorted. "You're the only person I know who tries to make himself comfortable by putting a briefcase over his head."

"Oh this, it's just to block the sun, Kidd." So I lied...

The sun had set below a distant band of cirrus that tinted everything with an orange-yellow hue just as we pulled into camp. Abby ran out from the kitchen to meet us before we had time to exit the vehicle, saying, "I sure am glad to see you, Boss."

I asked, "What's the problem, Ab?"

"It's that oven, Boss. I was making some cake and that oven wouldn't get hot, Boss."

"Well, help us unload some of this junk, Ab. I'll take a look at it as soon as I get a chance."

"I can't help now, Boss. I'm cooking cakes on top of the stove, Boss. I got to watch for them to rise." Our chef turned and began a full out run back toward the kitchen.

Sophie said, "I'd better go and check this out, Jim. From what I've just heard, I'm afraid to go look." Soph sprinted off toward the kitchen close on Abdul's heels.

I followed. Soph was right, baking cakes on top of the stove didn't sound quite right. It was intuitive, something was dead wrong and I had to go see, too.

I stopped at the screen door. I saw three-foot flames dancing above the stove. Soph had the fire extinguisher in her hands and was spraying white foam onto the stove and all over Abby's cakes. I stood there and watched. I had no intention of entering *hell*. Soph, who had exercised great patience and had been Miss Congeniality up to this point, lost it. Her mental fuses began to blow, one by one.

"Jesus H. Christ, Abdul. What in the fuck are you trying to do, get fired?"

"No, Miss Soph. I'm making cakes."

"Cakes?" Soph screamed, "Cakes? This isn't how you make cakes – this, is how you burn the fucking building down."

Sophie was hotter than the fire she was fighting. Abby yelled back at her, "I'm going out to help the boss, Miss Soph."

"Oh no you're not! You're staying right here, Buster. You've got yourself one big mother-fucking mess to clean up, Chef." Yeah, there was murder in Sophie's voice and an outright anger written all over her normally, angelic face.

Abby looked to be on the verge of tears, "Will you help me, Miss Soph?"

Soph screamed, "Help you? Help you? Yeah, I'll help you. I'll help you pack your fucking suitcase, you, you goddamned pyromaniac. That's how I'll help you, you Bozo. Now get yourself busy and start cleaning."

Abby went into a big smile, "That my nickname, Miss Soph."

Sophie, undaunted, fired back, "Yeah? Which one? Bozo or Pyromaniac?"

Abdul, now shuffling his foot, shyly responded, "Bozo."

Soph looked toward the door and saw me watching. She turned into a General, commanding, "Come in here, Jim."

"No way, Babe." I turned and headed – ran – for the bunkhouse.

Sophie burst open the screen door, yelling, "Mister Morgan." Heavily emphasizing the, "Mister."

I stopped in my tracks, turned, faced my blond enemy and said, "This is every man's dream, Soph."

"What?" She angrily demanded.

I repeated myself, "It's the fruit of every man's dream."

"Just what in the hell are you talking about?" She had her hands on her hips in a gunslinger's stance – ready to draw and shoot me dead right between the eyes.

I elaborated, "It's every man's dream, to have a beautiful blonde chase him into his bedroom." I turned, took two steps toward the bunkhouse door and stepped right into the open pit that Abdul had dug for the French drain. He had done a fine job. The hole was a good six-feet deep. I hit the bottom hard, not realizing immediately what had happened as I had forgotten about the drain.

I lay there a moment to feel if I was hurt. The pit was about the size of a grave. I rolled over on my back and thought about how silent it was below the ground. I looked up into the now black, star-studded sky; it was an eerie few minutes, very strange.

Then, Soph's pretty face appeared above the hole, her blond tresses cascaded down around her face as she gently asked, "Are you alright, Jim?"

"Yeah, I think so." Then I had to add, "Like I was saying, Soph. It's every man's dream to have a beautiful blond chase him into his grave."

She stomped her foot, "Damn you, Jim." Then she went away.

I lay there several minutes; it was neat to watch the stars from the hollow silence of a pseudo-grave. My mind wandered to the chores that I needed to do before Monday when we'd go into town to pick up the scientists. Actually, all I really needed to do was to hang the lab lights, pray for the toilet to come in on time, and…

Sophie appeared above the hole. She was holding a spade full of Malagasy dirt. She said, "When the beautiful blond runs the man into his grave, she expects him to stay there." She then threw the full shovel of dirt right onto my face. Spitting sand, I climbed out of the coffin-less grave only to see her storm off toward the station wagon, obviously mad, and looking very determined.

I thought, "Oh shit, she's going to leave."

I called out to her, "Does this mean that you're angry with me?" She didn't answer. I brushed off the clinging dusty earth as I went to her.

She was sitting on the Ford's tailgate, crying. It wasn't a hard sobbing cry. She wasn't bawling, ranting or raving. She was just sitting there with silvery tears streaming down her velvet cheeks.

With a forced vehemence, she said, "Can't you see when a girl needs to be left alone for awhile, Mister Morgan?"

"Actually Soph, you wanted me to come over here, it's the one place that you knew that I had to come to (I pointed) to unload all this junk."

Slowly she began, "Boy-o-boy, you and Eunice make a perfect match, you both think you know everything, don't you?" Her tears poured out in uncontrolled profusion.

I produced my handkerchief in a show of masculine understanding, "Here, Babe. I'm going in to help Abdul clean up. When you're feeling better, you can put this stuff in the lab."

On hindsight, I may have been a bit brash that evening. Sophie did empty the station wagon and put the load into the lab; however, she also moved all her personal things out of our bunkhouse. She decided to take up residence in the expedition's field laboratory.

Now I ask you, "What's a man supposed to do?" She knew damned well that my next priority was to fix up the lab. Right?

Chapter Twenty-Eight

Abby and I worked into the wee hours of the next morning repairing the fire-damaged kitchen. After scrubbing down the grease and smoke residue with soapy water, we painted the back wall with an old gallon of construction yellow equipment paint. The smoke odor was barely detectable above the scent of a stewing cabbage, which was Abdul's answer to the odoriferous paint smell. Actually, the kitchen looked much brighter and cleaner, in contrast to the original shade of pea-green that had been applied by some Malagasy forefather.

I repaired the stove's oven, it was just dirty, then gave Abby a stern lecture on the proper use of the camp's aged, but hardy, Philco appliance. And I hoped, with all my heart, that at least one of the incoming scientists would have some culinary skills.

Unfortunately, Antananarivo doesn't stock TV-dinners. Yeah, there are occasional drawbacks to being a field Engineer; a shortage of quality domestic help, and the non-availability of a quick TV-dinner have always been two of them. Now, I'd even have to make my own bed. With Soph in the lab, I'd even have to sleep by myself, which I did on that very morning – quite soundly.

Sophie's road alarm shattered our Saturday sleep-in. At nine in the morning the damned thing sounded more like a Civil Defense siren than a doorbell. In shorts, and half asleep, I fumbled around for the .357 Magnum, which I had stowed carefully under my bed. I went to the door and saw Soph run out of the lab strapping on her holstered .38 while heading for the dining hall.

Abby opened the screen door as she approached, she told him to stay put and continued her sprint up to the bunkhouse. I opened the door and she slowed, announcing, "We've got company, Jim. You'd better get dressed." She looked sullen.

I told her that I'd be right out and began dressing. I threw on a pair jeans and a Purdue sweatshirt. Not bothering with socks, I put on my deck shoes barefooted. My mouth was dry, so I took a deep draw from a fifth of J&B as a mouthwash substitute. Then, finding nowhere to spit, I was compelled to swallow. And *that* made for one *hell* of a wake up call.

Gasping, I ran out into the courtyard, *ready.*

Standing together, we listened for our visitor's vehicle. And it came, a high-pitched whine, the dead giveaway of a diesel truck pulling a heavy load. It had to be the contractor, no doubt. We put away our guns as soon as we actually saw the overloaded semi-truck come inching into view. Yeah, it was comforting to know that Soph's alarm system was working. It was even more comforting to know that it wasn't the crazy bitch Margolova sneaking in on us.

The twelve-man construction crew worked like a team of army ants invading a company picnic laden with cake. Uncle Bobby's brother came up to me with a set of blueprints that still smelled of ammonia. With the chewed tip of his fat cigar, he pointed out, that from the kindness of his heart, "I'm including screen doors, here and here, at no additional cost."

I think the man was having guilt feelings about his fee; but then again, he may have just been a considerate human being. Whichever, it was a real luxury to have screen doors put on an outhouse, especially one being built in the rugged, wild outback of west central Madagascar.

By noon, the project was complete. The twelve-man crew was reloaded on the now empty flatbed trailer and were preparing themselves for the three-hour plus trek back up into Tanan. They were singing, something equivalent to, "Lift that bag, tote them coffee bean sacks." They had sung this in a broken French, and a pigeon English that was quite moving, at least to me. No doubt, the young Polynesian crew had earned their pay. I wondered how much their pay was. But I never asked.

Throughout the morning, Soph gave the men an American beauty show. She decided to sunbathe, in bikini, while the Malagasy men, shirtless, sweating muscular laborers, cat-called and whistled at her wares, her most ample wares. It was somewhat disgusting, but as a virile male myself, my own personal observation time was split 50/50 between Sophie and the raising of the toilet. Hey, what can I say?

I gave Uncle Bobby's brother a fifth of my Scotch and a sincere thank you for his craftsmanship and the concerted professionalism that he and his entire crew had exhibited on that beautiful Saturday morning. In return, he handed me one of his fat Havana stogies (a stogie by definition is a long, slender, roughly made cigar. Bob's bro insisted on calling his smokes, stogies. If you caught this inconsistency, you're pretty sharp.). I, in turn, gave it to Sophie. She deserved it.

I spent the next hour inspecting our new building. I had this keen sense of achievement. It was as if I had built the whole thing with my own two hands. Occasionally, Engineers get like that.

With the departure of the workmen, Sophie also disappeared. She was maintaining a low profile. After all, it was her time of the month, that time when women lament their femininity and all its associated inconveniences. I did my best to avoid her, also. My thinking was thus; "She'd come looking for me as soon as she was ready to apologize. After all, I surely didn't do anything so bad. At least, that I could think of – right then."

Yet, I did need to wire up the lights in the lab. The exact spot where Sophie was hiding out. I killed time by stoning in the French drain. Abdul is an excellent hole-man. Then, Ab and I painted the toilets, inside and out, a clean washable white. This took us right up to sunset. It was now time to confront the CIA, it was a simple fact of life – Sophie had to move.

I went to Soph's door, the laboratory door, and knocked on the screen portal. I might add that I did this with an extreme amount of innate trepidation. I knew she wasn't going to like my alternatives. Which were to take a tent or to move into the kitchen with Abdul. Of course, she could always move back into the bunkhouse. But that would have to be her suggestion, and her suggestion alone. Right?

She answered, "Who is it?" She sounded cheery, charming.

"It's Admiral Halsey. I'm here to moor the USS Enterprise and to assist you in finding some other, safer, harbor." And, I really said this nice. I didn't want to show any animosity. I just wanted to get her moved and get my work done.

"Come in, Admiral Halsey. You may move my things back to the bunkhouse, if you must."

I rattled off, "Well, it's either there or a tent. Whichever you prefer, Miss Alberquist?"

Sophie sat down on her cot, hard. She stared down at the oak floor and said, "Things have really gotten out of hand, haven't they?"

"Yeah." Then, without thinking, "You ready to apologize?"

She looked up at me. She brightened, "I was." She began. "I really do want to bury the hatchet, Jim. But, you keep going on and on with your nonsense. Why, at this very moment, I'd like to bury the hatchet right between your shoulder blades." She was getting angry.

I thought she was going to start her crying all over again. Then, all of a sudden, I get this terribly strong sense – an *intuitive* insight.

"It was time for a truce." I could have a few weeks in heaven or a few weeks of pure hell. I opted to be, condescending.

I said, "Aw, I'm sorry, Kidd. I really thought that we were having fun, and believe me; I do want to have fun out here. To enjoy this adventure, and I was doing my best to make things – entertaining."

She looked up at me with daggers in her eyes, cold, and tears began to seep from their corners, and get this, at the risk of seeming insensitive, her lower lip began to tremble. Damn, PMS is one hell of a bad trip. She said, "Yeah, fun. Abdul screws up the kitchen and I clean up the mess. He starts the place on fire, and you ...you run away. That, Mister Morgan, is not my idea of having a fun day."

"Aw. He means well, Soph." We were quiet. I went to the door and looked toward the kitchen, contemplating what to do about Abdul. I had to do a double take – was that smoke rising from the roof? No, thank god. I was mistaken.

I turned, "Okay, Kidd. I'll go have a talk with him. I'll fire him as camp cook." I looked out the door again. Again, I thought I saw smoke. I added, "As a matter of fact, I'll go do it right now. It's something that has to be done."

Soph wasn't through, "And you, Jim. Just because I came into your bed, doesn't mean that you can run all over me. I'm a human being, too. I have feelings just like any other woman. I need to be treated with, at least, a little respect. I'm not down here for your amusement...for your sexual pleasure, James Morgan."

This pissed me off, "You sound as if Eunice enlisted you as an expeditionary whore, Soph. Quit building a negative case against yourself. I, for one, thought that we were having a meaningful relationship. Furthermore, I had hoped that it would go a little bit farther than a simple sexual fling." I had raised my voice. On this issue I was going to be heard.

I looked for smoke again. I couldn't tell.

Sophie cooled, "You happen to be a very desirable man, Jim." She was going to say more but she didn't.

I went over to her and sat down next to her, close. She has a wonderful scent, she smelled clean like jasmine and wild flowers. She sat, looking introspective, childlike. She was quite still, frozen, like a statue, a Madonna. Another tear welled out from the corner of her eye and oozed down her soft peachy cheek.

This was a terribly awkward moment for me. I felt like I was wearing boxing gloves while trying to rearrange the animals in a glass menagerie. I was on the verge of whispering to her, "I love you." But I couldn't. And yes, "I *did* love her."

Deep, deep in my heart, I knew, I knew that our love could never go farther then this, which was, a behind the barn lover's tryst, kiss and never, ever tell... And, I knew, that she knew it, too. And, I believed that she; *she* loved me dearly, too. So, I attacked her. Her underarms, with a tick tickling, wiggling, finger assault.

She pleaded, "Damn you, Jim Morgan."

I kept up the assault. We rolled to the floor. Then she hit me "hard," it was a karate chop right to my esophagus. Oh, how it hurt. I was choking and on the verge of blacking out. I rolled, gasping for air, out the door and into the courtyard grasping at my throat, dying, gagging, right onto the shoes of – Major LaCruel.

Deadly, with her blouse askew, exposing a healthy chunk of her left breast, flew out the door with her .38 leveled at LaCruel's head, yelling, *Freeze* in Malagasy.

Still gagging, I looked up at the Major. His hand moved in a slow, slow arch up to his red swollen eye where he began to gently massage his ugly, afflicted socket. His good eye looked into mine, and he spoke, "Mister Morgan, I presume."

"I rasped out an almost intelligible and very painful, "Yes."

He looked at Soph, "And you my dear? Miss Deadly?"

Soph lowered her thirty-eight. "It's Kidd." She quickly corrected. "Sophie Kidd, with two D's. And you are ...Major Cruel?"

He corrected, "LaCruel, just call me Major, it's simpler." He stopped rubbing his eye, "You won't need your weapon, Miss Kidd. Let me assure you this is purely a social visit."

Sophie began to bumble in the face of authority, "Oh, this. Well, I'm security. We weren't expecting anyone today, I mean tonight." She was smiling, being subservient, stupid.

"How may we help you, Major?" She was ignoring me, my pain. I still couldn't get my pipes working. She broke something, I knew I was doomed, I was dying, and I needed an ambulance and a whole team of doctors.

Through watery eyes, I watched the two karate masters sizing up each other, looking for some exterior weakness, for some wee fault in the other's being, so that one day, the other might capitalize on it if the chips fell in the wrong direction. Yeah, they were communicating in the sixth sense, that silent language of the karate masters. It was a silent mime exchange of physical résumés.

As their respective studies continued, I managed to raise my head and gulp in some badly needed oxygen.

Sophie's voice broke the awkward silence. "I was just showing Mister Morgan how to defend himself during an attack of nonsense, Major. The Master has taught him a valuable lesson tonight. He will remember this lesson for some time to come."

I tried to comment. I needed to get out a few "responsive" expletives on the merits of Sophie's "valuable lesson," but I couldn't. The harder I tried, the more grief and agony I caused to myself. I concluded that I was going to die, and collapsed.

I heard LaCruel say, "You must show me that move sometime, Miss Kidd. It appears to be a most effective nonsense deterrent."

His eye-rubbing hand reached down and rested briefly on my forehead. I was down on all four. He pushed my head to one side with a quick wrist movement. My head snapped backward, countering the sideways shove. Something popped in my throat and, hah! I could breathe – I was going to live. Ah, life once again became beautiful.

I stood and immediately tried to thank the Major, "Thank you Major." Although I could now breathe, I still couldn't talk. I sounded like a croaking frog.

The Major knew that I was thankful, he said, "I couldn't remember if that was a move to cure or to kill, Mister Morgan. I'm glad it was the cure."

Sophie had adjusted her blouse and placed her thirty-eight inside the lab door. Stepping back out, she asked, "What brings you out here so late in the evening, Major?"

"Purely social, Miss Kidd, I'm here on behalf of the Malagasy Republic."

The Major's English was heavily accented, but very understandable. He continued, "It is an army empiricism that I visit every expedition that comes here to explore our island. It is our Republic's way of saying, welcome. And, it is my way of keeping a leash on foreign activity."

Sophie was being more than polite, "May I give you a tour of Shell

Camp, Major LaCruel?"

They were off. Leaving me painfully alone lying in the dirt under the sparkling stars of the southern hemisphere and the onrush of a too quick nightfall. I went into the lab and began gathering up Sophie's gear. I decided that she wanted to move into the bunkhouse. Besides, I wanted her.

I heaped everything onto her old bunk in a big pile and returned to the lab. I began to install the workbench light-system that we had purchased the previous day. Soph had led the Major off toward the rocks where we spotted the spies. I had considered joining them, but I did need to finish the lab. Abdul came in carrying a quart of canned tomato juice and several sandwiches. His mouth was full. I asked him what was up.

"Want some juice, Boss?" He held the can up to me. I was on a ladder.

"No thanks, Sport. I'm having a little trouble swallowing right now."

"That Major, him a mean bastard, Boss."

"You know him, Ab?"

"Everyone knows him, Boss. He kicked Luke's ass all over the airport last Christmas, Boss."

"I stopped doing what I was doing and asked, "Why did he do that, Ab?"

"Luke said it was because he was fuckin' LaCruel's mama." Ab took a big swig of juice, "The guys at the airport say it was because Luke called the Major a one-eyed Jack."

I couldn't help but smile, "Kicked his ass, eh?"

"Yes Boss. Luke stayed in his cockpit a whole week, Boss. He couldn't fly because his eyes were both swollen shut. Luke was real mad. Luke said he was going to bomb the Major's house as soon as he could get a bomb." Abby emptied the juice can.

Do you think he would have done that, Ab? Bomb the major's house?"

"Ha, Boss. Luke couldn't get a bomb. Everyone he asked to get him a bomb just laughed, Boss. Luke wanted the bomb, but no one would give him one, Boss."

"If he had a bomb? Would he have dropped it on the Major?"

Abby shook his head in a confident, yes. He had stuffed a whole sandwich into his mouth forcing in the last inch with his chubby finger. He couldn't talk. Ab waved bye-bye and left, no doubt, to drain another quart of tomato juice.

I finished the lights in an amused contemplation of Luke dropping a bomb on LaCruel's house. I toyed with the idea of relating Ab's story to the Major, but never did. I tested the lights. They worked perfectly. I closed the door and started for the kitchen, it was time for the Malagasy News and a ham sandwich.

Ab was approaching the lab as I pulled the door shut and Sophie and LaCruel came out from between the buildings all at once. There was a moment of confusion, almost collision.

LaCruel asked, "How is your throat, Mister Morgan?" He sounded sincere and extended his hand in a show of friendship. We then shook a strong firm handshake. It was an avenue he controlled to transmit his power, his confidence and strength of character. His handshake said I'm in command and dominate all those about me as mere mortal entities. And right then I made a vow to myself that I would neither screw around with this man's mama, nor would I ever call him a one-eyed Jack – at least not to his distinctive and somewhat ugly face.

I tried in vain to spot LaCruel's missing pinky finger, but it was simply too dark in the courtyard.

He turned to Abdul, "Ah, Mister Abdul, when these Americans quit hiring you, you must come and join the Malagasy Army. We can always use a man of your stature to help us protect our noble and worthy Republic."

Abdul didn't like the Major, he edged backward while the Major spoke and slunk back toward the kitchen. It was rude, but Ab is Ab. Although his escape was obvious, it was blatantly ignored. I think the Major had expected as much, after all, he did kick the shit out of Abby's last boss.

I offered, on Abby's behalf, "Abby is a fine working man, Major. He's dynamite in the kitchen – one *hell* of a fine cook. Perhaps your army will get him, one day."

"Indeed. Armies do move on their stomachs."

Sophie excused herself, she had to go somewhere and laugh.

Suddenly, I found myself all alone with LaCruel, I asked, "I hear you can karate chop a sword in half with your bare hands, Major?"

He reached for his eye, "There was a time, Mister Morgan. My government has formally asked that I quit destroying their property, including their swords." He then went into a wry smile. Yeah, he enjoyed telling his little pinky quip.

I said, "I see." But I didn't, not really.

I walked him to his car. "Come back anytime, Major. It was nice to have met you."

"Yes, indeed." He reached for his eye and began his nervous pre-occupation. He had kept his hand on face until he was out of sight.

I have never been intimidated by authority figures. But this man, LaCruel, was something else. He had a dark sinister element about him that made me feel terribly uncomfortable. I didn't like him. However, the man did save my life.

I went in search of Sophie. I wanted to hear all about her visit with LaCruel. I wondered if he had taught her the art of breaking swords with one's bare hands. Ha, as if she wasn't deadly enough already, eh?

Chapter Twenty-Nine

Sophie was leaving the bunkhouse wearing a fat white mono-grammed bathrobe (stolen) from the Hilton. Over that, was her ever-present .38, snuggled and snapped down in its tan leather shoulder holster. On her feet was a pair of unlaced L.L. Bean designer hiking boots.

"Cute outfit, Soph." I had to ask, "Got a date with a moon shiner?"

She smiled, then did a model's spin, saying, "It's Fredericks' of Detroit. You like?"

There was no denying – on her, it looked good. If she were to throw on an oily tarpaulin, slick down her hair with a jar of grape jelly, and not brush her teeth for a week, she'd still look better than most girlie-magazine centerfolds.

Obviously, she was heading for my freshly painted showers. I offered, "I'll walk over with you, Soph. I need to check out the plumbing." To which I received a very queer look, I was caught up in a fax pas, a bit of CIA argot. Around Chicago, it would be deemed an innuendo. What Sophie had thought, was that I had wanted to check out her own individual plumbing... well, back to the adventure.

I offered her my arm and she accepted. How often can you find an escort service "serving" that late at night, eh? I left her at the ladies door and did a quality control Engineer's inspection of the external water pipes. This was good material for my daily report back to Eunice. I walked the PVC pipe down to the creek. Not feeling any squishy spots I professionally concluded that we had no leaks.

When I returned, Soph had already entered the shower. I yelled through the walls, "Hey Kidd, need a back scrubber?"

"What do you have, Jimbo, a Brillo pad?"

"Very funny, Soph. By the way, watch out for snakes when you go to get dressed. I hear that this island is full of them." I lied, Madagascar is a virtually snake free island.

Soph, it seemed, had done her homework on the reptile popu-lation. She shouted back, "The only snakes around here are you men, Mister Morgan."

I couldn't tell if she was being humorous or serious. So I gave it up. I went back to the bunkhouse and got a towel. It was as good a time as any to test out the men's side and see how long it would take to run out a sixty-gallon hot water heater. And at that moment, I hoped that it would take a long, long time.

Soph was still showering, women's side, when I entered the steaming water on the men's side. "Is that you, Jim?"

"Yeah. Isn't this great?"

Then she yells out, "Damn, I'm running out of hot water." Then, in a serious plea, "Jim?"

"Yes?"

"Can I come over on your side and finish, with you? I still have soap in my hair."

"No."

"Why not?"

"Because."

There was a brief pause before she answered, with laughter in her voice, she yelled out, "You're an asshole, James Morgan."

"Okay, you can come over. But you have to wash my back."

We used up the sixty gallons in about thirty minutes, along with a lot of soap, and a whole lot of physical energy. Clean, we dressed, and then took a cool stroll back into the real world.

Abby was watching TV as we passed the kitchen. He was eating a ham sandwich. We called in to him from the door, like a caring mother and father, "Goodnight Abby." To which he acknowledged with a huge arm wave, announcing that all was well in his culinary domain.

I asked Soph what she thought of LaCruel as we entered into the bunkhouse, she said, "Oh, he's interesting...predictable, too. If it weren't for his eye, I'd consider him quite handsome."

Soph's radio was set out on the makeshift desk. She moved to it and began packing it away, while saying, "Want to hear the latest on Margolova?"

"Yeah. When did you call in?"

"While you were pulling LaCruel's chain."

Sitting on my bunk, I said, "You're so perceptive, Soph." I reached under the bed and withdrew an unopened fifth of J&B and made a silent offer of sharing it with her. She made a sour face and shook her head in the negative. I replaced the bottle *unopened* back into the case and lit a cigarette. Soph took off her holster and set it on the table in front of her. I thought she was going to clean it. Instead, she kicked her long legs up on the card table and started into a narration of her call to Langley.

"No one has seen Margolova since she entered the Turk's villa. She's supposed to be under constant surveillance by LaCruel, but... he was here tonight and not at the Turk's. So, our intelligence on her appears to be suspect."

I propped myself up on some pillows and listened, intently.

"Well, that's the good news, Jim. The bad news is, she has more company now. Three of her old associates, expatriated Russian bad boys, have legally entered Madagascar since this morning. They're all holed up at the Turk's.

I learned this from LaCruel – *not*, from Langley."

Sophie was pleased with herself, pleased that she got something from LaCruel. And I asked her how she got LaCruel to talk to her about Margolova.

"Men like talking to pretty girls, Jim. I simply asked him if he was doing anything dangerous. He couldn't resist telling me all about the evil terrorist, Margolova, that he was assigned to watch. He hinted at the possible assassination of the president. He never came right out and said it, but it was a definite insinuation. I didn't pump him as he was talking quite freely. He said that his wife isn't interested in his work."

"Yeah? Ever hear that line before, Soph?"

Soph smiled, "Not since I got to Madagascar." She stared off into space a moment, probably contemplating where she had heard that line before, then continued, "Actually, I wanted to talk to him about Margolova, I wanted someone to listen to me, too. But my keen training kept me from blabbering. One learns more by listening, than by talking."

Sophie's story about LaCruel telling her about his secrets made me feel a lot better about myself, in the way that I blabbered on and on to Soph and Bess at the Washington Monument. It now lumped me into the livable category of being a human being. And, at the time, I didn't even *know* that I had anything to hide. But LaCruel, you macho son-of-a-gun... At least I was only telling stuff to my own domestic spies. While you, master of the cloak and dagger, you, go off telling foreign agents all your top secrets just because you're little wife-e-poo isn't interested in your little ol' Peeping Thomas work.

Oh, for shame, for shame.

And I seriously thought, "The next time I'm talking to a cute girl, I'm going to keep my conversations on the topic of poetry or stamp collecting and let the chips fall where they will."

I said, "You know... you really *are* a good spy, Soph."

Arrogantly she replied, "I know. That's why I'm here." She batted her long eyelashes confirming her cuteness, and her professionalism.

"He also told me of another expedition that's going on down at the Channel. There's a group of English scientists there who are studying Pimakeel Bay and its estuary. He said that they might come up this way because Travelle Creek is the fresh water feed down to the bay."

"Well, I hope they're not ecologists. Our drainage up here isn't exactly state of the art."

Sophie shrugged her shoulders. Either she didn't know or simply didn't care. She asked, "Do you think our group of scientists will want to visit them?"

"I don't know. If they do, I'm supposed to go out of my way to please them. If they want to go down there I'll arrange it. Yeah, it might be fun to go down to the beach. Besides, it *is* my job to keep them happy.

Soph interjected, "Oh, I almost forgot. The boss is going to send me the MAV-861." She was excited about this. I was dumbfounded and immediately apprehensive. Now I'd have to worry about this kid driving a dirt bike off some hidden cliff, or worse.

Teasing, I asked, "What's a MAV-861, a bazooka?"

"No silly, it's a trail bike. Remember?"

"Oh great. D. Deadly Kidd gets a scooter. Wait until daddy hears about this one. There'll be all kinds of new safety laws proposed on the hill. All aimed at little girl scooter riders on tour in third world countries."

She ignored me completely. She continued, "Since there is only one road into Shell Camp, I suggested that we have one here... as a lifeboat. If the road gets blocked we could ride out down the creek. It also gives us an in-the-field test opportunity by a woman, me."

"When does *that* get here?"

"Nine A.M., tomorrow. It's coming in by special courier, a U.S. Air Force Lear jet. We can pick it up on Monday morning before we get the scientists. That is, if it's okay with you? I mean... I'm supposed to ask you... if you'd mind? First."

I think I was being had. It sounded as if her getting her trail bike was dependant upon my approval. I didn't question her on this, I simply said, "Yeah, we can pick it up. We'll leave a little early. Say, three in the morning – no problem."

Soph, elated, snuggled into my cot. She listened to me prattle on about the generators and the food supplies. Then, we decided to take a holiday. We would drive down to the coast, go swimming, have a picnic, and, if we had time, we'd visit the English expedition. It was a great and spontaneous idea, a lark. We agreed to leave early next morning at eight a.m., sharp.

I fell asleep with Sophie curled up against my chest. It was very pleasant. Confining, but very pleasant.

And I dreamt a very weird dream.

I was in a very dank place. Wispy swirls of steam spiraled around old green pig iron lampposts. The street, a red inlaid brick street, was wet from recent drizzle. I thought it was a San Francisco street, and then I thought that it was a Detroit street with a dense fog blowing in from the east, off Lake Saint Clair.

It was dark. There were hollow doorways all along the sidewalks that vanished into the mist. There was movement. Phantoms flashed out from the corners of my eyes making me turn quickly to see them, to catch them slithering, dancing in and out of the varied gray and blackened shadows.

And then I thought, "No." It was the Hudson River. But no, it was the Potomac River and I was on a brick path to Eunice's Tudor. The tennis courts had moved. They were now in front of the house, hung with moss, and a grayish smoke was streaking up through and around everything obscuring all detail, all color.

And I became ebullient, excited, because the Austin, my own little 3000 was there in the grass, purring. No, not purring – *growling*. It was an angry growl. I moved to the painful revving and saw, rusted chrome highlights and a garish sea moss dripping off its rounded, finely molded fenders like a drab holiday garland. And the windows, what? What was that on them? It looked like wet glue or a petroleum jelly. I tried to get closer. I was forcing my legs onward but they didn't move. Then, I was moving backward away from the Austin and I had no control over my movements. I was a metal being pulled by a loadstar and to where I didn't know. And the lights, the amber parking lights of the Austin, began a fade and then died, extinguished and out of view. And I turned. My entire body was floating uncontrollably toward the patio doors of the Tudor. I was off the ground, levitated by – I didn't know what. But I did know this, it was very... *very* scary.

I braced myself in preparation of smashing into and through the glass panes, but the doors burst open just in time for my flying entry. The doors functioned like a mouth. As they opened I was literally sucked in. Then dropped in a heap. I rolled once in a slow motion head-over-heels tumble and then came to an abrupt stop with one big bounce that left me sitting upright right in the room's darkened center. A bolt of lightning, a sustained flash, lit the interior with a powerful explosion of white molten light forcing me to cringe in an even deeper fear than that which had already set my soul to trembling. I was like a Jell-o mold shaking in the after-shocks of a major Los Angeles earthquake. I jumped to my feet, looked around. More lightning. Crisp, reverberating thunder pounded my ears. The Tudor's tiled floor vibrated in a sick harmony to the accompanying din.

I called out for Eunice. My voice was tiny and weak and it lacked of resonance and volume, my screams were innately stifled. I shouted again but only a hoarse whisper left my throat. Yet, I continued to call out. And once again the magnetic force grappled with my being compelling me to move against my will, against my very survival instincts. I fought the pull with gritted teeth, but forward and forward I glided under the ethereal, mystic, ectoplasmatic energy that had now buoyed my being hurriedly into the foyer, where, swathed in a lime-green glow-in-the-dark focused circle of pulsating light was, Eunice – *hanging*.

Her bare feet were a good ten inches off the ground. The hangman's noose around her neck extended upward toward the ceiling, but I couldn't see to where or to what it was attached to, it just went up, to nowhere. Then I could see that her hands and feet were strung with fine wire, marionette wires, and puppet lines. The fine threads were barely visible. Visually I traced them up to the balcony where I could see that they were attached to a crossed set of huge sticks, a puppeteer's hand control. The control was being held by a hooded, faceless figure – the Grim Reaper. It was death, personified. Our eyes met. His were a dull red glow. And mine? Mine had opened wider than a pair of forged iron manhole covers.

I broke off our stare to look at Eunice. Her head lay limp on her shoulder. Her mouth was taped shut with a wide strip of white medical tape. And her eyes, they were closed tight, into flat slits. She was motionless and didn't look well, and I thought, "She's dead."

She was wrapped in a big blue ribbon. It was a bungled job. One breast was exposed around the nipple. I reached out to cover it by pulling down on a piece of the blue silky cloth. It began to unravel, more. I pulled my hand back in the realization that I was screwing things up more than they already were. She looked – so pathetic. I reached for the tape across her mouth and pulled it off. It didn't come off easy. It made a ripping sound and I feared that her flesh was going to come off. But it didn't. Her lips were cracked under the tape and showed dark purple creases, like stitching, vertically across the length of her entire mouth. I tried to replace the tape in order to cover up the exposed, *yuk*. But the tape wouldn't re-stick.

Then, like a jack-in-the-box, her head shoots upright and her eyes opened. They begin blinking rapidly, then stayed open, wide. They started to look around in quick glances. Right then left like a robot's eyes gone berserk, back and forth, back and forth. And then, they lock onto mine. Sad eyes. Pleading eyes. And she stared right through me, right into my very soul. I tried to turn my head but couldn't. I tried closing my eyes – I couldn't. I was compelled to stare at her. I had no choice, no alternative. Her cracked lips parted ever so slightly, her brow furrowed and she emitted a chilling sound that sounded like, "Herrrtz."

Tears formed, oozing from the corner of her milky eyes. They narrowed, as if to plead, to beg, then, that eerie sound again, a groan, "Errrrtz."

I asked, "What? What is it, Eun? What is it that you're trying to say, Babe?" Her eyes became even more focused. It was upsetting me, I said, "I can't understand you, Eun. Are you all right? What?"

The controlling force propelled me closer to her. I was now within an inch of her totally exposed breast. The ribbon had unraveled and was hanging down beyond her toes twisting down onto the cold inlaid marble tiles. She began to sway and her breast brushed soft against my face. I couldn't move, I couldn't back away, I couldn't even look up at her face or down at her legs. She swayed out, away, a good six – seven inches, then slammed back into my face, her flesh felt cold as it plowed into me, cold, like an ice water filled balloon.

Death began to laugh, a slow giggle, a sadistic, tee-he-he. Her body swung out again, two feet – three. Then it came back rapid, slapping me hard, hurting me. I couldn't escape. She flew out again, further – eight feet. Her eyes kept clicking back and forth. And they would occasionally fixate on me. Then, back to the oscillating, back and forth, tapping in their socket's at the extreme. Then, she flies back at me again, even harder than before. And smack. My lip splits, and warm blood runs down my chin. My nose was broken. I was dizzy. I felt the onset of a blackout. I fought it off by sharply shaking my head.

Out of desperation, I asked, "Eun? Are you mad at me?"

"Fa-whooop!" She slammed me again.

"Is it because of the daily reports, Eun? What?"

"Fa-whooop!" Another slam, she was really banging up her teats, my face was splitting open, and "my" blood was splattering everywhere.

"Oh!" I challenged. "You're angry about my little fling with the Senator's daughter aren't you?"

Her now grotesque torso stilled before me, a pallid, ghastly lump just hanging idle. Her right arm lifted determinedly by the thin marionette strings into a horizontal position and then made a slow move backward into a cocked and ready position. Ready, to unleash a roundhouse of limp flesh directly at my head. I tensed in preparation of a well-telegraphed onslaught. And it came, fast. I was totally helpless as her limp limb raced forcefully in at my grimaced face. I felt like I had been hit with a sopping wet mop. Eun's bloodied hand, stained by my own oozing wounds, lowered calmly to her side. Her entire body went motionless, completely idle.

A husky voice, not Eunice's, emanated from her closed mouth. It was the Reaper's voice, he was a ventriloquist throwing down words into her aura making it seem like it was Eunice who was doing the speaking, "You're damned right it's your little fling with that Alberquist bitch. What did you think it was? The way you change light bulbs?"

In an effort to sound chastising, I said, "This isn't a good time for making jokes, Eunice."

Death called down again sounding much more like Eunice this time. But, it was Death who spoke, "I really loved you, JIMMMM BO – ho-ho."

The Eunice puppet collapsed. The wires went slack and the hand controller slammed down on top of her lumped and lifeless form with a heavy thud. I heard myself say, "Wow, you're really taking this hard, Eun." But it was just a ventriloquist's trick.

The walls began to heave and creak as if they were alive. I looked for Death. He was on the balcony, laughing. I watched him float backward receding into a darkened room, his red-glowing eyes disappeared behind a violent slam of Eunice's hand carved, highly polished, bedroom door.

Everything went black. The nightmare was over. I tried to wake up. But I couldn't. I hated the total blackness. I wanted light, color – life. The blackness continued. I was walking in it. Yet, I couldn't feel the ground. I couldn't even see my own hands. A long time passed. Then I saw it, a tiny wisp of smoke. It was a small glimmer of hope, vague and elusive. I reached out to it in a vain hope to grasp it and hold it with my hand. No use...

It was all too frail, too fleeting. It was life. And it was not to be had, not meant to be grasped or held or to be controlled by the mere flesh of a mortal. And I called out to my god. But, before the word fully formed in my mind, a tiny dot, a wee point of silver light showed up before me, and it began to grow. Larger and larger, the dot became a small circle and the circle as it grew, grew fins, and soon – all too soon, I discerned that the circle wasn't a circle at all, it was a bomb, a bomb dropped from a B-25 bomber and it was headed right at me, right at my head. And I yelled out in panic – *screamed* out at the top of my lungs, "F u c k."

• • •

And there was Sophie – on top of me. "Wake up, Jim! Wake up."

"Soph?" I blinked quickly. I wanted to know for sure that I was awake. "That bomb was really close, Soph."

She was on top of me, naked from the waist up. I looked at her firm youthful breast only inches from my face. *She* was real. She bounced the bed and her breast bounced in unison with my head. I flashed back to my dream and saw the bomb. I forced my head up into the softness of her nudity and with a muffled plea asked her,

"Where's the coffee, Kidd?"

She says, "It's eight o'clock. I thought we were going to the beach? Wouldn't you rather have lemonade?"

My muffled reply, "Coffee now, lemonade later."

She says, "Ha. Who do you think I am, your secretary?"

Still in a muffle, I declared, "No. . . . Concubine!"

Chapter-Thirty

The drive to Pimakeel Bay took us all of four hours. It was a hot, sweltering, trip in the un-air-conditioned station wagon. But not at first, the higher elevations were actually cool and the first hour, an hour of twists and turns, was quite pleasant. It was fun. Until we hit the arid plains, the semi-desert, the rocky outcrops of massive boulders and sparse vegetation. That's when it got hot, ninety or even hotter.

As we pulled into Pimakeel Bay our shirts were soaked through with sweat. Soph's head was nodding, bouncing methodically to the bumpy, rutted dirt road. It was an in and out dozing that would leave her oblivious to the lush coastal scenery that quickly surrounded us. And then I saw the first thatched roof way off the road nested in a clump of tall island palms, then a second, then a whole bunch of them – all the same, yet individual and distinctive, like fingerprints. Soph sat up straight and tall, instinctively alert upon our arrival. Perhaps my gentle poke to her arm had something to do with her instant alertness, but then again, maybe no, as our CIA is infamous for cultivating such alacrity. I was told this by a high-up official who has since demanded anonymity – an undisclosed source (if you will).

The temperature dropped significantly as we entered deeper into the village. We had run into the afternoon sea breeze, a daily ritual along the channel that was a most welcomed relief from the exhausting heat that we had just experienced. I saw a topless native scurry into a doorless hut. A large dog, a huge Malagasy mongrel raced out from under an adjoining hut, it ran directly at us lunging right up to my opened window barking, growling out in a savage, "You don't belong here," notification.

I braked while rolling up the window. Soph was thrown up against the dashboard and we skidded a little, sideways.

"Jesus Christ, Jim. You're going to kill somebody. I knew I should have driven."

A native kid, about seven, came out of nowhere carrying a long stick. He ran up to the dog and starts beating it, yelling, "Get down, Spike, get out of here."

The blows were vicious, the kid demanded absolute surrender, and got it. Spike ran off with his tail stuck between his hind legs in a yelping whimper. The kid ran after it shouting something like, "Bitch." A misnomer for a dog tagged and titled, Spike, but maybe not?

I eased the Ford back into the grassy wheel ruts. Apparently the villagers didn't own cars, or – I really *had* gotten us lost. On a clothesline I spotted a distinctive "Hard Rock Cafe" T-shirt. It was a dead giveaway as to where this backward culture was heading. I pointed it out to Sophie, "Ready to do some jammin', Dude?" Soph pointed out a TV antenna. I did a quick look for power lines but didn't see any. Alongside one of the huts I saw an outboard motor. I didn't see any boats – not until we went up a small rise and saw the bay. It was a genuine breathtaking view. The water was a bright aqua-green, very similar to the way water appears above the coral reefs in and around the Hawaiian Islands, and very beautiful. A short pier stuck out into the bay. A fishing trawler, the only true sign of modernization, was tied up neatly to the rickety, should have been condemned, moorage. There was several hand made dugout canoes resting along the bank, but no sign of life.

We drove cautiously down the rise and past the trawler, which was flying a British flag. It was a good thirty-five, maybe forty foot long. Up close, it was much older than it had looked to be from up on the knoll a minute earlier. It looked more like a Gulf Coast shrimp boat – like the ones around Galveston, Texas, or one of the salmon boats of the Pacific Northwest. Seattle. Portland...

The boat was named, in bold black letters, "Gretta." In red paint, in small letters, someone had added a prefix, "re," making her the "re-Gretta," – ominous – to say the least. Boats have always fascinated me as their designs are almost always functional; however, I'm a sailor by nature and used to be quick mouthed to say, "If a boat doesn't have a sail – it's not a real boat." (I have subsequently purchased a twin diesel Chris Craft cabin cruiser. It's a blast to buzz my old sailing pals. It scares the hell out of them... err...back to the adventure.)

We parked just past the "re-Gretta" and walked to the water's edge. The water looked deep. We could see bottom but it sloped out and disappeared quickly. Some good size fish were swimming a short ten feet out. Soph asked if I brought my fishing pole. I told her, "You don't need one here, Soph. You just dive in grab what you want then go about your business."

I had this compelling urge to grab Sophie and toss her off the bank. And I would have. But she was saved by a thin, demanding voice, a heavily accented voice that had called out, "Hello there, mates."

We looked toward the English greeting. Bounding down from the clumped palms we saw a short, bearded, barefoot, hair tousled, khaki shorted, shirtless, shell necklace wearing castaway waving at us. He was old – late fifties, maybe sixty, deeply tanned and very muscular – in the way that old people get when they loose weight in their advancing years. He was smiling, showing some very white teeth – they were *too* white, they had to be plastic. And, as he neared, I saw that his necklace was made of small shark's teeth, not puka shells like I had first thought. Everything about him was clean, white teeth, white hair, white beard and white shark's teeth. He had on a huge diver's watch – probably capable of AM and FM radio reception – which was also white. He looked, retired.

At ten feet away he extended his hand out toward Sophie, saying, "I'm Doctor Maroo. Not of the H.G. Well's variety. Eh?"

His smile was warm and seductive, he continued, "Doctor of Estuary Biology, actually."

He took Sophie's hand and grasped it firmly then cupped it with his other hand, holding on to her, *too* long. He was eyeing her from top to bottom, as if she were a biology specimen or soon to become one.

He looked at me and gave me a simple nod. To Sophie he says, with a note of incredulity, and hints of I hope *not*, "Is this fellow your bloke, Miss?"

Sophie introduced me. The professor gave me a nano-second hand touch, in the way that one would touch a hot stove, then returned to surveying Sophie's body. I think his mouth was drooling as he grabbed Soph's hand and insisted that we join him for tea, at *his* laboratory, "Come, come. I insist." It was all quite sickening.

We had found the English expedition that was comprised of six biologists, three men and three women. Doctor Maroo was the leader, guru, field rebel, and catalyst for scientific inquiry. He was also making an open and determined play for Sophie's charms.

We sat down to a nasty English tea (Abdul's ham sandwiches, the one's that were in a cooler out in the wagon would have tasted much, much better than the dried out crumpets and moldy old seaweed marmalade that the castaway Maroo had proudly claimed, "...made them myself, this very morning."). Which, upon serious reflection would have tasted okay if anyone other than Maroo had made it. I tried to like the man, but I simply couldn't. Sophie was sucking up his shit like a hog lost in an apple patch. I had to excuse myself. I left the table and went outside for a taste of fresh air. Lust, I mean "love," can be a real bitch. I was battling my first bout with jealousy, a new emotion, and I didn't like it, no sir, not at all. It stunk. I picked up a stone and threw it toward the bay – it didn't make it. I watched it kick up a puff of Malagasy dust then roll to a stop several yards short of the inviting water. I went back inside to join the scientific circle jerk.

In the name of social niceness I made some small talk, asking if their expedition members had to pay their own way like our own scientists. Of course, Doctor Maroo elected himself group spokesperson, "Oh, save the queen, Mister Moonygan."

I didn't correct him and I'm very sure that it spoiled his obnoxious fun.

"Our universities support us, completely." His voice had trailed off, no doubt in recall of some covert funding similar to our own CIA's silent backing. The funding subject was quickly changed.

We discussed swimming spots along the coast, picnic spots, and nearby scenic locations. Maroo insisted that the only safe place to swim, within fifty miles, was right there at Pimakeel Bay. It was a conclusion after a twenty-minute dissertation on shark and eel attacks that he had personally gathered from the natives who fished up and down the Mozambique Channel. "The Bay has neither shark, nor eel...safer than one's own private swimming pool." ...Is what he said.

And as he rattled on and on, I thought, "If he swims there? Then there's at least one shark to beware of – a Maroo shark."

Sophie got Maroo to show her their radio setup. Like us, they had access to satellite communications. They exchanged frequencies and I heard Sophie request that he call her sometime – to chat.

Maroo asked if I'd look at a faulty air pump for him. I did. It took me two minutes to repair it. He then went on and on about how great I was for repairing the pump. He went so far as to gather his entire expedition for a diplomatic proclamation, "We shall not go forth on expedition "ever again" without a Field Engineer being in attendance." As he popped the cork on a cheap bottle of champagne, I noticed that he was the only one to drink. The other biologists, all five of them, had already gotten Maroo's number. He was Doctor Baloney – and he simply had no bun.

Somehow, suddenly, we were outside the lab. Doctor Maroo had a monocle squeezed into his eye and was pointing to the bay, saying, "There. Just by your motor. The best swimming spot in all of Madagascar." He smiled flirtatiously then lowered his voice to a nasty whisper.

"Needn't bother with swimming apparel. We've all gone native here." He turned and moved toward the lab door. Over his shoulder he continued, almost in a giggle, "Have fun children. We'll join you very, very shortly."

Soph was moving toward the car removing her clothes. She called out to me, "Come on, Jim. Last one in is a rotten egg." It was a classic display of youth and reckless abandon. Soph was naked by the time she reached the Ford. She tossed her bundled clothes on the car's hood (Maroo called it a bonnet, later, while he inspected Sophie's underwear), then, in a jiggled dance, she tiptoed to the edge of Pimakeel Bay, grabbed her nose, and leapt into the seventy-eight degree water. Just before hitting the surface I heard her yell out, "Cheerio Jimbo."

I sauntered over to the car, opened the tailgate, and took off my clothes, methodically, reluctantly. It felt strange to stand out in the open air naked, but it was also fun. It felt good. I sauntered to the bank and jumped in – shedding innate inhibitions all the way to the bay's warm and rocky bottom. When I surfaced I watched all six biologists come leaping into the bay, it was not pandemonium, it was laughter and joyful freedom, childlike shouts and pure unadulterated fun. These pseudo-natives, these scientific children, *knew* how to enjoy their paradise.

My personal sense of propriety was for evermore shattered. Yet, I still have a problem with mass nudity. I swam away from the group to further adjust my American attitude. I needed to put things into a workable perspective. It was a psychologically difficult moment for me personally. I treaded water watching the playful group from a distance. It was a simple case of situational ethics, the social norm was established, it was put to a democratic vote and the people's voice was heard. So – etched in stone – island law was enacted, swimsuits were taboo. My psychological world was in a mild upheaval. I penned an imaginary letter home:

Dear Mom and Dad,

Hi. I've landed in paradise. Early this week I had my first encounter with loneliness. I didn't like it. It was very discomforting. I was sitting on this runway and I had no one to talk with.

And now – I've fallen in love. At least I think I have, but I'm not sure.

Yesterday I learned intimidation by this guy who rubbed his eye until it bled. And…well…I've never been intimidated before. I hated that feeling.

And now, today, I'm experiencing severe bouts of jealousy. And these really, really suck.

Right now, I'm in swimming with a group of *naked* scientists. The Chicago school system didn't prepare me for this. Purdue may have tried, but – I was probably goofing off that semester. I think I should have attended more toga parties. What should I do?

Love, Your Confused Son, Jimbo…

I swam back toward the intellectual nudists who had put Sophie under their biological microscope – the monocle eye of Doctor Maroo. On my way in, I was met by Tina a tall, dark haired lass from Devon, England. As she swam toward me, she said, "I simply must chat with you, Mister Morgan." She stopped a few inches in front of me. Her eyes were shamrock green, sparkling, vivacious, and danced with scientific curiosity. She took a deep gulp of air and submerged herself. She grabbed my hips with both hands. A second, or two, later she let go and surfaced. Treading water with her feet she pulled back her black youthful hair and flashed me the emerald green of her beautifully sparkling eyes.

Then, with laughter in her voice, said, "You don't appear to be any larger than the average Englishman, Mister Morgan."

This pissed me off. I said, "Yeah? Well, I think you're mistaken,

Sweetheart. You'd better take a closer look."

Her eyes danced in a seductive playfulness. She submerged again, grasping my manhood in a biological comparison study. After a whole minute she released me from her extracurricular study. She popped out of the water and joyfully expressed, "You've got a yellow butterfly imprinted on your thigh, Mister Morgan." She turned and swam back to the others.

I followed in a slow dog paddle. Tina was cute, not Sophie cute. But intellectually cute, and her eyes – oh how they dazzled. I was touched, literally. Yeah, I was in love again, or was it more lust? Tina had made a profound impact on my confused psyche, and of that – I was very sure.

Sophie broke away from the herd (or should I say pod?) and swam out to me. We were fifteen yards from the school of scientists. She grabbed me low, playfully. I had a slight erection – from Tina's biological inspection. Soph cocked her head, "What's *this* all about, Jimbo?"

I said, "It's from the warm water. And quit calling me, Jimbo."

"So, the brunette's name is Warm Water, huh?" Soph was hotter than the water.

"I sure didn't hear you making any formal protests over Mister Monocle trying to make you float while under the guidance of his grimy little test tube hands, Miss, Nudist of the Month."

It was a verbal epee. I had thrust the blunt blade deeply into Sophie's naked chest, and then twisted the gilded handle to its full hilt.

"Everyone's naked, Jim! And besides – they're all biologists, you're acting like you've never seen a naked body before." She was trying to placate me but I wasn't buying.

I swam around her and up to Tina from Devon, England. Sophie remained behind treading in her own shallow thoughts – watching me.

"Can I try floating you, Tina?"

"I'm quite sure that you, can, Mister Morgan. The proper way to ask is *may* I float you?"

"Oh. Yeah. May I try my hand at floating you, Tina?"

"Yes, you *may* try, Mister Morgan." And her green eyes and smile were saying that I could try much, much more than just floating her.

With a British rump in one hand and a Devon back in the other,

I did my level best to float the tall, tanned brunette biologist named, Tina. And as I did so, Sophie swam slowly past our act ignoring the intense effort I took to make my point. Her swim was wave-less and passive – a silent crawl of feminine resignation.

All three Englishmen, the men, followed Sophie out of the bay. To their surprise, and to mine – she picked up her clothes and went into the wagon, closed the door, and dressed. Monocle and his fellow blokes were rebuffed. Comically, they stood in front of the Ford shrugging at each other in their nakedness. They didn't know it, but their game was over. The next thing that I saw, from the corner of my eye, was three white English butts beating a lonely path back up to the sanctuary of their field bio-lab.

To say the least, I still had my hands full. Tina is a very pretty, young woman. I guessed her to be in her early twenties. Tina has the smallest, darkest nipples that I have ever seen on any woman. Although, she is not well endowed with a healthy set of knockers, she is not what one would consider being flat-chested, either. Her belly is firm and taut, indicative that she worked-out, often. And, I couldn't help but notice that her hair color was natural and consistent from head to toe.

In comparison to Sophie…well, there was none. These two women were as physically different as gold is to silver; they were both just as precious and desirable. But Soph, well, she was, – by far, the bird in hand. And then I recalled the whole proverb, "A bird in hand is worth two in the bush." I looked down at my hands but I couldn't see them, they were both full of Tina.

I looked onshore for Sophie. She had dressed and I saw her walking toward a clump of bushes.

I let Tina down while I mentally penned a P.S., to my earlier imaginary letter home:

P.S. "Dear Mom: I really *am* in love – with a "CIA" agent."

Then (My readers may not believe this – but it's true.), and I'll swear to this on a whole stack of Bibles, Tina says, as her feet hit bottom of Pimakeel Bay, "I say, Mister Morgan…a bird in hand?"

I let go of the firm little buttocks from Devon and grabbed her gently by the waist until she settled into the soft sand. Tina gave me a warm and knowing smile, one that said – "I tried." Then says, ruthlessly "I'd have been worth your effort, Mister Morgan."

"No doubt, Tina." I looked away, deliberately looking for Sophie. "Perhaps another day. The pleasure would certainly be all mine."

Tina's friends, both within earshot of our talk, acknowledged Tina's jilt with a tandem set of "Ooooooos" accompanied by the two nastiest leers that I had ever experienced. One would think that I had just knifed their best friend, or something. I released Tina's hips and waded into shore. I never looked back. Sometimes, a man's got to do what a man's got to do.

Tina did call out, "I think the pleasure might have been mutual, Mister Morgan." To which her biological friends deeply chanted a "whooha" and low catcall whistle. Believe me! It crossed my mind that I was making a big mistake.

I dressed without drying, Soph had returned to the station wagon and was slunk down in the passenger's seat, her head was down and she was ready to leave. I knew this because she was holding the keys out for me to take them and get going. If she was conveying some other message, well – I totally missed it.

Chapter Thirty-One

We pulled out slow, the Ford bounced and swayed as it climbed up the grassy knoll and returned to the wheel ruts that ran twenty odd miles back to the paved roadway. Pimakeel Bay and its backward village were a good seventy miles behind us when I made a feeble attempt at conversation with my, Deadly, companion. But, it was not to be. I was getting the cold shoulder. My lovely was upset, or too tired to converse.

We flew past a kilometer marker doing ninety. I converted it to miles and figured that we had gone 150 miles. I made another feeble attempt at conversation, "I had a nice time today, Soph. How about you?"

"Oh! You had a good time." There was a negative edge in her voice, a sardonic edge, her words were cutting, and they were said with the sharpness of a rusted gardening hoe.

I answered, "Yeah, I think I could get into that Biology shit. It could be a lot of fun. Don't you think?"

She answered, "What you really mean is that Tina Johnson looked like a lot of fun. Right?" Her hoe ripped into my jugular.

Being pragmatic, I opted on silence. There is no safe way to answer such a question. If I said, "No." I'd become an accused liar. If I said, "Yeah Baby, I sure would like to boink that little piece of British fluff-butt. Yes sir-reee-bob, Baby." Well, I'm sure you get the drift.

I kept my eyes on the road. In the windshield I had a vision of Tina's pear-sized breasts bobbing on the surface of Pimakeel Bay as I held her, floated her. But, my image was shattered, quite abruptly, as Sophie insisted, "Right?"

I didn't answer. She reached her thirty-eight and strapped it on her shoulder. I was thinking, "Shit, she's going to shoot me."

I offered, "I think I'm riding with the proverbial woman scorned. You do have the safety on, on that cannon of yours, don't you?"

She didn't answer. She just stared out the window watching the jagged alien landscape, content with the title of "A Woman Scorned."

Boulders, tumble weeds, scraggly palm stubs and an occasional jack-rabbit gave way to the deep green, wooded foot hills leading up to the Shell Camp turnoff. It was pitch dark by the time we hit the mountain switchbacks and were forced into a 20-30 MPH, up and down, side-to-side, intense bit of steering drudgery. Finally, we reached Shell Camp Road. We made the sharp left turn into our own little piece of island paradise and headed safely into a most welcomed sight, Shell Camp.

Abby was standing in the parking lot waving his arms. He had a serious look on his face. It was obvious that the poor guy had really missed us, or...I pulled up alongside of him and through the window, asked, "What's shakin', Pal?"

He squatted down, his head even with mine, "They're here, Boss."

"Who's here, Ab?"

"The people from America, Boss."

"Yeah? Where are they, Ab?"

"*They* are right here, Jimbo." Chortled, Eunice.

Chapter Thirty-Two

Sophie screamed, "Daddy!" As I shouted, "Eunice?" Indeed, visiting day had arrived at Shell Camp. Eunice and the honorable public servant (and parent), Senator Alberquist, had (on a whim?) just dropped in to surprise their respective globetrotting adventurers, us.

The last time that Eunice just dropped in on me was, indeed, a colossal surprise. At least, this time, I was wearing my pants. However, my surprise on this particular night was as genuine as it had been some two years earlier. My face reddened in the darkness. Of all people, the love of my life, Eunice and – slap my knee, Sophie's father.

I tried to say, "Oh my! What a pleasant surprise." But I couldn't. God had struck me dumb. My jaw muscles had failed, and I could only sit there with my mouth hanging open. Yeah, I had turned into one proverbial, biblical pillar of salt.

My mind raced frantically – had Sophie picked up her underwear? Had Eunice gone into and inspected our "love-nest," the bunkhouse? Had Abby compromised our intimate relationship? I was going ga ga – did I love Eunice? And my thoughts slammed to an abrupt halt with a mental "neon" flashing light in my head that read, "Damn."

Sophie bounded from the car and embraced her father. I could only stare at my love, my "beautiful" Eunice. The car was still running, idling, and the thought crossed my blown mind to throw the gear shifter into reverse and run away – all the way back to, Alaska. I grabbed the key and shut off the motor. I was unable to break my ogle on Eunice.

Eunice moved close to the car window, "Are you all right, Jim? You look like you've seen a ghost." She was seriously concerned. And, I'm sure, that I must have looked as ill, as I actually felt.

I managed to blurt out, "I'm dumbfounded, Eunice. How did you get here?"

"Taxi. It took forever, Jim. The map says sixty miles, but it took us almost three hours to get here. Aren't you glad to see me?"

"Well. Yeah! Sure. I'm just overwhelmed, Eun. It's a wonderful surprise." And I hoped with all my heart and soul that I sounded, at least somewhat, convincing.

Eunice was dressed in an all black-jean cowboy outfit that included a hat. I looked for boots and sure enough, she had on a pair of snakeskin, square toed, high heeled, Durango Debby shit-kickers. In place of a red bandanna, she had chose to wrap herself in a solid red silk scarf. It was tied very primly around her neck. It would have been a cute outfit on a Texas ranch for serving up a western barbecue, but – a bit too much for Shell Camp.

Eunice came yet closer to the window, "We flew in on the private plane with the scientists." She bent down placing her hands on the windowsill, smiling, happy, and then elaborated, "We have to leave at sunrise. I'm so glad that you came back, Jim. We were afraid you'd gone into Antananarivo to meet the expedition. How was your swim?"

"I take it then that you've met your new employee, Abdul?" To which I quickly added, "I hope he hasn't talked your head off. He's a real talkative kid – can't keep him quiet."

Eunice looked at Abdul and then back to me, "We've only been here an hour. I had to twist his arm to let us in. Then I had to beg him, literally, to tell us where you were."

"Ah – yeah, he's in charge...he, ah – wasn't supposed to let anyone in – Soph, ah."

Eunice cut me off. She had heard enough of my dribble. She opened the car door, saying, "Come on Jimbo, get out of the car and make us some decent coffee. Your man, Abdul, has been trying to poison us with a black molasses he swears is, quote, "The best coffee in all of Madagascar." Eun had tried to imitate Abdul, but she fell short by at least five octaves.

"Yeah, he makes a mean cup of java. You didn't drink it, did you?" I was out of the car, stretching, and had to openly yawn. The four-hour drive back had worn me out both physically and mentally.

"I need to stretch my legs, Eun. How about I give you the grand tour – jeezes, you're looking good, Babe. Give me a second and I'll have Sophie put on some real coffee."

Soph agreed. Then I button holed Abby, "Go clean up the bunkhouse for me, Pal. This woman is my boss and may want to inspect it. Make sure all of Miss Soph's things are on her own bed. Got it?"

Ab shook his head, he understood. He questioned, "That Miss North said that she is my boss, too, Boss. Is she my boss, Boss?"

I told him, "She's your biggest boss, Ab. She writes out your paycheck. But if she asks you to do anything check in with me first. I'm your doing the work boss. Okay?"

"Okay, Boss." Ab looked confused, it was obvious that he did not want to work for a woman, – especially for one who was wearing a spaghetti-western cowboy outfit. He skipped off toward the bunkhouse.

Soph and her father had entered the kitchen. I jogged after Eunice who was heading toward her $14,000 "disposable" bathroom. I didn't know if she received the bill, as yet, but I'd soon find out.

She was peeking inside when I caught up to her, and said, "This is one hell of an expensive bar of soap, Jim."

She had received the bill. I kidded her, "It's not that bad, Eun. Wait until you see what it cost for the swimming pool."

Eunice's face went slack, "What swimming pool?"

"Just kidding, Eun. Ah, how's things back at the ranch?"

She smiled, "Mureatha misses you terribly. She sends you her love. I think she's waxed that car of yours every day since you left. What were you doing, banging her behind my back?"

I couldn't help but smile, "Cute, Eun, I'm glad you can still make a joke after buying this." I pointed to the shit-house. She frowned and shook her head in a slow negative.

She said, "Speaking of humor, have you tried getting into Alberquist's pants yet?"

"No, *he's* way too old for me, Eun."

"You know damn well whom I'm talking about, Jimbo. And it damn well isn't her father."

"Well, I don't think she's pregnant – she's been raggin' all week, being a real bitch, too."

"What kind of sleeping arrangements do you have for us, Jimbo?" Eunice had that sultry look in her eye, and I knew right off that she wasn't talking about sleep. Her suggestion had thrown me into an emotional upheaval. I was sure that I had fallen in love with Sophie, but now, my allegiances were all screwed up. Eunice, my beautiful love, the Goddess of my passions was once again standing at my door and I couldn't choose. But I did know this, in my heart, "I genuinely loved them both." And it was ripping me apart that I wasn't an Arab or at least one part Mormon.

I pointed out to Eunice, despondently, "If you're going to catch a plane at sunrise you're going to be sleeping in the backseat of the car, Eun."

Eunice came close, hugging me as she whispered in my ear, "I didn't mean to sleep, Jimbo."

Man-o-man, she felt so soft, so cuddly, and she smelled like French heaven itself. We kissed, wet and greedy demanding each of the other – *this*, this was love. And I knew, right then and there that I wanted to spend the rest of my life with her, and her alone. No ifs, ands, or buts about it. She was magic and it was time – time to do it – right then, but not there. – No! No. *Not* where Sophie might catch us, no way.

Eunice reiterated, "I can *sleep* on the plane, Jimbo."

"Well." I offered, "I would love to show you my generator room. It's a bit noisy, but there is...an old...sofa."

Eunice grabbed my arm, ordering, "Lead the way, Cowboy."

We left Shell Camp at three o'clock on a star studded, chilly, mountain morning. Abby sat in the third seat facing the tailgate. Sophie and her father sat in the middle behind Eunice and myself. The tedious drive up to the airport was a tense venture, to say the very least.

Eunice insisted on a show of lover's intimacy. She sidled up close to me; so close that I had to keep checking the door lock to insure that the lock was locked. Irrespective of the social complications that I had created for myself – I still had no desire to fall out onto the isolated and badly rutted tarmac.

Sophie, newly turned master of the snide remark, prattled on and on as we raced up into the higher elevations, "Oh Daddy, isn't it cute to see an older couple sitting so close together?" And, "You're so lucky to have latched onto such a no-nonsense Engineer, Misses North."

To the latter, Eunice quipped, "Thank you dear, but its still miss I'm afraid. Mister Morgan here has some psychological hang up over institutionalizing himself into the holy bonds of matrimony."

Eunice began to laugh. I hadn't seen anything humorous in her remark and was forced to ask her what was so funny. "Oh, I was just thinking. When you get back to Washington I'm going to get you down on my couch and eliminate those wedlock fears of yours. And not through the art psychoanalysis either."

"Yeah, that is funny. It might even work." For that I received a sharp poke in the ribs.

Sophie interjected, "It sounds like a deep-seated case of blatant fear to me, a *fear* of responsibility. What do you think, Mister Morgan?"

I tried to avoid the issue by not responding. Eunice wouldn't let it go. She jumped on Sophie's twisted wit with a whole new interest, "I'd like to hear your answer on that one myself, James."

I was caught in the middle of a mental gangbang. I kept my mouth shut hoping that they would tire of their barrage and maybe even fall asleep.

Then the esteemed politico, Iowa statesman, oratorical philosopher, and manipulative friend, Senator Alberquist, came to my rescue. With a silver-tongued soliloquy that was meant to pacify the raging sea of feminine, double-teaming. "I dare say, Mister Morgan, you'll have ample time to exhibit your sense of responsibility once you tie those nuptial knots."

"Yeah." I said, "I was just going to say that, Senator."

Sophie wouldn't relent, "Just when do you think that will come about, Mister Morgan, the tying of those nuptial knots?"

Everything went silent. I could hear the gas gauge move, a pebble had lodged itself in the tire treads and was making a rapid tick, tick, tick, as everyone waited for my reply. I had to break the silence, I asked, "Any tax reform coming our way, Senator?"

The crusty old pol was enjoying his daughter's wit. He was also poised in wait to hear his daughter get an answer, he said, "Everything tends to favor the joint return these days, Jim."

Eunice piped in, "Let's see you weasel out of that one, Mister Subject Change Artist."

Sophie jumped in with, "America doesn't need tax reform. It needs men reform."

Eunice and Sophie, now turned ERA specialists, raised their fists in a vote for male reformation. To the elder, and wiser Alberquist, I said, "I think it's time for us to buy some aprons, Senator. Someone has to stay home and do the dishes, it may as well be us men, eh?"

The Senator hedged, "I'm forced to advocate the voice of my constituency, Mister Morgan. Personally, I abhor the domestic life. Were I to enter my wife's kitchen, I'd be chased out with the fat end of a broom, tarred, feathered and ran out of town, probably, clean out of Iowa, on a rail."

And so it went, mile after mile, jab, jab, ka-pow, jab, jab, ka-pow. Shadow boxers all punching verbal stabs to nowhere. Only because they were socially created phantoms to begin with. Sordid all. Yet, to them, they are so very real, too. Their illusions of masculine subservience and protectionism are all so unfounded. We still chase our women until they catch us. Will we ever wise up? Nah, it's too much fun. Right? And then our night passed into day.

I was the only one awake as we entered the Cargo Only entrance to the mile high airport. The security guard, a much older cop than Tanan's own Chief of Police, waved us through without looking up from his paperback novel. Under a pretty sunrise, I nudged Eun.

"Where to, beautiful?"

"There, that big one." She pointed to a huge 747. It was a red and white corporate monster labeled, "Toys Inc. USA."

Our farewells were made with a lot of interspersed yawns. As soon as they entered the door the stairs were rolled away and the fan-jets whined into life. Eunice waved from a window once, and then pulled down the portal's shade. Our visit was now over and we were "dismissed."

As the "Big One" rolled off for its takeoff, we drove back to the cargo ramps where we were to pick up Sophie's scooter. Soph asked if I was tired. I responded, "No." And added, "I'm exhausted." This exhaustion wasn't solely from my lack of sleep. I felt more exhausted from just having Eunice around than anything else.

It took us twenty minutes to find someone who could authorize the release of Soph's MAV-861. It came in a wooden crate, a badly damaged crate. The forklift driver said, "Its the way it came. If you want to make a stink about it, see the boss. If not, sign these."

He then handed Sophie a huge stack of forms, and she began signing. I would have personally opened the crate and inspected the bike before signing anything, but life goes on.

In French, the forklift driver said, "Doctus cum libro." Which means something on the order of, "You're a book smart jerk.

Sophie pleasantly answered, "Thanks," with a quiet addendum of "asshole." She said it in French, quite emphatically, and I for one, was quite impressed. Soph does have some international spunk.

We used the car's lug wrench to break open the rest of the broken crate. It was mostly intact, but it did take an hour to get it assembled and ready to roll. The only problem was, gas and oil, which were not included. It was like Christmas morning, the sun is rising, the kids are waking up, and you've just finished the last few nuts and bolts on Space Station Alpha and you read, "Batteries Not Included."

Abby lifted the ugly, camouflaged, and chrome-less motorcycle onto the Ford's roof without uttering as much as a small grunt. He held it in place, from the back seat, as we drove slowly, safely, from the airport leaving the crate, the bike's windscreen, and a few spare parts strewn out across the loading dock. After all, what should one expect from a, "Doctus cum libro." Neatness?

Gassed, oiled and ready to roll, Soph climbed on her, all aluminum, 1000cc, hedgehopper, revved up its engine and like some hard outlaw-biker prepared herself to do some kick ass road battle. She looks at me intense, morose, and then gives me thumbs up sign. She pulls down her sunglasses, and with gritted teeth, pulls up on the handlebars and does an Evil Kinevil wheelie all the way out of the gas station, and maintained it for half a block as she headed off to the Hilton. Impressive, and, "stupid."

I watched her for a few seconds, wondering if Antananarivo had 911 services. I also thought that, "Soph was way, way too wild to ever be harnessed." And, I wished, with all my heart, that I had never fallen in love with her for that particular reason.

Ab and I fueled the Ford and headed for the Hilton. When we got there, the scientists were already loaded into the bus. Sophie had already tied the MAV-861 to the rear end of the bus. How she managed that in such a short time, was beyond me, but "she had."

Soph came up to the wagon, saying, "One of the Doc's wants to drive, says he drives a church bus every Sunday and wants to help out in any way that he can. Okay with you, Jim?"

I told her, "Hell yeah, sure." I was dreading the thought of having to drive that thing all week. "Have him follow us. We'll take it real slow and let them sightsee. Ab can drive while we sleep."

Soph saluted, "Aye, aye, Captain."

So. Soph would be lieutenant and I'd be the captain. She was adept at following orders and I was good at saying yes, or no, to her suggestions. We were going to work well together. It would be somewhat militant, but what the hell. When she turned, I returned her salute. She didn't see me. But Ab did.

"Hey Boss, you a captain, Boss?"

I told him that we were just goofing off, "Can you find the way back to camp, General?"

Ab liked this game; he saluted while saying, "Yes sergeant, sir, ha ha, Boss."

Yeah, he learned quickly. I told him, "Go slow, keep your speed way down, 20-25, don't hit any bumps, stop if the bus stops, and if you get tired wake us up. Any questions?"

He looked confused, puzzled, I asked him, "What's the matter, Ab?"

"If I drive all the way to camp." He paused, "Should I wake you up when we get there, Boss?"

I was really tired. I had to think hard about what he was saying. Then it dawned on me, I told him, "Oh, sorry Ab. If we're still asleep when we get to camp wake us up. Okay?"

He smiled big and happy, proud of his forethought. He said, "Okay, Boss. I mean, Sergeant." He saluted, and I quickly returned his snappy salute.

Soph took the rear seat, as I was already sprawled out across the middle seat (Rank *does* have its privileges). Then, with "Commander" Abdul at the wheel, the tortoise expedition had officially begun.

Chapter Thirty-Three

It was near four o'clock when our convoy entered Shell Camp. Abdul, our detail minded watch hound, woke us as soon as he turned off the motor. I was stiff and disoriented, my mouth was dry and I felt like there was sand under my eyelids. Waking Soph, I had noticed that she was experiencing the same sleep arousal symptoms that I had. I got out of the car and stretched. The camp looked beautiful. It had now become home, and there's no place like home. Right?

I put on my Camp Director's hat and shuffled everyone into the dining hall. It was time for camp orientation over a late, but welcomed lunch.

Sophie helped me serve up ham sandwiches, potato chips, cold beans and Pepsi Cola. Abby, up-loaded with a stack of food, went out and downloaded the crew's baggage. Yeah, everything was going smooth, it was actually pleasant, everyone was cheerful, "...downright, puppy-happy to be out of that bus and eating." Which is a quote from one of the scientists, but I can't remember which one.

It was about the same time that I heard, "We're all done pigged out." Which is attributed to one, Dr. Altie.

I started to set up a makeshift podium by using one of the smaller dining tables. That's when I saw Sophie sneaking out the front door carrying two sandwiches a quart of cola. She had her cycle keys dangling from her teeth in a big grin. Yeah, she was running out on me just when the fun was about to begin. However, she did mouth a, "Good luck, Yogi." Before the door hit her in the ass.

I introduced myself as the, "Camp Counselor." I started out with some light humor, "If anyone needs anything, anything at all, you'll have to give me two-weeks notice – in writing."

No one laughed, the scientists just sat there, stone-faced and quiet. It was horrible. So I added, "Just kidding, that was supposed to be humorous."

That earned me a murmur and two smiles. So, even though the comic is dying, he must continue – right?

So I said, "Actually, I need six-weeks notice, in writing, in triplicate and on letterhead stationary. And (slapping my hand down on the table for emphasis), they must be notarized."

This they liked. They all laughed. I had hit their intellectual funny bone. The audience was now mine. I had won their confidence and their respect they'd listen now, because they "wanted" to.

It took me thirty minutes to cover all the dos and don'ts of Shell Camp. All basic stuff, don't wander off alone, what to do in an emergency, what was public domain, what wasn't, how to call the States in an emergency, and blah, blah, blah.

When I had finished and asked if there were any questions. One lone hand rose out of the crowd, it was the hand of Doctor Arnold Balifourn. He asked, "Is there a Notary Public in the house?"

Eleven scientific hands raised in unison. And I asked, "Any other questions?" There weren't. The rest of the evening was spent unpacking and settling themselves into their new environment. I helped them as much as they would allow me to help, but scientist are a very picky lot by nature and insisted upon doing most things for themselves. And I thought this, "I'm glad they aren't Engineers."

About sunset I noticed Sophie sitting on the bunkhouse steps. She was reading the MAV-861 schematics, underlining each word with a wrench as she read. She looked confused. The MAV was parked alongside of her and it looked as if it was also reading the MAV schematic, and it looked just as confused as Sophie.

I slipped up on her, "Having fun, Kidd?"

She looked up, saying, "These suck. Look." She tapped the page with the wrench, "There's no red wire. I can't get the lights to work. Engineers suck."

"You've got them upside down, Priss." She turned them over before I could add, "Just kidding."

The red wire had been camouflaged into multiple greens. It took me all of thirty seconds to repair the lights, due to an excellently drawn wiring diagram. I said, "There. Piece of cake, Soph."

She grabbed her helmet, straddled the bike, and without as much as a thank you, putt-putted away. She left the schematics and her tools strewn in the Malagasy dust. This was very "unlike" Sophie, and it worried me – for about a minute. Until I realized that she was expressing her anger at me, a hate, because of Eunice.

I busied myself checking on Ab and his cooking duties, making fine adjustments to the generators and for the most part, being available to the expedition. For all practical purposes, I had become,

Camp Overseer. Which is like being the absentee owner of a time-share condo along Florida's gold coast. During an annual IRS audit, your CPA mentions it, once, along with your other tax shelters. Or, better yet, it's like sitting on a corporate board and no one has accused you of being the stockholder's gadfly. Yeah, that's what I was, Camp Overseer. A tough position, but someone had to do it.

The entire camp was a beehive of harmony. If things continued to go as smoothly as they were I'd feel guilty when it came time to cash my paycheck. And, if you believe that, I have a little business venture for you to invest your money in.

By eleven o'clock, Sophie hadn't returned. As C.O., I must say, "I was concerned." I took a quick shower and wrote up my daily report to Eunice. I lay down but couldn't sleep. I was tired, it had been a long day, but I needed to find Sophie. I was having all kinds of sick mental visions, like Soph being shot by Margolova, Soph driving her bike off a waterfall, Soph being gang raped by a heavily armed band of Polynesian banditti, and Soph lost and weeping for me, or anyone, to rescue her.

I dressed, sticking the .357 into my waistband and hanging Soph's binoculars around my neck. I threw on a jacket to hide the magnum and headed for Travelle Creek, to where I had last seen her and her metal quarter horse. Yeah, I was overtly concerned, but maybe not. Margolova was a genuine fact of life, like it or not, which at that moment, I didn't. Besides, I was...sort of, really missing her.

I searched the horizon and saw, nothing, nothing but blackness. And I heard nothing, nothing but a never ending din of insect noises. Confounded and worried, I went to the granite outcropping on the west side of camp. Still nothing, the focused Halogen headlight on the MAV should have shown up if it was on. Befuddled, I lolly-gagged back to my bunk.

It was a dilemma, I couldn't go looking for her and I couldn't let it drop. I began to prioritize my responsibilities. My job was to care for the scientists. That was clear, I had to stay with them. They had no knowledge of Margolova that I knew of. Were she to come into camp, they would probably invite her in for coffee and a chat. I didn't like the situation. It wasn't fair. Soph goes off for a joy ride and...oh well. I decided to wait until sunrise. If she didn't show up by then, I'd alert the world, organize a search party and hunt down her body for a decent burial.

Back in the courtyard, tent city was alive with after-hour activity. All but two of the tents were lit, typewriter clicking filled the air, and at least one member of the expedition was taking a late shower. I stumbled on the pseudo-city's myriad of extension cables and wondered if Madagascar had an OSHA program. I made a mental note to reorganize the power lines, first thing in the morning if I wasn't out beating the bush for Sophie's badly dismembered corpse, idly rotting away on some sun baked Malagasy rock pile where she had tumbled dramatically off her motorized CIA tinker toy.

Steam bellowed out of the woman's shower. Abby was sleeping – one could hear him snoring all the way out in front of the kitchen. And there, standing silent and ugly in front of the bunkhouse, I saw the MAV-861. And it made me angry. I had a terrible urge to go kick the damn thing over, but I didn't. I went storming into our former love nest ready to chastise my daughter – like the delinquent child she was.

Sophie was on her radio and gave me a shush sign with her finger as I entered. The room speaker was on and I heard Dawn, the CIA matriarchal saint of all field agents, saying, "No – not the president's son."

I sat down and listened as Dawn continued. "Damndest thing, Kidd. The think tankers still think that your project is small potatoes. Those graybeards, as if I've got room to talk, are saying that her target has to be the president himself. Their one guiding light is the fact that junior has flown off to meet his girlfriend in the Bahamas. Must be nice, eh Kidd?"

There was a long pause, a whole minute, then Dawn says, "Oh well, Kidd. At least the old man is on your side, if he weren't, you wouldn't have the MAV, Honey."

Sophie looked at me coldly, but spoke to Dawn, "How come I didn't get any warning on daddy coming out, Dawn?"

"Don't know, Honey. We should have been told. My guess is, they got a bug up their ass to take a trip and just went. Maybe the Senator is porking North on the side. We just don't know. Shit happens, eh Kidd."

Soph turned off her icy stare and began talking into the transmitter, "It was actually kind of funny, Dawn. You should have seen Morgan's face when Eunice walks up and says, "They! Are right here, James (Soph was doing a bad imitation of Eunice)." You'd have died,

Dawn. I thought I was going to piss in my pants."

When they quit ha-ha-ing, Soph continued, "Yeah, that's about it, Dawn. The important thing, is the English expedition, it's dirty. There's something covert going on down there or my name isn't Alberquist. See what you can dig up. I'd really like to find out what they're up to, Dawn. I'd sleep a little better if I knew. Okay?"

"Kidd, you can sleep like a bug in a rug. We'll have something for you by your morning. The C5 blokes play a fair game these days. They'll tell us what's going on, I'm sure of it." Dawn paused, then asked, "Speaking of the MAV-861 (which they were not), how is it, Kidd?"

"Well, it needs a few hundred more horses, knobbier tires and a readable schematic. Aside from that – it's a blast."

"Oh Kidd, you crack me up, Doll. You go get yourself some sleep now. Four hours in a back seat wouldn't be enough for my old bones, but you are a mite younger then me, eh?" Dawn's voice sounded old as it trailed off and off the air.

Sophie closed the conversation, "Talk to you tonight, Dawn. Take care." She pulled the plug and began to replace the radio into its padded aluminum case.

I began to remove my hiking boots. I was glad that Sophie was safe and my anger had subsided while I listened to her radio talk. I threw my legs up on the bed and observed her. Her shirt was soaked with sweat around her underarms. Her thirty-eight's holster was tinged a deep brown around its' edges, again from sweat. She looked radiant, cute, and in a way, *very* dangerous.

I noticed that she had tracked in mud and that it was still caked on her boots in wet clumps. Miss, all business, hadn't bothered to wipe her feet upon entering our cozy little love den, and, I made the terrible mistake of pointing this out to her.

Pointing to the mud, "Been wallowing in the mire, Soph?"

Without looking up from her packaging, she retorted, "No more than you and your stint in the generator room, Mister Morgan."

Chapter Thirty-Four

The elite dozen, the twelve expedition members, had democrati-
cally elected their own leader for the scientific end of things. Their
choice was the dynamic, Doctor Ludwig A. Strongbow. Everyone
called him, Bo. Except me, I felt that he deserved a little more respect
then "Bo." I called him, Doc. Behind his back, I called him other
things, my favorite was, Wiggy. It made Sophie laugh, sorry Doc. –
By the way, did you enjoy my Scotch? I'm specifically talking about
the bottle that we pissed in, just before we left.

Doc was "Mister Organization" personified. I was "his" Abdul,
well, I suppose that I'm being somewhat hyperbolic here, but it's not
too far from an axiomatic truth.

Doc was in his early sixties. He held some of the most impressive
educational credentials that I had ever seen dumped on any one individual. To name just four of the Universities that he has earned
degrees from, Harvard, Yale, Princeton and MIT. – Not to mention
where he has held full professorships, Duke, The U. of Chicago,
U.C.L.A, and don't let me forget "Berkeley" where he taught in a
tie-dyed T-shirt during the early Hippie 60's.

He has advised several presidential administrations, and now, most
recently, he writes "romance novels." His literary pseudonym, pen
name, is a household word. I have promised not to divulge his name
in this writing; in return, he has introduced me to his agent. But, that
is another story, one that I have further developed in the sequel to
this book.

Doc is a university unto himself. One day, a college will – no
doubt – be named after him. At one point, I had suggested to Sophie
that Margolova might have been sent out to kidnap Doc, pick his
brain, or worse, to seduce him and have his baby. And then sell the
offspring on the black market.

Sophie blew me off. She said, "No, Jim. He's way too old for
seduction. Besides, most of his theories haven't been proven yet.
And, he refuses to work for the D.O.D. (Department of Defense),
what good would it do for her to kidnap someone like that?"

I guess she's right. So, when you read the moniker Doc, you'll know a little bit about him and why he acts like such a big jerk.

Tuesday morning came much faster than desired, I did hit the snooze alarm but had knocked the whole thing off its stand and it then bounced under the bed. Getting out of bed to shut it off, Soph yelled, from across the room, from her own bed, "I'm not getting up until you bring me coffee, Morgan." These were the first words she had spoken to me since pointing out that I was, philandering about in the power plant. At least now, she was talking to me.

I readily agreed, anything to keep my darling love happy.

I did do a quick glance around the room, if I had seen a bucket of cold water, she'd have gotten up quicker than an SST climbing out of Orley. I didn't see anything, so I dressed and headed for the kitchen, it was only six a.m., blah!

It was a chilly morning. The tents had dew on them and it gave the camp an eerie, surreal appearance. The next thing that I saw was a line of bathers waiting to enter the showers. Eunice would have been proud of her purchase if she had seen the eager campers, greedily waiting their turn to primp. Looking out of the kitchen door was Doctor Strongbow.

Stalwart, chipper, dynamic and with power, Doc chirped out, "This is a fine day brewing here, Jim." He didn't say this loudly, but his voice has this reverberation to it that made his greeting resound all through Shell Camp. I'm sure that everyone heard him, including Sophie who had five blankets covering her head.

I said, "No doubt, Chief. No doubt." I tried to emulate his voice projection. But it just wasn't there, what can I say? Some people have it, and some don't – I still sounded like me.

I added, without trying to shatter glass, "Ready for some breakfast, Doc?"

"Ah yes, about your cook, Abdul. I've taken the liberty to replace him, not totally, but I have asked Doctor Gnancy to assist him in the kitchen. I'm sure you'll find this satisfactory, Jim."

This was a statement of – your camp shenanigans have been exposed. I could only say, "Excellent, Doc! Excellent." In my mind, I danced an Irish jig, a little soft-toe dance in abject appreciation. Doc had just solved my worst nightmare, Chef Abdul.

Doc continued, "I've also posted a shower schedule. I'm sure that you, and Miss Alberquist, of course, will find it satisfactory."

Doc placed a confirmatory hand on my shoulder, "Have you made arrangement for more fuel oil, Jim? I believe we're about to run out, unless I've inadvertently misread the gauges."

"Oh, don't worry yourself about that, Doc. The fuel truck will be here by ten this morning, or my name isn't Jim Morgan." I did calculate the camp's fuel consumption rate, but – I hadn't checked my calculations to see if they were accurate against our actual consumption. I had an overwhelming urge to excuse myself and run to the gauges and read them.

Instead, I simply asked, "Can we make it until ten, Doc?"

"Oh yes, they'll run until twelve-fifteen. It does depends on the fuel grade, I didn't do a lab test...but..."

He turned in mid-sentence, "Let's get some of Gnancy's coffee, Jim. It's going to be a busy day. A busy day, indeed."

As I filled two mugs with Gnancy's brew, I wondered if he had checked Sophie's alarms, cleaned her weapons, and made a call to Langley for her. Hell, it was only five after six and he had me ready to retire, without a pension.

Abdul was awake and standing next to Doctor Lotty Gnancy. He was watching her mix, what looked like, a huge bowl of pancake batter. He left her side and joined me at the coffee urn.

Gnancy called after him, "Get back here, Abdul. You don't get a coffee break until breakfast is over, Chef."

Ab yelled at her, "I *got* to see the boss, Lotty." He was adamant, unflinching, emphasizing the "got."

Distraught, Lotty said, "Oh, go ahead. Ask him for another pay raise while you're at it, too."

Lotty is ageless. She is both young and old. She has been married, and then divorced, three times. She has one son from each of her marriages, is considered to be marriage minded, and looking to produce son number four. Eunice had remarked, back in Washington, that if I were to get horny down here, "...just give Gnancy a wink or two. I hear that she has a penchant for younger men." ...And we laughed.

I strained to get a look at Gnancy around Ab's bulk. It was the first time that I had seen her alone, away from the crowd. She is a cute woman, short, and dark haired, full-bodied from the waist up, but slim, too thin, in the haunches. I caught myself in an unconscious act

– I was practicing a wink.

"Something in your eye, Boss?"

"Ah, yeah – it's okay, Ab. How are you getting along with Doctor Gnancy?"

"She says that I don't know the difference between a pot and a pan, Boss. What's the difference, Boss?"

Doc spat coffee when he heard Abby ask me what the difference was. It was one of those involuntary acts, choking, he excused himself and went outside to recuperate. He had a world to run, why spend time differentiating pots from pans, indeed.

"She wants me to wear that hat, Boss." Ab pointed to a stovepipe chef's hat that had to have come right out of a French cooking school.

Trying to keep a straight face, I offered, "Well, you are the site's cook, Ab. Site cooks wear those kind of things."

Ab retorted, "Miss Lotty say I ain't no cook, Boss. She says that I could ruin a slice of bread, Boss." Sulking, he added, "I don't like that Lotty, Boss."

I gave my pouting cook a slug on the arm, "Just hang in there and help her any way that you can. Okay? Do it for me – as a favor. Okay Pal?"

Abdul smiled big, showing white teeth, as big as a farmer's planting thumb. He lowered his chin to his chest and said, with reluctance, "Okay, Boss."

I told him to take a walk around camp, that I'd talk to Lotty in an attempt to make things go more his way. He thanked me and headed for the door. Outside, he stopped, turned around and asked, "Hey Boss, can I have a pay raise, Boss?"

I relented, "Yeah. But don't be asking for one every day, from now on, you have to earn your pay raises."

Again, the big Ugandan showed his grin. He said, "Thanks, Boss." Then skipped off across the courtyard. I was sure he would go all the way around camp before returning. I hoped to god that he'd go slowly. I took a deep sip of my coffee, thinking, "God I love this job."

I topped off my coffee and entered Gnancy's new world, the Shell Camp kitchen. I introduced myself, "Compliments on the brew, your talents are well appreciated."

Feisty, she stopped her cooking, leaned back against the counter and began to inspect me from head to toe. I felt that I was being stripped naked, in her mind. I had a wink hanging below my forehead but restrained myself with great difficulty, this thought had crossed through my mind, "Lotty would be a fun tumble, fleshy, pert, but...probably, too dominating."

She stopped my thought, "Your man, Abdul? He isn't a cook." Her cold blue eyes locked onto mine, they were filled with wit and bespoke of fun and a worldly zest for life. Her eyes were painted up with an azure blue pigment that highlighted her crow's feet, tiny wrinkles from a life of laughter and gaiety.

With a genuine acceptance of her stated fact, I pleaded, "I know, but he's the best shovel and pick man east of the Mozambique Channel. I need him, Lotty."

"Eunice says that you smoke too much, got a cigarette?"

And then, I did wink. I gave her the whole pack while requesting that she keep her ashes out of the pancake batter. – I turned my attention to Soph's cooling mug of coffee and left the sumptuous Lotty, new Chef and Camp Matriarch to her nicotine and flapjack beating. She was busy; we'd talk later, much longer.

Soph was balled up under five blankets, her alarm was on and making a horrid racket. I wondered who she had short-sheeted, as we didn't purchase that many blankets that she should wind up with five, how she manages these things is beyond me. Another thing that I simply hate is the way that she sleeps while her clock is screaming out, wake-up! Her alarm clock buzzes at about 110 decibels. That's about the level where a person needs to put on a pair of earplugs for OSHA safety requirements. I set down her java, shut off the clock, and had a thought of fondling her awake, but I didn't. I didn't think it very wise, after all, I was still on thin ice, and I knew it.

Actually, I was under the ice. I was ten feet under and sinking rapidly. I had two five-hundred horsepower generators lashed to my ankles and they were pulling down, deeper and deeper into the deepest ocean trench of all the ocean trenches in all of this vast world's seven oceans and seven seas. No, it was worse, "much" worse than that, it was the whole damned generator room *and* Eunice, pulling me down like mega-tons of lead.

I'm not sure how long I stood there and contemplated our relationship, days, weeks, and years had passed as I looked down at my sleeping beauty, contemplating, pondering the proper way to wake my precious love, take her into my arms and tell her how much she really meant to me, that, "I loved her," and, in spite of my noisy fling with Eunice, I still wanted her, and her alone.

But, nothing came. She lay there before me, a taboo. To wit, I had ostracized myself from her sensuous graces. I felt that I no longer had the right to even breach her slumber. Gently, I set down her mug and left the bunkhouse.

I walked aimlessly toward the showers not wanting to arrive anywhere in particular. I was hopelessly dazed by romance and a sorely illicit love. I was ill from the grievous loss that stemmed from a most wanton relationship, sick, with confusion, the confusion of loving two women with an equal passion and with an equally hot and burning intensity. Yeah, at that moment, I was not a very happy camper.

Chapter Thirty-Five

It's odd, the way a handful of little pressures can mount and cause one such "silly distresses." – Especially on such a distant adventure where one is thrust into many contrary concepts and ideals. Yeah, the mind *tends* to the familiar. It latches onto those things that it readily recognizes within one's own accessible memory, ingrained knowledge, local familiarity, and one's own innate ease with time proven socially accepted norms.

It's good that we humans can adapt so quickly to these mental atrocities. After all, it's not every tree that can bear an apple, some really big ones, like the giant California Redwoods, refuse to bear anything, except time. And yet, the coconut, weighed down with milk, and meats, hang heavy on the palms of most islands.

Like a good human being, naturally confused, I threw myself into my work. I walked the water pipes looking for leaks. Finding none, I returned to the kitchen for more coffee.

As the front screen-door banged shut, Gnancy yelled out to me, "I need a few supplies if this crew is going to eat sensibly, Jim Morgan."

God himself, or herself, must have been smiling down on me that morning, just when I needed some "think time," time to sort through my personal conundrum of feminine woes, up jumps a grocery run to Tanan. "Thank you lord, thank you." The trip was under Doctor's orders; a Gnancy prescription, a tonic task to invigorate the cupboard. Yeah, Doc was right as usual, a fine day was indeed brewing at Shell Camp.

"Have you put together a list, Lotty?"

"That I have, Mister Morgan." She waltzed up to the coffee urn and handed me three sheets of culinary demands, "I'll need it for lunch. Can you get back by noon?"

"Settle for dinner and I'll bring you a bouquet of flowers."

She held out her hand and stated, "Deal." I shook her hand to confirm the food run. It was a very soft hand that firmly gripped mine, as she added, "If you pick `em in a field, you're going to eat `em in your next salad, Morgan. I don't bribe easy."

Lotty is a lovable person, she has a knack to make one love her, and she does this, without trying. Cupid must sit on her shoulder and shoot little errant love arrows at everyone she comes into contact with – plink. If Freud were to get Lotty on his couch, she'd have yet another son, no doubt.

Jubilant over the trip to town, I headed for Sophie's bed, to wake her. I stripped off her swaddling; it was time to face the realities of camp life, "Okay, CIA, up and at 'em, Sarge. You've got an expedition to defend. I'm making a supply run into Tanan. Do you need anything?"

Yawning, reaching for her cool coffee, "Want me to go with?"

"Nope. I need the room. I don't want to rent a truck. If I go alone I can probably get by with the wagon. Besides, I need the think time."

Soph came wide-awake with her first sip of coffee; she downed the mug and asked, "Any more of this? This is great." She had worn flannel pajamas to bed, they weren't flattering, they were actually anti-sexual, yet – she still looked desirable.

I handed her my mug and she drank it down in three gulps, "Anymore?" She held the cup out to me, flashing me her blue, pleading, eyes.

"Yeah, in the kitchen." I set the cups on a crate. "You can have all you want, as soon as you change out of those awful flannels."

Ignoring me, she started into an excited tirade about finding a ruby mine, "...just up the creek. I want to go back there. I want to find one – a ruby."

I suggested, "I'd like for you to stay around camp, Soph. I've got an oil truck coming in this morning. It would be best if you were here. In case your friend, Margolova, shows up. It would make me feel better just knowing that you were here, on site."

She pouted, "I'd much rather go into town."

"No." I insisted. "I want you here. It's better if you stay put and hold down the fort – safer." I turned to leave.

"What about tonight? Want to go up there with me? It's a really neat mine, Jim."

"Yeah, sure, sounds like fun. See you later, Kidd." And I slipped out, quick, not listening to what she had added. I think that pissed her off; but she could have told me about the mine last night, instead of putting me on a guilt trip, right?

I knew that my allegiances were in an upheaval, and now, I believe that Soph's were, too. It sounded like her highest priority was to poke around an old mine and just screw the camp. Yeah, we were both on a vacation and we both knew it. Our personal lives, our natures, had turned us into a pair of bugaboos.

It felt good to pull away from camp, to enter into a temporary escape from the simplicity of just having to be there. My bi-polar love orientation had to end. Loving two women is not the healthiest mental existence known to man. One of them, maybe both, would have to go by the wayside. Of this, I was certain. It would be hard, but, it had to be done, and until I made a decision, I was playing with dynamite. And I thought, "Damn, I'm actually becoming responsible." And I concluded, "What a bitch."

I passed the incoming fuel truck and my spirits brightened. At least something was going my way. The camp would have electricity and my name could still be, Jim Morgan. Doc will be pleased, and I thought, "Did I check the mistresses, the generators? Shit." I hadn't, and then, I mentally passed the buck, "Doc will handle it." I pressed down on the Ford's accelerator. Yeah, it was time to screw off a little, do some cruising, and a little shopping.

I fiddled around with the car radio and found some nice classical guitar. It was indeed a beautiful morning. I stopped at the tarmac highway that led from Antananarivo all the way down to the coast and Pimakeel Bay. The radio was blasting out a Spanish hat dance. The sky was blue. A few puffy white cumulus clouds were forming in the west. A cloud of white dust hung in my wake and a light breeze began to carry it over the stopped wagon. For an instant, I thought, "Tina Johnson."

I looked down the road for traffic, first left then right, the road is seldom traveled and that day was no different, there was no traffic. I conjured up a sketchy vision of Tina. "...I'm sure the pleasure would be mutual, Mister Morgan." Involuntarily, the wheel turned slightly to the right toward Pimakeel Bay. And I sat there in a mental stupor, then, I listened to the powerful engine idle away above my silent reverie. I envisioned Sophie in the new showers, soaped and wet, demanding that I take her, then and there, under the steaming creek water. And then Eunice, her cowboy shirt opened, her breast bouncing, not bothering to remove her hat, or boots, saying, harder, harder. And then Gnancy winked at me from the windshield, and said nothing, nothing at all.

I turned the wheel left easing onto the tarmac and crawled slowly into the mountains and the shadowy side of the Antananarivo outskirts.

Our food supplier, our grocer, and the owner of the Prisunic Department Store, had said, "If I don't have what you want, than it can't be had." That is what he told me when I set up a line of credit with him a week earlier. I went to him and presented him Lotty's list. He told me that the meats had to be dry-iced for delivery, that he would rent me a freezer and that his son was an excellent cook if we were to be in need of one. Uncle Bobby had mentioned this to him – we might be looking for a cook, on that very morning, during Catholic mass, just before they had Holy Communion.

I agreed to the dry ice, rented the freezer, but declined the son. The seven hundred dollar order would be delivered by 5 p.m., for the tiny fee of a mere 400 dollars, American, to which I readily agreed. I left the Prisunic with a complimentary bouquet of mixed Malagasy flowers for our cook. This was actually a kick-back, I asked for them as a kickback. Ah, shopping can be fun, eh? It was going on noon; it was time for a decent meal at the Hilton. I was ready for anything, except, a ham sandwich. I was thinking of something hot, hot and spicy.

Uncle Bobby was standing in, as bartender, when I entered the Hilton's lounge and ordered up a double Scotch, on the rocks. He leaned over the bar and confided to me, whispering, "A dark haired woman, fiftyish, has been asking about your expedition, Mister Morgan. I think she is a European, perhaps German."

"Oh yeah, what kind of questions is she asking, Bobby?"

He smiled wryly, then, put his hand out, he began to rub his thumb and index finger together in that international sign which calls for a bit of palm greasing. I pulled out a twenty and slipped it into his waiting fingers. I was enjoying this spy business, it was a fun game, and, I really wanted to know more about Margolova. I must admit I was concerned about my twenty. I wondered if it would be a valid item to put on my expense account.

The twenty disappeared and Uncle Bobby began to relate his encounter with Margolova. "She wanted to know what your expedition is searching for, Mister Morgan. Of course I could not tell her, because, I myself do not know this, eh? She then offered me French notes, francs, if I were to find out this information and call her. Ah, what is it, that you are seeking out there, James?"

I said, "Marsupial Butterflies, they're very rare."

"Ah, I see. I myself have never heard of such things. And this is my home."

"Yeah." I continued the lie, flagrantly, and I'm not a good liar, "No one has ever found one yet."

I continued, "What else did she ask, Bobby?"

She asked about the scientists, and she was most interested in Miss Kidd." He lowered his voice, "She wanted to know if Miss Kidd carries a weapon." Caught up in his information service, he asked, "Does she carry a weapon, Jim?"

"Only her charm, Bob. Only her charm."

"I see." He said, "Yes, she is a very charming woman, very pretty." He looked off into space, "Yes, very pretty. But no weapons, eh?"

"Not a one, Bob."

He continued, "She wanted to know when you were leaving our country. She asked for you departure reservation dates."

"Did you give them to her?"

"Yes, yes. Such things are not confidential, Jim." Uncle Bobby gave me his finger-rub to show that Margolova had paid for the information – he was bribed.

I asked again, "What else?"

"That is all. She gave me her phone number. I'm to call her, if I should hear anything. She specifically wants me to inform her, if you should decide to leave earlier than planned."

He paused in a serious stare, then says, "Mister Morgan, please understand, I only take these monies to help with the huge medical expenses of my crippled child, do you see?"

"Oh yeah, I get it." I reached into my pocket and produced another twenty. I asked him for Margolova's phone number. With a rapid search of his pockets, he produced a matchbook cover with the number and a note that said, "Ask for M."

As I jotted down the number I asked Bobby if there was anything else going on that we should know about.

He asked, "Do you know, Major LaCruel?"

"Yes, I've had the pleasure. Is he asking about us?"

"No, no. He was following the European, M. I think she knows this, that he is following her."

It comforted me to know that LaCruel was following Margolova. For whatever it was worth, I went ahead and asked Uncle Bobby to keep our conversation confidential.

He agreed, "As you wish, Mister Morgan. As you wish."

I then sat down to the biggest, juiciest steak that I had ever eaten. When Uncle Bobby served it, he was the stand in waiter, he said, "I picked this one out myself, enjoy, enjoy." And I did.

I even tipped him another twenty – on behalf of his crippled child.

Chapter Thirty-Six

It was three-thirty when I arrived back at a very deserted camp. The generators were humming, the coffee urn was hot and Soph's MAV was in front of the bunkhouse, idle, and cold to the touch. It was strange, eerie, I called out, "Hello, anybody here? Hello?" Yeah, the camp had turned into a ghost town. Everyone had vanished.

I returned to the dining room in search of their whereabouts. On the east wall, a set of photos, maps were pinned to the bare wall. The maps were very detailed – one even showed the old outhouse and the path that lead up to it. Scanning the photos I noticed one that had a circle drawn on it and was labeled, Search Area 1, with that day's date scrawled in alongside of it. Hell, I thought, I'm not only a great spy, but also a fair detective.

The circled area was just to the west of Travelle Creek. I grabbed a quart of pop, went to the bunkhouse, got Sophie's binoculars, then – leisurely, strolled out to look for them. Through the field glasses I saw one, then two, of the scientists with large sacks thrown over their shoulders. They appeared to be returning, they looked hot, their sacks looked full, and then I saw Abby, his sack looked empty, he was following Soph, her sack seemed to be a little bit fuller than Ab's, but not much.

As I scanned the area further I found their leader, none other than the esteemed, Doctor Strongbow. Doc was striding out ahead of the others, the natural leader, one pace quicker than his nearest follower, Planchard, who was openly exerting himself, forcefully, in a losing battle to maintain pace with the old bugger who was their shepherd. I watched him stop and openly count his straggling sheep. Content with his count, he turned and pressed on. Hup, toop, threep, four, turn and count, now march some more. Hup, toop, threep, four, turn, count, turn and stride, go Doc, go. You sick old bastard. I stood there and laughed, it was a hilarious looking scene.

Doc yelled something at Sophie. Sophie threw down her sack. I watched Abby pick it up. He was drenched in sweat, looked hot, tired, and angry. I looked back Doc, he was counting cadence. Yeah, he was their driving force, their motivator, if it weren't for him, the entire camp would be on siesta, or worse, still in bed.

It would take the expedition a good twenty minutes to return, maybe longer if Doc were to relent his pace. I went back to the bunkhouse in an amused state. Being tired from the drive, I opted for a quick nap, truly happy that I had missed the day's hunt.

Our cabin was a mess, let there be no doubt – Sophie is a slob. One would think that, when one shares a building with a woman, that the woman would keep the building clean. At the risk of being labeled a misogynist (one who hates women), I do believe, that it's the woman's job to keep things orderly, isn't it?

Although sweaty, I plopped down on my, unmade, ruffled bed and fell directly into an unusual and disquieting dream.

I was inside of a maze. The walls were high and smooth, but opened at the top to expose a blue but cloudy sky. One that rushed past rapidly as if the tufts were projected there by a movie camera that someone had deliberately fast-forwarded its film, and then slowed it until it came to an abrupt halt. As fast as the puffy cumulus had stopped, they once again began to build, skyward, upward in a bil-lowing, roiling turmoil of huge, white cumulonimbus monsters that quickly blackened the sky into a rumbling, thundering, nightmare.

Lightning fissures shot around the base of the rolling black heav-en. They were continuous and erratic. Bold fiery filaments stabbing, slicing strands of un-harnessed electrical energy seeking brash havoc while issuing an ill notice that their being was indeed to be taken as a real and justifiable fear.

A thick plasmatic bolt hit down on the maze and lit the walls with a sizzling curse of impending doom and destruction, the jagged streak sped off, down and across the curved walls roaring out in a loud and absolutely terrifying hiss of sparking and decaying magma shards, and then it was gone, as fast as it had appeared, charging manic out of its roiling mammoth pouch, it had vanished, then, silence, in pitch blackness, the storm had abated, dissipated into night, into a black, tranquil, low quietness akin to that of a heavily padded listening booth.

And I began to glide, genteel, very slow, down along the plastic lined maze, on a carpet, a magic carpet, that flew close to the ground, so close to the ground that the carpet had merged with the floor in a continuous symbiotic flow like a surfboard descending its wave. Poky slow at first, then faster and faster I sped on through the curved passages careening left, then right, and again right, and then I'd be whipped left again – only to whip back once again to the right, and yet again, with stomach tingling – in a jolt, from the mighty centrifugal force that had been applied only a mere second earlier from a tight left-handed switchback.

I reached out and touched the polished wall with the tip of my finger and the walls screamed like a blackboard being erased with a handful of razor blades. My speed increased, the maze had dropped into a descending tunnel, an icy tube, and, the carpet transformed into a sled, an Olympic sled, and I plummeted yet faster – faster into the narrowing innards of a frozen blue void.

Then I saw the light, the tunnels end, and I knew this, in a euphoric sense of knowing, knew that I was being shot from a cannon and with the quick snap of one's finger I was out of the huge dank barrel and soaring wildly out into the distant mad yonder, wind whistled about my ears and face, and my cheeks became distorted, contorted, from the gushing, rushing air as I shot up, up and away into...an old... Yeah, I was flying an old, old airplane, a barn buzzer with an open cockpit and a rudder stick jammed up between my legs, one that I had to grip with two hands as I had now entered into a deadly tailspin, one that had me gritting my teeth so tightly that my gums had begun to bleed. I had on an old brown leather helmet with a set of pop-eyed oval goggles snapped to the leather above a white silk scarf, one that flagged out behind my neck due to a rushing wind that pushed past the crescent windscreen that was badly splattered with moth fuzz and red streaks from impacted, almost dried bug bits, and, some frail, transparent, still wiggling in the wind, wing fragments.

The craft's body was covered with yellowing shellac that was mostly translucent and exposed a thinly woven gray canvas underpinning that was applied, glued, to a wooden framework. The mad spin ended into a swooping glide and a slow roll to the west that gave me a breathtaking view of patchwork farm lands, pastures and widely scattered farmsteads. The plane responded to my commands and I dove down, low, over wheat and corn and scraggly soybean beds, close, ten feet, nine feet, I put out my hand and touched the baby soft wheat as it rushed past the wings, it felt like an elongated peach fuzz, the plane leveled and I withdrew my hand, I was in laughter, I was ecstatic, it was a wonderful feeling. I flapped the wing tips along the wheat tops as I raced along the farmlands and I recall singing, "...carry moon beams home in a jar...and be better off than you are...or would you raaa-theeeerrr-beeee – a spy?

Pulling full back on the rudder stick, I shot up into a bank of towering cumulus, pillar clouds. I zoomed around them like so many pylons on a parking lot racecourse, then through them, leaving remnant cartoon holes where I had been. Yeah, it was great fun. I loved that dream. Until the propeller fell off and the right wing ripped out and *away* from the fuselage and went spinning off into oblivion, and the wheels, old baby carriage wheels tore loose and began to bang relentlessly against the undercarriage like a storm shutter let loose in a gale, and the straight-lined twelve-piston engine popped a ghastly snort and began a gush of white, steaming hot, fumy, acrid smoke, right back into my army issue flying goggles. And then, I didn't like the dream any longer.

Yet, it continued. The plane began a horrendous vibration, the varnish began to peal away from the canvas and the canvas began to strip away from the strutting, and, I began a climb out of the cockpit as the ground raced up to meet the, rapidly disintegrating, monoplane and its scared shitless pilot, me. Who in mid-dream discovered that the plane and its accouterments weren't designed to accommodate its pilot with such luxuries as that of a silken parachute.

So, I'm standing atop of the last wing, air-surfing toward "doom" and I get this bright idea, "When the wing gets to about five, six feet from the ground, I'd leap upward off the canvas, and then, as the wing goes shattering into a million bits of thread and wee slivers of yellow varnish, I'd softly land, upright and "unharmed" standing on my own two feet amongst the newly dropped hunks of broken and widely scattered aircraft debris."

The ground came up quickly, fifty feet, thirty – and then ten. I was poised to leap, and I thought, "Hell, things don't work like this, at least, not in our world, the *real* world."

It was Deadly, Sophie D. Deadly, the Kidd, who woke me at four feet, just as I began my leap off the...falling... "What? What?" I bolted upright, waiting for the impending impact, I was panting deep, mumbling, saying, "Fuck me."

Sophie said, "No thank you." She was dirty, sweaty and red-faced; her hair was mussed and she looked angry, perturbed. She quickly added, "There's a grocery truck here and the guy wants to know where he should put the freezer."

She continued, "How was your trip to town. It must be a hundred degrees out there. How was your nap – how do you manage to get a nap?" She trailed off her tirade catching herself in a fully developed rant.

I pulled the sheet back over my head trying to see the outcome of my dream. I hadn't answered Sophie. I did hear her turn on the shower. I kicked off the sheet and got up, I was anxious to relate my story of Margolova and her approach to Uncle Bobby.

Soph had her back to me and didn't hear me get up. She was undressing. I hoped, preparing to shower. Without turning she repeated, in a yell, "The grocery truck is here – get up, damn it."

I yelled back, I was standing right behind her, "Thank you!"

She spun around, "You're weird, Morgan." She went into the shower still dressed in her jeans and bra drawing closed the plastic curtain with a brisk snap, one that demanded privacy.

Peeking out our window, I saw the scientists unloading the truck. Doc, of course, was directing the show. I decided to shower before going out, as I was sweaty from sleeping in the heat. I asked Soph not to use up all the hot water.

"Too late, it's already cool." But she did turn it off, saving me what little warmth was left.

I yelled in another, "Thank you."

She muttered, "Yeah."

By the time I dressed and made it to the kitchen the truck was unloaded. The freezer was plugged in and the groceries were neatly stowed, and Lotty, Kitchen Master, had already started the ball rolling for an evening – steak – barbecue.

Baked potatoes were already cooking on the oil drum grill that had rested, rusting, behind the generator room. Lotty and Doc had carried it up to the kitchen door while the hunt still straggled in from the field. Where she found charcoal is yet a mystery to me. I know *this* as fact – there wasn't any around and it wasn't on the shopping list. When I asked Lotty about this, she said, "It's residual ash from an old bridge, don't ask."

And I let it go, then. Today, well, it's a conundrum, a puzzle that I haven't yet solved (Hey Lotty, drop me a line, I need to know as it's driving me crazy, Where'd you *really* get that charcoal?).

A comradeship had overtaken Shell Camp. As the barbecue progressed, it was quite obvious that a community of harmony had been established, everyone helped, everyone pitched in a hand, or two, to make things work, to make things fun, to make every moment of their expedition a memorable activity. Even Abby, with his stovepipe mushroom hat had joined in, adding a unique flavor to the scientific gala, I personally saw him chopping lettuce with a two-pound ball peen hammer. And now that I think about it, I don't know where that (the hammer) came from, either. It must have been in with the charcoal.

Lotty was stirring up a pitcher of powdered milk, Doc was setting tables, Soph was washing something in the sink, the others were chatting, sipping on a red wine (I know where that came from), and generally splattered around, cooking, talking, nibbling and in general, enjoying themselves. It was nice. It was intellectual camping and it was fun.

I went over to Sophie, "Ah, you're every man's dream, Soph. A woman who washes dishes." I grabbed a towel and took an old and rusting serving platter from her soapy hands and began to dry it.

She ignored me, but said, "I never realized that a bunch of scientists could have fun, Jim. I've had a really nice time today. I actually had fun, they made me feel like I belonged, know what I mean, Jim?"

"Yeah, keep washing their dishes and they'll nominated you for a Nobel Prize. I've seen it happen, Kidd. One day your kissing ass in the kitchen, next thing, you're queen for a day, and then you have to do all the dishes. And the worst part is, no one comes over to help you dry, because you're the Nobel Prize winner, you can't be helped. See how it works?"

She answers, "You shouldn't take a nap in the heat of the day, Jim. You've baked your brain."

She reached another platter, "We found all kinds of turtles. Until today, I've only seen their shells. It's amazing how they can hide, right out in the open. You can walk right over one and never know it. Now, I see them everywhere. I find it most interesting, James."

"Uh huh, you've only been with these kooks for one day, Soph, and already, you're beginning to sound like one of them."

She says, "Ak-chu-lee, James. I believe that I've missed my calling. As soon as we get back to the States I'm going back to college to become a scientist."

I thought to myself, "Well, so much for suburbia, rug rats and a lawn mower." Out loud, I said, "We're Americans. You can do, what ever you want to. Be, whatever you want to be – just do it."

Then I asked her, "Have you ever considered having a few kids, living in the suburbs, washing the dishes every night?"

"No."

Abby looked up from his lettuce pounding, "I like this hat now, Boss."

I nodded him a smiled reply. To Soph, I said, "I've got some news on Margolova."

Her eyebrows shot up, "Let's go for a walk, Mister Morgan."

Soph grabbed me by the arm and forcibly dragged me out the back door, past the sizzling steaks, and twenty yards away from the din of the diesels. Stopping abruptly, still holding my arm, she says, "Lets have it?"

I relayed the whole scenario, including the bribes. Then, with concern in her voice, she said, "Let's eat. I'll inform command post when we're through. Maybe they can get us a bug on her phone line. We should get something, at least a list of who's calling who from the local phone company."

She paused, gave me a look that said I was stupid – then says, "You know of course, that Uncle Bobby will call Margolova back? Probably as soon as you were out of his sight, right?"

Although she affected a chastising glare, it was filled with a kind and deliberate humor. It said, "You're playing the game, Jimbo. Don't screw it up inadvertently, if you hadn't already."

"Yeah. I hope she finds the story about marsupial butterflies as interesting as Uncle Bobby did." It was an attempt to show how smart and intelligent I was during my clandestine meeting at the Hilton. Yet, somehow, I knew I had blown it. Just how, I didn't know. I shouldn't have spoken with Uncle Bobby, his job is information, and mine (arguably) is changing light bulbs.

As we walked back to the barbecue, Soph asked if I was going to go with her to the ruby mine.

I made this joke, "Yeah, but, we have to get a "steak" first, don't we?"

"Yes. I'm hungry, too." She said, missing the point and pun.

My sense of humor had gone sour. I needed to work harder on my delivery. Perhaps my timing was just off. And for a brief instant, I thought to myself, "I wonder if Gnancy would have laughed?"

Chapter Thirty-Seven

Our steaks were medium-rare, light pink, tender and very, very juicy. Even the ball peen hammer salad tasted fair, too. Although! Abby does have some serious work ahead of him if he's ever to perfect the hammerhead salad. I used the whole-bottle-of-dressing technique to make mine palatable, as did Soph.

Soph had a lot to say about the art of tortoise hunting, she had had a great time, based on her recanted tales of that day's events. Including the one's on how Doc kept expressing his heart's desire to experience her charms, "...some starlit evening."

Soph hardly touched her 18-ounce steak, she did pick at the salad, and I think she had two bites of her potato. It's the price one pays to maintain a model's figure. My steak disappeared so fast that David Copperfield, the infamous illusionist, would have been awestruck, and be demanding that I eat another so he could pick up on my trick. But then again, "my waist line isn't a model's."

We dumped off our plates with the one man Ugandan Dish Corps and retired to the bunkhouse. Soph had her call to make. I had my rounds to do – check the water system, oil the generators, let Doc know that we'd be gone for an hour, pat Ab on the back and, generally ask around to see if anyone needed anything.

Everything was on the up and up, I was earning my pay, the expeditionary force was happy. Everything mechanical was working and my staff, Abby, was sincerely content. When I returned to the bunkhouse, Sophie was changing clothes. She had on a red flannel shirt and skin-tight jeans, her holstered .38 looked natural around her shoulder, it was meant to be there. As she put on a blue jean jacket, I asked, "Where's your horse, Annie Oakley?"

"Right outside the door, Jimbo."

I kicked off my Docksider's and put on my safari-issue hiking boots, and following Sophie's lead, I threw on a light jacket. She was already outside stroking the MAV, revving its engine, which isn't all that loud, I should have said, purring, engine. She was having fun. She was a teenager with a new toy. It wasn't exactly a Harley Davidson, but with each rev of the 1000 cc engine she began to look more and more like Marlon Brando, in that movie classic, "The Wild One, Woman."

She says, "Hop on, Gramps."

I ignored the gramps. She isn't *that* much younger than me. Although, she is in better, physical, shape. First it's Eunice calling me chubby. Now it's Soph calling me gramps – it's enough to give an open-minded pragmatic Engineer a psychological complex.

The MAV - 861 is not designed to carry two passengers. But it certainly beat walking, and it was nice having Sophie close to me. As a matter of fact, it was down right pleasurable. We pulled out slow, no wheelies, no showing off. The bike was our mule, and we were two prospectors, plodding up the creek on rubber horseshoes – the bike's tires. I felt safe as we meandered up the riverbed. Soph had a feel for the creek, when it got deep we skirted the bank. She had been there before. She does learn quickly, no doubt.

We did have to dodge a few palm fronds and duck under a few deciduous tree limbs, and once, we had to dismount and lift the MAV over a small waterfall. And once, I almost fell off, but I grabbed onto Soph's chest, her braless chest, and after that, I knew exactly where to hold on to maintain a healthy balance.

The ruby mine is only a few miles up Travelle Creek, but even so, it took us a good thirty minutes to get there. It was a fun ride, it was scenic, and a nice diversion from the drudge work that we had left behind, cleaning the kitchen, watching TV, and listening to Doc.

The sun was lowering in the west. When we stopped, the orange and red sky had turned into a dynamic tapestry of light refraction. We stood there without speaking for a good ten minutes. The colors began to fade into grays and night blues highlighted by a few early stars. A few more popped out as we watched just to announce the end of what was a sensuously pleasant pastel sunset.

It was a splendid experience. My entire body was tingling from the vibrant bike ride. I was still warm, from bodily contact with Sophie and still in awe of the now passed spectacular light show. Had I experienced nirvana, that state of peace and harmony that sages and meditative yogis devote their entire lives to for that one brief second of universal oneness?

– My spiritual oneness with nature was short lived. Sophie had broken my trance; my transcendental ga-ga-hoop-a-la went its way and was instantly replaced with that old capitalistic, materialistic, dilemma – instant wealth. This time, a plethora of red rubies were begging to be collected, damn the beauties of a Malagasy sunset, they happen every day, but – rubies? Rubies aren't just strewn about like so many light refracted cirrus ice crystals, no sir. Rubies are only found here, right here, in this old abandoned mine guarded by an old, hand painted, deteriorated sign declaring ownership with the words, "Jake's Ruby Dig."

"Come on, Jim. – It's getting dark, we don't have much, time."

Ah, the cry of all mankind, "...we don't have much, *time.*

Inside, in a timely manner, we found big rocks and a lot of little rocks. They all looked alike, except for the igneous quartz that streaked through the ragged granite, called veins. These veins were of a pastel pink unlike the white quartz of California rock, the kind we were allowed to handle in a box in our classroom back in the (my) Purduvian geological epoch.

I lighted my Zippo and looked for the deep red, red-red, of a ruby. It was liken to reading my lottery tickets back in Illinois, nothing matched, nothing red, yet, the intense hope, easy street is only six numbers away or – hey, how valuable is a ruby? Did I need to find just one, or ten thousand? And, where was this Jake? Did he hit it rich? What's his story? Suddenly, I had more questions than answers, I snapped the Zippo shut and crept onward toward the light, Sophie's light.

She shouted, "Found one!"

The light glowed ahead of me as I hurried to see, it was an eerie dull dancing yellow light, she was holding the lantern, it was swaying slightly, hauntingly, it cast monster shadows before me and I felt a chill, a scare, or – perhaps, an excited flush that she had indeed – found one. I stumbled, not seeing on what and immediately said to myself, "Sorry Jake."

Joining her, I took the gem from her extended hand, studied it under the kerosene lamp, and then handed it back to her, "Sorry, Babe. It's a fake."

"Fake? What do you mean, fake? It's as real as you and me, Jim. It can't be a fake. I just found it."

Elaborating, I said, "What I mean is – it is *not* a ruby. It's a nice piece of quartz. Probably, a rose quartz."

She looked at it again, turned it around in her fingers, then, looking up at me while putting it into her pocket said, "It's a ruby."

Yeah, it would now take an official decree from the president of the American Geological Society to prove her wrong, she had found a ruby, and that was that, the end. We spent the next thirty-forty minutes sifting through a huge pile of soft and multi-colored stone. Jake hadn't left much behind. If rubies were there, they were still there imbedded deep in the granite. Jake was thorough, and probably broke. Jake's dig was *done* dug and I, for one, was ready for some fresh air. Jake was obviously not very big on soap and water – the air inside the mine was permeated with sour odors like those found in an athletic, gemnasium – pun intended.

I knelt down next to Sophie, saying, "The only jewel in this hole, is you, Kidd."

Without looking up from her search, she retorted, "Have you used that line on Eunice, Jim?" She said this quietly. Dry worded as if she was thinking out loud and I wasn't supposed to hear her, but I did.

The proverbial light at the end of the tunnel was getting dim, I said, "We'd better get going, Soph. If we stay much longer, we may have to spend the night – together."

She stopped pawing through the quartz. She looked up at me. The light was indirect but there was enough to show a tear streaking down her cheek. She says, "You know, Jim. I still want to sleep with you. I know that things won't be the same – like they were. But I do like you, that much. Shameful, aren't I?" She didn't look at me for a response, she went back to her ruby hunting, sifting rough stones through her delicate fingers.

I lit a cigarette, wanting to say, everything. Nothing formed. My mind went blank. I was speechless. She had yanked on my heart with a pair of vice-grips, she had locked them on and was tugging at my soul with both hands, and I don't think she even knew it.

I did finally say, "I mean it, Soph. You *are* the only jewel around." I moved toward the mine entrance grinding stone under my boots, feeling my way slowly along the jagged walls. As I neared the opening I saw a few stars twinkling against a dark, blue hued blackness that was simply breathtaking and I knew, Jake had found something more precious than gems every time he exited his dig and – I envied him. He certainly was one of the richest men on this earth, or now in it – wherever he may be.

A low shimmering glow began to exit the mine behind me. Soph had finally thrown in the towel. Too bad she was carrying that lantern, she'd miss the star gate, that priceless portal out of reality. Yeah, it would escape her because of the lantern's flickering flame. I thought of calling in to her, but didn't.

Suddenly, I was gripped with a mortal fear, a chill raced through my body tingling my flesh, and – I wondered, just what it was that I feared? And I knew – it was, *love*.

Soph ducked out into my night holding out her hand, "Look."

She rightfully smiled, "And don't go telling me "this" is a fake, Jim Morgan."

I took the ruby from her hand and held it up to the brightest star in the Malagasy heaven. I had to whistle, deep and low, it was "brilliant." It was pure, and intense. Yet, it was not as beautiful or pure, as Sophie, D. Deadly Kidd.

Chapter Thirty-Eight

Back at the bunkhouse, we shared a quick shower, poured some light Scotch and joined in on the camp's entertainment. No one had missed us. No one had even left the dining room, except Doc, who was in the lab doing his thing. The solo guitar twanged on and on until midnight, when the tired, yawning crew, drifted off in piecemeal to their respective tents leaving Lotty to tidy up under the drone of Abdul's nasal snore.

Sophie was antsy. She left several times during the evening, to scout our perimeter. She'd return now and then, then be off again. Once, I went with her. She'd stand still and listen. Yeah, looking around for lurking spies is definitely hard work. I wondered how many times a day she had to tell herself that she isn't really a paranoid, and that her suspicious leers at every moving grass was actually an integral part of her CIA job description. It was boring and I didn't go with her a second time. Besides, the music wasn't all that bad considering my Scotch intake.

Soph decided to call Washington a second time. She didn't need to, or so she said, but she was mentally preoccupied with her work. Perhaps, she just wanted to tell someone about her ruby find. I listened in as Dawn's, now familiar, voice echoed out from the desktop room speaker.

She was in, what Sophie called, a prattling mood. She had categorically listed several agent reassignments to the Middle East areas. Washington was in a buzz, subtle war signals were emanating from the Arab community. I'm quoting Dawn, "Iraq is heading for some heavy international embarrassment – how blind can that king be?

Oh, gods of greed and avarice soften your hearts and let the poor man see. World opinion has a big foot on his head and he doesn't even feel it. These opinions are getting stronger every day, heavier by the minute, and soon – he won't be king. You'll see, Kidd." Soph was listening intently, not interrupting, just listening as Dawn prattled on, "...even the Russians are scratching their heads, and they'd probably become some kind of support for him. This is enough to make a grown person enter politics, or start going to church, and things like that..."

As she continued, Soph covered the speaker with her hand and said, "It sounds like she made all of those reassignments by herself. Rest assured, Dawn is at the helm, and the world *will* be saved." She began laughing.

Personally I didn't see the humor, I was thinking, "Come on, get to the point, it's late and I'm ready for bed."

Soph stopped Dawn's tirade, "Dawn? ...Dawn? What do you have for me, anything?

Dawn paused, "Ah... We got a line on that phone number, Kidd. It's a real moneymaker for the phone company. They get calls there from all over the world, including, get this, "Hollywood." Isn't that something, Kidd? Of all places, Hollywood."

She paused, we could hear papers being shuffled in the background, "and... we are...working on the phone numbers right now. The Russian calls will be the hardest, but we've got the Recheeka task force going through them as we talk, Kidd. I hear they're excited, it's a new link for them, Madagascar."

Soph broke in, "What's the latest on Margolova, Dawn?"

"She's still holed up at the Turk's, Honey. The Malagasy Army has pulled their surveillance. Junior's in the Bahamas... Hold on a sec, Kidd. That report on the English expedition has just come in, can you hold?"

"Standing by." Sophie turned to me, "I'll bet that Tina bitch was a whore back in Devon." She was happy, unable to hide her own vehemence, her feminine nature was tossing some nasty venom directed directly at her charming rival.

I could only shake my head in bewilderment. Women can really be ruthless, one to another. Soph turned back to her radio as her face was reddening. I think that she may have realized that she was out of line, but maybe not.

Dawn's voice hammered into our silence, "Get a load of this! Kidd. That whole English expedition is a cover story for a covert study on Pimakeel Bay – as a potential submarine base. We've been asked to assist them, Kidd. Code 48. Repeat: Code Four Eight. Copy in blood, Honey."

With a heavy note of reluctance, Soph answered, "Copy. Code 48. Repeating: Copy, Code Four Eight." Actually, it was a note of resignation. Whatever a code 48 was, it surely wasn't something desirable, at least, not to Sophie. She looked at me and made a sad face, then went back to her radio.

Dawn continued, "Your C-5 link is, Tina Marie Johnson. She's one of England's finest, Kidd. Want a profile?"

"We've already met, Dawn. What's her weaponry?"

"Ah – not listed, assume a standard issue, Kidd."

"What's her specialty, Dawn?"

"She has a doctorate in Biology. Her specialty is "wave mechanics." She's really deep cover, Kidd. There are *way* too many unknowns written in her file. Think you can handle this, Soph?"

"Oh Dawn, 48's are easy. If she says jump, I jump."

"Well, you got it, Honey. There isn't anything else I can give you. Want me to call Papa on the 48?"

"No. I can follow orders with the best of them. Anything from the boss

"Date, time and initials – your on your own, Kidd-o."

"Do you know if Papa's seen the 48, Dawn?" Sophie asked this with a desperate hope in her voice, a hope that someone had goofed and that her Code-48 notification was an honest mistake. Her tone said, "Papa wouldn't approve a 48 for his Kidd, check those records one more time, Dawn, something's not *quite* right."

Dawn broke in, "It's signed, Kidd. He's read it, and it's approved. Do you want further clarification? Assistance? – Anything?"

"No. I guess not, Dawn. It's just that I had this Johnson broad pegged as a whore."

Dawn was cracking up at Sophie's comment, "You crack me up, Kidd. I'm sitting here looking at her picture and I was thinking she belonged in a nunnery." Dawn let out a bash of laughter.

Sophie wasn't sharing in Dawn's joviality, and tiredly said, "I don't have anything else on my end, Dawn. If your through, I'd better get some rest. If you know who, says jump, I'd better be ready to ask how high."

Dawn's laughter subsided, "No, that's it, Kidd. Unless you want to hear about my mother's lumbago?"

Sophie flipped off her radio without responding to Dawn's question; and to this day, I still don't know what a lumbago is.

I asked Soph, "Hey, what's all this code 48 stuff?"

She stopped stowing her radio, walked over to my cot and sat down next to me, she seemed glum, no – she was *obviously* glum. She was looking down at the floor, "A code 48 is an international signal agreed upon by certain international organizations to lend a hand in their operation, normally a covert operation. England's C-5 section, which is similar to our own CIA, is a subscriber to the code 48 program."

"If Tina were to knock on the door right now, I'm obligated to assist her in any way that I could – no questions asked. She had to have asked for it, the code 48. I'll find out when we talk. If – she asks for assistance. Once she officially asks, I'll no longer be working for the CIA. I'll be working for England. Tina will be my direct line supervisor, code 48's are approved by presidential order and everyone involved has to concur to be a part of that mission."

She continued, "When I said, "Copy 48," I concurred. I agreed to drop whatever I was doing and assist the requesting agency. My supervisors had to approve it first, or I wouldn't have been asked. Now, I'm committed. Once Johnson evokes her authority I'll be Code 49, Johnson's agent."

She paused, she hadn't told me everything. She looked into my eyes, "Actually, this could get really exciting." Suddenly her gloom turned to excitement; she had been thrown into the limelight of international super spies.

My thoughts, which I immediately expressed, "Yeah, exciting. So, if you're protecting me, and Eunice's tortoise, and Tina snaps her fingers – you go? You leave me on my own?"

"Technically, that's true."

"Yeah, well you can just drop that technically crap. Are you going to protect me or not?"

She began to tease me, erotically fingering my neck, cooing, she pushed me down on the cot, "Is my little Jimmy afraid of losing his Sophie's protection?"

I pushed her hand away, "Damn right, Soph."

Sophie was enjoying my apprehension, and her sexual effort to placate me was downright disgusting, and working. We entered into a playful wrestling match that left us naked under the bed sheets. Sophie was crazed, I couldn't fend her off, not that I tried with all my might, but she had her way. And I wondered if she had learned those moves at spy school. Although, perhaps, and maybe – she was just horny.

She fell asleep cuddled in my arms, snug, and very cozy. It was nice, I smelled her, felt her firm breasts against my arm, studied her flesh, her calmness, and contemplated her as a wife, and that – didn't seem plausible. No, Sophie wasn't designed to run around suburbia barefooted and pregnant. No. She was designed to do what she was doing, spying, riding experimental scooters, loving when she wanted, karate chopping bad guys and protecting a turtle and its captor from unseen enemies and assisting our allied governments by secret code at the drop of an international hat. Yeah, this is what she was suited for. Could she be an Engineer's wife? – Nah!

No, she could no more fit into a picket-fenced neighborhood than could a herd of Indian elephants. Like myself, she *needed* adventure, she needed to fly, free, free from all nuclear family commitment, freed of that loving entrapment – babies, and most certainly, free of social bondage, neighborly gatherings, and the PTA harness of subservient motherhood. And I fell to sleep thinking of my own serendipitous life and how I would fit the mold of a T-ball coach, or a little league umpire. In my mind's eye, I socked Margolova in the face with my balled fist. She grabbed her bloody, squashed to a pulp, nose and ran back to her native homeland, Russia. And, as she fled, Sophie emerged from a dark recess of my one-act mental play, falls to her knee and pleads, "Please, please marry me, James."

And that was all I recalled until the alarm clock buzzed me awake at exactly six a.m. Malagasy time. Sophie looked at me in a somnam-bulist daze, rolled off my chest, and, bundled herself away under the sheets and covers, then mumbled, "Turn it off." I showered until the hot water was gone. The bunkhouse was layered with a cloud of steam when I exited the water and began to towel myself dry.

That's when Doc knocked on the door. I peeked through the cur-tain and told him to give me two minutes while I dressed. He said, "Meet me in the dining room, Jim. I need a minute of your time." He turned and left.

I watched him as he marched across the yard, and I sensed that he knew I was watching, because he did march, and, he looked like General George S. Patton himself, booted, and striding boldly to his dining room office. I looked at his hands to see if he were holding a riding crop. He wasn't, but if he had been, it would not have been out of place. Doc, most certainly is, one of a kind.

I hurriedly put on my own uniform, Levis, white sweatshirt, my Rolex, sweat-socks and Docksider's. I had chopped off the sweatshirt's sleeves near the elbow. I did this for a macho look, but I also think it is more comfortable.

Exactly two minutes later I was in front of the coffee urn with Doc. He held up his wrist and studied his own Rolex, "Ah, two minutes exactly."

Not to be out done, I held out my own wrist, mimicking Doc's flair at showing off his gold, "You need a minute, eh Doc?"

A few layers of crust fell off the old bugger's back as he said, somewhat condescendingly, "Time isn't always of the essence, I suppose. Have a cup of coffee, James. It's quite good, I made it myself just an hour ago."

We sat down at a corner table, Doc's office, and sipped the master's brew. And, of course, it was excellent. I threw him a sincere accolade on his coffee. He accepted the compliment openly in the way that people who excel have learned to do, graciously, with only a "slightly" big head.

Just then, Lotty Gnancy burst through the door like a Mack truck with a broken brake hose, stormed right past us (I don't believe that she saw us), up to Ab's kitchen bed and began some hefty, organizational shouting, "Abdul Amin, why aren't those eggs boiling? Where's your hat, Chef? You should have been up hours ago."

And then we heard grunting, ugly grunting, it sounded profane but the words, if they were words, were muffled, smothered under a bundle of wool blankets and un-cased pillows.

Gnancy wouldn't listen to his vehement protests, she shouted, "Up and at 'em cup-cake. We've got a hungry crew to feed this fine morning, how come you're still in bed?"

Abby's head poked out from under the blankets, "I don't know boiled eggs, Miss Lotty. You do it, Miss Lotty."

Lotty was up for the fight, "Oh no, Buster. I'm only here to help, not to do everything for you, Abster-Flabster, now move before I get myself a bag of ice cubes. Today, I'm going to teach you how to make pies, Mister Chef."

Amused with the dynamic duo's culinary plans, but not wanting to intervene, Doc suggested we move to the lab where he wanted me to look at a laser pen, to see if I could repair it. He had a ton of shells to engrave, and, a broken laser. As we left the dinning room we could still hear the continuing combat between the student and his teacher, Abby was losing, and I was beginning to think, "This battle is going to cost Eunice another pay raise by day's end."

• • •

A new odor filled the laboratory, the odor of alcohol. Doc used it extensively for various and sundry cleaning purposes. I commented on the powerful smell. Doc drew in a deep breath, "Ah, love that fragrance. Women should wear it in public." He took a second deeper inhale. Doc was a laboratory odor junkie.

I looked about the lab and saw tortoises everywhere. Tubs, boxes, bins, all full with clawing, wiggling heads and feet and various colored shells. Some boxes were stacked three deep with them, bumping, clawing, yet voiceless in a continuous attempt to escape their opened-at-the-top containers. Big ones, little ones, there must have been three hundred of them.

"How did you get so many in just one outing, Doc?"

Doc glanced around the catch, "These tortoise fields were discovered many years ago, Mister Morgan. They haven't changed in three hundred years, maybe a thousand years. The creatures are quite easy to collect, they aren't very cleaver, or fast."

He held up a five-inch wiggling tortoise, a yellowish one, like dried grass, it was tagged with a small brass plate that showed an eight-digit number and a date, 1957. He then continued.

"Shell Camp has been a study site since the 1850's. The oldest tag that I've personally found was dated in 1879, it was on a broken shell, not of much use to us, but it's early, we'll find more, older ones. Some of them are over four hundred years old. Did you know law protects them? We're not allowed to remove them from the island, that's why we're here. They're extremely fascinating, some of them grow to an excess of 500 pounds."

Doc handed me the laser, saying, "Here, it doesn't work. Can you fix it?"

I asked for a schematic. He didn't have one. "How soon do you need this, Doc?"

"Right now, I'm afraid. We need to etch these fellows and get them back into the field. We've lost a few already, they need their space I fear."

I plugged in the cord and turned it on, nothing happened. I grabbed the plug and wiggled it around in the outlet. The laser lit. The plug prongs were not making a solid contact. "There we are, Doc. Good as new. First rule of every repairman, check the plug."

Doc asked, rather humbly, "Can we keep this little repair job under our hat? I was preparing to have a new laser shipped out from Stanford, Jim. You've just saved us a considerable expense, and me personally, a considerable amount of embarrassment. I thank you, sir. From the very bottom of my heart – I thank you."

And there you have it; five years of intense study at one of the world's finest engineering colleges had finally paid off. One day, I may return to Purdue and teach a class on plug wiggling. Yeah, it's that old joke, "It only takes one Engineer to change a light bulb, but the light bulb must want to be changed." Whoops, that's a Freudian, sorry.

Chapter Thirty-Nine

I did my camp chores, oiled the mules (the generators), rid the creek pump of debris, walked through the showers to insure their cleanliness and to see that everything was working, checked the tent pegs, and finally, wrote up my daily report:

Dear Res. Dir. Eun,
Everything on the up and up!"

Sincerely,
J. Morgan, Rural Field D.

I threw the envelope in my briefcase. If a mailman happened by, I'd mail it.

It was eight o'clock, I woke up Sophie and physically aimed her toward the shower, and she went, reluctantly, mumbling, something about a monthly visitor, or that she had a monkey sister. I'm sure it was some feminine thing and I let it drop. While she showered I went to the kitchen, she'd want coffee and I needed a refill myself. Besides, I needed to practice my winking.

Breakfast was over, Abby was washing dishes, Lotty was making pie dough, and two doctors, who had mated for the expedition, sat in a darkened corner dazed with fresh love and romance. They were sipping coffee in a blurry eyed ceremony of consummated sexual adventure that had left them wading around in a cesspool of guilt and shame, they were both married and they both had children, and I won't mention their real names because they are noted members of our scientific community, and because, they are both human.

Abby said, "Hey Boss, boiling eggs is easy, Boss. Miss Lotty say I'm number one egghead, Boss." He smiled big, adding, "Miss Lotty say I can ask for more money now, Boss. Can I have more money, Boss?

I responded, "Maybe. When you finish with the dishes I want you to clean up the showers. If you do a good job, we'll sit down and discuss it. Okay, Pal?"

He shook his head in a positive reply, saying, "Okay, Boss."

Lotty had a big hunk of dough on the table and was rolling out circular pie crusts, I watched her a minute, then asked, "Pancakes again, eh?"

She raised the roller, tomahawk fashion, "You, Mister Morgan, can become number one potato head, real quick." Once again, her eyes twinkled. And once again, I caught myself winking.

I moved close to the Chief War Horse's ear and whispered, as I threw my thumb toward the cooing lovers, "What do you think about our young lover's, Lotty?"

She said, "Flagrant, isn't it?" And then, she turned up the corner of her mouth. I had believed that only Eunice had the facial plasticity to perform such a mouth curve – I was quite in awe of her feat, down right surprised, as a matter of fact.

She added, "Speaking of steaming windows, Mister Morgan, a lot of eyes are glued on the bunkhouse, including mine. Want to talk about it?"

I was caught with my hand in the cookie jar. I smiled, and said, "Nothing going on, Lotty. A little smoke – no fire. If you want to see some real steam watch Strongbow and Sophie. I hear that the old fox is pouncing on the chicks while beating the bush. Of course, this is just between you and me, okay? I wouldn't want it to get out that Sophie made me her confidant on the Doc's advances."

Lotty gave me a nod of confidentiality. Grinning she said, "Why that old bastard, who'd think?" She trailed off her verbalized thought while scanning the kitchen for an answer to her own question.

She shook her head in a shake of disbelief, or dismay, saying, "Thanks again for the flowers, Jim. I really got a kick out of the note."

I scanned the kitchen looking for the roses. I recalled the note, "Thanks for saving our stomachs, better tell Abby they ain't parsley, With Love, the Grocery man."

Lotty, seeing me look for them, said, "I've got them in my tent, drop in and see them sometime, they really are beautiful."

She grabbed my chin with a heavily floured hand and kissed me full on the lips. And, as luck would have it, Sophie bumbled into the kitchen. Just as our lips separated from the platonic, thank you, kiss.

She looked at me in a dumbfounded glare – she wasn't fully awake, even after showering, and says, "Your lipstick smeared, Mister

Morgan. Been checking the generators this morning?"

Abby broke an awkward silence, "I can check the generators, Boss. I always checked the oil in Luke's plane. It's easy, Boss."

Lotty said, "The lipstick is mine, Sophie. I just gave him a thank you kiss for the flowers."

Sophie asked, with a thick note of confusion in her voice, "Flowers?"

Needless to say, it turned into an awkward morning. I found myself explaining, way, way too much. Sophie was actually being silent, not eliciting excuses, but I kept giving them. The more I explained – the more I needed to clarify. The more I clarified – the deeper I sank into a justification muck-a-muck.

Exasperated, I opted to escape. I decided to drive into Tanan. Then, I made a foolish mistake. I asked Sophie if she'd care to join me. To which, to my utter surprise and dismay, she readily agreed. It's hard for a man to understand his woman at times, and this was one of those times.

On the way to town, I ironed out the lipstick thing, cleared up the flower controversy and made an adult effort to rationalize my quick-ie with Eunice in the generator room. The latter turned into a major bug-a-boo. Sophie was diametrically opposed to everything that I started to say. I say, "started, to say," because she didn't want to hear my side, my perspective of what had happened and the why. She had her point of view, the end, finis, case closed, "A man cannot love two women at the same time." Especially, if one of them is named, "D. Deadly Kidd," nee "Alberquist." Amen, adios, "Up yours, James Morgan." And she added, "What's done is done. Don't bring it up again – I don't want to hear it." And then we rode in silence for a good ten miles, at 20 miles an hour.

Then, she slides across the seat and snuggles under my arm. From there on in it was a leisurely ride. We listened to the radio and made a sincere attempt to enjoy the noise on a Malagasy rock station, we had ultimately switched back to a classical station that was playing piano solos. Some things are universal, classical music is one, and, a warm, sensuous woman under one's arm is another.

We mailed off my last eight daily reports at an ancient post office near downtown. We bought ice cream cones from a street vendor and strolled through a small park with a green statue of an old horseman wearing Spanish armor plate and a carrying a lance. The horse had all four on the ground which Sophie said had significance as to how the soldier died – old age, was her recollected guess. The nameplate was missing so we guessed at who it might be. I suggested it was, Jimmy the Greek, sitting on the last horse that I placed a C-note on during the Kentucky Derby. A real flat hoofed bastard, stood just like this statue through the last furlong (eighth of a mile), with all four touching the track, at full gallop.

The Deadly Kidd says, "I've seen a movie that proved a horse can run with all four legs off the ground, but I never heard of one that can gallop with all four *touching* the ground."

"Yeah? Well, just watch the next horse that I put a C-note on, you'll see what I'm talking about, Kidd."

"Oh." She said. "I get it."

Soph suggested we tour the city, "...maybe drive past the old Turk's villa, see what it looks like, see where the bitch is holed up, just for fun."

It took us nearly an hour to find the villa. It was fenced in by an eight-foot stucco wall and was painted a pale pink. As we drove past the wrought ironed, arched gateway, we could see that the main house was also painted pink – it looked expensive. Soph said there was an armed guard patrolling the gate, but I didn't see this, as we had driven by rather quickly and the traffic happened to be heavy at the moment we had passed. I wanted to go around the block and take a second look. I really wanted to see the armed guard, but Sophie discouraged me.

She said, "Not a good idea, Jim. If Margolova was to spot us, she'd probably take a pot-shot at us, no sense aggravating her."

I said, "You know, we know, that she's in there. Right?"

"Oh, she's in there. Believe me."

"Well, why don't we call in a B-52 and bomb her and her rat pack of friends, right to hell, eh Soph?"

She poked me in the arm, hard, "What do you want me to do, lose my job? Without people like them, I'd be out of work." – I couldn't tell if she was kidding or not.

"Oh-oh." I announced. "We've picked up a tail, Kidd."

She didn't turn around but quickly responded with an emphatic, "Shit."

"It's a black Saab, he's followed us through four turns now. It's two cars in back of us. What should I do? Should I try and lose them?"

"No." She sounded calm, collected, "As soon as you can, pull over and stop. We need to know for sure that they really are following us. It could be a simple case of coincidence." As she said this, she unbuttoned her jacket and unsnapped her thirty-eight's holster flap and loosened her weapon away from the leather.

I eased the Ford to the curb and stopped. "Don't look now but they're stopping, too. They are a half-block back, same side."

"How many of them, Jim?"

"I'm not sure – at least two. That's all I can see."

"Here's what I want you to do, Jim. Pull out slow. Drive back to the Turk's villa. Drive past the gate and park just beyond the driveway. Okay?"

"Okay." And I added, nervously, "I hope you know what you're doing?"

"I do." She smiled, "If it's Margolova, or her henchmen, they won't want to start trouble right outside the Turk's front door, would they? Let's move it, Jim, before they figure out what we're doing."

I did exactly as she said; I drove slow but deliberate and made sure they could follow, which they did. At the Turk's, I pulled two car lengths past the driveway and stopped, but left the motor running. The Saab pulled up, too, about a hundred feet behind us. Sophie said, "I'll be right back." And was out of the car before I could object and was walking rapidly toward the Saab.

I leaned over the seat and watched her through the tailgate window. She was at the Saab's driver's window. Her hand was in her jacket. Probably gripping her .38, although I couldn't exactly see. I lowered the rear window, the distinct servo motor whine was loud and worked slow but I soon had a clear, unobstructed view of the confrontation. I couldn't hear them distinctly but they appeared to be arguing, heatedly. My heart began to race, I wanted to join her, but she had specifically told me to stay at the wheel and be ready take off, quick.

Soph was the expert. I did like she said and stayed put. I didn't know what I would do, if trouble did start. I wasn't prepared, and I had no plan.

Then it started, the passenger opened his door and began an exit from the Saab. I threw the gearshift into reverse and powered the Ford backward, screeching the tires and coming within an inch of the

Saab's bumper before bouncing to a stop. The punk stopped his exit midway and watched the smoking Ford advance. From the corner of my eye, I saw the armed guard that Soph had mentioned earlier come running up to the closed gate, and indeed, he *was* carrying a rifle.

The Saab's passenger jumped back into his seat pulling his door closed. I got out, leaving the Ford running and my door open and ready, for a quick departure. I joined Sophie at the driver's side of the Saab. The villa's guard had reached the gate and had jammed his face between the black iron bars and stared intently toward us, just watching. He had slung his rifle over his shoulder by a shoulder strap. It was an obvious statement that he wasn't going to shoot us, at least, not real soon – he was just watching.

Sophie had pulled out her thirty-eight and had it stuck, flush to the driver's forehead pushing him backward against his seat. "Meet the two punks who visited our camp last week, Jim. Dumb, and his baby brother, Stupid."

I looked at them close, studied them for distinguishing marks, I wanted to recognize them in case our paths were to ever cross again. They were just kids, eighteen? Nineteen? Dirty, they had probably just waxed the Saab, their hair was greasy, and their skin was dark – Polynesian – maybe Samoan. They were trying to look tough, they were wanna-be hoods, wanna-be bad Asses. They both had thin black mustaches and wore matching black T-shirts. They both had brown, bloodshot eyes and a good guess was that they were both on drugs, or were sniffers, – paint, glue, and hair spray... I didn't see any weapons, no guns, no knives, brass knuckles and they surely weren't muscle, no powerful builds – they weren't about to grab us and break us in two. Far from it, they were undernourished, skinny runts. Two social dropouts – they probably signed their names X and X – illegibly.

They were pissed, they had bonged their tail, they would probably be sent to bed early, without supper, – again. At that moment they were a pathetic looking duo. They sensed that they were in trouble, not only with Sophie, but – with the Turk, and for sure Margolova, for causing a scene so close to home. Soph was right, if their names weren't really, Dumb and Stupid, then they should have been. It was a most accurate description.

Soph jabbed the .38 against Dumb pushing his head back even further than it already was, saying, "Keys please."

Gritting his yellow teeth, he reached them and handed them into her free, waiting hand.

She holstered her gun, and then threw the keys over the Turk's privacy wall. I looked at the guard; he was frozen into the bars content to just watch. I was nervous. I wanted to leave. A large truck rolled past kicking up dust, rustling a nearby tree, vibrating the street.

When it had passed, Soph told the Saab's driver, Dumb, "The next time you follow us or come sneaking around our camp, I'm going to personally break off your arm and beat it over, pointing at his partner, Stupid's head. Got the message?"

The driver's eyes narrowed in a show of anger, he understood, but didn't like being threatened, especially by a cute blond.

Sophie told me to get in the car, motioning toward the Ford with a nod of her head. Keeping her eyes on the duo, she says, "Let's get going before this turkey starts to cry, Jim."

I backed to the Ford and got in, I waved to the guard, as he was looking right at me, studying me. He didn't respond. He shifted his weight, straining to see Sophie, no longer interested in me. I pulled my door closed, reached over the seat and opened Sophie's door. I restarted the car. It had died when I slammed on the brakes to avoid ramming the Saab. I watched Sophie through the side-view mirror. She took a side step to return to the Ford. The punk spat a defiant wad of spit toward her retreat.

Soph bolted back to the Saab's window. I watched her reach in the window and grab the insolent teenager. She grabbed him by the hair and pulled his head full out of the Saab's window. Then she hit him, *hard*. I had turned around in my seat just in time to see her balled fist knock the little bastard right on the button. I heard her fist make contact with his face. It made me wince.

And I mean to tell you, it hurt me – and I was just watching. The passenger, Stupid, grabbed Dumb and cradled him back to his seat.

Soph had knocked him into next week, he was out cold, and from my position – fifteen-feet away – I could see blood smeared all over his face.

My blood was pounding, my heart racing, the guard was fumbling with the lock on the gate, frantically trying to open it. Soph walked back to the open door of the Ford and got in, swiftly, she was panting but only slightly. She pulled the door shut, and with a smile, offered, "Let's go get a drink. Jim Morgan."

As I pulled away I saw the guard set his rifle against the Turk's outer wall and run up to the Saab. The passenger was out of the car and had opened the driver's door, Stupid flashed us his middle finger as the big V-Eight fishtailed into the middle of the Malagasy avenue leaving behind a stench of blue smoking tire fumes and some very upset, bad Asses.

"Are you okay, Soph?"

Ah, the classic question, not, "Hey, nice punch, Kidd." Or, "Wow, did you feel the bone break as you hit his nose?" No. It was just an old, "Are you okay, Soph?"

"Yeah." She slightly panted. "Now slow it down. I want to see what the guard is going to do."

I hit the brakes and it threw Soph forward against the dashboard. She gave me a horrid look that said, "Fool." Then, looked out the back window as I inched along at below five miles per hour to let her watch. But very soon, I had to speed up due to the flow of on-coming traffic. She turned around and squared herself in the seat looking at her knuckles, they were red, not from blood but from impact, impact with Dumb's brash attitude. I said, "Yeah, I can use a drink right now – a triple."

Chapter Forty

The world is full of puzzles. Sophie hitting the kid who had spit at her from the window is one of them. The event replayed over and over in my mind as we drove back to Shell Camp. I was trying to rationalize her actions in terms of ethical merit, and I couldn't. If there were some positive moral concept as to what she had done, it wasn't expressed to me. My thinking at that moment was this, "Sophie has a dark side, a sadistic, instigative and down right mean, side to her personality." Those two kids, the Malagasy punks, were probably planning some retaliatory action, some punitive act, at that very moment as we drove down away from Tanan. And, they would probably carry it out because they were really dumb and stupid, and very immature.

Ten minutes away from camp I confronted her as to what goal she had hoped to achieve by busting the punk's nose.

She pursed her lips in contemplation of my question, then, as if the question was a stupid question, she answered, "That little punk back there is my enemy." She paused briefly mulling over her forth-coming answer.

She continued, "The next time we cross paths, he will either run the other way, or attack me with his heart and soul. If he attacks me – it will be to kill me. From here on out I will protect myself accordingly. If he comes after me, I'll kill him before he kills me. I won't be pulling punches, and believe me – he knows it."

We rode in silence. I needed to absorb her logic but was having major difficulty in rationalizing her CIA thinking. I guess she was, too. Because she added, without a prompt, "He didn't respect me before I tapped his nose. He does now. And believe me, it may save our lives one day. He now knows that if he pokes around the beehive he's going to get stung – big time."

I felt that I had to say something, even though I disagreed with her, at least, in principal. She drew first blood. She opened herself up for all out reprisal. I said, "I just don't understand, Soph. That's all."

She gave me a, "Humph." She gave it to me quietly, as if I weren't to hear her, maybe I wasn't, then says, almost as an apology, "I just wanted to show him that I meant business, that's all."

The camp came into sight as we continued down the rocky road without elaboration. Once again, I was experiencing a new sensation, that of openly confronting my pre-developed beliefs. My concept of right and wrong was undergoing a rapid flux in meaning, the truth, the cardinal laws of existence were not as black and white as I'd have liked them to be. The "golden rules" were being modified, rapidly, under the age-old guise of survival.

Then, I recalled my stint in Nome, Alaska where I announced that I could lick any man in the house and wound up with my bottle scar. But, that was different. Wasn't it? Yeah, I was mixing apples and oranges, and as we pulled into the tented courtyard of Shell Camp I decided to compromise my beliefs into, "Applornges."

I filed this idea for future discussion with the camp's visiting lexicographer. It's always fun to bastardize the English language when there's a lexicographer lurking in the wings, eh?

Abby ran out of the dining room and came bounding up to the car door. He stopped about three feet away and said, "Hi, Boss." Then just stood there. I thought, "Gee, I forgot to bring him a cookie." I said, "What's up, Ab? – Lotty treating you okay?"

He shook his head yes and continued his idle stand. I got out and stretched, as did Soph. Doc and his crew were coming in on the bus. We watched them pull in, singing, "99-Bottles of Beer on the Wall." They were on verse 52, my guess was that they hadn't gone too far away as they all looked fairly chipper. Thankfully, they quit singing. We all helped unload the day's find, which was considerable.

Doc, in scientific excitement, came up to me and announced, "We may have found the Rex, Jim. I'll know for sure in an hour or so, I've a few tests to run, then we'll know." He hurried off to his alcohol pit, whistling, "Pop Goes the Weasel." The crew must have had a fine day in the field, a fine day indeed.

I had another thought, "The bus load of tortoise harvesters was not unlike a bus load of migrant farm workers. They both had meager quarters, they both worked from sunrise to sunset, but, these migrants were paying hefty to do their hard day's work and loved every minute of it."

Soph poked me out of my trance, "I'm taking first shower. Hey, earth to Jimbo, come in Jimbo."

"Oh, ah, applornges, no, you go ahead. Get your shower, I'm

going to lay down awhile." I pointed to the car, "The drive down wore me out, Kidd."

I left her in the courtyard and headed for a nap. The heat had taken its toll. The drive from Tanan had now become a chore, a boring, tedious, and redundant necessity.

Abby followed me, calling out, "Everything is peaches and cream, Boss. That what Miss Lotty say, Boss."

I stopped and said, "I'm glad that you two are getting along, Ab. Keep up the good work, Pal. I really appreciate your effort."

Ab had stopped some five feet behind me, "What is Einstein, Boss? Lotty says I'm a real, "Einstein." Is Einstein *good*, Boss?

"Yeah, Ab. It's kind of a compliment. It's like Luke saying AOK, when things are going well."

Ab looked confused, he said, "When I got something right, Luke would say, "It's about fucking time."

"Well, being called Einstein is a lot better, Ab. – Miss Lotty calls you that because she likes you. You keep up your good work and she'll call you that often. Okay?"

"Okay, Boss."

"By the way, what's for supper tonight?"

"I don't know, Boss. Lotty say if I touch anything in the kitchen that she would beat me with a wet noodle, Boss."

"Well, Lotty's in the kitchen now. You'd better go in and help her. I'm sure she'll be needing you, Ab."

"Okay Boss." He smiled big, adding, "A-OK, Einstein."

Chapter Forty-One

An orographic wind hit the camp around sunset causing a thick deck of clouds to form and build westward, outward from the higher elevations, the updraft winds were sustained at 30 MPH and I'm sure that the gusts we had experienced easily exceeded gale force. Two tents blew down as we watched helplessly from the dingy dining room windows. Everyone had huddled around the room, some reading, some writing, two of them, holding hands. Fine sand had filled the outside air and it stung the exposed skin of those who chanced a run to the bathroom. The freak storm was unexpected. Tanan was forecasting rain, but the weatherman said nothing about the brisk, howling winds.

From the door we could see rain falling, heavy rain, only a few hundred yards to the east. In the dusty, sandy courtyard we could see an occasional rain drop splatter up a puff of dirt that left dark splotches, like baby mud pies, scattered widely across the tented yard. From the kitchen window we observed a bright reddish sunset below the growing cloud canopy. It was a rare sunset. One that none of us will ever forget.

Sophie's electronic doorbell was activated twice before she had to shut it down. On both of these occasions I accompanied her out to investigate the road. We concluded that nobody would be out our way, not this night, no, not even Margolova.

At nine o'clock, Sophie retired. She said that she would be up when the storm ended, "...if I were going to sneak in here, I'd pick a night like tonight. No one would expect it, just like we had thought earlier."

She told me to wake her up when I got tired, and that I was in charge, as she handed me her .357 Magnum, adding, "She could be at the window right now, listening, we wouldn't even know it."

Leaving me with that comforting thought, she crawled under her blankets and in short order began a low humming, cute snore.

The winds subsided about one A.M., the camp had began to retire quite quickly, the tents were put back up, and the other ones were tightened down by Doc and myself while Abby – helped. He was an excellent flashlight holder, I even heard Doc thank him for his steady aim on more than one occasion. Once, I heard him say, "Can't you even hold a friggin' flashlight still." I'm not sure, but I think I heard the word "moron" being used most freely. The temperature had fallen below the fifty-degree mark and two of the women asked for an extra blanket. So, now you know who stole them, Ab. – Ha, ha.

At two o'clock, I roused Sophie. I took two of her blankets and crawled snugly into my bed. She asked if it would disturb me if she were to call Langley. I was almost asleep when she asked, but answered with a reluctant, "No."

She says, "No, you mind? Or no, you don't mind?"

"Make your call, Soph. You won't bother me, not one bit."

Then, with more noise than a bulldozer, she began setting up her radio. It was most deliberate and most annoying. I finally sat up and asked our night watchman if she'd like some company while she protected the camp.

"Oh no, Jim. You get some sleep. I'm fine." And then, she drops the aluminum case on the floor, very deliberately.

"Sorry." She chides, "It won't happen again, Jim."

By then I was wide-awake, I listened in as she yakked on and on with Sally, her *wonderful* roommate.

They talked about flies for their fake plant, about how Phil does 200 sit ups, before he jogs his five miles into work every morning, about spies massing in Damascus and how a quart of milk had soured and turned lumpy, "...you left it out, Kidd. If it weren't for that awful smell, I might not have noticed it, just think how bad it would have smelled if I didn't smell it last night?"

With a sarcastic note in her voice, Soph answered, "Yeah, I'm glad you're there holding down the fort, Sal."

Soph went on to relate her encounter with the Malagasy punks. She was being very descriptive, "...a big green honker, Sal, right at my feet." And, "...felt the bone break." And, "...blood was squirted everywhere, Sal."

Finally, Soph did ask for an update on Margolova. There was none. Then she asked for the latest on the English Camp at Pimakeel Bay. There was none. And then she asked Sally to inform Papa that Tina Johnson hadn't contacted her, so far.

Sally knew about the code 48, she said, "That Johnson doesn't really need you, Sophie. You know how them English are, always wanting someone else to do their dirty work. She probably wants you to wash her clothes or something. What do you think, Soph?"

Sophie was giggling, "Oh Sal, quit being so cynical."

After a long silence, Soph asked Sally to start her Corvette, "...to keep the engine oiled."

Sally says, "I don't know, Sophie. Is there an N on the shift lever, it's a stick shift, isn't it?"

Soph says, "Oh, don't worry. I've got insurance, Sal."

Their conference ended with a, "Kiss, kiss." Sophie began to stow her junk with as much noise as humanly possible.

Something was needling her. She needed to talk. It was quite obvious that I was not to go to sleep, at least, not until Sophie wanted me to. I asked her, stifling a yawn, "Are you sure that you don't want some company while you stand guard?" The yawn broke through; after all – I was tired.

"No. Not really. I know thirty-two different games of solitaire. It's an occupational necessity to know so many different variations. She was disquieted, resigning herself to sit out a lonely camp vigil, it's the fate of every night-watchman, be it a CIA suit, making sixty-grand a year or a junkyard dog, working for his master's pat on the head, it's a lonely occupation.

I asked, "How about some gin rummy at a penny a point?"

"No." She says, withdrawn and intoning an air of ho-hum, "You'd just beat me."

Persistently, I goaded her, "How about some Scotch?"

"No, not while I'm working." This was said with an actor's flair for the dramatic.

Resigned to let her brood, I offered, "Well, if you get tired, wake me up. I'll keep you company or spell you awhile."

"No, it's my job. I can handle it."

Finally, I said, "Okay. See you in the morning."

"Yes." She says, moronically, "See you in the morning."

She turned off the light. She sat down on her bed. She was being quiet, totally silent, not moving, not breathing. It was a horrible distraction. After listening to nothing for a good two minutes, I asked, "Is something wrong, Soph?"

"No." She answered in a small voice. Then, she begins, "I was just thinking."

That, is a phrase that always scares the hell out of me, "I was just thinking." Especially when it comes from a woman and it's after two o'clock in the A.M. and you're dead tired and about to fall asleep and she had just slept for the last five hours and to make things worse, you love her.

She continued, "I'm hopelessly in love with you, Jim."

And there it was, her gloom had surfaced. It didn't come over a nicely flowered luncheon with a sparkling wine. It didn't come over a leisurely hand-in-hand stroll through a freshly hewn field of clover with sparrows chirping in the surrounding trees. It didn't come over a candle lit dinner served by a gloved hand with a violin soloist attending her ear in a suite at the luxurious Four Seasons in Downtown Chicago, no. Absolutely not!

No, it came from a darkened bunkhouse at two in the morning on the side of a ragged mountain south of the equator on a backward third world island nation called Madagascar. Tired, sleepy, living under a constant intrigue, deadlines and international spies roaming all over the place, comes the primeval scream, "I love you."

"And I love you." I said this in the sincerest manner that I could muster while laying there in our darkened den of overly taxed emotions, and let there be no doubt, I did love her dearly, totally and passionately; but not in the same way that I loved Eunice.

And I went to her, despite the icy floor and chilly air, in spite of only wearing a pair of Jockey shorts and, most assuredly, despite the waning hour and my openly displayed need of sleep; and I took her in my arms, cradled her softness close to me, kissed her tenderly in a shared need of oneness and unrequited rapture.

Our bodies, albeit our souls, commingled in the heated passion of wants and flagrant needs to give, to share in the wild ecstasy of one torrid, sexual, fulfillment, and it was right, it was equitable and it was downright phenomenal. Our love was an axiomatic reality, it was live and vigorous, impassioned and, yet, pure, above the carnal lusting of a mere sexual romp, yes, pedantic logic be damned, we had capitulated into a social norm, ousted ourselves from the emotions of lust, and entered into the majestic realm of un-requited, "emotional" satisfactions, love.

And it was after five am, the stormy skies had cleared and the dawn and its first shimmer of a pale twilight infiltrated our very beings, and we slept. Naked to any fear of intrusion or clandestine attack upon anything, especially our love.

And I slept. And yes, I dreamt. Here it comes:

• • •

Sophie was carrying a small brass cannon. I was helping her, but from a distance. I was carrying something, too. But it wasn't a know-able thing. She needed what I had, but like myself, she didn't know what it was. It was heavy and I told her so. She said not to mind and beckoned me on, "Come along, come along."

We were in a huge building that had a continuous grass floor. We were moving toward a large hill in the middle of the expansive arena, the hill extended upward toward a stained glass ceiling, a ceiling made of stained glass panels not unlike those found in old gothic cathedrals, yet, they weren't holy scenes, no, there was no theme, just multi-colored geometric shapes haphazardly intertwined to avoid any logical grasp of an innate purpose. Ropes and lines hung from the roof but they were so high that one couldn't tell to what they were attached to, or, if they were attached to anything at all. The entire room was in a fuzzy, blurry state.

Sophie was dressed in a white dress, a wedding dress. I asked her, harshly, "Hey, why the cannon?"

With laughter in her voice she called out, "Come along, Jim. Come along."

Pausing, I set down my unknowable object. I sat down on the grass and watched Sophie trudging up the knoll. She turned, saw me sitting, and screamed, "No! I need that, I really do."

This big white limo pulls up, between us, and stops. The passen-ger's door opens, real slow, and I'm instantly transfixed on a pair of shapely legs that come dangling out, clad in glass slippers over-set in pure white diamonds. My eyes follow the perfect forms, legs, up to a pale yellow hem of a mini-skirt, and exposed is an ever so tiny shot of white silk panty.

From my sitting position I bent my head slightly to improve my perverted view up the shapely, slightly parted legs, but – when I did, the toes began a little tap dance that averted my caddish, inquisitive search, and I was forced to refocus my gaze on the diamond studded glitter of the tap-tappity-tap, tap-tap of the two dancing feet. Then they stopped and retracted up into the limo's darkened interior with the sound, and accompanying motions, of a pneumatically driven robot, slow, solely computer calculated and extremely precise. The door closed with the click of a solidly built machine. The back tires began to spin on the turf spitting up dirt and grass as the long, stretch, sped away and out of sight behind a grassy hillock, where Sophie had been only seconds before.

A focused stage light illuminated the brass cannon, highlighting Sophie's absence. I called out to her several times, only to hear my own voice echo helplessly around the gigantic enclosure.

The cannon began to roll down the mound. It hit a rut and went into a wild tumble, end over end, it was coming directly at me. Somehow, I managed to sidestep the bounding metal, but it was close, I felt a cool breeze as it flashed past my face a mere millimeter away from ripping off my head.

My defensive lunge threw me on top of the unknowable package, I hit the box pointedly with my left shoulder smashing the wrapping and shattering the wooden slats that under laid its outer cover. It made a sordid crunching noise as it imploded under my own body weight. The crate appeared to be empty. It was filled with nothing more than an unknowable void.

At least, I couldn't discern anything amongst the debris or around the spot where I had pulled myself back into an upright, sitting position at the foot of the indoor grass mound. I reached the package remnants and began sifting through them, there had to be something there. Didn't Sophie say, "I need that – I really do." Surely she didn't need an empty box. And again I called out for her, if only she came when I called, everything would be so clear, and – "knowable."

I dug around the bits and pieces in a frantic search for anything. Inadvertently, I happened to scratch the earth, and when I did, a most amazing thing happened, I discovered that the grass was all a "fake" along with the soil that it was growing in. I began to scrape away the bogus sod to expose a large and expansive cavern, one that bottomed out some four hundred feet below my rooftop observation point. I suddenly became dizzy looking down into the gaping pit and had to look away, I continued digging away the lumps of counterfeit soil, fixating on the stained glass ceiling another four or five hundred feet above me.

Freakishly, the plot of ground under me gave way and I started to fall into the cavern, with a life saving grasp I latched onto the edge of floor-ceiling with both hands, a few loose divots gave way but I finally got a grip on some solid – fake, whatever it was terra firma and then hung there swaying back and forth like the pendulum on a grandfather clock. And then, things became worse.

A switch was thrown and the upper area went black, everything became nothingness above me. Hanging there by my fingertips, I looked down while pondering my fate. The cavern below was lighted a dull gray, the floor looked solid, my guess, cement. A hairline crack appeared between my hands and began to split out and away from me sending a cold chill, a doom chill, down my spine. I tried to get a better grip and while doing so my hand touched something, something metallic and cold just an inch to my right. I grappled with the object and moved it to the edge of the pit where I could see it, holding on by one hand I lowered an old golden key, level with my eyes. – That's when the ledge gave way with a quick, snapping crack, like the sound of one's own leg breaking in a skiing accident – muffled, yet, sickly audible.

I closed my eyes. We all have our own little inbred defense mechanisms and closing one's eyes is one of them, gritting one's teeth is another, and I gritted my teeth, too, but nothing happened. I opened my eyes to find myself suspended in mid-air below the hole that I had fallen through. I looked down, sideways, all around, and, there I hung, suspended like a helium balloon in free space. I fixated on the key, panting rapidly, uncomfortable with the mid-air suspension.

It was gold, a golden skeleton key. A four-inch key with a row of tiny diamond-chips imbedded haphazardly around its finger-crown. And then, I sensed a downward movement. It was almost imperceptible. I reached out my hand to touch the ceiling and sure as taxes the roof moved, or I had moved – a good ten inches lower than just a few dear seconds earlier.

I tried to jump up to the opening, but it was not to be. In my desperation to grasp anything tangible, I ...bobbled the key, and it went spinning end over end toward the floor accelerated by the earth's ever present gravitational pull, which at that moment, was "not" affecting "everything" that it should have been, namely – "me."

And then, I craved the key. I wanted it, *so* badly, I was overwhelmed with a desire for it and I screamed out, "I want my key." And I tried in vain to reach it, I could see it, at least I could see a speck, a shinny speck where it had dropped, but – it was no use. The harder I tried, the more anxiety I felt, I had become the junkie with-

out a fix, a pyromaniac without his flame, a nymphomaniac without...
"I wanted that key!"

And then I remembered Sophie's plea, "I really need it." And
that's when I knew... Sophie was a "key" junkie, too.

And I was overtaken by a great sadness. I began to pity her and
her illness, her pain, her agony. And I called out to her, "Sophie."

Not, unlike the call for "Stella" from, "A Streetcar Named
Desire." And it was superb, so pleasurable, to call out her name,
"Sophie, Sophie, Sophie..."

• • •

And she heard me, and she woke me up.

"Jesus H. Christ, Jim. The whole fucking camp must think that
I'm banging your brains out. Wake up, wake up, damn it, Jim –
wake up."

And I did, and I was hot, and I was sweaty, and my mouth was
dry, and I didn't know where I was, and... Damn! I hoped it wasn't
one of those dreams that Eunice called, "Prophetical." And, as my
head cleared, I thought, "Soph won't need no cannon to get me up
to the altar, no sir. Not at all." Yeah, I really *was* disorientated.

Chapter Forty-Two

I lit a Camel and carried it into the shower. I was still pondering my dream, the significance of the key, and I recalled a Freudian interpretation, Freud was big on phallic symbolism, then I recalled the work of his protégé who split away from his totally sexual themes, Doctor Carl Gustav Jung. Jung labeled keys as being symbolic to education, the thing that could open many worlds, many doors, hearts, and secrets. Describe a key, imagine a key, and express your concept of knowledge. Freud shook his head, "Ah, such a pity Jung – the key is Phallic. Pass me another cigar, and prescribe me a little heroin for my mouth cancer, please."

Yeah, Jung was right. Sophie did say she was going back to college to become a scientist. But then again, she sure does like sex. And, as the water turned cold, I thought, "Maybe she'll become a Sex Scientist."

And what about the cannon? – Definitely a Freudian phallic symbol. And those beautiful dancing legs, the ones that came dangling down out of the big white stretch limo? I'm "sure" they were sexual. "Oh well." As I toweled off I made a mental note to mention the dream to Eunice. She'd have it ironed out in nothing flat. After all "dream analysis" is one of her better talents. As a matter of fact, it's probably way, way up there with Tasmanian witch doctors, rabbit's feet and divining rods.

I peeked out the window to see if there was any activity about the camp. The first thing I saw was Sophie. She was sitting on the wood porch whittling on a stick. One of the women was exiting the new shower, fluffing her wet hair in the bright, warm morning sun. It looked like a beautiful day, a golf day, a picnic day, and a tennis day. Ah yeah, maybe, a beach day.

I dressed hurriedly, not wanting to miss any more of the day's invigorating glory. When I made it out the door, Sophie had left her whittling and disappeared, to where? I did not know. I made a beeline to the dining room, for coffee.

Inadvertently, I had interrupted Doc's morning tortoise brief.

The coffee urn was near the front door and I was so intent on filling my cup that I hadn't realized a meeting was in progress. With my back to the old bird, he had stopped speaking when I entered, I said, to wit, trying to emulate his own dominate vivacity, "Beautiful fucking day, eh Doc?"

I hear Doc's reply, "Ahem." My back still turned to him while adding sugar to my brew.

I continued, "You couldn't ask for better weather than this. Hunting down them little pricks will be a piece of cake today, eh? ...Doc?" And then I turned around and saw the smiling staff sitting silently behind one red, and furious, Doctor Strongbow, hands on his hips, feet spread in a challenging-all-comers blockade to his sanctified lecturing grounds.

I reddened, vainly trying to recall what I had just said in my spontaneous moment of masculine heehaw-good-Malagasy-morning-gaga bit of unnecessary and highly frivolous Engineering hoopla, I said, "Sorry."

Deserving of his chastising stare, I tiptoed quietly out the door. Leaving the angry king and his amused subjects to their vast and varied scientific efforts.

Once outside, I went to hunt down Sophie and my employee, the Absteer. They weren't hard to find, they were behind the kitchen, laughing their ass off. Well, Sophie was, and Ab was just laughing at Sophie – it was contagious.

I whispered, "Isn't *this* a beautiful fucking day?"

Soph was about to pee in her pants. Abby stopped laughing, he said, "I don't know what's so funny, Boss." Sophie had fallen on the ground. She'd lost it, completely. I was personally amused, but nowhere near as amused as the CIA. Ab farted. Soph *did* piss in her pants. I could only stand there and hope for composure. Soph ran off toward the bunkhouse. Ab said, "Sorry, Boss."

Yeah, it was a beautiful fucking morning...

Soph returned wearing a fresh pair of Levis. Her eyes were wet from laughter-tears, she was still grinning. She grabbed my arm, and spilling my coffee, pulled me away from my eavesdropping on Strongbow's, "Tortoise Habitat" lecture.

Past the generator room, she says, "Did you see the look on Bo's face? – He'd have shot you dead if he was carrying, Jim."

I said, "Aw, he'll get over it. Besides, how often can you interrupt God – and still get a laugh?"

Soph had finally calmed, she was still in an amused humor and wouldn't let the dead dog lie. "Oh, I wish I had my mini-cam...the look on his face. If you were working for him, you'd be walking back to the states, Jimbo."

"Well, I said I was sorry, besides, Engineers can get away with stuff like that, it's expected."

Soph, all calmed down, joined me on my rounds. We walked the water pipes looking for leaks and removed some flotsam above the creek pump. We started the bus, checked its fluids, and when it was time to inspect the generators, Soph said, "I'll wait out here, if you don't mind? I have this thing about shared nests."

I shrugged it off. A man's got to do, what a man's got to do. The oil level was low and the cps (cycles/second) had dropped to 50. I was pretty sure that Doc would point this out to me, real soon. I topped off the fluids and reset the cps at a harmonious 60. Patting the blue monsters I left to join my lovely who was listening in on Doc's continuing narration, which had moved on, to "Tortoise Fungi."

I handed Sophie my coffee mug, "I'll give you a dollar if you go in and fill this up for me, Kidd."

"Up yours, Jimbo."

We listened in on Doc's talk for a good five minutes. Doc had a real presence. His years of teaching had honed his public speaking skills to the proverbial razor's edge. I had a vague idea as to what he was talking about, but I was more enthralled with the "way" he was speaking, rather than, what it was that he was actually saying. He was charismatic, animated, and had a way of emphasizing every word he spoke with a bodily nuance. I had only wished that he had been speaking on an Engineering subject, and not on some controversial issues of tortoise enzyme production.

Soph, bored with the fifteen letter words, whispered, "I'm hitting the shower, want to wash my back?"

"You go ahead. I want to listen to this awhile longer. Do you mind?"

And "that," was probably the first time in Sophie's life that anyone had ever refused her, her come-on, for a sexual interlude. She was struck dumb. Her look of dismay was catastrophic. She had snapped her manicured fingers, and received a negative response. Her tools, her weapons against the male species had faltered, and failed. She was shattered, and no doubt, quite bewildered – beyond belief. With her mouth gaped, her lips looked like a grouper's lips, pursed before it gets the gaffe in its gills on the transom of some chartered fly-bridged sport's boat. Her eyes hazed, and she staggered a few steps backward.

I said, flippantly, "Get yourself wet and soapy. I'll be along in a minute, promise." But it was too late. The damage was done.

She weaved off in delirium. Surely pondering her wares, her age, her weight, her hair – she'd be demanding a trip to Tanan for another perm. Yeah, I had my foot stuck in my mouth, and I needed a cup of coffee, badly, to wash down my argyle socks.

Then, a miracle happened. I heard Doc say, "That concludes my lecture on Extant Metabolic Sera Protein Derivatives. The bus will leave in – fifteen minutes. Good luck, and good hunting."

The sound of chairs and a hum of conversation poured out of the kitchen door, the lecture had ended, amen.

I entered the kitchen and eased toward the coffee urn as the coven began to disperse. Doc, eyeing my trek to the java, took a step in my direction, his face said, "Time for some rudimentary, disciplinary, brow beating, get ready, your ass is grass, you know it, I know it, it's a universal, you've had it."

God smiled on me, Doctor Franz buttonholed Bo for some vastly higher priority, a mere four feet from certain impact. I continued around Franz's back and made it to the almost empty pot.

Camp rule, a Doc rule, written in red above the silver cauldron, says, "Last Cup Builds New Pot." It was signed, in what looked to be Sophie's handwriting, Adolph Hitler. I tilted the pot, filled my mug, and had almost made it out the door.

Lotty had blocked my path handing me two neatly typed sheets of supply demands. I took the shopping list, it was typed on her university's letterhead. I scanned it for notarization – it was missing. Flippantly, I shoved them back at her, "Sorry, not notarized. Re-submit in twenty-four hours."

She pleaded, "It's for the lab. We need it by the time the bus gets back this afternoon. Will you do it, Jim? Please?"

"Well, Lotty, I know that I'll be missed on the day's hunt, but if you really need this stuff? I'll get it, just for you."

Doc called out, "Morgan. I need a word with you, as soon as you're through there."

I smiled at him hoping to disarm him. I nodded in the affirmative.

My stomach sank, I'd have to face the music, rap music, and there was no way out. I checked the list with Lotty, gave her a wink and, reluctantly, sauntered over to Doc's table, mentally I think I was prepared to knock the old goose on his ass if he started any shit with me. But, he didn't. My fears were totally unfounded. Docs, understand such things, after all, shit happens.

Bo was studying a map. Without looking up, he says, "I want to hunt this ravine today." He tapped the map for me to look, "It seems to be somewhat isolated. Can we get in there from the road?"

I studied the map, and then suggested he walk in from a place four miles west of the turn off to Antananarivo. – West toward Pimakeel Bay and the English encampment. I said, "Hell Doc, even Ab could find that spot."

Doc gave me a weird look, he asked, "That's not a racial slur is it, Morgan?"

"No way, Doc. That's a fact."

He bobbed his head, "Indeed, indeed." He paused momentarily, staring off into outer space, maybe inner space, and then asked, "Will you be going with us? We leave in about ten minutes."

"No, I'm the gopher today."

"And pray tell, what is *that*, Mister Morgan?"

"Oh. Well, a gopher... He goes for this, he goes for that – goes here, and he goes there."

"I see. I take it then, that you're going into town?"

Scientist can really be dense at times. I think that they have to surrender all their common sense when they're handed passing grades on their doctoral orals. Hell! Doc was the biggest gopher in camp. He just didn't know it. I said, "Yes. I'm picking up chemicals for the lab. I should be back by three or so."

I pointed to his circled location. I can lead you out there. I'll be leaving about the same time as you."

"Splendid Jim, splendid. By the way, while you're in town, will you pick me up a fifth of whiskey? It's purely medicinal. Understand? – Purely medicinal."

"I've got a case of J&B under my bunk for the same purpose, will a bottle of that do?"

"Of course, of course, an excellent whiskey. It's a Scotch I believe, isn't it?" Doc had been whispering. Now, he whispered even lower, confidentially, "Let's keep this between ourselves, Jim. My position, you know?"

"Of course, of course." I mimicked the old buzzard. "I'll meet you out front in ten minutes. Did you want that J&B now?"

"No, no, James. Tonight will be fine." He then dismissed me with a nonchalant wave of a well-manicured scientific hand. Regardless of the old coot's ways, one had to admire his tenacity and flair.

Meanwhile, back at the bunkhouse, Sophie had entered into a deep, snoring sleep. She was out, probably for the day. I went back to the kitchen and placed Abby in charge of the camp. He would wake up Sophie if any problem were to arise. He had on his cook's hat and when he nodded a positive response it fell off. He smiled, reached it, and replaced it on his head.

"Ab." I said. "I think you've found your calling."

"What that, Boss?"

"Being in charge." And I left a very happy commander washing up our breakfast dishes, indeed, I did.

The bus was warming up, Doc was at the helm, Lotty was loading coolers and sandwiches with the help of Doctor Franz and the weedy, frail, Doctor Polus.

I decided to take along my jacket, just in case, and ran over to the bunkhouse to fetch it. When I grabbed the jacket, I saw the .357 Magnum and wrapped it up in the coat. I thought, "...just in case."

I lead the expedition out to Papquin Valley. It was ten A.M. when I turned the dusty, dirty Ford east and headed for a quiet day of shopping and, for some real sightseeing. What could go wrong?

Chapter Forty-Three

Having turned Lotty's order over to the clerk, and being told to return in an hour, I opted for lunch, at the Hilton. Perhaps Uncle Bobby had some news on Margolova. Upon leaving the store I ran physically into – Tina Johnson, from Pimakeel Bay and Devon, England.

Her green eyes were even greener with her clothes on. She said, smiling seductively, while eyeing me up and down, "I say Mister Morgan, I hardly recognize you with your clothes on."

"Well! Ah… This is, ah – certainly is…a, …pleasant surprise. What brings you to town?"

"Groceries. And you?" She was radiating, talking quick, too quick. She is a most exciting woman to be near.

"Supplies. I've turned in an order. I've an hour to kill before it's ready. I'm just on my way to the Hilton for lunch."

"Oh, how keen. May I join you, Mister Morgan?"

"Oh, it would be my pleasure. Did you want to do your shopping first?"

"No, no. I'll come back later. I've only a handful of things to pick up. I actually came in for the post, and I've already seen to that. Shall we go?"

Tina suggested we dine at a small outside terrace diner that she had wanted to try. Her countrymen at the English embassy had suggested it to her on several occasions, but as of then, she had not had the opportunity to try it. There was no way that I would refuse this beautiful woman her choice of a restaurant. If she had said, come back to Pimakeel Bay and I'll make you biscuits and a spot of tea – I'd have made the drive. No, I'd have walked, just to share a few minutes, an hour, with this stunning English princess.

We rode in her Landrover which needed cleaning as much, or more, then my rented Ford. Along the way she pointed out many points of interest, expressing her vast knowledge of Antananarivo's people, its government, and history came natural to her, she could easily become the city's historian. Actually, I was enjoying her accent so much that I missed some of the places that she had pointed out. I had a terrible time looking at her, although she was pleasantly dressed in acid denims, my mind kept wandering back to when I had held her, floated her, in the warm Pimakeel Bay waters. Aggravating my active imagination was her braless wardrobe. Every time she pointed something out to her right, her blouse would open just enough that I'd focus my attention on her chest instead of the quintessential architecture of Tanan's historical sections. Nothing, and I mean nothing, was built quite as well as Tina's body.

As we dined, we chatted bookishly on the cultural aspects of an island nation. Tina never once divulged her hand in the spy business. And, of course, I was not at liberty to discuss my own knowledge of her involvement, nor of Sophie's ties to the CIA. It was a stupid game, but it had to be played. It was killing me to ask her about Her Majesties Secret Service. Was she C-5, MI-6, or what? Not that I knew the difference, but maybe she'd tell me.

Boldly, I asked her, indirectly, "When I first met you, Tina, I had you pegged for an English spy."

She reddened ever so slightly, her deep tan hid a full blush, and she said, "Actually, I'm Double 0 – Sixty-nine." She stared into my eyes with a keen sexual intensity, and then added, "Just kidding." She laughed, warmly and easily in an effort to save her secret identity. It was good – but not convincing. But then again, I knew much more than I was supposed to know. Our tit-for-tatting had become quite the afternoon sport.

She asked me back, "And you, Mister Morgan? Are you the latest version of your American hero, John Wayne?"

"Oh no. Not me. I tried kissing a horse once. It still came in dead last, didn't do a thing for me sexually, either."

Tina didn't understand my weak attempt at humor, she asked, "And Miss Kidd? She is your American Wonder Woman?"

"Oh, yeah, yeah. *That* she is. I'm in love with her you know. I've only known her for a couple of weeks."

"I suspected, I didn't know." Her face became somewhat drained, she poked at her salad, thinking – whatever – I did not know. It's at times like those that I wish I could read minds. Intuitively, I read her look as a look of disappointment. A disappointment in the following sense – "I was making myself unavailable to her." At least, to her immediate feminine pursuits, whatever they may have been.

I decided to open the door slightly, "Yeah, I'm a typical male, I think. Every time I meet a pretty girl, I want to take her home to meet mother."

It worked. She brightened ever so slightly. The games could continue, if that's what they were. She placed her napkin on the table, saying, "I really must be going, James. Can you make it down to Pimakeel, for another swim?"

"When?"

"This evening would be cozy." Her words were brimming with ebullient innuendo, a sexual, yet – humorous ebullience.

I had to say, "Can't." But added, "How about tomorrow?"

"Splendid. And, oh, do bring, Miss Kidd, she seems to be such a cheery young lady. I simply must get to know her better."

"She's working nights. She may "choose" not to join me. Would that be okay with you?"

She gave me a sultry smile, a smile that said, "Yes! Oh yes."

Out loud and in perfect Queen's English, she said, with articulate verbal acumen, "Her presence would be most interesting, don't you think?" And she blushed. She had ordered herself a desert off the feminine menu of sexual intrigue, knowing damn well that the extra caloric intake would involve her in some intensive exercise to maintain her as an international figure.

Tina Johnson, oceanographer, wave analyst, double 0-69 and male libido activator, paid for lunch. "Lunch, is on the Crown, James."

On our way back to the store we had cause to pass the American Embassy, with great pleasure, I was able to point out our modern structure, which indeed, is quite impressive. Tina offered me a tour of the English offices, "...one day. You'll find them most stuffy, it's an image you know?"

I found myself comparing Tina to Sophie. Sophie was tough and rugged, and, although very cute, she exhumed an air of don't mess with me, I'm deadly, and she'd make it well known that she was wearing a thirty-eight in her shoulder holster.

Tina, on the other hand, looked sweet and approachable, it was only clear that she was deadly when one smelled her fine perfume and looked into her emerald eyes that bespoke of mystery and international intrigue. These weapons, beauty weapons, were more deadly than any bowl of hemlock, deadlier than Sophie's .357 – at a whim, she could destroy a man by simply looking at him and teasing him into desiring her.

Yeah, if Sophie had to register her karate knowledge as a real and viable weapon, then Tina should have to register her charm as piece of her nation's assault artillery.

Both of these women were plagued with poisonous venom, their beauty. And that gave them a license to kill. I thought, to myself, that this adventure was getting out of hand. Something had to give – soon.

Lotty's chemical order was ready when we returned. Tina saw me out to the station wagon and gave me a platonic kiss on the cheek. As she brushed up against me I could feel her radiance, her softness and sense her desire, and I knew right then, why some Englishmen refer to their women as birds. Tina, a cuddly little dove, so fluffy and free, could never be in hand; she was destined to the bush. And when I looked at her, standing there on that Malagasy street, and I found myself studying her, in the way one would study a Monet – looking for some impressionistic imperfection, only to find that her overall beauty had multiplied by a factor of ten.

As the English lovebird went off to shop, I – the American eagle on a short leash, went off to the Hilton, for a chat with Uncle Bobby. With a light heart and a swimming party floating around in my head I parked the Ford and headed for the Concierges' office. The door was locked. I roamed over to the bar and was told that Bobby hadn't come in today. Which, according to the dark and very ethnic barmaid was, "...quite unusual." She had fixated herself on the TV so intently, that it surprised me when she spoke.

It was obvious, I now knew as much about Bobby's whereabouts as she did. I filled my pocket with a handful of complimentary matchbooks and meandered out to the front desk. I picked up a couple postcards picturing the hotel and left. I was thinking to send mom and dad a short greeting, for real.

Once again, the orographic winds began their upward climb from the heated mountainside. Clouds had already begun to edge outward from the higher elevations. Rain was forecasted for Tanan. I got into the dusty Ford with the hope that I could get back down the mountain before the rains started. A swirling clump of leaves blew across the gas station's lot as I gassed the big V-8. Then I headed towards home, to Shell Camp, and my sleeping beauty, Sophie.

Fiddling with the radio I locked onto a Greek station that was playing, Zorba the Greek, dance music. It was great music to negotiate the afternoon traffic, too. I was digging the beat as I approached my final turn west, the last turn before descending into no man's land. That's when I spotted the "black Saab." The two brats that Soph and I had encountered back at the Turk's villa occupied it. They had pulled up behind an old dilapidated corncrib, they were watching the road, monitoring the road, the "only" road that lead to Shell Camp. They had to be waiting for me, or Soph. It was too much of a coincidence for them to just be there. – And let me tell you, it scared the hell out of me.

I reached the .357 and adjusted it to where I could grasp it easily, quickly. My heart began to race and I saw the passenger point at me through their windshield. I pressed down hard on the accelerator and the Ford leapt into action reaching 90 MPH before I looked down to see just how fast I was actually going. I had my eyes glued to the rear view mirror waiting for the Saab to follow after me, but it remained blank. I checked my speed again and I had reached 120, still no sign of the punks. I then became more concerned with my speed than I was about the Saab. I was going way, way too fast for the conditions of a rutted secondary road and for one being in the state of panic. I slowed to under a hundred, and again to below ninety, as my fear subsided. The black Saab wasn't following, at least, not to where I could see them.

I drove another twenty miles then slowed again to a safe fifty to sixty MPH. My mirrors remained blank, void of pursuit. I was approaching the switchbacks, the tight curves that would slow me to twenty miles per hour and slower, the curves that Sophie had previously pointed out to be, "excellent ambush spots." My fears renewed as I envisioned Margolova placing myself in the cross hairs of a high-powered riflescope and pulling gently in on the sniper rifle's hair trigger.

What was it that Sophie had said, "If they come after me now – it will be to do me physical harm."

So, I had to know. I had to know if the punks were following. I pulled the Ford off the road at the first turn following a four-mile descending straightaway. The curve where I stopped would protect me from being seen because of its boulders and dense brush. It was a perfect spot to watch for the Saab. If they were following, I'd still have time to make a run for it, as they would have to slow for the forty-five degree turn.

I hefted the huge .357. I checked how many bullets were in the cylinder. There were six. I didn't bring any extras. Hell! It was dumb to have even taken the gun along in the first-place, and it would have been down right idiotic of me, to have along extra rounds. But then again...

I left the Ford running and moved to a huge pine outcrop that afforded me cover, and still gave me a clear view of the rising tarmac that I had just traversed. The road was deserted, very empty. The winds were howling at my back, a wisp of dust blew up the empty road, the sky kept darkening beyond the road's end and all too soon it would storm.

There I stood, apprehensive about my action, wondering if what I was doing was right. I should have continued on to camp and let the CIA do her job. Better yet – I should have stayed in Alaska. My only enemy there was the alcohol closet and bad poker hands. A gust of wind screamed through the pines knocking me slightly off balance. The Magnum was getting heavy. I lowered it to my side. I was safe. The Malagasy punks weren't following. If they had been, they'd have appeared by then, and they hadn't. I lit a Camel and relaxed, thankful that they weren't coming.

And then I thought about the bus and the scientists. If the Saab was coming, it would be better to meet them right here. Yeah, it was my job to protect the scientists, indirectly. Not in the same way that Sophie was to protect them, but – I felt it my duty to keep them from harms way. I decided to wait another few minutes just to make sure. I aimed the gun down the road and imagined the Saab in front of the sights bead. I said, out loud, "Pow, pow, pow." And the Saab exploded into next week, a rolling ball of flame and flying metal. Again out loud, "Yeah. Just call me Walter, Walter Mitty."

I was there for twenty minutes. They could have walked to where I was in that much time. They weren't coming. I placed the .357 down on a boulder and began to relieve myself before continuing back to camp. My vigil was over.

Zipping my pants, I saw a vehicle shoot over the rise and come speeding towards me. It wasn't the Saab, it was Tina's Landrover and she was flying. She must have been doing a hundred... Then, the weirdest thing happened, a huge staggering bolt of lightning shot down out of the black roiling clouds and danced around the tarmac beyond Tina's Landrover sending new fears back into my every vein, now pulsed frantic with the ugly vision, the real black Saab, as it came flying over the road's crest and came blasting down, hot on Tina's rear bumper, only two, maybe three car lengths behind her.

Of this, there was no doubt – it was Tina. The Saab and its two goons were after *her*, not me. I picked up the .357 while yelling out, "Mother fuck, son of a bitch. The dirty bastards – fuck, fuck, and a double fuck." I walked deliberately from my rock and up to the stone apron of the highway bend. I was caught between a rock and hard spot and wasn't sure as to what I should do, but I had to do something, and I had to do it fast. Tina would be at the curve in ten seconds. Intuitively, I raised the Magnum and leveled it at windshield height while cocking the hammer back for a faster, smoother shot.

Tina began breaking for her entry into the curve, with her tires smoking and squealing she rounded the curve in a slide, all four wheels barely in contact with the road's surface. I think she saw me but – I wasn't sure. Surely her attention was on the curve as she flew past me or she would have lost control. The Saab was braking, screeching into view, I aimed the .357 at where the driver should be and fired. The .357 kicked up my arms, but not before I saw the windscreen spider web outward from where the bullet had penetrated into the careening Saab and its very stunned driver.

The Saab never finished the curve. As it left the road, it hurdled silently into a nameless ravine some thirty feet from where I stood. The car didn't explode, there was no fire, and there was no noise, except for the ringing in my ears from the gun. Yeah, it wasn't like in the movies, not at all. I saw the back end of the Saab whoosh into the scrub bush and disappear with a rustling of the local fauna, and, just that fast, it was gone.

I stood looking at the bent grasses and crushed saplings where the car had entered, hell? The only sound was that of the wind whistling past my ears. I looked down the road to where Tina had gone, she was backing up the road, slow and deliberate, she had put on her emergency flashers and was looking at me instead of the road as she pulled up some five feet ahead of me and I heard her, pull set, the Rover's hand brake.

I held the gun up in the air, the way a good gun handler holds one when he may have to fire it again. Tina jumped down to the tarmac. She had a small weapon in her right hand, held upward, ready. We met at the end of the Saab's skid marks, where they entered into the mashed and now rutted weeds. When she lowered her weapon, leveled it at the weed tops, I saw that it was a German Luger. It was very black, and I thought...well... it really looked – like a toy.

Without looking at me, she says, "I'll handle things from here on in, Mister Morgan. You may stand down your weapon."

Chapter Forty-Four

Tina was adamant that I remain on the road. Her professional demeanor gave her all the authority she needed to take control of a nasty situation. I did question her, once, "You sure?"

Without hesitation her green eyes bore into mine and she said, with all the conviction of a Supreme Court Judge, "Quite!" And sternly added, "Now stay put, Mister Morgan."

With great reluctance, I stayed. – But not for long. My adrenalin was pumping higher than a kite as I watched her tiptoe into the crushed fauna and then descended into the gorge, disappearing from sight.

I looked around the barren curve and my mind flashbacked to the bullet entering the windshield. Shaking my head to clear the vivid apparition, I decided to follow Tina. It was simple logic, I needed to be with someone – I was scared.

Like a cat preparing to pounce upon its supper, I followed the barrel of the .357 into the scrub. Besides, I had to be doing something. Standing on the road was driving me nuts. What was I supposed to do – direct traffic?

Twenty feet into the bush I came to a deep sided ravine that dropped at a sixty degree angle straight down to a rocky floor that was barren except for the Saab and a splattering of browned out tumbleweeds. It was a good hundred, hundred and twenty, feet to the bottom. Tina had already reached the ravine bottom and was moving stealthily toward the Saab that now lay on its left side with the driver's door down. I couldn't see any sign of life from where I stood on the gorge's rim. Except for Tina, who was rounding carefully up to the front end of the badly crumpled vehicle with her arm extended, and her Luger pointed at the windshield.

I pushed over the edge and began a very rapid descent down the soft and crumbling side of the ravine. For the most part, I was following in Tina's tracks, but where she had left footprints, I was leaving five-foot long lunge marks.

When I had almost reached the bottom I heard a gun shot. I tried to stop my descent but couldn't, I had built up too much momentum and had to continue my slide to the floor, luckily, still on my feet and still in possession of the .357. Tina was walking toward me rapidly – she looked pissed, "You should have stayed on the road, Mister Morgan."

I pushed past her and ran to the front of the Saab. The driver was partially out of the missing windshield and the left side of his face was missing. The passenger was slumped over at an odd angle still wearing his harness-type seat belt. There was a small hole, a *bullet* hole, right between his eyes. A lot of fresh blood was pouring out from his head. His right hand was twitching ever so slightly – but maybe not, for when I looked closer it had stopped. He was dead. Of that I was sure. Tina had shot him. I was sure of that, too.

I went back to Tina. "You shot the passenger?"

"Yes."

I asked her, "What do we do now?"

She asked back, "Are you with the CIA?"

"No. Sophie is. I'm just an Engineer. I work for the Institute of Intuitive Thought. But I know about you. Sophie told me. She said. I had – a need to know."

Tina looked tired, she said, "I thought that you knew. But I didn't know for sure." She turned toward the car, "I'm going to burn the car. Will you help?"

"Yes."

She looked up the rocky wall. "There's ten gallons of petrol on the back end of the Landrover. Will you get it?"

"Yes." I didn't ask why or what for. I headed up the embankment without waiting for any more instructions. It was a difficult climb up the gorge due to the loose, sandy soil, which kept breaking loose with each step that I took. For every two steps up, I came at least one step back down. I was still carrying the .357 and it was getting really heavy. I was puffing like an old locomotive and swore to God almighty that I'd quit smoking, soon. When I reached the top, twenty minutes later, my shirt was soaked through with perspiration. My legs were burning and I had to gasp for oxygen.

I bent over to rest while looking back on my climb, panting. My hands began to rub my aching knees, I couldn't think. I just wanted to regain my breath and have my muscle pain subside.

I could see Tina removing the gas line from the undercarriage of the Saab. She had a wrench in her hand and apparently knew what she was doing. I hobbled off, stiff legged, over to the Landrover. I removed the two, five-gallon gas cans. They were full and heavy, but I held this consoling thought: it would be a down hill climb and gravity would save my ass.

I turned off the jeep's emergency flashers and placed the .357 under some packages on the passenger's seat. I fumbled around for a cigarette and then just sat there regaining my strength, not thinking, and not wanting to think. I just sat there recuperating. The cigarette didn't help. I snubbed it out in the ashtray. Then I forced myself off the seat and back to the gas cans.

Like I had figured, going back down was easy. The jerry cans acted as ballast and I literally slid to the bottom using the gas can weight, for balance. A few times the cans would hit a rock and I had a vision of them exploding, but they didn't. My shirt was caked with mud made from my own sweat and my pants had a huge rip down one leg. When I looked closer, I found that I was bleeding, but it wasn't serious, just a long ugly scratch, just deep enough to bleed. My shoes were full of sand and I sat down on one of the cans to empty them. My breath and most of my strength had returned by the time I rejoined Tina alongside the crumpled Saab.

She had formed a dirt mound around the car and the Saab's fuel was pouring into her moat quite rapidly. She grabbed up one of the cans and began pouring petrol onto the bodies through the top of the car, now the passenger's side window. We didn't talk. I opened the other can and held it up to her when she had emptied the first one. The stench of gas was formidable and I hoped that the engine had cooled enough to keep it from igniting the heavy, noxious vapors.

We moved the empty cans a good fifteen, maybe thirty feet away form the car and stood there silently studying the scene. Tina finally asked, "Got a light, Mack?"

I wasn't sure if she being humorous or if the Mack was an English accent thing, I didn't ask. I handed her my Zippo, asking, "Want me to do it?"

I noticed that her hands were bloody when she took the lighter. She saw it, too. She knelt down, set the Zippo on a small rock, and began to wash her hands in the sandy soil.

I asked, "Should we say a prayer or something?"

The green eyes looked up at me quizzically. Quietly she said,

"Thank the Queen that it's them, and not us." She smiled ever so slightly, and then added, "Amen."

Her hair was a mess. She was soaked in sweat and had big splotches of blood on her acid denims. She is one of the "beautiful people." One of those beings that no matter what they do, and in spite of what may happen to them, they always look appropriate and still manage to exhume their beauty. Tina, rubbing the drying blood off her delicate, and well-manicured hands, looked gorgeous.

"Start climbing, James. I'll catch up to you." She picked up the Zippo and walked primly toward the Saab stopping to pick up a stick as she went. She dipped the stick into the gas filled moat and retreated backward a good twenty feet. She looked at me and yelled, "Get moving, James."

I was already holding the two jerry cans and was backing up the gorge slowly so that I could watch. I really wanted to see, and I did.

She lit the stick and threw it, flaming, toward the Saab. Before the stick landed the fumes exploded in a dull, "Whomp."

A huge fireball rose in the air and roiled into a white cloud of smoke – the funeral pyre was lit, and I wondered how long it would take before the gas tank would explode.

Tina caught up to me and took one of the two cans. They weighed a good fifteen pounds even though they were empty. She didn't appear to be straining but she was panting slightly – I was dying, but refused to let on, one of those stupid macho things. My thighs were gone, my calves were swollen and my whole back felt like I was carrying a fat jockey to the wire on a two-mile track, in the mud.

Tina says, "Most invigorating, eh James?"

And I said, "Yeah." But I had to stop. I couldn't go on. My body wouldn't respond to my mental commands. It had simply shut down. The only sensation left in my body was muscle burn. I had to rest. I lay prone on the gorge wall and then felt myself slipping down, ever so slowly. I was sliding backward, and I didn't give a shit – I didn't care.

Then Tina calls out from the canyon's rim, "Are you alright, Mister Morgan?"

I lifted my head and saw her, thirty feet above me, sitting on a rock, looking concerned, and rightfully so. I said, "No. I need to rest a minute." And that *was* being macho – I really needed to rest an hour. I looked back at the burning wreck and thought again about the fuel tank exploding. It was a real possibility. I took a deep breath and forced myself onward. Somehow, it didn't seem so bad. As fast as my body had resigned itself, it was now back, and my strength was somewhat returned. I made it to the top, exhausted, tired and sore, but, very, very happy to just be there.

The smoke rose straight up until it left the valley where the strong gusty winds above its rim forced it westward just above ground level. The dark swirling puffs were scented with the acrid odor of burning rubber, and that – hopefully – masked the scent of burning flesh.

Tina was at the front of her Landrover washing herself from a water pouch that hung from its grill. I retrieved Sophie's .357 and carried it over to the Ford where I put it in the tire well and then pulled a bushel of cooking apples over it. – Dumb, right? Well, that's what I did.

I went back to Tina and related the events that had led up to my shooting of the Saab

(– I still prefer saying, " I shot the Saab." Instead of saying, "I shot the punk who was...")

Somehow, this works for me, psychologically.

Tina listened intently, never once disturbing my narration or questioning my interjected reasoning. When I had finished confessing my soul, there was a long silence. Tina was sitting on the ground. We both were... Her eyes developed a kind of sadness, perhaps she was exhibiting tiredness, she said, soulfully, "You saved my life, James. What you did was very brave."

Tina was sincere. Indeed, I may have well saved her life. No one will ever know for sure. The punks may have simply lost control of their Saab as they entered that curve. Tina might have stopped, and shot them both in a gun battle. Hell! – They may have quit their chase anywhere between there and Pimakeel Bay, and *nobody* would have died, not one single soul.

But, that is conjecture. The facts, for me, will evermore be shrouded in maybe and more maybes, evermore. When I say that I shot the, Saab. I'm saying that I didn't shoot the idiot who sat behind the wheel. And, there's no *proof* to the contrary. Well, so much for me in this "hind-sight" perspective. Tina now, is a horse of another color. Did she shoot the passenger in cold blood? Did she put him out of his dying misery? Did she? Well, I never did question her actions. Amen.

It was already four o'clock and I'd have to speed to meet up with the busload of scientists. Tina agreed to meet me back at Shell Camp. She needed to confer with Sophie. War had been declared. The allies needed to bond, to plan for the next battle, an episode that would surely come soon, fast, laced in a grandiose flurry of rage and inhumane madness. That's what she said, as she kissed me at the Ford's window, adding, "You're a very special man, Mister Morgan."

Then, I peeled out, leaving "Dead Man's Curve" and some even deadlier curves standing in my wake as I sped recklessly westward to meet up with my destiny – the elusive, Malagasy Tortoise.

Chapter Forty-Five

When I arrived at the crew bus, Doc and able crew were still in the field. I scanned the field with a strained eye but was unable to discern a living soul. Shutting off the motor I began to contemplate the day's events, shooting the Saab, burning the wreck and the pleasantness of being around Tina Johnson, undercover agent for Her Majesties Secret Service. I concluded that my actions were justified. Were I to be confronted again with the identical situation, it would be hard to act in any other way.

I switched on the radio to get the latest weather report and I noticed that my hand was trembling. It was more of a slight tremor than tremble, but nonetheless, I had the shakes. A stiff Scotch, perhaps two, would have done wonders for me at that moment. A few pelts of rain splattered the windshield as a sustained and howling gust rocked the wagon. Having found an English news channel, I fished around the groceries for a snack. The only thing I found was the cooking apples that held down the tire-well lid, the lid that covered up Sophie's .357 Magnum. Grabbing two, I settled back for some local news, fully expecting to hear about an auto accident just west of the mile-high city.

Just as I tossed the second apple core out the window I heard the newscaster announce a breaking news story. My ears perked up like a pair of parabolic dish antennas.

The announcer said, "Just in, a local businessman was brutally murdered this morning shortly after leaving his affluent Garden District home. Local police discovered the body of Roberto De Santos during a routine patrol of the posh western suburbs. The Chief of Police, who is reportedly a relative of Santos, believes the murder to be drug related due to the severity of Mister Santos' wounds. It appears that he may have been tortured prior to his murder."

"On the International scene..." Click.

My mind was reeling, "Roberto De Santos – Uncle Bobby? Mutilated body? Torture? – Margolova. – Holy shit!"

I got out of the wagon and climbed up on the roof of the bus. I still couldn't see anyone. It was almost five-thirty – they were an hour late. I climbed down and sounded the bus horn. I was really getting hyper, I needed to tell Sophie, I needed a drink, I needed to ask Abby what Uncle Bobby's real name was, and, I needed a nap, I felt drained, and I was. I went to the tailgate of the Ford and withdrew the .357 and placed it under my jacket on the front seat and I waited, biting my nails, something that I hadn't done since the fourth grade.

A very few minutes later, Doc tapped on my window. I had dozed off and was startled to see him. I rolled down my window to hear his chipper announcement, "We've found one, Jim. I'm sure of it! It's a perfect specimen, perfect."

The rest of the group was straggling in, piecemeal, waving to me, and then climbing aboard the bus. They were a jovial lot. I was not. I tried hard to be pleasant. But it was very difficult. Finally, they were loaded and we pulled away with me as guide, a dazed guide that was mentally preoccupied with some vivid ghosts. When I made the last turn onto the road leading to camp I waved out the window and sped ahead of them knowing that they couldn't get lost, even if they tried.

Sophie and Tina were standing at the Landrover waiting for me. They were quiet, and they looked serious, intent. I got out of the wagon while saying, "We've got to talk – in the bunkhouse. The bus is coming right behind me. – Margolova may have killed Uncle Bobby."

The girls looked at each other, dumbfounded, then followed me into the bunkhouse. I went directly to my case of Scotch and removed a new bottle twisting off the cork as I reached for an old Anchor Hocking water glass and filled it full, over-spilling some to the floor, and then gulped it all down, the whole glass of it. Then poured another, only half full and set the glass on my makeshift desk and took a deep draw out of the bottle itself while the girls looked at me with self-righteous and abject disgust, not saying a word, but communicating deep dissatisfaction with my – to them – drinking problem.

Then, wonder of wonders, Sophie picks up the fifth and fills my glass to the top, shoved it toward me while saying, "Margolova *did* kill Uncle Bobby. We just got word from Washington, it's official."

I looked down at the drink that Sophie had just topped off. As I tapped the glass with my index finger, I said, "I'm not *this* macho,

Soph." I stood and carried the drink to the shower dumping half of it behind the plastic curtain. I sat down and toasted both the spies with a glass salute, "I'm only this macho." I threw down the golden liquid in two gulps and then refilled it, another half way.

The girls were not impressed, I said, "Doc Bo has found the Malagasy Tortoise." And as I related this, the first drink hit the old cranium and the room begins to spin ever so beautifully, and then, that gentle numbness reached my hands and I noticed that I was no longer the victim of nervous tremors, and, it felt so very, very nice.

And I asked, to no one in particular, "How do we stand on Code 48's on this wonderful Malagasy evening?" – Yeah, I had to ask.

The spies were still silent, they looked at each other with their eyes, not their heads, then focused back on me, still silent, calculating, wearing their dead-pan spy faces.

The second Scotch hit home, the buzz was on, I poured another half glass and announced, "I need a nap, anyone care to tuck me in?" Sophie did an imperceptible gasp, opening her – up to then, closed lips.

The girls were not amused. Tina smiled slightly, saying, "I must get back to Pimakeel, I do hope that we'll meet again, Mister Morgan."

I smiled at her, my lovely, Tina. There was a huge smudge of blood on the front of her jacket. Soph walked to the door with her. I noticed that Tina was slightly taller than Sophie. I heard Soph say, quietly, "I'll walk you out Tina – before I tuck in our hero." Soph had thrown a thumb in my direction to delineate who the hero was. They both smiled. – I think I was experiencing, an insanity.

I poured yet another half a glass and threw it down as neat as the last four. I stripped off my muddy shirt and threw it toward my laundry bag. The booze had really hit me hard, the room had become too bright, and I turned off the lights. The winds shook the cabin's shingles and I think I heard a splatter of rain dancing across the tarpaper roof. I sat on my cot and removed my sand filled shoes. My socks were muddied and I threw them under the bed. My torn pants followed the socks, and I said out loud, "Just call me, Soph." Which was in reference to the way that Sophie undressed, everything went under her bed. I wobbled to the shower while removing my shorts and I no longer remember where I had thrown them.

The shower felt good. I felt good. I wondered, too – about how good I'd feel in the morning. And I laughed to myself – "Ha." – Some hero."

Chapter Forty-Six

Whether it was the Scotch or the previous day's events remains a moot question. The fact that I had slept from six pm. until seven A.M. the next morning was a bona fide testimony to my innate need for some uninterrupted Z time. Mental exhaustion aside, a half-fifth of J&B Scotch Whiskey is enough to send most of us mere mortals to bed, with or without a bona fide, trumped up, excuse.

I showered again, a wake up shower, and found my head clear – no symptoms of hangover. Sophie was asleep, in her own bed, and the camp, it was active with the sounds of exotic birds singing wild chirps and screeches as they dug recklessly through the edible wealth discarded in Abby's hand dug garbage pit.

As I dressed, my recollections of firing the .357 into the Saab and the Luger's bullet making a hole between the punk's eyes kept returning to my mind's eye, fuzzy at first, then more and more vivid. Again, I was thinking around the facts, the Luger's bullet hole, instead of Tina's bullet made the hole. It seemed so much more civilized. I pulled on a white Purdue sweatshirt, one that I had whacked off at mid-sleeve just below the elbow, and then moved to the kitchen for coffee.

Doc was sitting there scanning his maps, looking for a new field as intently as a teenager scans a nude foldout within a girlie magazine. As I filled my mug, Doc said, "I hear you're leaving us today, Mister Morgan."

Surprised, I prompted, "Tell me more, Doc. I haven't heard the news yet."

"Oh!" He exclaimed. "I thought you..." He stopped in mid sentence, collecting his thoughts, he continued, "I've been given control of the expedition. I thought you knew."

"Well, congratulations Doc. When did all of this come about?"

With grandiose pride, Doc boasted, "Effective last night. Shortly after verifying that we had indeed found the Malagasy Rex."

He lowered his voice and gave me a most curious look, "Why weren't you informed, Jim?"

"Oh, I wasn't feeling very well last night – I turned in early."

Excusing myself, "I'll be back in a minute, Doc. I've got to rouse Sophie." As I left the kitchen, I could only think that the expedition had been placed in very deserving and competent hands.

Sophie was disoriented when I woke her, but soon went into a nonstop tirade of what had transpired after my plunge into sleep on the preceding evening.

Once Strongbow certified that the team had "indeed" found the Malagasy Tortoise, Sophie immediately contacted Washington, who in turn, contacted Eunice. Decisions were made. Air transportation was activated. And Doc "demanded" that he be placed in charge.

We'd be picked up at five pm that very afternoon by an Air Force Lear jet. Sophie's Code 48 had been rescinded, to which she smugly commented, "The little tart is on her own." Sophie, my personal escort, would hold my hand, all the way back to Eunice.

She concluded, "That's it. I've got to start packing, you too."

Having purged herself, she jiggled her young charms toward the shower, naked, and openly excited to be leaving Shell Camp. She asked, demanded, "Bring me some coffee, Jim."

Yeah, my role at Shell Camp had been reduced to one of CIA subservience, or Federal gofer, if you will. I deliberately didn't tell her that I had exhausted the hot water. I yelled into the shower, "I'm off to get your coffee, Boss." She'd need it, too. As soon as the cold Travelle Creek hit her pristine curves, and *that* would be a "nude" awakening. Pun intended.

The idea of Tina being on her own concerned me terribly. Soph and her snide remark, that the "tart" was now on her own was shallow and undeserving. Miss Priss, love her dearly, deserved the cold shower. And, that's just what I thought as I strolled contentedly back to Doc's kitchen.

Abdul was serving up oatmeal and hard boiled eggs to a pair of hungry scientists as I entered, Lotty was stirring some bubbly brew on top of the stove; and, the lovers, trays in hand, were snuggling into the dining room's darkest corner, as if in darkness their affair would not be noticed, right. I moved over to Doc's table, the camp Overlord's table, and sat down in wait for the Prime Minister to acknowledge my presence. – And sure enough, after a few seconds, he stated, "Back again, eh?"

"We've some business to conduct, Doc. I have a whole briefcase full of contracts, bank letters, hotel reservations, checkbooks, and a list of who's who in and around this paradise. I also have a few thousand dollars that you can sign for, as soon as you can find time, of course.

Doc continued to write in his ledger, not bothering to look up from his intensive task. With a smooth nonchalance, he says, "At your convenience, Mister Morgan. We'll be doing lab work all day today, I can break loose at any time."

I continued with a thumb motion toward the kitchen, "My man, Abdul. He's done an excellent job for me since he joined the expedition. I'd like him to stay on with you. Can you find room for him under your wing?"

Doc didn't answer me right off. He looked up from his writing and stared toward the kitchen, at Abdul. Abby was licking the serving spoon from the oatmeal pot. Doc shook his head in a show of disgust at Ab's grossly exaggerated, candid, spoon licking and went back to his diary.

I added, "I've stumbled onto a case of Chivas Regal yesterday, know anyone who might take it off my hands?" He kept writing. I upped the ante, "There's also a half-case of J&B under my bunk, and I'm debating if I should ship it back or..."

Doc interrupted me, "I see. A little backwoods blackmail, eh, Morgan?"

"Well. I picked it up for snakebites. One never knows?"

Doc riveted his eyes toward the kitchen, "Mister Abdul does have a unique way of doing things, I must say. Personally, I don't see how the camp could survive without him. I'm afraid he'll have to stay – at least for the time being. You may leave the snakebite medicine in the bunkhouse, I'll be moving in there as soon as you've moved out."

The Scotch was accepted. Abby could finish the tour. Just then, there was a loud crash in the kitchen. Doc cringed, and Lotty said, "Oh, whoopsy daisy once again, eh, Ab?"

Abby responded, "It just slipped, Einstein."

Doc looked at me, "I dare say, Mister Morgan. You drive a hard bargain, a very hard bargain, indeed."

I filled Soph's mug and returned to CIA Headquarters, Soph was back in bed covered with all the bedding – mine, and hers. Her teeth were clicking, "There's something wrong with the shower, Jim. There's no hot water." She reached a hand out from the bedding to accept the coffee, "You're a life saver, Jim."

It was the second time in 24 hours that I had saved someone's life. Ah, being in the right place at the right time, a circumstance that has thrown so many men into the limelight of heroism. I sat down on her cot and pulled her into my arms, still swaddled in blankets, "I took an extra long shower just before you got up, Kidd. You'll have hot water in about twenty minutes, guaranteed."

"I can't wait that long. I've got too many things to do. We've got to leave here by eleven. We have to be at the embassy before two and we take off at five." She looked past me to the oak nightstand, "Hand me that list, Jim."

Sophie had everything prioritized. Everything she needed to do before we departed was down and in chronological order. I scanned her list: shower, dress, pack, and "connect" Morgan to the DLIDS...

When I read that, I looked at her, asking, "What's this, connect me to the DLIDS business?"

She grabbed the list, "Give me that, Jim. It's for my own personal benefit, not yours."

I did scan the note down to where it said, "fresh panties." I stood up from the bunk and said, "I've a ton of things to do too, Soph. Besides packing and everything else, I need to locate myself some *fresh panties.*"

Whoomp. She hit me with a pillow. I picked up my briefcase and let her know that I was off to transfer authority to Doc. At the door I paused, and said, "I think you'll find a fresh pair of black lacy ones, hardly used, under my bunk."

Sophie can imitate a drunken sailor's vocabulary with great ease, and that's what she was doing when I left her, screaming at me like a drunken sailor. Where one learns so many expletives is beyond me.

I found Doc in his lab peering through a microscope. I set down my briefcase and asked him if I could see the Malagasy Rex.

Without looking up, he said, "It's in the sink, be careful, he'll bite."

I lifted the tortoise by its shell holding it up to eye level. He, Doc called it a he, was five inches long, three inches wide, and two inches tall. Its shell was a sandy brown and had a slight gloss to it. His flesh was different from the other tortoises that I had seen. It was almost blue, not like the sky, but a deep aqua blue. His shell was much rounder then the other ones. Indeed, it was almost a perfect circle. I set it back into the sink. It wasn't *all* that impressive.

I said, "He doesn't look like he deserves all the attention that he's getting. What do you think, Doc?"

Doc had left his microscope and was making notes on a clipboard, "It's what he eats that makes him so potent, Jim. He diets on poisonous ticks. The ticks are toxic enough to kill a rabbit or even a small dog within hours of its bite. It's a biological wonder as to how it breaks down the poison. Doctor North's people will figure it out. They'll be able to make a tick anti-toxin from him. It'll be a valuable asset to the world community. Especially here, in the southern hemisphere, where the ticks are epidemic. They are causing the Africans all sorts of horrid ills."

"So, what do I do when this little guy gets hungry, look around for some poisonous ticks?"

"No, no. He won't eat for a week now that he's in captivity. I'm preparing him a tick paste right now, you'll take it with you, just in case."

That's when my left ankle began to itch, then my right, and then my wrists. I had become a psychosomatic tick-hypochondriac in less time than it takes to say, poisonous ticks. Yeah, I was feeling them everywhere from head to toe. To myself I was saying, "Tick tack paddy whack, leave those ticks alone." Out loud I asked, "Any of those poisonous ticks around here, Doc?" I began to rub my neck with my fingernails.

"Oh yes. The lab is crawling with them. The tortoise is a natural host for the Salmonellaenidea Ixdoes, it's a Melophagusovinus, which means, they suck blood for their livelihood. They bury their heads into the tortoises skin, and then spend the rest of their life sucking out the renewal, healing, and fluids. Quite nasty."

"Well, son-of-a-bitch. You could have at least posted a sign or something, to warn us." I was getting pissed, hadn't anyone heard of OSHA, surely they make rules for the handling of poisonous ticks – they have one for everything else on our industrialized earth, don't they?

Doc began to laugh. "We "have" posted warnings, Jim." He walked to the door, opened it, and pointed to a six-inch, red lettered sign, which read, "KEEP OUT." – A sign which had been posted by myself, only days earlier. A sign that any five-year old child could read from half-block away and know that he shouldn't enter; because, "KEEP OUT" means what it says, "keep out." Doc couldn't stop laughing, he had tickled his own innards – he had gone goof ball.

Then, I had this terrible thought, "Eunice was out to get me."

I said, to the manic laugher, "Yeah, but it doesn't say, POISO-NOUS TICKS, you, crazy old fuck."

Still laughing, he says, "There's many hazards in here, Jim. We can't list them all. Keep out, is a cover all."

I grabbed up my briefcase and headed out the door, saying, "When you're through laughing, Doc, I'll be in the bunkhouse." And I left before he answered. I wanted a shower, a hot soapy, disinfecting shower, ASAP, and as I crossed the courtyard I could not help but loath the idea of carrying poisonous ticks, even in paste form, half way around the world, chained to my wrist. Yeah, it was time for a major pay raise, at the very least.

I was thinking to call Eunice and have her come up with an alternate plan of delivery. No, I wanted to do much more than just discuss alternative shipments – I wanted to shove the Malagasy Tortoise and all its hosted ticks right up her intuitive ass. Things weren't developing well on that last morning at Shell Camp – no, not well at all.

Sophie was in the shower – strike two. I hefted the case of J&B out from under the bed and opened a new fifth, snakebites be damned, this, was a *real* emergency. I cupped the golden liquid and began rubbing it on my neck, shoulders, arms and ankles. I called into the shower, "Soph, can you save me some hot water?"

"Too late, sorry." And I heard her turn off the water – strike three. I went to the window to see if the showers were in use and found my view blocked by the striding Doc Strongbow, intent, no doubt to get his *power* papers.

I told Sophie, "Dress quick, Kidd. We've got company coming."

Strongbow knocked at the door as the naked agent exited the shower with a towel wrapped around her head, asking, "Who's coming over..." And she ducked back into the shower and accidentally pulled the curtain off its rod. She ended her incomplete statement with a very emphatic, very un-feminine, "Fuck."

I stepped out on the porch to allow Sophie time to dress. Doc said, squiggling up his nose, "You smell like a brewery, Jim."

Then, figuring out what I had done he began to grin, verging on another crack-up.

"Tic repellent." I mused, what else could I say?

Doc somatically mused, "You needn't worry about those ticks, Jim. They avoid Americans, has to do with our diet. You'd have to live here, in Madagascar, for a good six months before they'd consider you, tasty."

Doc was very amused, and me, I felt like a total ass.

Soph opened the door, her hair was damp, but she had dressed, "Thanks for waiting, things have been rather hectic this morning. Come in, Bo." And she smiled like she was caught with her pants down, and she was.

As Doc passed her into the bunkhouse, she gave me a scowling leer. Intuitively, Sophie didn't want his company. As I followed Doc past her, she asked, "What's that smell? Jim! You smell like a brewery."

I could only answer, "Tick repellent." And received another, an even more graphical sneer, one that verged on a growl.

She said, emphatically, "Yuk."

Sophie went about packing up her things as Doc signed his life away to the Institute. The various transfer forms were prepared prior to our departure from the Institute, and they only needed to be signed, about fifty-five times, in triplicate. I conceded to take responsibility for the purchase of the booze up to the transfer. I signed Abby's pay vouchers, and made out his last paycheck – I would take *that* heat, not Doc.

Doc looked at Abby's paycheck, whistled, then said, "The next time you need a field consultant, "call me." I had no idea that one could demand such a lucrative salary, especially in this neck of the woods." And then, in a whisper, he asked, "You getting a kickback on this, Morgan?"

"No, just some personal satisfaction. It's a bit of old "one ups man ship" on Eunice. Look the other way on this one, Doc. You can deny any knowledge of it. By the way, the Scotch is under that crate in the corner." I pointed toward it with an itchy finger.

Doc looked to the corner, "It's not stolen is it?"

"No, no, Doc. – It was a birthday gift."

"Well then, I bid you a happy birthday, and a bon farewell."

As we shook hands, Doc announced, "I must prepare the Rex now, time is wasting." And he left, with a nod and smile toward Sophie, and, a sweeping survey of the bunkhouse, "Yes, this will do nicely, nicely indeed."

I showered and began my own packing, a male dread. I decided to discard my dirty laundry, and suddenly, I was done. I offered Sophie a hand, but she refused, ah...she's my kind of woman. I then took a fully clothed, Malagasy siesta. It felt good to be going home, which is an integral part of every adventure.

Chapter Forty-Seven

We loaded down the Ford, inside and out, with what seemed to be a ton of luggage. It surely didn't seem like we had arrived there with as much baggage as we were departing with, but Sophie had readily assured me that we had.

Our departure plan was simple. I'd drive the station wagon. Soph would ride the MAV-861. She'd leave the experimental bike at the American Embassy and we'd turn in the rental Ford at the airport. It was time to attach the DLIDS box, say our farewells and hit the road, it was eleven o'clock – Malagasy departure time.

Connecting the DLIDS box was easy. I looked into an eyepiece and dialed in a four-digit number of my choice, and I choose, 0007. It was an easy number to remember, and besides, Tina would get a kick out of my choice, if I ever got to see her again and relate the experience.

I was told not to divulge the number to anyone. When Soph asked me what number I had picked, I refused to tell her and it pissed her off, which surprised me. After all, it was her that told me not to tell "a living soul." She pleaded, "I thought we were friends, Jim?" I was quite amazed that she wanted to know. On hindsight, I'm even more amazed that I never told her.

The Malagasy Tortoise was placed in the box and the lid was secured with the iris reading lock that only matched my eyes. The chromed steel bracelet was then clamped on my wrist. The only key that could open the cuff was back in Washington – probably around Eunice's neck.

Saying good bye wasn't, too hard, as we hadn't become intimate with the expedition, we were always busy doing other things. Ab had become my pal and I thanked him sincerely for his culinary efforts. Soph did not appreciate him much, but I certainly had. If it weren't for him, I'd still be digging the garbage pit and washing up the breakfast dishes.

"Doc Strongbow is your new boss, Ab. Call him Einstein often, he'll appreciate it, and, you'll get along just fine. Okay?"

He simply answered, "Okay, Boss."

We got into and onto our vehicles and headed out. In my rear view mirror I saw Ab waving bye-bye like a three-year old child who is seeing his daddy off to work. Yeah, Major LaCruel would get himself one hell of a good cook when the hunt ended. And if he were really lucky, Ab would return to Uganda and his pregnant girlfriend.

It was agreed that I would follow Sophie out to the tarmac, because of the dust. From there, she'd follow me to Tanan.

The first thing that I noticed was that Soph had wore her helmet. It made me proud of her, her sense of propriety and safety consciousness pleased me tremendously. I really cared for her, loved her, and it made me feel good that she cared about herself.

Then, as soon as we were out of the camp's sight, she removed the helmet and flung it out into the brush. Then, she puts on a pair of bright blue shades, silvery blue. Yeah, she was cool. The whole world would *see* that she was, too. Well, so much for propriety. I blasted a Camel and enjoyed the scenery, namely, Sophie. It turned out to be a splendid, splendid, morning after all.

Chapter Forty-Eight

To match her silver blue shades, Sophie chose to wear a white baggy sweatshirt that read, "I LUV N.Y.," and, what appeared to be, a brand new pair of Levis, very snug Levis. She had on her, as she called them herself, Scooter Boots, which looked very Italian.

She said that she'd change after delivering the MAV. She wanted to match me, is what she said. I was dressed in a simple short sleeve Arrow dress shirt with a pastel floral designer tie, summer gray slacks, and tan Docksiders. Soph said that my shoes, "sucked." However, I'm more into comfort – she's into scooter boots and reflector sunglasses. I threw a pale blue lightweight sport coat into the front seat. I had only packed two suits. And of course, I wore my two pens, my Engineer's badge.

It was getting hot on the plateau as we headed south along the tortoise and tick infested scrub fields. It was probably eighty degrees or better, and climbing. But it would be considerably cooler up in Antananarivo, which was visibly clouded over as I looked out and up to the west.

I looked at my sport coat and wondered how I'd put it on if I needed to, over the DLIDS box and its thirty-nine inch chain. One doesn't always plan ahead, does one? I pushed the thought out of my mind – hell, I'm an Engineer I'd think of something, when the time came, right?

By the time we reached the tarmac highway leading into town, I had grown used to the DLIDS appendage and its dangling chain. The entire package weighed about seven pounds, including the tortoise. I was told that the chain would separate from the cuff with a ten-pound pressure application. This was a safety precaution for the wearer, me. It was designed to save arms. And I wondered if Margolova knew that? And, I wondered, if indeed, it was a fact? I'd sure hate to start playing tennis, left-handed. And then, I wondered, would Sophie marry a one armed man? And then, I wished that I had Sophie's .357 Magnum sitting on the seat, next to my jacket. But, Sophie said, "We won't be needing this anymore." – As she locked it into an aluminum carrying case with a double set of combination locks above its handle. And when I protested, she hit me with the logic handed down to her from the Washington think-tankers, "Margolova is after the English bitch and her submarine data. She doesn't care about our tortoise."

And then, we were there, at the road leading up to Tanan.

Soph had stopped the MAV and dismounted. She wanted to talk, or rest, or something. As I watched her approach, I was comforted to know that she wore her thirty-eight snugly strapped under her N.Y. sweatshirt. Even if she, Margolova, wasn't after our turtle it made me feel a whole lot safer knowing that Sophie was armed.

She came up to my window and said, "Show me where you killed the punks, Jim. It'll make my final report much easier. Okay? I'll follow you."

I said, "Okay." However, I was deeply reluctant to stop and revisit the past, especially one with a death scene. I don't believe in ghosts, but hell – why tempt fate.

As we neared, "Dead Man's Curve," my mouth became dry and I actually began to get light headed. I knew it was wrong for us to stop there. I wondered if Sophie really *needed* to stop, or was she just being curious? My heart said, race on past and tell her you missed it, and that the curves had all looked alike. But by all means, "don't stop." And then, I found myself slowing down and looking for the spot where I had pulled off and waited, panic stricken, for the black Saab and its sinister passengers.

I pulled off the tarmac and bumped onto the same grassy spot where I had previously parked and turned off the Ford's abused engine thinking that I might actually vomit. And I thought about the big gulps of Scotch, and it made me feel better, my ills were of the stomach, not the mind, and I knew – that if the events of my yesterday were to repeat themselves this day – that I'd act the same way that I had previously acted and shoot the Saab all over again, "Ka-pow."

Once out of the car I began to feel better. I showed Sophie where I stood and waited, watching for the Saab. She stood alongside of me listening intently, looking up the road, trying to envision what I was describing to her in her own mind's eye. I retraced my steps down from the boulders and stood at the exact spot where I had fired her .357. I even pretended to fire an imaginary gun, saying, "Ka-pow." Then pointed to the mashed shrubbery where the two idiots plowed headlong into the gorge some hundred and twenty-feet below.

She began a brisk walk toward the mashed and broken foliage.

A chill came over me; my desire to accompany her was a big fat zero on a scale of one to ten. I just stood there, frozen. She calls out, "Come on, Jim. We haven't got all day."

I followed after her, reluctantly. On the one hand, I wanted to see how completely the car had burned, but, on the other hand. I didn't want to look; I didn't need a mental image of mayhem lodged in my mind, an image that I had helped to create, by simply being in the wrong place at the wrong time. I stopped, and said, "There's nothing to see, Soph. Let's go. I don't want to get my pants dirty. Okay?"

She said, defiantly, "I'm going to look. Stay here if you want, I've got to see." And she headed into the crumpled weeds and was gone.

I called out to her, "I'm coming, Shithead, wait up."

When I caught up to her she had transfixed her eyes on the charred Saab, she said, "Jesus." Then added, "Not much left. Is there?"

I was experiencing a sense of vertigo. The shell of the Saab was grotesque. And, – I had this false odor overwhelm me, the false scent of burnt flesh. I went myopic and no longer saw the wreck but a panoramic view of the Malagasy wastelands spread out before me. I said, "I've seen enough, I'm leaving." I turned and began a dizzy walk back toward the sanctuary of the packed up, ready to roll for home station wagon. What was done! Was done.

Soph yelled out an emphatic, "Shit." I turned around, and she pleaded, whining, "I've got to go down there."

I said, "Go ahead, I'll meet you at the airport." I turned and continued out, not looking back, knowing that she'd follow. She said damn it a few times, and then I heard her kick the ground to release her frustration. The brat wasn't getting her way.

Crossing the road I stopped and looked back at her, she was bending down to study something on the tarmac, I asked, "Looking for blood?"

"No. Glass. Didn't you say the windshield exploded?"

"Yeah, inward." It was more of an implosion than an ex..."

I stopped in mid-sentence, "Soph, get over here. Quick! A car's coming, hurry up." And one was, and it was coming fast.

She raced over and we ducked down behind a dense clump of pine boughs, we could see the car, it was black, and big, and as it got closer I made it out to be Mercedes Benz, a big Mercedes Benz, not a stretch, but a really huge one. One, just like the one I had seen parked inside the Turk's villa behind the armed guard a few days earlier, and Soph said, "It's Margolova. It's the same car that I saw at the Turk's." And before she finished saying this she had her thirty-eight out. She was checking the cylinder to insure that it was loaded and ready.

I agreed, "Yeah, I make six passengers, how about you?"

The Mercedes began to brake for the up coming turn. Sophie leveled her.38 at the driver's position. The car swept into the curve doing at least sixty, squealing tires and leaning stiffly to its left, and then it passed on – in less time than it takes to pull the deftly fingered trigger on a Policeman's Special. I never heard the shot – the one that I had fully expected to hear from Sophie's aimed and steadied .38. No, she simply didn't shoot. Her weapon didn't jamb. The bullet didn't misfire ... she just never pulled the trigger.

The Mercedes whizzed off and around another curve while Sophie kept the silent barrel locked onto its rapidly fading trunk lid. Then, she lowers the weapon and looks at me. "It was Margolova. I saw her plain as day."

"Why didn't you shoot?"

"Shoot?"

"Yeah, she'd be down there with her pals." I stood and walked to the Ford. Soph sat in the pine needles flabbergasted at my question or at my suggestion that she should have fired on her archenemy, Margolova.

From the car I called out, "Where do you think she's going?"

She stood and said, "Pimakeel Bay." – As she nonchalantly dusted off her Levis.

She holstered her gun, and when she pulled up her sweatshirt, she revealed that she was wearing a bra. It must have been terribly condescending of her to wear it. I wondered if it was a courtesy extended to our embassy – coat and tails, bras and panties... How civil.

I said, "We've got to warn Tina."

Soph looked at me with a look of incredulity, "It's no longer our concern, Jim. – She's on her own."

This pissed me off, I said, "Oh, she's on her own? Well let me tell you what I think about you and your whole rat pack of CIA bug-a-boos. I think you're all "fucking pathetic idiots." You stand right here and watch a whole carload of spooks racing down to kill a group of biologists, and you can just say, "They're on their own."

Well, you're a fucking nut case, that's what I think."

Sophie turned red face. She spat back, "It's the risks we take in our business. It comes with the territory."

I got into the Ford, saying, "Yeah, get on your little toy and go. Enjoy your fun, Miss Deadly. I'm going down to warn Tina."

She got hotter. She was screaming, "Our job is to be at the embassy by three o'clock. That's my orders."

I said, "Oh no. Those are *your* orders. Not mine, I *quit*."

I got out of the car and set the DLIDS box on the ground, placed my foot on the chain and pulled with all my might. The cuff didn't give, the chain held, so much for that ten pounds of pressure, nothing happened. I was stuck. The tortoise was going with me.

I got back into the car, saying, pointing to Sophie's DLIDS contraption, "Any more secrets I should know about?"

Sophie began to laugh hysterically, "What you going do – go down and hit Margolova over the head with your tortoise?"

I got back out and sat down on the ground placing my feet on the box and exerted as much force on the chain as I could. I was sure that my wrist was going to break, and I had to give it up and call it quits. The chain held. I probably exerted a hundred-fifty pounds of pressure on it – it was useless. The only thing I wound up accomplishing was to get grass stains on my eighty-dollar slacks.

Sophie began laughing again, "I can see the headlines now, MAN FOUND ON ROAD BLUDGEONED TO DEATH BY BOX. POLICE SUSPECT – TORTOISE."

"Very funny Soph. – Very funny."

"The key is in Washington. – Give it up, Jim." The anger in her voice returned, she was back to being – really stupid.

She stood with her legs spread in an intimidating stance, one that said, "We *are* going to the embassy, and we are going right now."

I climbed in behind the wheel and started the engine. "I'll meet you at the airport by five, I'm going down to warn them."

She withdrew her .38 and stuck it in my face, yelling at me to, "Turn it off! Now."

She looked pretty serious, she said, "You and that tortoise are my responsibility. We are *all* going to the embassy – *together*. Now move over. I'm going to drive."

"What you going to do, Soph? Shoot me?"

"I'm *authorized* to..."

I said, "Fuck you." I threw the Ford into reverse turning my head away from her to see where I was backing and hit the gas."

She screamed, "Okay! Okay. You win. We'll be a little late for lunch, but – who's hungry anyway – you big jerk. All of this hero shit has really gone to your head, Morgan."

I hit the brakes. Soph rounded to the passenger door and got in, nesting the .38 in her lap. She was disheveled, totally unsure of her snap decision. She had momentarily lost her cuteness. It was surrendered to the frustration, and agony, of not following dictated orders.

Yeah, she was as *unsure* of her decision as I was *sure* of mine. To say that we were at odds with one another...well, that would have been a most definitive understatement.

Chapter Forty-Nine

We drove recklessly through the curves and switchbacks swaying left then right and finally wound our way down to flat stretches of open road that seemed to never, ever end, it just narrowed away into oblivion, yet would still be there, its end, always just out of reach.

We rode in silence until we hit the flat lands; the dry arid semi-desert area that extended, down and out, right up to the Mozambique Channel itself.

Although the Ford was fully overloaded, we still managed to reach speeds of 110 MPH, on the straights. I kept the pedal floored, when possible, and it surely helped that we were moving downhill. Soph had suggested that we dump the luggage, but we didn't. Every now and then we'd hit a rise in the road and several times the wagon felt like it had left the road, then it would pound back down, hard, with a sharp lunge to its right, it was scary at first, but the grab was so persistent that it became a standard operating procedure. I told Soph that it was probably due to a low tire, but she didn't seem interested.

I asked her for the .357. She didn't answer, but leaned over the seat and extracted its aluminum case and set it in her lap and opened it. Still not conversing, she loaded its cylinder. She then placed two full boxes of bullets on the dashboard. She closed the case, and silently, mechanically, returned the empty gun case back over the seat. She then set the weapon down next to me, and the DLIDS box. She still hadn't said anything, and I supposed that she was just mentally preoccupied, planning a strategy, designing a war plan, or maybe – praying.

When we neared Shell Camp Road, I slowed and asked Sophie if Margolova might be raiding Shell Camp. She finally spoke, "No."

I pressed back down on the gas and Shell Camp Road was behind us, way behind us. Soph said, "I don't know anymore. Everything has me confused. I think she'll go to Pimakeel, there's nothing for her to steal at Shell Camp."

Soph was biting a fingernail. Her answer was an out loud thought, an expression of surfacing doubt. "The think-tankers are usually right. That's probably where she's going, Pimakeel. But, I just don't know."

I said, "The Saab could have followed me yesterday, but they waited for Tina – they're going after Tina.

Soph nodded an agreement, more of a nod in resignation to her commitment. Then, after a bit, she says, "Yeah. Submarines!" I get sent on a turtle hunt, and Johnson – she gets submarines."

We bounced along the road for a good ten minutes in a stone dead silence. I had no intention of answering her comparative allegory. I was personally quite happy to be looking for a tortoise in the tropical warmth of Madagascar; it beat the hell out of hunting for oil on the frozen slopes of Brooks Range, Alaska. But on the other hand, the oil fields were comparatively safe.

Soph began, "Jim?"

To which I responded, "Yes?"

"Oh, never mind."

There it was, that old, "Never mind." That feminine plea to tie her up, torture her, snap her teeth with a pair of pliers, put hot coals on her belly button, but at all costs, extract that passing thought. I said, "Okay."

A heat mirage formed in the distance, it was getting hotter as we descended through the deserted wastelands. Soph says, "We're going to shoot first and ask questions later. Okay Jim?"

"Sounds fair to me." I added, "Maybe we can get them all in the back."

Soph concluded, " – We should be so lucky."

Ten more miles slipped past before she spoke again, "I'm sorry for threatening you back there. I was only doing my job."

I shook my head in acknowledgement and lit a cigarette. I asked her if she had any idea as to how we might get rid of the DLIDS box.

She suggested, "We could try shooting it off."

I took my foot off the accelerator, saying, "Let's try it."

The wagon slowed to a stop, we were in an area that resembled a moonscape. It was hot, and a lone vulture circled lazily to the west in a clear but slightly hazy sky. It was windless and quiet, the only sound was that of the engine ticking and some bug clicking for a mate somewhere off in the distance.

Yeah, it was a weird area, an eerie spot. It was void of vegetation, lifeless, and – hot, hot, hot.

Soph wiped sweat from her brow, "You could have parked in the shade, Jimbo."

I looked around, "Yeah, see any? Point it out and we'll go park in it."

I set the box down and looped the chain in an arch away from me. "Blast away, Kidd."

She moved behind me and pointed the .357 down at the chain. The gun was only ten inches from my ear. "Hold it! Hold it. Your not going to fire that thing right next to my ear, are you?"

"Here." She handed me the gun with a disgusted look on her face. "Do it yourself."

I put the barrel next to link about ten inches from my wrist and fired. The bullet hit the link and damn near pulled off my wrist. The power was so strong that the box had turned over. The chain held and there wasn't so much as a scratch on the chrome plating.

I tried it a second time, making the chain taught between my left foot and my wrist and prepared for the jolt. I fired again, and nothing. It was useless. Sophie said, seriously, "I've got a hand grenade." Well, maybe not so seriously, because she also suggested that we dump water on it and let it rust away. Getting back into the car she further suggested that we fly up to Washington and get the key.

To which I told her, "If you get another bright idea, put it in writing and then mail it to me, okay?"

We were nearing the road to Pimakeel and I slowed to around sixty, looking for our unmarked exit. Sophie busied herself and reloaded the .357. I asked her, "Do you really have a hand grenade?"

"Yes. I have four of them." She fished around the back seat and pulled out another aluminum case. She opened it and showed me the four pineapples nesting in a thick black foam rubber pad.

I said, "Jesus, you're a regular James Bond, Soph. Can you use those things?"

"Of course."

She removed one and gave me a step-by-step lesson on how to use one. It sounded simple, pull the pin, throw it at your target, then duck, while holding your ears.

She set a grenade next to the magnum then removed the other three, they were latched in with metal bands that secured them tightly to the case. I think the case was designed to make one, think twice, before pulling one out. When she removed the last one, she tossed the empty case out her window. This was a strong indication to me that the grenades were not going back to Langley, at least – not in their original package.

She set them on the floor and said, "When we turn, stop a minute so I can get the rifle out, I need to align the scope, it'll only take a minute.

I was wholeheartedly subservient, "You got it, Babe."

It was obvious that "Sophie D. Deadly" had come to life. Even her voice bespoke of her highly trained commando expertise. She was preparing for battle, and, she was going to win, every trace of doubt had vanished. The Kidd was in control, and her collected countenance gave me a renewed confidence in my own self. "We," were going to kick some ass, *big* time.

I stopped the Ford at a knocked down sign, it read, in French, "Pimakeel Bay 20 Kilometers." I hadn't seen it before. It was old and made out of concrete. I sat on it while Sophie attached the Lancia scope, and filled three bullet clips that were stored in its case. She did this all in a quick minute. She then lifted the 30/30 Winchester and fired off one round. It startled me. I wasn't expecting her to actually *fire* the damn thing. She made a small adjustment to the scope and fired it once again.

She told me that it was set at a hundred yards. She gave me a brief lesson on how to use the weapon, "Aim and pull the trigger..." Then she did a textbook summary, "Any questions? Your life, or mine, may come to depend on this." She shook the rifle for emphasis.

I felt comfortable that I could use it and I told her so. We got back in the Ford and sped off fishtailing through the grass until the wheels fell into the tire rutted road trail. Right or wrong, we were off to war. There was no more room for hedging, no more room for second thoughts. We were totally committed – and nearly out of gas...

Chapter Fifty

Moving north to Pimakeel Bay was tedious. We went slower than we wanted to, we had to go slow, the over laden wagon and the badly pitted roadway had roguishly conspired against us, denying us any speed, or comfort, even with our seat belts on we were being slammed around like a pair of dice in a shaker cup. But, we were at least moving, attacking.

Soph stated a plan. We would enter the bay area slow and as soon as we saw the Mercedes, we would stop and proceed by foot. It would give us the element of surprise. Soph's thinking was that Margolova wouldn't enter the village directly. "She'll walk in, sniper down the entire expedition, then, walk up and take what she wants. – She's done it before."

This amazed me. How can someone get away with so much, out-and-out, evil? I asked Soph, "How many people has she killed now, a thousand?"

She answered, "Forty-three that we're sure of, twenty more are listed as strongly probable, double that, and you'd be fairly close to an accurate number."

Soph was mentally preoccupied and her answer was given in a monotone. I should have left her alone, but pressed her, "It hardly seems possible, she knocks off some hundred people and still roams the earth. It's beyond my comprehension. How does she get away with it? There ought to be a law..."

"There's plenty of laws against her and she's broken every one of them. She's wanted, dead or alive, in about nine countries. You shouldn't have any qualms about shooting her in the back, if you get the opportunity, shoot her. Think of her as a rabid dog drooling slime through multiple countries giving the world a genuine heartache. Chop her down, quick. She'd slit your throat for a dime and never bat an eye. She's a shark, Jim. If you get half a chance to shoot – shoot. Don't hesitate, don't even think about her as a human being, she's scum, vile scum, and she won't hesitate to kill you, she don't play around. Remember, she's really bad, and don't you *ever* forget it."

"What about her henchmen? Are they wanted, too?" Aren't they, just following orders? Like in the military, or like you?"

"Believe me, Jim. Every one of them will show up on a want-ed list, somewhere. If you can get one of them, get him. They're bad, they're all wanted and they're all guilty of something. You can't go up to one and ask him if he's guilty – not today. Today, he's guilty by association."

She looked at me with total sincerity, "Understand?"

I answered, "Yeah, got it."

And as soon as I said, "...got it." I was overwhelmed with the truth of my situation – "I was only following orders, I was only Sophie's flunky, and if I shot someone, I'd only be following orders."

Wasn't I guilty by association, too? By association with Sophie, I had made myself an enemy to Margolova and her clandestine entourage. By association, I was their target, and I could almost hear Margolova telling her troupe, "...if you get the chance, shoot him, he's guilty by association."

Mentally, I began running through reasons that would justify my killing Margolova and her associates.

One, Sophie said it was okay. She's a CIA field representative backed by the USA. If she says it's okay to kill these people, then they are surely fair game.

Two. They're assassins. Assassins are murderers by the very nature of their business, assassinating. Assassins are therefore bad. Yep, I have never met a good one. Actually, up to that moment, I had never met one at all. Yeah, I thought, I can kill an assassin, especially, in self-defense. And it was already established that I was guilty of association with Sophie, which made me, their enemy.

Three. They were here to steal something that didn't belong to them. They were showing intent, according to Soph. So that made them crooks, robbers and thieves. Yeah, I could kill a thief, certainly one who was stealing from a good guy. In this case, stealing from one of our American allies, England.

Four. I was – I still am – an American. Americans are the good guys, right? So, I'm an American, I'm a good guy. Now, Margolova, an old school Russian, is a bad guy because old-school Russians were the bad guys. Therefore, Margolova is a bad guy. And the good guy always kills the bad guy. Right?

Yeah. I could shoot them. Shoot them all. Shoot the whole bunch of old-school Russian assassins dead on the spot. Because they are bad people, crooks, robbers, thieves, murderers, and terrorists. Yeah, I'd shoot their black Mercedes, too. Yep, Soph's .357 Magnum would get them all. Yes sir.

We were getting close. I lit a cigarette. I thought further, "I'm a Catholic. If all else fails, I'll go to confession and atone for my sins." "Dear Father bless me, blah, blah, blah... I have killed six bad guys...no, make that eight bad guys – blah, blah, blah...Amen."

I slowed to five MPH and asked Soph, "We're only doing what rational people would do, aren't we?"

"What are you talking about?"

"Sorry! Just thinking out loud." Then asked, "We *are* the good guys, aren't we, Soph?"

"Yes. Now quit thinking about it. We'll be saving a lot more than just your little whore from Devon, believe me."

"I wonder what she thinks of you, Soph? Do you think she calls you, the whore from, Washington?"

She looked at me with a deadpan face, then says, "I think she's prettier than me. I'm jealous of the way she throws herself at you. And she's smarter, and more intellectual than myself. Is that what you wanted to hear, Jim?"

"Well, I must admit, the thought had crossed my mind. Although, I never thought that I'd hear it from you, Soph."

She answered in a whisper, more to herself (I'm sure) than to me, "Men are such assholes."

She whispered out a scream, "Slow down."

"If I go any slower we'll be going backwards."

"Stop. Pull in."

"Which one? Stop? Or, pull in?"

"For Christ's sake, Jim. Pull in, there – now." She was pointing off to the west, to a clump of trees surrounded by dense vegetation, growth that got ever deeper and thicker to the north.

I drove a good fifteen feet into the brush, and when I felt that the Ford could no longer be seen from the road, I turned off the ignition, and everything became instantly silent. My heart was pounding. The moment of truth had arrived.

Soph got out, opened the tailgate and pulled out a black sport bag from under some heavier bags. Not talking, she tromped around to the hood and set the bag on it. The bag was tied shut, I hadn't recalled seeing this bag before, but... She twisted off the wire and removed a camouflaged suit, a hooded, ninja suit. Then she began stripping off her clothes, throwing them to the ground. Naked, except for bikini panties, she slipped into the oriental garment.

It was the most amazing thing that I had ever *not* seen. She was gone, vanished, right before my eyes.

She spoke, "It's the latest technology, Jim, it's called, Low Island Invader."

I said, "You'd better keep talking, Soph. Right now, you look like a pretty good spot to take a piss."

"Very funny, Jim. Stay here. I'm going to see if Margolova left a lookout with the Mercedes. It would be a standard operating procedure for her to do that. I'll be back in ten minutes. If I'm not... You can try driving in to warn your sweetheart. Okay?"

Speaking to the body-shaped shrub with blue eyes, I said, "I only have eyes for you, my little bushkin."

The piercing blues blinked, "Ten minutes, Jim. Check your watch, and, save the bull shit, okay?"

Nonsense was out. Soph had entered the world of chop, kick and kill. Sincerely, she asked me, "Do you love me, Jim?"

"Yes."

She stared at me deeply, a full interminable second. She had penetrated into my very soul. Then she says, "Good luck, Jim. – Be careful." She said this with such finality that it actually scared me, she knew, she might not come back, and had just stated that fact in so many words, and a few cryptic eye nuances that were impassioned, sincere and reeked with a deadly and eerie earnestness.

She turned and ran into the roadway. She looked like a puff of wind rustling through the coastal vegetation, her camouflage was that good, I only knew she was there because I strained with a total effort to watch her. And then – she disappeared. I looked at my watch. It was two minutes past three. I looked for Soph, but it was no use. The chips were down. It was time to show our hand. And I thought, "The chips are indeed down, now, for a slight of hand, go get them, Soph. Kick some ass, Kidd."

I gathered up Soph's clothes and threw them in the back seat. Her thirty-eight was on the ground. – I hoped it was deliberate, surely she wouldn't have just forgotten to take it. And I felt a pang of panic. I looked at my watch. One minute had passed. I put her gun on the passenger's floor. I removed the scoped rifle and edged toward the road, ducking down. I looked through the scope trying to see the Mercedes that Soph said was a mere hundred yards ahead of us. I couldn't see it. I didn't dare to move farther into the roadway. I went back to the Ford. Two minutes had passed. My mouth was dry, my pulse was beating rapidly, I was sweating and I wasn't so sure that it was from just the heat alone. Toss in a bunch of fear and idle waiting, hell – just the waiting...

I tried to be functional. I began a forced recall of the road as it entered into the village, to recall the village huts, their locations, where the "re-Gretta" was moored, and the position of the English laboratory. How many buildings did they have? One? Damn. I should have been more interested, looked at their set-up and not have spent so much time disliking the Moo-Roo fag, or whatever the hell his name is. Four minutes had passed.

I thought I heard a drum, but it was only my heart thumping. I forced myself to pace back and forth alongside of the wagon in an effort to make the time go faster. I thought of emptying the Ford of our luggage. I set the DLIDS box down and studied its configuration and thought about how I might rid myself of it. I hated it and I hated the tortoise.

I got into the driver's seat and thought about starting the engine, to be ready. I grasped the key, only seven minutes had gone by...we were low on gas...I released the key and waited.

I got out, leaving the door open, ready. I practiced removing the .357 from my belt. It was awkward to do, because of the stupid chain. I studied the road for signs of Soph, nine minutes had passed, "Come on, Soph." I went back to the car door. She wasn't coming. She had ten seconds left – I started the Ford. She hadn't come. The whole ten minutes were gone. I was getting numb. I had an icy chill invade my being. My heart was up in my throat.

I placed the rifle where I could reach it, picked up the .357 and backed into the road ruts, bouncing the car frame hard to the ground. I threw the gearshift into low and floored down on the gas pedal. The front of the Ford reared its head and leapt upward. The rear tires were spinning and spewing dirt and dust until a sand cloud had engulfed the wagon, not until then did it actually edge forward, leap forward, toward the black Mercedes, Pimakeel Bay, and my sweetheart, Tina Johnson.

I hadn't seen the limo when Soph had said to turn in and stop – I was looking at her. Now I saw it. It was only a hundred yards or so, ahead of me. I couldn't see anyone near or anywhere around it. I couldn't see Sophie, even if I had, I wouldn't have known it. The speedometer read 30 MPH as I came alongside the now sinister look-ing Mercedes. I was fully prepared to be shot at, and had scooted myself down in the seat, to hide, presenting the smallest possible tar-get to my *unseen* enemy. Yeah, I could hardly see out the window as I picked up momentum, and then I saw the lone clump of bush move... I slammed down on the power brakes, hard. The DLIDS box, the rifle and two suitcases from the back seat came flying for-ward into the passenger area, and then – the engine died. The mov-ing bush opened the door and slid in. Propping her legs on top of shifted cargo. Soph slumped back in the seat, panting heavily, and said, "One down."

Stupidly, I asked the old adage, "Are you alright?"

"Yeah." She was still panting, deep. "I had to break his neck. It wasn't like in the movies..."

I was momentarily speechless, then asked, "What do we do now?"

She said, "I don't know. I've got to catch my breath. I need to think a minute."

Reluctantly, I stated, "You forgot your gun."

"Yeah. I didn't want it." She was breathing easier, but, still strain-ing, still winded, "I used a ninja star. Hit him square in the forehead. He pulled it out and came after me. He knew karate and he was very good." She pulled off her hood and looked at me with drained eyes, "He scared the hell out of me, I thought he was going to get me. I was only lucky, I wasn't worth a damn, Jim."

Soph searched the car, found her thirty-eight and put it on, right over the ninja suit, it looked out of place, but it sure made her feel better, instantly. I don't think she once thought about appearances, not then.

I sat silent, listening, Sophie D. Deadly Kidd had the floor, and I was not going to interrupt her. She continued, "We've got to move, we've got to warn them. These are really bad people and I'm feeling "very" inadequate. Lets roll; maybe Johnson can give us some help. If Margolova's other henchmen are as tough as this guy was, well, we're in some deep shit."

The Ford fired up under a shaky key and we pulled out slow and controlled, accelerating quickly to forty, then fifty, as we bounded across the grassy, rutted bumpy entrance to Pimakeel Bay and its attendant village. We were about to enter paradise, with our guns at the ready, and I for one – was honestly praying.

Chapter Fifty-One

The grass lane changed to dirt as we hit the village with a cloud of dust billowing out from behind our tailgate. The speedometer was reading sixty when I slammed down hard on the brake in an attempt to miss the village dog, obviously, he had never seen a car enter his domain doing 60, because he made a vicious attack, teeth bared, right into our front bumper. It was a heroic gesture on behalf of the village's protectorate, to attack us, the intruders – but not too bright. I had to keep going, I did offer, "Damn. I hope there's a doggy orthodontist in the village." To which I received a very, *very* angry stare from my ninja woman. No, it was not a good day for dark humor.

Braking hard, we managed to stop just short of submerging the Ford into Pimakeel Bay. We had slid a good twenty-five yards, before coming to a halt. We were just east of the empty pier. One more foot and we'd have needed ourselves a rudder, we were that close.

"The re-Gretta," was out to sea. Soph said, "Thank God, they're out in the boat. We've got to get to their radio."

I threw the Ford into reverse and backed all the way up to the lab with our wheels spinning up a flurry of coral dust and shell imbedded sand. We paralleled the lab's front door with Sophie's door, and then ran headlong into the screened, unlocked, plastic walled, tin roofed, army constructed, field building. With our guns at the ready, we were prepared for anything. But inside, we only found an empty lab, dark and void of any human activity.

The interior was aglow from aquarium lights and it gave the lab an eerie quality, it made me think of Captain Nemo's Nautilus, as the bubbling tanks calmed and relaxed one's senses causing me a momentary lapse into forgetfulness as to what was actually going on in the here and now. The sensation only lasted a few seconds, but it was mentally a startling moment.

Soph scanned the room from behind the nose of her .38. She had both hands on the weapon, ready to drop anyone, or anything, out of the norm. Suddenly she then holstered it, quickly with a snap, slap. She trotted toward the radio, while calling, "Hello, you *bloody* blokes. Anybody here?"

I stayed at the door and peeked out. Everything seemed calm, peaceful, quiet – too quiet. Soph had reached the radio and was throwing switches, firing up the equipment. Then I hear, "English camp to Gretta ... English camp to Gretta ... Come in, Gretta. This is an emergency, Gretta. Come in Gretta. This is an S.O.S., a real emergency. Please respond, Gretta. Over."

She threw some more switches and we listened to a loud and irritating static. No one was responding. After a short minute, she repeated her plea. Again nothing. Nothing but static!

Soph looked up at me and said, "I don't know if I've got the right frequencies, Jim. I feel like I'm wasting my time."

Her self-confident nature was under attack for the second time in the same half-hour. Her frustration level was peaking and it worried me. – If she were to crack? I'd probably follow suit. We'd both be out under a palm tree muttering ga ga in a pair of matching straightjackets. I offered, "Give it your best shot, Kidd. "I then turned my attention to the islanders who were out to retrieve their watchdog's crumpled carcass.

One native was crouched over the dog, and yet another was approaching him, pointing toward the Ford and the lab, they looked mad. They would come to the lab, soon. I yelled this development over to Sophie. She chose to ignore me as she was making a fourth effort to contact, anyone.

She threw the radio into receive, then moved rapidly past me on her way out to the wagon, saying, "Listen for a response. I need to call Washington." And she was out the door before I could question her as to where she was going.

From the lab window I watched her dig through the luggage and pull out her CIA radio case. She was on the front seat leaning into the back and throwing stuff everywhere, looking for...something? I was still holding the .357 in my right hand and the DLIDS box in my left. They were getting heavy, both of them, not to mention the chain.

I looked toward the natives. One of them had lifted the dog and was carrying it toward us. They were now joined by one of their woman.

"That's when the shit began."

A bullet puffed through the rear window of the station wagon leaving a one-inch hole webbed across the glass. A second bullet shattered the driver's window sending glass grains splattering into the interior and onto Sophie. It was in a mad scramble for her to get out of the Ford while carrying – dragging, her radio gear.

Finally she had to abandon the radio on the ground and make a headlong dive through the screened door. Soph literally rolled into the room. She stood, shook her hair, and said, "That, pisses me off. Those bastards are shooting to kill, Jim."

I looked for the natives, but they were gone. The dog was discarded in a heap. It was no longer such an important issue – compared to the value of their individual dark carcasses.

Yeah, I couldn't see anyone. I didn't know where the shots had come from, and I didn't know what to say, or do. I just looked out the window, dumbfounded, wondering why Sophie would want to call halfway around the world, to Washington.

She joined me at the window. "Those were two separate shots. The first one came from the west and the second one from the bank somewhere by the canoes. I think we're surrounded."

I seriously said, "We'd better surrender, Soph. Bullets will come right through this shit." I tapped the wall with barrel of the .357.

She says, "Not yet." And bolts out the door, grabs the radio and lunges back in like a yo-yo on a tight string. A bullet kicked up sand behind her heels, missing her by a mere inch. She smiled, grinning at the rush. Or, she was just "stupidly glad" that she hadn't been shot. I hoped it was the latter. I remained silent. I didn't quite know how to respond to her blatant show of idiotic bravado.

She stood and took a deep breath, looking at the Ford, she said, "We need the rifle." And before I could protest she was out the door and into the driver's seat.

Many shots were fired; bullets ripped away the rear window, several new holes appeared in the windshield, and tufts of leather from the suitcases flew into the air. Then I heard the feminine call to, "Cease Fire, cease fire." It was, no doubt, Margolova.

Soph had grasped the rifle and as soon as she had heard the cease-fire, she was out of the Ford and diving back through the door like a human cannonball shot from a circus cannon. – She tumbled over the rifle, and sprang upright to her feet. It was most impressive. She held up the rifle and two grenades. – Again, the grin. This time, it was an obvious victory grin.

She set down the grenades, went to the door, and fired off an errant round blindly towards the east. She didn't aim. She just shot. She said that she wanted them to know that we would fire back. It would make them think a minute, or two, before rushing us.

She stood back and surveyed the car. "I hope you purchased lease insurance?"

"I think it was a package deal." Then added, "Ah, Soph? I left my cigarettes on the dashboard, would you mind?"

Ignoring me, she plugged in the radio. She then withdrew a three-foot fold-up parabolic dish antenna and began to fan it open. She then attached the focal horn and connected up with a coaxial cable that was probably 30 feet in length, maybe longer. She then stood, picked up the dish, and flew out the door trailing the cable behind her. She placed the antenna on top of the luggage and was back in before we heard a double round of shots make a thip, thip, into the wooden doorjamb of the lab.

The British camp's radio set crackled in, "Gretta to base...Gretta to base...Come in Kate."

Soph ran to the set and threw down the send switch. "Base to Gretta...Base to Gretta. This is Sophie Kidd from Shell Camp. Do you read me? Over." Then threw down the toggle to receive.

"Gretta to base. Tina Johnson here. Go ahead Kidd. Over."

Soph gave Tina a complete rundown of what was happening, she started with the sighting of the Mercedes at Dead Man's Gulch and finished with, "...we haven't seen Kate or the Landrover."

Tina asked Sophie to verify that Margolova was indeed there. When she did, Tina asked Soph to burn her files. "Burn the whole bloody building down if need be, but destroy them, quickly. Over."

Soph asked, "What's your ETA, Tina?" And then the whole lab shook to a mighty whomp and the lights and pumps and radio all went deader than the native's dog. Margolova had blown the generator room with what sounded like a full stick of dynamite. Simultaneously, bullets began to riddle Sophie's dish antenna. We went to the window and watched it disintegrate before our very eyes. Once again, Margolova called out for her men to cease firing.

Soph yelled to me, "Come on. We've got to burn her files."

I followed her to a row of file cabinets, there were nine of them, and each had three drawers. She read the content tags, and said, "Here, these two." One was opened and the other was locked. I turned the locked file on its side and showed Soph how to unlock it without a key.

"Where'd you learn how to do that, Jim? Purdue?"

"Yeah, during finals."

We balled up the papers and started a fire right in the middle of the aisle, it would indeed, burn the whole bloody building down, eventually.

Soph said, "Margolova will figure out what we're doing any second. She'll rush us and try to recover what she can."

I said, seriously, "Maybe she'll realize what we're doing and go away."

"She can't, Jim. I've punctured her gas tank and threw her keys into the jungle. She needs the Ford or Tina's Landrover to go anywhere."

Goose flesh formed on my arms and I asked, "Did Tina say how far out she was?"

"Yes. She said they were five nautical miles west."

"Well," I said. "Unless she's got a supper charged spy engine, it's going to take her twenty…thirty minutes – maybe more, to get back. She did say that she was a double-0 agent. Double-0, sixty-nine."

Soph looked at me with what could only be described as a look of incredulous disbelief. Then says, "You're a real fucking idiot, Jimbo."

We finished balling up the papers. Our fire was a good four-foot high, and smoke was quickly overtaking the lab. Soph stood and ran to the back door, she ran in a low crouch, carrying her rifle in only one hand. I followed, clumsily toting my wares, feeling dumb, and wondering why in hell I had let myself be chained up to a tortoise in the first place. Yeah, it was dumb…dumb…dumb.

When I caught up to her, I empty-mindedly asked, "What do we do now? Make a run for it? Hide in the jungle?"

"I don't know. Margolova has probably sent her best man to the west of us. Her second best will be positioned in the back of us. The worst of them, she'll keep alongside of her – so she can keep an eye on him, watch him."

"What about the fourth man?"

"That'll be her real henchman, somebody who would die for her, someone who idolizes her. A lover… She's probably sent him after the Mercedes. He's the only one that she'll remotely trust, but not very far."

"That's sick, Soph. Where does she find these people?"

She shrugged her shoulders, "There's some real weirdoes out there, Jim. The world's full of them."

"Well, I think we should do something. What? I didn't know.

She offered, "Our best bet is to sit tight and wait for Tina. I just hope she's as good a spy as she is a flirt."

I was getting tired of Soph's snide remarks, but let it go. Yeah, If Tina was able to sail in, walk in, or even crawl in and save our ass – Sophie would probably change the tune she'd been whistling. Personally, I had a lot of respect for Tina Johnson. I also wanted to get to know her a little bit better. Actually, I wanted to get to know her a lot better.

I said, "If Kate drives up now she's in for one hell of a big surprise, eh Kidd? By the way, is Kate a spy, too?"

"No, just Tina. For Kate's sake, I hope she's hiding in the woods, maybe, she's gone into town."

Soph suggested that we look for an escape route, out front. The back was wide-open field for forty-feet up to the edge of the jungle. We moved to the front and studied the area. It was even more open then the rear. We were pinned down and our cozy lab fire was spreading like – wild fire? The smoke was getting thicker and intensifying by the minute. Soon, we'd have no choice *but* to make a run for it.

Soph suggested, "Maybe we can get them to use up all their ammunition." And she was out of the door and leaping, back into the already bullet-riddled Ford.

Bullets began pounding into the wagon, fripp, zing, plink, and thip, it was a relentless volley. Soph tossed a suitcase out of the car door, and, no less than ten bullets ripped into my Arrow shirt bag, the same bag that held a dozen designer ties at over sixty bucks a pop.

Soph was playing a dangerous game, a game that could backfire at any moment and leave her dead, and me, begging to surrender. She threw out a second bag. One shot was fired hitting the bag full center. And, for the third time that afternoon, Margolova had to yell out a ceasefire. And when she did, I aimed the .357 out toward her witch voice and loosed off a round in her general direction. And before the smoke had cleared my barrel, Soph was back inside the smoking lab. Her plan had indeed cost our enemy a good fifty-rounds in wasted ammunition.

The rear window of the lab imploded. Shards of glass flew in the air... I turned in time to see a hand grenade rolling across the floor, to mid-building, some thirty-feet from our stand. Soph jumped sideways behind a desk and I – I had nowhere to go. But out the door and throw myself into the Ford, leaving the DLIDS box dangling below the Ford's rocker panel.

Bullets came pinging into the car and I just knew that I was hit, somewhere, because I was in pain from head to foot. Then the grenade blew, a rush of smoke bellowed out the door and encompassed the wagon. I scooted backward, into the smoke, and entered the lab choking and calling for Soph, to see if she were still, alive.

Two shots rang out from the rear of the lab. I dropped to my knees and leveled the .357 through the smoke toward the back door.

Soph called out, "Jim?"

"Yeah."

"You okay?"

– "I don't know."

Soph emerged from the smoke with a rag covering her mouth to block the smoke and mumbled out, "I got another one."

"Great!" I said. "Now get the other four."

She smiled, mumbled, "I'm morking on it, mashole. – I'm working on it."

Without any warning, Soph dashed four-feet out the door, and quickly ran back in. She didn't draw any fire. "They're onto our tactic, Jim. They've got to rush us now, they know they're low on ammunition – it'll be a last ditch effort."

I stood, feeling myself for wounds. I had heard that people have been shot and never knew it, until someone else came along and pointed it out to them. I told Soph, "I bet this tortoise is shitting ticks."

We looked at each other, smiling. Then, Margolova calls out, "Americans. Come out, now. Before you die. I will treat you fairly. ...If you act quickly...no harm will come to you. You have five seconds before I blow up your building."

Chapter Fifty-Two

Sophie shrieked, "It's a diversion!" She whipped out her thirty-eight and leveled it at the back door and began firing. I counted four shots before she stopped and we both listened to a dying scream retch through the perforated plywood door at the rear end of the now flaming laboratory.

Soph grabbed up the rifle and we ran to the back of the lab shielding ourselves from the building heat, the entire left side of the lab was on fire, soon, the entire lab would be engulfed. She kicked open the door and fired her rifle, point blank, into the dying assassins forehead. There were now two bodies behind the lab. One was already covered with flies, the other one, headless from the nose up, would soon match his brother-in-crime as an insect delicacy.

Soph said, "Cover me." And dashed out across the field and into the dense growth of jungle and wind waved palm fronds.

I said to myself, out loud, "Oh great. Cover you. I can't even see you. What am I supposed to cover? Nothing?" And I added, out of frustration, and much quieter, and with a forlorn note of resignation, "Son-of-a-bitch."

I looked back down at the bodies from the lab door. It didn't take long for a mass of flies to cover the second body. The head was already covered with a black molten swarm of bluish-green coastal bottle flies. I turned and headed for the front door. I'd soon be diving headlong for the Ford as the fire was now hopelessly out of control. After taking two steps toward it, it banged open. And *there* I was, face to face with Margolova. – Yelling out a most memorable and ear piercing – "*Freeze*, Mister Morgan."

Chapter Fifty-Three

And I froze. I really did. I couldn't move. My mind went blank. A second person, a young boy, with a thin mustache and dark greasy hair entered right behind her. He couldn't have been more than eighteen, probably younger. They both had big weapons, .357's, maybe bigger, they looked like cannons, they looked nasty, and sinister. I fixated on Margolova's gun, I just knew it was going to fire, shoot, and blow me right into an afterlife. And there we stood – just looking at each other.

A piece of burning roof fell to the floor and sent a spray of sparks and a puff of hot white smoke across my being, and yet, I didn't move.

Margolova told the kid, "Get his gun, Stick." She waved him forward with the nose of her weapon.

I handed it over carefully without question. From across the lab, Margolova could have easily passed for thirty. She walked toward me. We were sizing each other up. She looked to be a *friendly* person. As she neared, she said, "You are a very handsome man, Mister Morgan. Your photographs do not do you justice." This was all said with a heavily laced, sexual connotation. And I thought – this is one *sick* bitch.

And where this aside came from I'll never know, but I asked her, "Wanna fuck?"

She was silent, calm, and expressionless, for a brief second, and then smiled ever so deftly. She turned to her batman and ordered, "Go watch the door, Stick."

Stick, seriously asked, "Ah, which one, Mag?" And I recall thinking, "Mag? What's that? A cute nickname for his mamma-maggot, Margolova?"

Margo grabbed the youth by his arm and violently thrust him toward the front of the lab. Stick stumbled and fell to one knee, dropping his weapon. He scrambled around for it and without looking back sauntered defiantly to the front door. Margolova never looked at him. She had her eyes riveted into mine, looking for something, something that only she knew what. Then said,

"The front one."

Stick took an exaggerated look to the east and then peered west, "Ah... I don't see nuttin', Mag."

Margolova said to me, "Good help is so hard to find these days, especially here, in Madagascar."

And I thought of Abby and I almost lost it. I couldn't help but smile, and I had to force back an out-and-out laughter, which had already given Margolova a misinterpretation of my thinking. She asked, "Do you find your situation amusing, Mister Morgan?"

I said, "No." And was hung on the edge, on the very verge of once again losing it, totally. I couldn't shake the thoughts of Abby that had come racing into my over-taxed mind.

Then Margolova said, "Would you please share your comedy "wit" me, Mister Morgan? I fail to see any humor in your current predicament."

When she dropped the "H" in with and said, "wit." I did lose it. I cracked up – laughing, insanely. I'm sure it was stress related. I had no control. I had burst into laughter and could only answer her with a giggled out, "No. – No, I don't want to share my humor *wit* you."

Stick called out, "What's so funny?"

And there I stood, cracking up, laughing in the face of death. And, I had yet another thought, a sobering thought – I was going to die, laughing, in a burning building, at the hands of a sex-craved mad-woman, because I refused to tell her what was so funny about her bastardized use of the simple word – *with*.

I sobered, saying, "I'm sorry. I'm only an Engineer. I'm not cut out for this spy stuff."

She motioned me toward the front door with a head nod, and I went. I think I had humored her. At least, she didn't pull the trigger and shoot me.

She called out to Stick, "Start their car and turn it around, com-rade. We're getting out of here...hurry."

Stick went to the car and had it running by the time we reached the door. Margolova stuck her gun hard into my back, it would sure-ly leave me a bruise, and, I could only pray that it wouldn't acciden-tally go off and leave a bullet hole into my spine. Margolova grabbed me by the collar with her free hand. Her fingers were colder than ice. She was a dead woman. She was void of body heat. Her icy fingers were a *dead* give away.

She said, "Do not try any heroics, Mister Morgan, if you do? I will hurt you, very badly." And I for one, believed her.

The Ford was running. Stick had turned it around as he was told to do. It now faced west, which was stupid. We had to round the car to get in on the passenger's side. I felt a new wave of laughter coming on, but stemmed the onslaught when Margolova poked the nose of her gun sharply and smartly into my backbone. It really hurt, and she knew it. It was a deliberate show of meanness to keep me in tow, and, as unnecessary as it was, it worked. I had no intention, none whatsoever of disobeying her demands.

I slid into the seat with her icy hands still clinging tightly to my collar, we were sitting on little cubes of broken safety glass from the windshield and I couldn't help but wonder if my pants were going to get torn. It was weird to be seated in a windowless car. I was pushed up next to Stick, with the DLIDS box on my lap. Margolova had moved her forty-five to my ribs. Stick smelled bad, really bad, I quickly placed the scent – it was from a pig farm, a pig's sty on a hot humid day, only worse.

We were moving and the dying Ford began to bellow smoke from the radiator, the lab was totally in flames, black smoke billowed eastward with the afternoon sea breeze. Margolova kept the gun barrel shoved hard into my rib cage, knowing full well that it hurt me. She was watching for native activity as we chugged slowly past the grass huts and then south, toward the Mercedes. And I thought, "Come on, Soph. Do something – anything."

Then I got a whiff of Margolova, she smelled of wet wool, sweaty wool. She smelled better than Stick, but not by much. I had a funny thought, and I almost laughed again, Margo had a dead fish in her pocket, and she had put it there solely to offset Stick's hog scent. Yeah, I was amusing myself, true. But at that moment that was about all that I had left, my sense of humor. And then came a sobering sight, Tina's Landrover.

It was pulled up next to the Mercedes. And as we neared, I could see, intuitively, that the driver was dead. Actually, I would have been more shocked to see Kate alive. *That* would have been contrary to *any* of my own personal-expectations on that particular afternoon.

Mag, Margolova, said to Stick, "Get rid of dat body, comrade. We're taking the Landrover."

We sat in the Ford and watched as Stick opened the driver's door of the Landrover and yanked Kate's body unceremoniously to the ground. He then stepped on top of her abdomen, reached in, and removed the keys. He held them up to show his – Mag, who nodded in a good-boy approval.

While Stick remained standing on top of Kate, Margolova opened her door, while ordering me, "Come."

She pushed the tortoise and me ahead of her. I was directed into the passenger's seat and climbed in. Margolova climbed into the rear seat keeping her weapon in contact with my head the entire time. Kate had emptied her bowels, probably at death, and much of it had oozed onto the driver's seat. Stick looked at it and made a grimace, then asked Margo if they could wait awhile – to let it dry.

"Nyet." She yelled. Which is no in Russian.

With a show of reluctance, Stick climbed into the damp seat and sat down. Kate would have some small revenge, albeit post humus, on at least one of her murderers, Stick, by way of his soiled pants.

The vehicle was rancid, putrid, with the remnant odors of Kate's demise, add Stick's "sty" scent, and Margolova's, "La dog-pissed-on-a-rug" perfume, and the entire vehicle could have been labeled a mobile toxic waste dump.

Margolova and Stick seemed oblivious to the odors as we pulled away from Kate, the demobilized Mercedes, the burning lab and at least three dead assassins, plus one dead and toothless dog. Stick had deliberately left the Ford running, it would soon freeze up and need a whole new engine.

I had to roll down my window…one, to breathe…and two, to validate a hope of seeing Sophie bound out from the jungle and affect my rescue.

Things began to look grim as the Landrover reached sixty MPH on the speedometer. Margolova even lowered her huge .45. As we bounced and swayed along the rutted path from paradise, one thing became self-evident – Sophie hadn't rescued me.

I set the DLIDS box on the floor. I couldn't help but wonder if the little fucker wasn't already dead. I looked in the side view mirror, I was looking for Sophie, and I couldn't help but wonder if she might be dead, too.

Chapter Fifty-Four

So. – In all due fairness to my reader. I must expose something. Something that I myself didn't find out about until much, much further along in this sequence of events. And that is: Six bodies were removed from the carnage at Pimakeel Bay, not counting the islander's dog. – One of them was Sophie's. "God rest her soul."

Chapter Fifty-Five

Margolova lit a cigarette and offered me one. I gladly took it. I needed the rush. It was an English cigarette called, Players. It was very similar to a Camel, and it gave me a moment to escape the dark thoughts that had filled my mind. I raced over and over them, trying to make some sense out of the day's extremely extraordinary events.

Stick kept the accelerator floored with a heavy army boot, one that had never seen polish. The Landrover would occasionally reach speeds of eighty miles per hour. All the while I kept a constant vigil for Sophie to appear, speeding in to my rescue. But the rear view mirror remained blank.

And, it was so damned hot. Soon the coastal foliage gave way to wasteland and a distant, shimmering mirage. We rode in dead silence. I glanced back at Margolova; the vulture was filing her talons with an emery board. The Colt .45 lay loose in her lap. I wondered how many lives it had taken. I pondered my own fate. I had difficulty coming to any other rationalization than the fact that – I was going to die.

I pondered the DLIDS case and its contents. It wasn't worth the agony and pain that it had already cost so many people. I gave the box a short kick in a worthless act of defiance. It turned out to be a stupid act, when I kicked it I had hit my anklebone and it hurt like hell.

Margolova yelled, "Be careful you fool. Your life depends on that box and its contents."

"I said, "It's only a tortoise."

Stick began laughing, not unlike myself back at the lab. He was caught up in some manic thought that only he was privy to and it made for an un-nerving moment. It was an inappropriate outburst and it not only befuddled me, but Margolova, too.

Mag shouted, "Shut up, comrade. We've got a long way to go. Pay attention to the road." Stick quieted himself.

We neared the road to Shell Camp. I wondered about Ab…about what he was doing? Cooking? Calling Strongbow, Einstein? Yeah, he was probably sitting on his bed picking his nose, and – I wished I were there to yell at him. And then I thought of Lotty and made an involuntary wink.

Margolova broke the silence, "What happened to my men, Mister Morgan? The two that I had watching you."

I said, "We ate them. They were last night's supper."

Margo said, "I see."

I looked at Stick and asked, "How come you didn't laugh at that one, Stick? It was a pretty good line, Pal."

Stick gave me a genuine look of hatred. He said, "Earl and Donny are my brothers."

"Oh?" I corrected, "You mean the two jerks in the black Saab "were" your brothers?" I turned to my window, and said, "What a pair of assholes."

Stick removed his foot from the accelerator. The Landrover began to slow. Stick was having an emotional crisis. He screamed out, "*What* ...did ...you ...do to *my* brothers?"

I said, "Oh, who cares."

Stick hit the brakes, shouting, "I'll show you who cares, Big Shot."

Margo leaned forward, angry, and said to Stick, "Don't stop you fool. He's just trying to aggravate you. Keep going."

I said, "Yeah, keep driving. I'd hate to wipe out an entire family in just under twenty-four hours."

Stick shoved his finger into my ribs, hard. It really hurt. He said, "I'm going to get you – you, mother-fucker."

Margolova said, "Behave yourself, Stick. I want Mister Morgan in one piece. Now settle down."

And she added, "And you, Mister Morgan. You had better keep yourself quiet. I need you, but not all that badly. You are warned."

The car was still slowing. Stick was hot. I said, loud enough for Stick to hear, "I pissed on their bodies."

Margolova began to ask, "What did you..."

Stick slammed down on the brakes. Margo was thrown forward. Stick was screaming, "You're dead! You're dead." Margolova put the barrel of her .45 against Stick's head. His face was crimson and he had spittle on his lips. The Landrover had come to a complete stop after sliding a good 100 feet. Stick produced a Bowie knife from his army boot and stuck it solid up against my neck forcing me back against the window frame, I felt the warm blood ooze down from its tip. It had easily penetrated my skin. I wasn't feeling pain. I was too scared to feel anything. The blood reached my shoulder and I could hear the knife separating my flesh. It was a horrid sound – the sound of having one's own throat slit.

Margolova pulled the trigger.

The sound was devastating, Stick's face blew off and onto the windshield in a red and white gut-spew that lasted no more than a split second, but it seemed to fly out in a slow motion. I felt the knife tumble from my neck and fall heavy to my seat.

This all happened at once, Stick's body arched backward against the seat and his legs kicked out straight. I reached out to keep him from falling on me and I had this sensation that I was pushing over a grave stone, it fell away very slow, then slumped against his door looking at me without a face, just a jagged, red and bloodied pulp. For a brief instant, I could see the hole in the back of his skull but then some brain tissue settled over it. I looked away and closed my eyes. I grabbed my neck and felt the warm sticky blood and kept my hand over the wound to stem the flow of blood. I opened my eyes to see how much blood was on my shirt sleeve and saw a lot and shut my eyes again knowing that I was going to bleed to death, right there, and probably quite quickly.

I opened my door and got out, deaf from the gun shot and dizzy from the scene, reeling from what I thought to be blood loss. I leaned against the hood, Margolova was at my side, her icy fingers probing my neck, inspecting the knife wound. She gave me a handkerchief and told me to hold it on the cut, she added, "It is not serious."

She put the DLIDS box on the hood and made me spread my legs, and back away at a forty-five degree angle while leaning against the fender with my elbows. She said, "Don't move. I'll shoot you if you fall – so don't fall."

The DLIDS box hid my view of the windshield. I heard her open the driver's door and drop Stick out onto the road. She ripped off his shirt and then, based on what I heard; she began to wipe the windshield from the inside. I strained a look around the box without moving my neck, and sure enough, that's what she was doing, cleaning up her mess.

The Landrover was in the center of the road and I could see backward slightly, the road stretched out into a thin ribbon where we had just traveled, I wanted to spot Sophie. But the road was as empty as Stick's head. I tried to think about anything to clear my mind of Stick. Margolova's squeaking rag was nauseating. I began to hum aloud in an effort to mask the noise. I don't recall what I hummed – it wasn't working anyway.

Margolova came back to me, jabbed the forty-five in my underarm and said, "Let's go, it will be getting dark soon." She said this soft. It was a matter of fact. She was being friendly. She had just saved my life. I was confused, but I followed her order to get in.

At the door, I balked, due to the milky film that spread across the inside glass, a milky pink. I asked, "What about him?"

She narrowed her eyes and said, "Are you worried about his comfort, Mister Morgan?" She had emphasized the word comfort so strongly that I didn't dare question her further. I got in the passenger seat and buckled in while holding the bloodstained handkerchief as solidly as I could against the wound in my neck.

Margolova got in and started the engine. As we moved away I looked in the side view mirror. Stick was there, on the road in a heap. There was no sign of Sophie.

My thinking was this: "Soph had called LaCruel via the radio on the "re-Gretta." By the time we got up to Antananarivo, the entire Malagasy army would have the Turk's villa surrounded. I'd be saved and Sophie would fly up from the coast on a chopper and we'd still make our scheduled flight to Washington. I tried to look ahead and watch for an army roadblock. Or, maybe, the Chief of Police and his heir, Rudy, would stop us for a routine traffic ticket.

But all too soon, the only thing I could see was the streaked, hazed, and opal tinged windshield glass. Margolova was not good at windows. No…not at all.

Chapter Fifty-Six

Once upon a time, I had read an article that was devoted to the beautiful-people. The jetsetters and our globetrotters who might one day find themselves precariously labeled as "hostage." The article strongly suggested, "*Befriend* your captor if at all possible." The reasoning behind the sentiment is as follows, "No one will deliberately hurt a friend; because, "When push came to shove, the captor will choose someone he/she doesn't know. Inevitably, the captor victimizes a person or persons that they know little or nothing about. One can kill a hostage without much guilt, but killing a friend is very difficult. A psychologist wrote this particular article, and I couldn't help but think that Eunice may have written it, under some CIA pseudonym.

The article went on to say, "This is no guarantee that one will not be murdered.

However, the chance of being murdered with *dignity* was greatly enhanced – by a factor of ten."

From the recall of this traveler's tidbit, I began to formulate a plan. I would befriend Margolova. After all, I for one surely wanted to die with dignity. Death "is" somewhat final, and one should make the most of it – when the time comes.

Working toward a little dignity while one was still kicking seemed like a noble enterprise at that particular moment in my adventurous life.

I pointed to the windshield, and advised, "You missed a spot."

She quickly answered, "I will not be so easily antagonized, Mister Morgan. Should you continue your nonsense, I will break off a few of your teeth, which will force you to keep your mouth shut. Have I made myself clear?"

"Yes. Very clear." What else could I say?

"If you behave yourself you may live to tell someone of your adventure. You are a cheap adventurer, aren't you?"

"Well… I haven't considered this expedition, cheap."

"I was referring to your file, Mister Morgan. It described you as a, cheap adventurer."

"Yeah? Well, it seems like everyone has a file on me these days, but you're the first person to call me cheap in quite awhile."

She smiled, "Cheap is a negative term for you capitalist, isn't it?"

I wanted to ask her if her perfume was extracted from a dead sheep. But I didn't. I stuck to my plan. "The file I read on you said that you were an old hag, pushing seventy."

"How old do you think I am, Mister Morgan?"

Nothing came to mind, except – treacherous sarcasm. I stuck to my plan and lied, hoping that I wouldn't choke on my own words, "Oh, you could pass for thirty...with the right clothes."

"First you try to provoke me, Mister Morgan. Now you try to flatter me. What is your game? – As you Americans say."

I responded, "Life, liberty, and the pursuit of happiness. What's your game, Margolova?"

"I dream of destroying the capitalistic system and all of the decadence it showers upon the hard working classes of the world."

"Would you care to elaborate on that? Personally, I think Capitalism is rather unique. It has certainly worked well for me."

With conviction, she elaborated, "Communism, old school Communism, was so pure, so social. ...It would have allowed all people to exist in peaceful harmony with nature and the universe. Marx and Ingles were brilliant. Their work, "The Communist Manifesto," could liberate the world from its slavery to rubles and kopeks."

I had to say, "Personally, I have always thought that Marx and Ingles were a brilliant pair of assholes who suffered from limited international insight."

Of course, I didn't say this to Margolova. To her, I said, "I suppose you're right. Too bad their ideas didn't work in the real world."

Margolova clouded over. Her beliefs were, truly, deeply ingrained.

She spat out at me, "It would work. – If it weren't for the likes of you and your pathetic Capitalism."

I interjected, "There seems to be a bit of handwriting on the wall in what you say. You should defect and loosen up a little."

She regained her composure, somewhat. "Capitalism is on its death bed, Mister Morgan. When it dies, people like me will unify the world's people and bring them all together under a socialist government. Then – universal peace, eh?"

I could only answer, "That's a very scary thought, Margolova."

"Please, James, call me, Margo."

We were nearing Dead Man's Gulch. I had a thought, Plan "P" for, Push Margo off a cliff. I said, "Your comrades, the one's in the Saab. They're just up ahead. About a mile, maybe two."

"I thought you had eaten them, Mister Morgan?"

"Please, Margo, call me, Jim." And she smiled ever so candidly.

I continued, "They had to swerve their car to avoid hitting Sophie's MAV-861. They lost control and went over a cliff. They were both killed. The Saab burned for hours."

"What is this – MAV-8, 6, 1, Jim?"

We had slowed to enter the curving switchbacks leading up to Dead Man's Curve. I had to get her to stop, if for no other reason, it would give Sophie more time to catch up with us.

I said, "Oh. Well, it's an assault vehicle. Sophie has it on loan. She was testing its adaptability to women. It's very hush-hush…a big Army secret. You probably know all about it, eh? It's just up ahead…at the last curve. Want to stop and see it?"

She said, "We will see." She sounded suspicious, I had been too eager to divulge an Army secret.

I added, "Yeah, it was designed to fight Communism."

Margolova looked at me with deep suspicion, a look of keen incredulity. She was curious, but had become more and more, openly cautious.

She said, "You will show me your MAV-861. I am very interested. I am also interested to know why you tell me about this?"

She smiled slightly. Perhaps she thought I'd tell her about my plan "P." She asked, "Why are you telling me about this, Jim?"

"There! There. Over there, by the rocks."

Margo reached the Colt that was resting between the seat and her door. She steered with the gun in one hand as she down shifted and slowed to exit the road. My mind was racing, searching for the courage to act. Searching for some small advantage, seeking that advantageous moment – the proper instant at which to overthrow my captor. It didn't come.

We stopped. She set the hand brake. She told me to stay put, taking the keys with her, she went out to study the bike. After a few minutes she came to my window and said that we were going to stay there until sunset, "You may stretch your legs, Jim."

I exited the Landrover and Margo turned her back to me to return to the bike. I acted! With my heart racing I swung the

DLIDS box around on its chain, timing an impact with Margo's head. The chain disengaged itself. The DLIDS box flew off and out into the scrub. It made a noisy clunk, and a loud metallic click as it rolled over in the rocky turf.

Margo turned and saw the chain wrap itself around my outstretched arm. She withdrew her Colt and cocked the hammer, as I dropped my Statue of Liberty arm. The chain unwrapped itself, and hung limply at my side. I shrugged my shoulders. Margolova released the hammer but kept the gun leveled at my chest. She shook her head and said, "You seem to have dropped "some-TING", Jim."

Chapter Fifty-Seven

Margolova waved her Colt toward the area where the DLIDS box had flown. With a deadpan expression, she said, "It is not nice to litter, Jim." Her emphasis on my name was challenging its use.

I said, without much conviction, "It was an accident."

She waved the gun, again. I moved toward the box dragging the chain at my side. I was ahead of her and expected her to shoot me at any moment, or, at least crack me on the head for having made an attempt to kill her. But, nothing happened. I found the box, picked it up, then turned to face her. I looked her in the eye, and offered, "...Chain broke."

She raised the Colt, pulled back on the hammer and aimed the gun right between my eyes. I got dizzy. Intuitively, she was going to shoot me, point blank. It was over. The moment of truth had come. I was going to die. She said, "Open it."

I found myself saying, "No."

She said, "Refusing to open the box makes you expendable. Open it, or I will kill you."

She was so matter of fact that I set down the box and made an attempt to open it. I flipped open the eye latch and placed my forehead on the rubber eyepiece. I started to tell her about the acid vials inside the box.

"Just open it. I know all about the acid."

I shut my mouth and set the combination, 0007. I watched for the grid to read, OPEN. It didn't. Instead, a wonderful message appeared, in big red letters, SATELLITE TRACKING ACTIVATED.

Excited, I looked up at Margolova. She placed the barrel of her .45 between my eyes, and then poked it hard on the bridge of my nose. Then retracted it, slow, deliberate, back a good foot-foot and a half, smiling...

I said, while looking into the barrel of her weapon, "It isn't working. I have to be relaxed before it will open, I'm under too much stress."

She released the hammer and placed the Colt in her belt, saying, "We shall try again later, if you are still alive. I have a lot of patience,

Mister Morgan, but not much time."

She reached out her icy fish hand to help me up. I took it. She balanced me up into a standing position. And, I thought, "Maybe, just maybe, that pamphlet on hostage survival was beginning to pay off. Perhaps, Margolova would back off and allow me some time to relax. After all, it would be to her advantage. Right?"

Chapter Fifty-Eight

We returned to the Land Rover and sat in its shade. I asked Margolova where she was taking me. Her answer came without any hesitation, "Moscow."

It was a foregone conclusion. My itinerary had been set. At least she didn't say that I'd be dumped into a garbage dumpster in the same manner as Uncle Bobby had been one day earlier. And I thought, "Russia? Well, I'd been there before. I pissed on its soil, once. Maybe this time, I'll get to piss on Red Square."

It was back to plan "P." I said, "Your pals are down in that gulch over there. I think they stole some papers from the English Biologists."

Margo jumped to her feet. She took the .45 from her waist belt. She commanded, "Show me."

She set the tortoise inside the Landrover and locked its doors, then motioned for me to lead the way by waving her pistol toward the road. I stopped on the tarmac and looked east hoping to see Major LaCruel and his army convoy racing down to save me, and to protect the expeditions at Shell Camp and Pimakeel Bay. But the road was vacant and desolate. No one was coming, yet.

I plodded into the brush hoping that Margolova wouldn't notice or question the Saab's entry line from east to west. She didn't, and I continued on and up to the canyon rim, where I pointed down at the burnt and crumpled vehicle, "There. They must have died instantly. It's a good 150 feet to the bottom. The fire probably destroyed what they took from the Johnson woman, don't you think?"

The apprehension and fear that I had experienced earlier that morning disappeared, the vertigo was gone. I tensed for the opportunity to shove Margolova and her nickel-plated Colt into the gorge. She could join her henchmen, in hell. I hoped.

She motioned for me to start down, which I did. She let me get a good ten-feet ahead of her before she started down herself. She was obviously adhering to her own plan, to avoid my plan.

Half way down I got my break; the Russian goat had lost her footing, her age had caught up to her, she began sliding in the gravel.

The Colt flew out of her hand and slid past me, only inches from my reach. I watched it surf for a good twenty-feet before it hit a rock and came to an abrupt stop.

I lunged toward it head first, sliding down the gorge on my belly. I missed it by a whole three-feet before I could stop my plunge, swing around, and dig my feet into the loose gravel. Margo was up and running toward the gun. I reached it first, aimed at her gut and pulled in on the trigger.

Nothing happened – the safety was on.

She jumped toward me with opened arms from some eight-feet above my position. I rolled right and watched her glide past me into a dusty ball, then tumble another thirty feet before she hit a scrub pine. She hit it with her back and lay motionless while the loose debris following her path built up against her idle body. She began to move, pulling herself up to her knees, holding on to the pine sprig that should have broken her back, but hadn't.

I undid the safety and inched myself toward the sand-spitting bitch with the barrel locked on her heart. I took every step with extreme caution. I had her! The tables had turned and I wasn't going to screw it up. No. – Not this time. I was going to shoot her cold in the heart, or between the eyes. I would do it just like Tina. The same way she had shot the punk who was strapped down and dying in the Saab's passenger seat.

My adrenalin was pumping ultra-high. Margolova's face was streaked with her own blood. Her hands were scratched and bloody. Sand had stuck to her open wounds, her face, her hair, and she was spitting out yet more dirt while wiping her mouth as I neared.

I said, as mean and as ugly as I could, "How was your trip, Bitch?"

She stood, smiled, and then made a desperate lunge toward me. I leveled the Colt with both hands, aiming it right between her eyes and pulled solidly down on the trigger.

Chapter-Fifty-Nine

Sophie would have been proud of "her" plan. The plan she devised back at Pimakeel Bay. The plan designed to exhaust our enemy of their ammunition. It had worked, and it had worked, very well, indeed. Margolova's "last" bullet had been spent on her comrade, Stick. The heavy, ugly Colt was empty. I pulled on the trigger over and over and over at the advancing, openly smirking bitch, Margolova.

She reached out and grabbed the barrel. Tugging it loose, she threw it into the depths of the valley not bothering to watch where it landed, as I had foolishly done. When I looked back at her, I saw a rabid dog, the smile and laughter had vanished, her teeth were bared and I could see sand encrusted over her grayed and aged enamels. Hate was etched in every one of her wrinkles, she looked ugly and very old, and – she was going to kill me.

I lunged at her. She saw it coming and dodged to her right, trying to use my attack to her own advantage as I had done to her only minutes earlier. But I grabbed her wrist and hung on with all my might and pulled her along with my own weight and momentum catapulting her over and down with me atop the loose gravel. I never let go of her skinny boned wrist and kept it locked tightly in my hand all the way down to the gulch basin where we slammed into a huge boulder some twenty feet from the Saab

Margo's back was up against the rock and I still had her left wrist tightly held in my own left hand. I grabbed her right wrist and held her there, pinned down, like a de-winged moth, still straining to fly. But, I was barely holding her down. She was very, very strong for a woman in her mid-fifties. She fought hard, struggling desperately to free herself. She knew, that if she did get free, she'd probably be able to kick my ass. I sensed it, too, and held on with all my waning might.

And then she relaxed, not fully, but kept her muscles taught enough that I couldn't let go to get a better grip. She was like a snake, coiled and ready to strike, conserving her energies while I had to use mine, openly, just to keep her down. As soon as I loosened my grasp, she'd strike. Her martial arts were well honed, ingrained to the point of reflex. I had been lucky to gain the momentary advantage. I knew, and she knew, it was only temporary.

I asked, "Had enough?"

She jerked hard and had almost broken free. I held on. Her wrists were turning blue. I squeezed down even harder, preparing for another energy burst. My heart was pounding, and, that's when I realized that she was calm, barely breathing, she was that calculating, and – it scared the hell out of me. I was in some deep shit. I couldn't hit her, not without letting go, and, if I didn't let go I couldn't hit her. I decided to deal, if she would?

I asked, "Want to make a deal?"

With gritted teeth and a blatant show of uninhibited hatred, she answered, "Of course."

I offered, "I'll open the DLIDS box. You let me go."

I knew she'd say yes. *That* was a foregone conclusion. I had even calculated that she *might*, and I stress might, be able to abide by her own agreement.

She said, nastily, "Alright."

I doubted her completely. She had answered with way too much vehemence. She was mad, insane, psychotic, and I was sure that she had killed people for lesser aggravations. And, to top everything else, she smelled terrible.

I questioned her, "No tricks?"

Still seething with hatred, she answered, "No tricks."

I questioned further, "Do you believe in God?"

She answered, "Nyet."

At least she was being honest about her beliefs. There wasn't any way that I could trust her, I was making a worthless deal. I asked, "Will you swear on communism, Carl Marx and Frederick Engle's grave?"

"Yes, yes, yes. Now let me up."

I hoped that I had kept her down long enough so that she would act with some sense of rationality. Actually, I couldn't pin her down any longer. My neck was throbbing and I saw fresh blood dripping from my wound. I had to let her go.

On the brink of my release she went *completely* slack. She offered, on her own accord, "I will personally see that no harm comes to you."

I wondered why she was dealing back, and, I couldn't come up with a decent answer, I said, "Okay."

When I released her wrists she immediately moved her hands to a defensive posture, she had expected me to strike her.

Standing, I offered her a hand up. She refused. I said to myself, "God help me, I'm really in for it now." She didn't attack me, she did state, "You are my prisoner. If you obey me, no harm will come to you." I nodded out in solemn agreement. And, I was very happy, ecstatic, that I was still alive.

Chapter Sixty

The sun had set by the time we returned to the Landrover. It was still light, but the evening stars had already appeared to decorate the otherwise clear Malagasy heaven.

I had questioned myself on my decision to surrender that evening many times since. Second-guessing the situation has never given me any peace – it has only given me headaches. Inevitably, I deduce that I'm still alive and go about my business; because, even though I surrendered, I had never given up.

Back at the car, I offered, "Want me to try the box? I'm a lot more relaxed now, now that I'm in your competent hands."

She opened the doors and immediately armed herself with Stick's Bowie knife. No, she didn't trust me. Perhaps, she even feared me. After all, I would have killed her if her gun were loaded. And who knows what would have happened if the DLIDS chain hadn't separated from the tortoise's cage. Well, there I go again, second-guessing what might have been.

I no longer feared her, even with Stick's Bowie knife. Oh, I hated her. I hated everything that she had done, and hated to think what else she might do in the future. She was evil, but I no longer "feared" her. She sensed this, too. Every time I'd look her way, her hand reached for the hilt of the Bowie.

I sat down and placed the DLIDS box on my lap and dialed in the 0007 code, opening my eyes big and wide allowing the sensors to easily read my irises. A new message flooded the message grid, "LOCATED STAY PUT" – The message went blank. I reset the combo and nothing happened, no message...nothing. I shut the lens hole and said, "I guess I'm not as relaxed as I thought, it's not opening. Got any Scotch?"

I set the box onto the back seat. Margo climbed in and inserted the ignition key. I said, "Can we hold up a minute? I've got to pee."

She released the key, came around and opened my door. I felt like a little boy being led to the potty. It was the only excuse I could think of to, "Stay Put."

As I was reaching for the door handle, I recalled the water bag that hung from the Landrover's grille and asked if I could have a drink.

I was allowed the drink and began to wash the blood from my neck. I had reopened the cut and wasted ten more precious minutes with a pressure bandage until the bleeding stopped. Pushing my luck, I asked if I should try the DLIDS box, one more time, just for luck.

"Nyet!" She yelled.

And even I knew that she meant, "Later dude. Quit wasting my time. Right now!"

I had run out of excuses. She turned the key and fired up the Landrover. She was reaching for the gearshift lever when I said, in a last ditch effort to remain at Dead Man's Gulch, "I think I'm going to vomit."

Margolova glared at me with suspicion, then, with apprehension she said, "Go. Spit up. Hurry."

I stood at the rear end of the Landrover and feigned illness. Acting is not my forte, my vomiting sounds were not convincing, at least, not to myself. I'm sure they must have sounded ludicrous to Margolova, too. I felt dumb. I stood there thinking of another excuse, but I couldn't think of a thing.

I was considering a dash into the bush. I'd hide in the rocks and wait quietly for Sophie to rescue me. It seemed like a good plan and... Margo got out of her seat and shouted, "Let's go. Now!" I returned to the window, stuck my head in and questioned, "Aren't you going to steal the MAV-861?"

"Nyet!" She was getting furious.

"Just what does `nyet' mean, Margo?"

"It means, no. Now get in."

That was my last card. My hand was played out. So much for staying put, eh? We pulled out of the clearing and bounced onto the tarmac heading east toward the glow of Tanan's city lights.

It was nine o'clock when we pulled into the Turk's villa. We parked near the service entrance in a slot that was marked, in French, "Reserved." Margo got out, and told me, "Stay." In the same manner that one would tell one's dog to heel. I stayed. A rifle toting guard enforced her order.

Margo returned in less than a minute carrying a small Luger in her right hand. It was identical to the one Tina had out on the road on the previous day. It looked like a toy. But then again, so did Tina's. She opened my door and told me to get the DLIDS box, which I did.

Being waved ahead of her, I entered the Turk's service entrance.

The extra wide hallway, it was a good eight feet wide, was carpeted up to the ceiling. A double door, marked kitchen, was to my immediate right. Margo pushed me past them, and said, "Wait." She rounded me, and went to a single door marked, "Laundry." She produced a key and opened the door. She motioned for me to enter. I went in and she closed the door behind me. I heard her lock it with the key. And there we were, the boxed Malagasy Tortoise and me – "prisoners" in a Turkish laundry room.

The room was lit by a single, naked, 300-watt bulb. There were others, but they were turned off or burned out. The room was twenty by thirty, and windowless. The ceiling was a good twenty-foot high and had a huge exhaust fan, turning slowly, mounted directly above a row of commercial dryers. There was a huge water heater, a boiler actually, six washers, and several large vats. Two of the vats were filled with sudsy water. The room was exceptionally clean. The walls were tiled and the floor was bare cement. The floor was contoured, sloping down to a twelve-foot drain-grid made of metal, which spread out in front of the six industrial washing machines. The room was secure. The only way out was by the door that I had entered – excepting the drain and the air vent.

There was a large sorting table in the center of the room. I set the DLIDS box on it and dialed in my code, nothing happened. I tried a second time, again, nothing. I dialed in a bogus code, 9999, the grid lighted, it read, INCORRECT CODE. I dialed in the 0007 again, and again nothing.

I boosted myself onto the table and lay down. The chain made a horrific sound against the polished aluminum. I studied the wrist bracelet and wondered how Houdini had escaped so many of them, so quickly. I cleared my mind by fixating on the slowly revolving fan blades, and waited.

Exactly seventeen minutes later, I had already began watching the clock, my Rolex, a key turned in the door. I sat up abruptly, and a guard entered carrying a huge set of wire cutters. He stood at the door and said, "I'm here to remove your chain."

Without standing, I held out my arm letting the chain drop to the floor. He approached slowly, carefully. He was big, probably two hundred pounds, I had no intention of overpowering him. I was actually glad to see him and his chain cutter. He looked at the bracelet and had me place my hand on the metal tabletop. He made two snips on either side of the cuff and it fell noisily to the cement floor. He dragged the chain a few feet away from me with his foot. Keeping his eyes on me he bent down and picked it up.

I said, "Thanks, Pal. I owe you one." He smiled and left, backing out of the room, and then pulled the door closed. I heard the key turn and he walked away. He was talking to someone, but his or her voices were low and muffled.

My wrist was black and blue, it was swollen and the skin was rubbed raw on both sides. It felt good to be rid of the chain and cuff. I went to the sink and took in a deep drink of cold water. It tasted great. I found some clean bedding in a dryer and made a pillow for myself on top of the table and lay back down to wait.

I sat up and tried the DLIDS box again, still nothing. I wondered if the tortoise was still alive. I put my ear to the box and listened to see if it was moving. I didn't hear anything and when I recalled the bit about the poisonous ticks I removed my ear and set the box under the table.

My thoughts were many and quite varied. I was hungry and I wondered if I'd be fed, I wondered if Margolova would get me a Big Mac when we arrived in Moscow, I had recently read that McDonald's was open for business there. And I wondered about Sophie. Why hadn't she come? Why hadn't she notified authorities? And where were, Tina, La Cruel, and Rudy? And just where was his mummy-Chief? And I envisioned them all sitting in a command room plotting their raid on the Turk's villa. And I lay there thinking about the Ford, and I did indeed wonder, did I, or did I not, purchase that lease insurance? I was pretty sure that I did.

An hour passed, it was almost ten-thirty when I heard a key turn in the door, and it was Margolova. She was dressed in a black pantsuit. It was simple and made a statement, it was a no nonsense, no frills presentation of subservience. She wore neither watch, nor any other jewelry. Her hair was combed, but still damp from a recent bath or shower.

She held out a plate of baked fish with two thick slices of black bread, it was garnished with a parsley sprig. I took it and set it down on the laundry table. She said, "I will bring you some water." She reached into a hidden pocket and removed a spoon and set it down next to the plate. She retreated, backing out, keeping both eyes on me. Before she closed the door, I said, "Put some Scotch in that water, okay?"

The door was locked behind her. I tasted the fish. It was good, but cold. I ate it all down, except for the parsley, before she returned with a plastic cup of water, no Scotch. She smiled at the empty plate, saying, "I'm glad to see that you have a healthy appetite, Jim. Was it good?"

It was. And I told her so. I pointed out that she had forgotten the Scotch. She made a pouting frown and left. At midnight I checked the DLIDS box. It remained blank. I piled all the dry laundry on the table and went to sleep. My last waking thought was that the laundry room was better than some old dark and damp dungeon, or a cell, with rats sizing me up for a snack. And then I slept...

Chapter Sixty-One

And I slept hard, and I had this dream. A full and cratered Easter-moon loomed out ahead of my aircraft windscreen. I was flying a super-modern jet – an Avenger. And a twin Avenger soared with me on my right, port (or is that starboard) wing. A beautiful woman, a woman holding a placard that stated, "Watch This!" piloted it. And of course...it was Sophie.

Reducing my throttle, I fell in behind her. It would have been foolish to watch from any other spot in the sky, right? – Wrong! In the dream, there was a much better vantage point to observe the totality of her aeronautical skills. Oh yeah! And I went there and I watched...it was so beautiful! But now, as I write this – I cannot recall just where it was that I went... Go figure. But I remember that I did have to get back into my designated Avenger at some minute point in time; because, I did wind up following her, from behind.

And...I knew, how superbly she manipulated the Avenger, it was sublime perfection – the knowing. The bluish white flame of her engine scorched a streaked path toward the distant city lights that all twinkled like a cluster of pure white diamonds, shaking helter-skelter, atop a black velvet jeweler's counter.

Soph's path was not an easy trail to follow. She did a four point roll completing a 360, with distinct "one counts" at 90, 180, and 270 degrees before leveling back and screaming out and onward toward the light. And I wondered where she had learned that 360-degree roll, because she hated flying... Or, was that, dying?

I stayed locked onto her flame only a mere nanosecond behind her. We blasted through the sound barrier in a mach one dive, slashing into the massive bulk of towering cumulus, and then broke out clean just below a ceiling of undulating mammatus, threatening and roiling to announce an oncoming violence. The canopy of her jet was only inches below the gray cloud-roof when she chose to level off.

And then she stopped. The Avenger was frozen in time. She gave me no warning, no notice. Red warning lights flashed, brighter than lightning across the entire length of my instrument panel, they read – they screamed out, "AIRBRAKE NOW."

And I did, as I swerved to avoid impact with her flamed-out engine. And then I stopped, right up alongside of her. Both Avengers now idle below the undulating downward percolating nimbo-fractus. And there we hung, dangling by the mythical sky-hooks of human imagination, implanted so magically by the wizardry of our own Para- psychologically misunderstood, ids. And, we smiled each to the other, knowing nothing, nothing more then this: that we were one, for the briefest instant, a spark had snapped across the distant and vast universal boundaries of space and time uniting our two beings in an subliminal neither world exchange, of cosmic intimacy, and our souls commingled, and no one could know, no one, but us, and such were our needs – so simple...

And then we reunited, somewhere, in the chaotic dream-either without our temporal homes, in a perceived, yet impossible scenario of jumbled, mumbled imagery hues that bespoke of high jinx, super-limits, and super-strings that upset the physical bounds of all known physical reality.

Below the glow of her cockpit, a story was stenciled, "Sophie D. Deadly Alberquist." The bright pink lettering, boldly outlined with black, said, "I am." And she was!

I slid back my canopy, a whistling wind mussed my hair, it caused me to squint as I strained my ear to hear what wisdom Sophie was projecting, vocally, through the now softly misting heaven, and I heard her angelic verbiage, penetrating the winds song, to state, "You're on your own, Jim. That's all I'm allowed to tell. I must go, and remember this – I loved you."

The swirling mist intensified and through a hazy gray fog two ephemeral hands, lifted her, and her jet, up into the secrecy of all mortal searching, afterlife. I begged her to wait, called out, over and over, in a useless – primeval beckoning that wafted off, unheard, into the vastness of a stormy, and turning uglier by the second, atmosphere of unpredictable, yet ominous violence.

I scanned the instrument panel looking for the start button. There were so many buttons, so many dials, Christ! The fucking Avenger isn't like a Cessna, shit. I read a lever that said, EJECT. I pulled it.

A siren began to wail, actually, it was more like a DEFCON horn, the gauges and meters and dials all lit red with the words, OH SHIT, and a computer voice, a female voice, announced, "Two seconds to ejection. One second to ejection. Ta-Ta...

I heard a champagne cork pop. And, just like a soaring champagne cork, I was blasted out and up into the nimbostratus, I began to rise through the molten cloud, my cockpit turned into a glass enclosed elevator on an express run to Apollo's penthouse. Then it slowed. Then it stopped. I was at apogee, and my descent began a slow start back down through the gray bleakness of an overcast and murky heaven.

The breaking out into clear sky was sudden and spectacular. The panoramic view had overwhelmed me with awe, a reverent awe, and an awe that demands one to weep at its majestic splendor. A small chute unwrapped itself from the pod and cockpit, it made a soft bump upon opening, a larger parachute began to stream out above me, and when it was fully deployed, a glass shattering whomp, slowed me and my prison, to a gentle, swaying float toward the center of – Red Square. Right smack dab into the Muscovite's May Day, cultural center, and according to a calendar that I was suddenly holding – it was only April, and I immediately felt very confused.

I looked up, and there, crawling over a stratocumulus cloud was a Mig, a Mig-29. Its wings were digging into the cloud vapor like a pair of cat paws so that it could peer down on my descent, and I swear, the Mig was laughing, snickering at my predicament as it watched me glide, ever nearer to the bulbous and colorful rooftop of an old Christian Orthodox Cathedral.

An old and wrinkled hand, extended out from the Mig-29. It was Margolova's hand. It was holding a Colt .45 the size of Texas, and she aimed it at my haven and fired. The sky lit in a pyrotechnic explosion of reds and oranges and as the burning papers extinguished, I saw the bullet racing toward me like a 3-D pop-out flower in a Hallmark greeting card. I closed my eyes and prepared myself for doom. Then I heard the whoosh of a bottle rocket, and I realized that the giant lead slug had missed its mark and went on to bury itself in some unknown place in the vast Russian Ural landscape.

Looking back to the Mig, I saw Margolova grinning in a mean and sadistic show of her own personal and inherent love, the love of treachery. The Mig-29 crawled off the cloud and slowly moved off, to hunt some other prey, shark-like, the huntress had slithered off into the night, where, she'd sneak unnoticed into dark corners of the Moscow International Airport.

And a deep cold chill ran through my being, because I knew, I just knew, that when I hit the ground, she'd be there, waiting, gun drawn. Waiting, simply to end my existence, just for fun.

And I woke, uncovered, staring at a gray cement floor, and on the verge of toppling from the cold, metal laundry table. I slipped myself down, and stood, dazed, not knowing where I was and – I had a revelation, a premonition. – Sophie was *dead*.

My watch was reading four o'clock. My neck wound stung, and I felt it to see if it had opened, and thankfully it hadn't. I thought about washing my clothes. I had a lot of dried blood on my shirt, and my pants, too. My slacks were ripped in several places, and my shoes, my ninety-dollar loafers, looked like shit.

I sat and recalled parts of my dream. It was one of those live and vivid ones, easy to recall. "Yeah, Soph was dead." She had to be, or she'd have rescued me. I looked at my Rolex, again, and it still said four o'clock. I took a closer look, to see if the second hand was moving – it was. I felt sad. I mumbled out, "Son-of-a-bitch." I laid back down feeling really tired. The slow turning fan blade on the ceiling wooed me back into sleep as I counted its monotonous revolutions, 236, – 237... 2, ...3. Out.

Chapter Sixty-Two

When I awoke, again, it was six o'clock. I retrieved the tortoise case. Still groggy, I placed the DLIDS box on the table and set the combination. The screen lit up, it read, LOCATED PLAY ALONG.

The screen went blank and wouldn't repeat the message even though I entered the code another seventy-five times. The message gave me a tremendous sense of security, "I was located." Soon, someone would rescue me. I was part of the *game*, PLAY ALONG. I was being manipulated, controlled. Only, I didn't want to play any longer. The game had gone sour. It had turned ugly and dangerous. People were dying. I had almost died. "Play along." Yeah, right. I'd play along – for Sophie's sake. "In loving memory of..." And I chuckled inwardly.

Yeah, Sophie was indestructible. She was a good guy, and nothing "bad" happens to the good guy. Right? I decided to leave the premonition business to Eunice. It was probably Soph herself who had sent the message, PLAY ALONG.

Margolova entered at a few minutes past seven. She carried in a plate of cold eggs, two slices of toast, and a solitary cube of white cheese, which tasted like tofu. And there was black coffee, very black, and it was cold. She handed me a pad of paper and a ballpoint pen, "Write down your clothes size, I've got to clean you up."

Playing along, I wrote down what she wanted. She was wearing the same jump suit as she had worn earlier. She had put on a watch and was wearing a string of wooden beads. Her hair had dried, and right then, she looked fairly attractive. I played along and said, "You're looking very pleasant this morning." She smiled ever so slightly and left, locking the door behind her.

She returned at nine with a guard, he was big and dumb, in French, he said, "Come whiff me." Yeah, he had a lisp. Like Margolova said, "Good help is hard to find these days, especially in the underworld of terrorism and international thievery." I'd have bet my last T-Bill that the guard's highest level of education was kindergarten, at a public school in Outer Mongolia.

I followed him and he never once looked back to see if I was there.

We went up three sets of stairs and then down two hallways. He opened a bathroom door and said, in French, lisping, "Take a shower."

I stripped and entered the steaming, soothing, shower. I had just soaped down when Margo entered and announced, "You are clean enough. Get dressed. We are leaving for Moscow within the hour." She threw a stack of clothes on a lone chair and quickly left. The guard said, "You her-her-heard her, hur...hur...hurry up." He also stuttered.

I dressed in the provided brown slacks, brown shirt, brown socks and a pair of brown shoes. I carried the brown jacket and looked for a U.P.S. monogram on the front, but there was none. I had also noticed that the clothes were de-tagged. Although they reeked from the scent of mothballs, everything fit well. The shoes were snug, but adequate, the guard from Outer Mongolia had probably picked them up at an Inner Mongolian oasis tent sale.

I followed my mentor back down to the laundry room. I was once again, locked in. I set up the DLIDS case and read a *startling* new message, "DO NOT ESCAPE." I sat down atop the table intent on following the CIA directive. A thought came into my mind, I wondered, "Who's prisoner was I, Margolova's? Or the CIA's?" They were both telling me to do the same thing, "Do not escape." And there I sat – not attempting to escape.

Margo and her comrade returned at a few minutes past ten. I was ushered out through the service entrance and into a waiting stretch limousine. It was diplomatically flagged, with both Russian and Malagasy flags. It was a most flagrant misuse of our international courtesies.

Margo carried the DLIDS box, the guard had a weapon out, but I didn't know what it was, perhaps a Glock .45. I don't know for sure, but it used a clip – it wasn't a revolver.

I made a small protest, "You can't really get away with this, can you?"

Margo answered, "No one cares what I do, until it is too late, Mister Morgan. You Americans always want someone else to do your bidding. Your favorite saying, "someone ought to do something," has given me a great advantage in undermining your people. My answer to you is, yes. I will get away with it. This, and much, much more."

We rode to the Antananarivo Airport in silence. We drove out onto the runway without being stopped or questioned. We boarded a Russian fan-jet with Margolova holding her Luger solidly pressed into my back. And I thought, "Someone ought to do something about this."

Margolova was right. She was going to get away with this, and probably a whole lot more. It was, indeed, the American way – let someone else stop her. Someone will stop her. Right?

The Aeroflot climbed out of Madagascar with a very light load. Aside from the crew, which I never saw, the load was only the DLIDS box, Margolova, her lisping Mongolian henchman, and I. When we leveled off, Margo produced a hypodermic needle with a greenish liquid in it, she ordered, "Roll up your sleeve."

I protested. The guard stuck his six inch fist on my nose and said, nodding toward the needle, "That! Or this? Take your pick." He may have said, "Or fist?

Some choice, eh? I rolled up my sleeve and watched the needle enter my arm and, "I never saw it come out..."

• • •

"Come on, Mister Morgan, wake up. You've slept long enough. Time for a little dinner." It was Margolova, she was holding out a paper cup filled with cold water. I took it greedily. My mouth was so dry that I could barely swallow.

"Where are we?"

"That is not important. We will be leaving soon. Your dinner will be here shortly...if you have a need to use a bathroom? There is a facility across the hall. Your door is not locked. There is a guard down the hall. If you try to escape he is ordered to shoot you."

I looked at my watch. – It was gone. "Where's my watch?"

"It will be returned to you. I will be back shortly. Enjoy your meal."

I looked for the DLIDS box. It wasn't around. "Where's the tortoise?

She had moved to the door, she turned and said, "By now...it is in Russia. You will open it for us in the morning." And she left.

So, my security blanket was on its way to, or already in, Russia. PLAY ALONG had somehow lost its meaning. DO NOT ESCAPE, was no longer a comforting set of orders either.

I poked my head out of the door and surveyed the guard.

Looking up from his newspaper, while resting his hand on the butt of an automatic weapon, he said, in perfect English, "You may go across the hall…no further.

"I was just wondering what time it was, do you have the time?"

"Ten."

I begged, "Can I have a piece of your paper? There isn't anything to read in here."

He stood, and cautiously handed me a section of his paper. He was huge and ugly, pockmarked, probably from birth. I thanked him with a sincere smile and returned to my cot. The paper was printed in Arabic, maybe Islamic. I was somewhere in the Middle East. I couldn't read the newspaper. I took it back to the guard. When I returned it, I asked, "Hey Pal. What city is this?"

Actually, I should have asked, "What country?"

He looked at me quizzically, and then answered, "Damascus."

"Syria?"

The big guard pointed me back to my room. "Don't ask any more questions."

I sat on the cot and tried to visualize a map of the Middle East. I knew that Damascus was the capital of Syria. I figured that I must be somewhere near the Red Sea. Iraq was to the east, Saudi Arabia to the south, Turkey to the north, and Israel, or Lebanon, was west.

Lying down, I contemplated my fate. Hours passed, Margo never returned with that promised dinner. I was feeling ill. It may have been from hunger, but it was probably from the drug that was shot into my arm. I was beginning to feel the horror of being a prisoner, a foreign prisoner at that. It was not a pleasant way to spend one's allotted time. Yet – I was thankful to be alive, "Praise Allah!"

Chapter Sixty-Three

Margolova woke me rudely with a sharp kick to the bed frame. Dazed, I bolted upright, and asked, "Time for dinner?"

"We are leaving. Come."

Her cold hand grabbed my collar and I was pulled hurriedly out into the corridor. As I was unceremoniously shoved past the guard I bid him an all-American farewell, "Later Dude." And I'm sure I heard him say, "Praise Allah, my friend." But I only heard this beneath Margo's shout of, "Shut your mouth." Then she jammed the Luger forcibly into my spine.

It was dark out. There were low mountains silhouetted off to our right. The moon was almost full. I was in a state of quasi-disorientation and the fresh air felt wonderful. However, that blast of fresh air was short lived. A black Lincoln pulled up to the curb and I was ushered into a carload of turbaned Arabs, seven of them. We were crunched in like two scrod being added to a tin of Mid Eastern sardines, there was some soft laughter, nervous laughter, because the door wouldn't close, but with a little body shifting, it did close. Margo took the wheel and we sped away from the mosque with screeching tires.

It must have been late as the streets were empty. We passed several minaret towers that soared high above their adjacent mosques.

We drove silently into an airport and right up to a waiting Aeroflot. Margo leaned over the seat and said something to the Arabs. The two on either side of me grabbed me, and the one on the right forced up my sleeve. A third turban was holding a needle and squirting a drop of the drug to clear the needle of air, it was the same green-colored serum. The needle entered my vein, and once again I was blacked out before I saw the needle removed.

I woke in a real cell. It had one-inch metal bars on it and they were spaced at four-inch intervals. King Kong couldn't have broken through them with a battering ram. Everything was painted a dark, battleship gray – the bars, the concrete floor, and the fourteen-foot ceiling. The cell had no individual light, no window, no toilet, and only the one cot that measured out at three-feet by five-feet.

I had the luxury of a one-gallon honey-bucket, but no toilet paper. The cot had one sheet and one grayish colored wool blanket and it smelled like Margolova. The way she stunk back in the Landrover. My view from inside the bars was limited to a carved block wall that was also painted, with many coats, of the same naval-gray paint. I was dressed in the same brown clothes, but the jacket was missing. My shoestrings had been removed and my belt was gone. I was depressed. I was hungry. I had no idea as to where I was, but assumed, that I was in Moscow.

My throat was practically swollen shut. I needed water, badly. I called out, down the hall, in a hoarse voice, for anyone. Nobody came. Time passed slowly. I'd doze off. And then get up again and then doze off...and get up... My mouth got drier and drier. I couldn't swallow. I couldn't produce saliva, at all. I looked for a bug, not a listening device, but a real live bug. I needed moisture that badly. I didn't find one. I went through fits of anger. I upset the cot and banged the frame against the bars. No one came. I sat on the broken cot and smoked *imaginary* cigarettes, and I dreamt of food every time I dozed off. – I went crazy! How much time actually passed, I didn't really know. My best guess was – three-four days.

I sat in a corner against the wall. I sat there because of a Carlos Castaneda book that I had read in college. He said that everyone had his place of oneness within his own environment, after testing many locations within the cell, I finally came to rest in that far corner, and I was resolved that I was going to die there. And, that's when I heard the footsteps come echoing down a distant, unseen hallway.

I didn't move, I couldn't move – I just sat there.

A uniformed guard set down a tray on the outside of the gray bars. He stood, peering at me through the metal, and then said something, in Russian. Then he went away.

When I was sure that he was gone. I went to the tray, I slid across the floor without standing, the cell was only seven by five, it wasn't all that far of a slide. The cold water tasted better than my first sip of a Dom Perignon. I drank the whole quart before I slowly ate the beans and the three-inch square of meat that was plopped on top of them. I wiped the plastic dish clean with my fingers, licking every bit up like it was my last meal – a thought that had crossed my mind, often, during the previous few days.

The meals began to come at regular intervals, once a day. I had eaten ten of them. They were always the same, a quart of water, a can of beans, and that slice of pinkish-green meat. I began praying. I tried thought transference, to Eunice. I spent long hours contemplating Sophie. I thought about joining dad's tool and die shop, but not for long. I promised God that I'd donate ten percent of my interest-income to a church if he'd get me out of there, alive. Hey, I was raised Catholic. I promised to quit smoking. That I'd give up Scotch, and that I'd go to church on each and every Sunday morning.

And I slept. And one day, I counted all the blocks that lined the outside of my cell. The blocks that formed the passageway, the passageway that allowed the Russian guard to bring me food and water. Today, as I write this, the exact number that I counted eludes me, but it was over three hundred, thousand – million. And I thanked God, that I wasn't tortured. – Or was I?

Chapter Sixty-Four

Sitting in my preferred cell-corner anticipating my next meal, I heard a new sound approaching, the sound of four feet instead of two. They were coming quicker than usual, too. It wasn't a food run. No. It had to be Margolova. I stood for the first time in several days and strained to see who was coming and prayed that at least one of them spoke some English.

The two uniformed Russians motioned me away from the door and unlocked it. It was the first time since I woke up from the knock-out drug that the door had been opened, and I recall this – I wept. The guard motioned me out into the hallway. I followed his directive arm gesture, not knowing what he said as he had spoken in his native Russian. I was ecstatic and barely able to contain my anxiety.

The guards manacled my arms behind my back with a heavy chain. It weighed thirty-pounds, maybe more. The restraints weren't neces-sary. I had no intention of running away. After all, I was "PLAYING ALONG." Although, they had no way of knowing that. I was also very weak. I couldn't have run very far, even if I had wanted to.

We marched briskly down the vacant corridor for some two hun-dred yards before coming to an open and waiting elevator. I was pushed into the stark wooden elevator cage rather brutishly. I stum-bled to the far wall where I remained slumped down on one knee. We rode upward, ultra-slowly for many, many floors.

I never learned how many, my guess at the CIA debriefing was ten, or twelve. The elevator finally stopped, and I was pulled out and pushed along a carpeted hallway. It was the first time in weeks that I had seen the light of day which streamed in through a curtain win-dow at the far end of a long, long, green wall-papered hall.

I was shoved into a small room and seated roughly on a wooden chair in front of a formidable looking desk. The two guards stood at attention, one on either side of me. They were whispering back and forth to each other. I remember thinking that I was a mess, I hadn't shaved or bathed in what turned out to be, three weeks. My teeth were probably as yellow as the beans that I had been eating and my breath probably smelled as bad as the meat.

The guards laughed quietly between themselves, they had probably wanted to hold their noses, but they stood solidly waiting for my interrogator to make his entrance. I asked for a cigarette. The guard on my left nudged me, saying, "Nyet." He at least understood the American word cigarette. I then asked for a drink of water. To which the same guard, simply said, "Nyet."

The door opened and a Major hurried behind the desk as the two sentries stiffened to full attention. He stood there reading a passport. He looked at me and asked, "James P. Morgan?"

I shook my head yes, and asked for a cigarette. The guard at my left made a nervous move when I made my request. I guess my plea was inappropriate.

The burly, gray eye-browed, KGB Major looked at me for a long time. He was studying me. He then said something in Russian and the guard on my right produced a package of Russian cigarettes called, "Pognu." He lit one, and then stuck it in my mouth. I noticed that the cigarette paper was stamped with the number 14. I about died when I took a puff on the thing. It was the strongest cigarette that I had ever deeply inhaled in my entire life. After chocking it out of my mouth, the same guard retrieved it from the top of the Major's desk. The guard returned to his position of attention and just stood there holding the Pognu down at his side.

The Major relaxed, visibly, and told the guards to undo my chain. He had spoke in Russian. The guards did as ordered rapidly. I asked for the cigarette back. I then took a baby puff, and survived – it wasn't like a Camel. It was probably made from tumbleweed branches during the Bolshevik Revolution. But it was good, in a sick sense of masculine pleasure. The Major said something else in Russian and they all laughed. No doubt at the strength of their cigarettes.

The sentries were excused and moved outside the open door, which was left opened.

The Major asked, softly, "How did you get into Russia, Mister James P. Morgan?"

His question shocked me. I said, "I flew in, from Damascus." I was dazed. I wholeheartedly wondered why he didn't already know this.

The Major angered, he threw my passport on the desk. It slid quickly toward me. I reached out and stopping it from falling to the floor. He was mad, and spat out, "There is no visa there for Syria, and there has been no visa granted to you by the Russian government. Why are you here?"

I took in a deep breath and asked, "Where's Margolova?"

The Major's eyes opened wide in a genuine surprise, he could have yelled out, Eureka! Instead, his face reddened to a full-blown flush. His eyes locked onto me, then narrowed, as if he were trying to peer right into my very soul. He grabbed up my passport and said, "You will excuse me, Mister Morgan. I will be back."

His temper had visibly cooled. Just her name, Margolova, had solved a lot of unanswered questions. Questions, that the Major no longer needed to ask.

He spoke to the guards momentarily and departed. The senior guard entered, speaking guttural English, he asked if I'd like some tea. I asked for coffee and more cigarettes. He left and the other guard came in. He set his pack of Porgu in front of me along with a box of wooden matches. I thanked him and he went back into the hallway. A fat mug of really hot coffee was brought in. I sat back, and enjoyed fully this simple, courteous, luxury. Margolova obviously had some pull. Just by mentioning her name I was deemed an instant comrade.

I had lit my seventh cigarette and was on my way to finishing my second cup of coffee, when the Major returned. He moved behind the desk and sat down very formally. He leaned forward placing his elbows on the desk and locked his fingers together, he had a most serious demeanor about himself as he gathered his words, then spoke, "We have a most serious situation here, Mister Morgan."

The Major told me how I was found, literally, lying on the Kremlin's doorstep. I had been deliberately dumped there, most likely by, Margolova. It took the KGB two whole weeks to figure out – that I really was the person depicted in my passport. The American Embassy had been demanding my release for the last ten days. Saying that I had been a kidnap victim from the island of Madagascar – as yet, my passport has not been stamped to show that I had actually been there. He concluded, "You will be picked up by your American Ambassador, very shortly."

I spent the next hour relating how I worked for the Institute of Intuitive Thought as an Engineer. How I was abducted at the hands of Margolova, about the Turkish villa, and about our work in tortoise research. I didn't say anything about killing two punks, about the shoot-out at Pimakeel Bay, or about the English submarine studies. Hands down, the Major believed everything that I had told him. And, everything that I *did* tell him was the absolute truth, a few omissions from my recollections were certainly prudent, especially when one considers to whom I was talking to at the time.

The Major, Major Rudolf Chernyayev, thanked me for my forthright narrative and insured me that Margolova and her Recheeka henchmen were dual enemies of both the Russian and American people. And, when I asked him about the prison meat, he just smiled, and then whispered, "Top Secret."

Chapter Sixty-Five

In a genuine whirlwind of events, I was rushed out of the KGB offices and carted off in a black stretch-limo with a young lady, 14, maybe 15 years old sitting across from me in the jump seat. It took her ten seconds to produce a handkerchief and cover her nose. She refused to look at me all the way to the Embassy. It was a simple case of her being in the wrong place, at the wrong time.

A crisp-looking Marine opened my door and led me straight to a waiting bath without any pomp or circumstance. Actually, he never said a word to me, not one.

The same rigid marine presented new clothes to me. He finally spoke, "These are for you to keep, sir. Compliments of the United States Marines." I thanked him sincerely and dressed. Everything fit, gray slacks, white short sleeve shirt and black loafers. The slacks required suspenders, which were produced within two minutes of my requesting them. The gray jacket was a bit snug, but looked fine as long as I didn't button it. I was given a dark tie, but chose to stick it in my pocket.

I was then taken to an industrial sized kitchen where I was served a cold chicken breast, coleslaw and a hot, buttered roll. It tasted wonderful, and I washed it all down with a quart of homemade lemonade. I mooched a few American cigarettes, and by the time I met with a young attaché named Andrew, my mind was a million miles away from dank dungeons and undercooked Lima beans.

I had no watch, wallet, or passport. Andrew assured me that I wouldn't need them. He said, "You'll be leaving for the States within the hour. You'll fly directly to Andrews and be met by a state representative." He studied his watch, saying, "You'll be there in about two hours – their time." His watch was reading noon. By two, Washington time, I'd be home.

I slept most of the way as we blasted across the Atlantic in a jet that proudly displayed the United States Air Force insignia across its tail. We ate a cold box lunch midway across, and I chatted with two young soldiers who where on their way home from the embassy. They were both being reassigned, one to the White House and the other one was going to Paris Island. I was amazed at how young they seemed, and couldn't help but wonder how old, I, had seemed to them. And I also thought, "Sophie would be too old for them – in more ways than just their age."

• • •

Eunice met me at the plane. She was escorted by a dozen of suited CIA personnel who shuttled me off to a briefing room above the Andrews' flight terminal. Eunice *did* grab me by the arm in a brief professional show of affection, and her smile was as warm as the flight line cement, that we crossed on foot to the terminal. After that short encounter we were separated. I didn't see her again until four in the morning. That was when the CIA people released me from their debriefing and allowed me to resume my private life as, "Jim Morgan, Engineer."

Eunice was waiting for me in the terminal. I said, "My god, Eunice, have you been waiting here for 14 hours?"

"No. Silly. I had them call me when they were almost through. I've only been here about thirty minutes."

We embraced tenderly, the way lover's embrace when they've been separated for more than a day or two. It felt nice, it felt right, and I did a mental flip-flop trying to decide whom I loved more, Sophie or Eunice. And I heard Tina's voice interrupt my thinking, she was saying, "A bird in hand, James..." and I stopped our advance to the waiting limousine and kissed Eunice deep and long with a built up passion that even surprised *me*, Jim Morgan.

And she was returning my embrace with an equal, and even more impassioned greed, a greed for intimate love that ought, only be displayed to one and the other behind the closed doors of one's darkened bedroom. And I knew, with every fiber of my being, that Eunice *was* the only woman alive, for me, Jim Morgan.

We entered the limo with Eunice telling the driver, "To the Institute, and step on it."

We kissed and fondled one another like teenagers on prom night right up to the front door of the Tudor where Mureatha stood in the door, pink curlers and all, to say, "Welcome back, Mister Mogins." Then disappeared with a chuckling laugh, sincerely glad to see me safely returned.

Eunice announced that a bath was drawn and that we'd bathe together so that I could give her the same debriefing that I had just given to the CIA. And I said, "Sorry. I can't tell you anything, Eun. I'm sworn to secrecy on the Capitalistic Constitution of America, apple pie, mom, and the old red, white and blue itself."

She made a pouting frown.

I said, "Besides, you probably know more about what really happened down there than I do. Right?"

She nodded out a maybe yes, maybe no.

And I asked, "By the way, how did Sophie make out?"

Eunice turned as white as a sheet and her eyes noticeably dilated, "Oh my god. They didn't tell you?"

And I knew... And as emphatically as I could, I whispered out a very loud and emotional, gut retching, "Fuck."

Eunice sensed, and/or probably knew, that I was in love with Sophie. I'm sure that she guessed many other things about Sophie and me, too. But never dared ask, ever. Eunice came to me, she placed her hand on my shoulder and she did it with such tenderness that I couldn't help, but cry. Something that Sophie wouldn't have wanted me to do, not at her expense. But that's the way it was.

I asked, "Do you know what happened?"

Eunice was gentle, "No one's absolutely certain. She died at Pimakeel Bay. I went to her funeral. Here, in Washington. I thought you knew, Jim. I'm terribly sorry."

Eunice was sincere. She *was* sorry. She had real pain over what had happened, and guilt, and she couldn't begin to hide her hurt, over Sophie's untimely demise. After all, she *was* part of the machinery that caused Sophie to be down there.

In an effort to sooth me, to take away some of my rising bile and hatred, she started, quite awkwardly, "We must admit, she died in the line of duty, Jim. She was doing what she wanted to be doing. She knew the consequences of..."

And I stopped her, cold, "Consequences of what, Eunice? Dying?"

"Let's not blow this out of proportion, Jim. Sophie was an excellent agent, she was doing what was expected of her."

A cold silence ensued. I had never lost a close friend before. The thought of never seeing her again was excruciatingly painful. Eunice sensed that she was saying the wrong things and wisely entered her own silent thoughts, leaving me to my own reflections of the why and the wherefores.

I asked, "Did you get the tortoise?"

Eunice wasn't thinking in that direction. She thought for a second, and then said, "No, it's in Baghdad."

"Baghdad?"

Eunice continued, "Well, the DLIDS box is, we're not sure about the tortoise."

I asked, "What about, Margolova?"

"She was last seen in Moscow. Shortly after you were picked up in Red Square. She's since disappeared. That's all I know. Is there anything else I can tell you?"

"Did you hear anything about the English spy, Tina Johnson?"

"You mean, you don't know about that either?"

"You mean...?"

"Oh no, no. She wasn't killed." Eunice curled up her lip, before continuing, "She's made you a hero. You're to be an Honorary Knight, Sir Morgan. It's a great honor for you. I heard how you saved her life, I've read the C5 report, I'm very proud of you, Jim."

I was befuddled. I needed to hide, to sleep. I said, "Yeah. Let's get some sleep, Eun. I'm really worn out."

It was getting light out. Dawn had broken. We passed on the bath and I procrastinated getting into Eunice's bed. I think it was out of respect for Sophie. After Eunice was asleep, I scooted in next to her and listened to her breathing until I fell asleep, which didn't take all that long, as I *was* mentally exhausted.

And I had a most vivid dream.

•   •   •

Sophie was at a podium lecturing me. I was the only student in her class. She said, "You must take the .357. You're going to need it. Then she got angry because I had insisted that it was unnecessary. I simply didn't need it.

She karate kicked the dais and screamed at me, "You will need it, Jim. You will! Believe in me, Jim. You *will* need it."

•   •   •

And I woke. The dream lingered on with me all the next day. It was so vivid, so real. I started to believe that I did indeed, *need* her .357. And then I laughed to myself, "Yeah. Just where in the hell would I go to find it? Back to Madagascar?"

Later that very afternoon, a package arrived for me from Senator Alberquist. It was Sophie's .357 Magnum. A letter was enclosed that read:

Dear Jim:

My daughter has been haunting me nightly. Her spirit insists that I present you with her .357 Magnum. It is the one that I gave her when she was accepted into the CIA. Please accept this as a gift on (Sophie's) – my behalf. Please come around and visit, soon. My door is always open to you. With the Utmost of Sincerity, I Remain…

The letter was signed, "Her Loving Father."

Chapter Sixty-Six

I took a month off without pay. Yeah, I went home and set up a small office in the rear of dad's shop. I made a few suggestions on how to turn bigger profits and they actually worked. The second week, I threw myself into the OSHA regulations and brought the shop into compliance with the Fed. It cost a few bucks and when dad saw the bills coming in he had a fit.

"This shop was here before OSHA came into existence, and it'll still be here when their tax payer funds dry up. – You're fired."

Actually, the argument wasn't over money at all. It was over the Austin. It was mine. And I wouldn't let dad play with it... Right dad?

I looked up my college buddies, they were all married or leaving town on business. No one wanted to party, no one wanted to chase wild women. That's when I decided to write this book.

Eunice called me almost every evening. We'd chat awhile, she would profess her love to me, and, I'd profess mine to her. Actually, I *did* miss her. I *loved* her, and my job was still open. Eunice claimed that she had a lot of work for me. – Especially around her bedroom, but I just wasn't ready. Although, I was close to being ready – I just wasn't.

I called her one evening and discussed my plan to write a novel about the expedition. At first, she was cool to the idea. She thought it would be "negative advertising" for the Institute. She suggested that I write a poem and get my ass back to work.

I "pretty-pleased" her, and she agreed to let me use her summer get away, a small cabin up in the Catskill Mountains, for six-months. It was under the condition that she could visit me often. To which I most readily agreed.

And so it went. I set up camp with two sacks of groceries and a second hand word processor. It was, a dream come true. I grew a full beard and was blasting away at my first draft like a man possessed – for two weeks. Then boredom set in (a fellow writer, Stephen King, suggested I say "...writer's block set in."). I was lonely. The silent nature of a mountain cabin was, too antisocial.

I'd write for a few hours, sleep a few hours, and then read a few minutes. Then run up the road and drink too much Scotch at a ski lodge, and then I'd lose a whole day's work due to a hang over. Writing isn't as glamorous as it sounds. It takes a lot of work. Right?

By my fourth week, I discovered a comedy club with a lot of cute hostesses. They seemed to be impressed that I was a writer for some reason. Reasons, way beyond my own personal insight into the writing life. So, over the next three weeks, I only wrote two paragraphs.

Eunice came up often. She'd send me flowers during the week. My best friend was the flower truck driver. We had coffee together three times a week. Then Eunice called and announced that she needed me. She was putting together an expedition to the Maldives Islands. Would I be interested in sun, surf, palm trees, and naked natives?

"No spies. No guns. No CIA involvement, none whatsoever."

I said, "I'll think about it." And let it go.

That's when I got serious about this novel. The pages started to jump off the old word processor like ticks off a tortoise shell sprayed with elephant poison.

The first snow fell in late October. Eunice was getting impatient with me. She stopped driving up every weekend, saying that the roads were too treacherous in the winter. The fresh flowers stopped coming as regularly as they once had...and I worked all the harder.

Then I received a note, by mail, it was an ultimatum issued by, Eunice May North, Resident Director of the Institute of Intuitive Thought, Washington, D.C., it read, "Finish by Christmas, or clear out of my cabin. My Expedition to the Maldives Islands leaves in March. – If you want this job? Be here for Christmas." Signed, E. M. North, R.D.

My back was up against the wall. I'd have to write fast. I went to bed for a nap. I'd get up fresh, and, I'd blast a whole new chapter by midnight. But, December came before I finished. I was wrangling with myself over the closing chapter. I didn't want the saga to end. Psychologically, I'd be burying Sophie with its, "The End." Somehow, it just didn't seem right that Sophie had died.

On the seventeenth of December, I fell into a fitful sleep. I had just penned, "The End," below my 146-thousand word manuscript. But, I knew it wasn't over because, Margolova, was still on the loose.

I fell asleep in my chair just staring at those last two ugly words. And I had this dream:

• • •

Sophie was sitting in the cabin on the cloth easy chair. She was covered with an old Arapaho Indian blanket. She told me that she was naked. She asked me to put another log on the fire, as she was cold, an occupational hazard of the netherworld.

And in my dream, I did, subserviently, add another log to the already glowing hearth. As I was doing so, Sophie said, "It won't be long now, Jim."

I asked her, "What are you talking about, Kidd?"

Before she could answer – the phone rang. It was Eunice. She said, "Margolova is on her way up to the cabin."

I said, "Big deal, Soph's here. Let her come."

Eunice was adamant, she screamed, "Get out of there! Right now, Jim. She's coming there to *kill* you. This isn't a joke, Jim. You've *got* to get out of there."

I hung up the phone and told Sophie, "It was Eunice. She said that Margolova is coming here to kill me."

Sophie says, "I know, Jim. That's why I'm here."

"I said, somewhat nonchalantly, "Oh."

Sophie said, in a matter of fact statement, "Don't worry, Jim. I'll handle everything." She poked her thirty-eight out from under the Arapaho blanket, pointed it at the door, the only door in or out of the cabin, and added, "Let her come. I *want* her to come. Don't you?"

• • •

And I woke. The dream had left me in a pleasant, euphoric state. I tried to recapture the essence of the dream, some meaning, some reason, but it was gone. Indeed, I too, would like a shot at Margolova. Just like Sophie – I thought, "Let her come."

And I went into my bed. My novel *was* done. I lay there thinking – I was planning my drive back to the Institute. That was when the phone rang.

Reluctantly, I climbed out of bed and answered it. It was Eunice.

"I have really bad news, Jim. – Margolova is on her way up to the cabin. You've got to get out of there, Jim. Jim? Do you understand? She's on her way up there, right now, to kill you." …Jim? …Jim?

I hung up the phone and unplugged it. Then, with calm certainty – I went to the dresser and retrieved Sophie's .357. I shut off the lights and settled myself into the cloth easy chair – the one that faces the only door into, or out of Eunice's cabin. I pulled her old Arapaho blanket up over my shoulders. It felt somewhat cool in the cabin, despite the fire that roared away in the open hearth. I positioned Sophie's .357 so I could easily cover Margolova's arrival. And I thought, "This is going to make one *hell* of a good ending to our novel – eh, Soph?"

The End

About the Author:

Mr. Halon was born in Hammond, Indiana on August fourth, 1946. He served as a Weather Observer, Weather Forecaster, Solar Observer and Astro-geophysical Data Analyst before retiring from the USAF. He later worked for the Department of Defense as a Nuclear Scientist in Radiological Control de-activating nuclear submarines at the Bremmerton Ship Yards outside of Seattle, Washington.

Mr. Halon now resides in northwest Indiana where he wrote a lot of poetry and published his first book, "Poetry." He wrote for a radio program called CRY, Concerns and Resolutions for Youth, while teaching English and Mathematics at a local college prep school. A dabbler in the arts, for the fun of it, he has published many cartoons, poems, and painted numerous paintings in water-based acrylics. He worked five years in the northwest Indiana steel mills as an Inspector on a continuous-roll galvanizing line.

Today, he just writes. He is nearing completion of the sequel to "The Malagasy Tortoise" and will title his second novel "The Maldives Island Incident" which is also a Jim Morgan Adventure.

Mr. Halon attended Chapman College in Orange, California; The University of Hawaii, on Oahu; Purdue University, Indiana; LaSalle University, Chicago; and the University of Wisconsin.

His interests lie in the para-normal and the Para psychological. He is a consummate and varied Philosophical-subject research reader. His favorite authors are: Aristotle, Hume, Walt Whitman, John Galloway, Jr., St. Augustine, Henry Miller, E. Hemingway, L. Tolstoy, Stephen King and G.B. Shaw.